The O. Henry Prize Stories 2007

The O. Henry Prize Stories 2007

Edited and with an Introduction by
Laura Furman

With Essays on the Story They Admire Most by Jurors
Charles D'Ambrosio
Ursula K. Le Guin
Lily Tuck

ANCHOR BOOKS
A Division of Random House, Inc.
New York

An Anchor Books Original, May 2007

Copyright © 2007 by Vintage Anchor Publishing, a division of Random House, Inc.
Introduction © 2007 by Laura Furman

All rights reserved. Published in the United States by Anchor Books, a division of Random House, Inc., New York, and in Canada by Random House of Canada Limited, Toronto.

Anchor Books and colophon are registered trademarks of Random House, Inc.

Permissions appear at the end of the book.

Cataloging-in-Publication Data for the *O. Henry Prize Stories 2007* is on file at the Library of Congress.

Anchor ISBN: 978-0-307-27688-9

Book design by Debbie Glasserman

www.anchorbooks.com

Printed in the United States of America
10 9 8 7 6 5 4 3 2 1

The editor wishes to thank Kris Bronstad, Katarina Dolejsiova, and Katie Williams for their good company and intelligent consideration of short stories, and the staff of Anchor Books, whose energy, skill, and enthusiasm makes working on each O. Henry collection a pleasure.

Publisher's Note

A Brief History of the O. Henry Prize Stories

Many readers have come to love the short story through the simple characters, easy narrative voice and humor, and compelling plotting in the work of William Sydney Porter (1862–1910), best known as O. Henry. His surprise endings entertain readers, even those back for a second, third, or fourth look. Even now one can say, " 'Gift of the Magi,' " in a conversation about a love affair or marriage, and almost any literate person will know what is meant. It's hard to think of many other American writers whose work has been so incorporated into our national shorthand.

O. Henry was a newspaperman, skilled at hiding from his editors at deadline. A prolific writer, he wrote to make a living and to make sense of his life. He spent his childhood in Greensboro, North Carolina, his adolescence and young manhood in Texas, and his mature years in New York City. In between Texas and New York, he served out a prison sentence for bank fraud in Columbus, Ohio. Accounts of the origin of his pen name vary: one story dates from his days in Austin, where he was said to call the wandering family cat "Oh! Henry!"; another states that the name was inspired by the captain of the guard in the Ohio State Penitentiary, Orrin Henry.

Porter had devoted friends, and it's not hard to see why. He was charming and had an attractively gallant attitude. He drank too much and neglected his health, which caused his friends concern. He was often short of money; in a letter to a friend asking for a loan of $15.00 (his banker was out of town, he wrote), Porter added a postscript: "If it isn't convenient, I'll love you just the same." The banker was unavailable most of Porter's life. His sense of humor was always with him.

Reportedly, Porter's last words were from a popular song: "Turn up the light, for I don't want to go home in the dark."

Eight years after O. Henry's death, in April 1918, the Twilight Club (founded in 1883 and later known as the Society of Arts and Letters) held a dinner in his honor at the Hotel McAlpin in New York City. His friends remembered him so enthusiastically that a group of them met at the Biltmore Hotel in December of that year to establish some kind of memorial to him. They decided to award annual prizes in his name for short-story writers, and formed a Committee of Award to read the short stories published in a year and to pick the winners. In the words of Blanche Colton Williams (1879–1944), the first of the nine series editors, the memorial was intended to "strengthen the art of the short story and to stimulate younger authors."

Doubleday, Page & Company was chosen to publish the first volume, *O. Henry Memorial Award Prize Stories 1919*. In 1927, the Society sold all rights to the annual collection to Doubleday, Doran & Company. Doubleday published *The O. Henry Prize Stories*, as it came to be known, in hardcover, and from 1984 to 1996 its subsidiary, Anchor Books, published it simultaneously in paperback. Since 1997 *The O. Henry Prize Stories* has been published as an original Anchor Books paperback.

How the Stories Are Chosen

All stories originally written in the English language and published in an American or Canadian periodical are eligible for consideration. Stories are not nominated; magazines submit the year's issues in their entirety by May 1.

The series editor chooses the twenty O. Henry Prize Stories, and each year three writers distinguished for their fiction are asked to evaluate the entire collection and to write an appreciation of the story they most admire. These three writers receive the twenty O. Henry Prize Stories in manuscript form with no identification of author or publication. They make their choices independent of each other and the series editor.

The goal of The O. Henry Prize Stories remains to strengthen the art of the short story.

To Sherwood Anderson (1876–1941)

Sherwood Anderson grew up poor in a small town in Ohio. His father was an entertaining but unreliable man. His mother took in laundry to support her six children. When Anderson was a boy, he gained the nickname "Jobby" because he accepted any work offered, trying to earn money to help his mother. He chose a career in advertising and manufacturing to make as much money as possible. But Anderson was an artist. He loved books and reading, and this changed his life.

When he was running a factory and trying to lead the respectable life of a husband and father in Elyria, Ohio, Sherwood Anderson kept a room of his own at the top of his house. Naked, he scrubbed it clean to make it a place for his writing. It was a physical manifestation of his determination to tell the truth.

In his stunning collection *Winesburg, Ohio*, published in 1919, the same year as the first *O. Henry Prize Stories*, Anderson wrote in the plainest, most direct language he could of the people and the life he knew. In "Adventure," he writes of Alice, who's waited long years for her young lover to return, as he promised he would when he left for Cleveland. Her thwarted sexual passion, loyalty, and naïveté have turned her into a grotesque (a word Anderson originally wanted in the title of his collection). One night, Alice runs naked through the rain, calling out to the only person she finds, a deaf old man who doesn't hear her. She crawls home, and Anderson ends the story: " 'What is the matter with me? I will do something dreadful if I am not careful,' she thought, and turning her face to the wall, began trying to force herself to face bravely the fact that many people live and die alone, even in Winesburg."

That hard truth, and the nakedness of his prose, are the essential Sherwood Anderson. Any reader who loves the short story, any writer who wants to work in the form, should read this linked collection, nearly ninety years old and as fresh and heartbreaking as when he wrote it. *Winesburg, Ohio* creates a town, its atmosphere and countryside, and gives us its people both as others see them and as they see themselves. The stories stand alone and together create a larger whole. One feels behind every sentence of Anderson's, however plain, clear, and quiet the words seem, his fervent desire to give everything he has to his reader.

Contents

Introduction

Reading the many short stories submitted to The O. Henry Prize Stories by periodicals each year would seem to provide a special perch from which to generalize and categorize, to proclaim the year's prevailing style or subject matter. At a recent dinner party I attended, the host declared that he didn't read contemporary fiction and didn't know much about it, but he wondered if people still wrote old-fashioned sentences like " 'I don't know what you mean,' Constance said coldly."

It was easy to reassure him that such sentences still enjoy life, along with many other kinds, and that writers today are publishing a healthy variety of stories. But nothing would induce me to stand on an O. Henry soapbox and preach about trends in contemporary prose.

By choice, my reading experience focuses on one story at a time, not on what kind of story it is. If it's a great story, it doesn't matter if it is a Western, an epic, historical fiction, a spiritual journey, a domestic drama, or a postmodern fable. What matters most is how effectively the story moves the reader from one world (her own) to another (the story's).

As the statements of this year's O. Henry writers reveal, the writers themselves come to their stories in many different ways. You'll find one writer who wrote a story to express deep grief, and another to enter a contest that required a certain genre. Another of our writers wrangled his subject from anecdote to part of a novel to a short story. Yet another writer found her story within the fiction of two centuries ago, when, we would like to think, women's lives were so different. Each story in the collection represents an individual writer's search for the story and the right way to tell it.

There's a distant intimacy in William Trevor's fiction. He observes his characters from the heights of a chilly god, not without sympathy but without sentimentality—a god with low expectations, perhaps. The reader of a Trevor story, whether she likes the characters or not, can't help but be drawn to their dilemmas. In "The Room" the much-wronged Katherine uses infidelity as a catharsis. Varieties of betrayal and a homicide shadow the story, yet its focus is not on violence or even conflict but on an intricate emotional balancing act. Katherine lives as though in a chambered nautilus, with each aspect of her life sealed off in a separate compartment. It's up to the reader to make the connections between them.

Three of our stories have war in the background: Justine Dymond's "Cherubs," Joan Silber's "War Buddies," and "The Gift of Years" by Vu Tran. In "Cherubs" the war is long past, and, at first, there are no signs of trouble at the charming wedding in France the story portrays. But as it unfolds, narrated in first-person plural by American guests with the breathy enthusiasm associated with nuptials, the past intervenes. The excitement and promise of the occasion is tempered by another time when other Americans, the liberating army, were terrible guests.

Joan Silber, whose story "The High Road" was in the O. Henry 2003 collection, sets her story "War Buddies" years after the war has ended, when the narrator takes stock of his life and, most of all, of his long-lost doppelgänger. They were a civilian pair of engineers sent to South Vietnam to solve a technical problem that was costing lives and money. The war, though terrifying, was almost the least of their troubles.

The third war story, by Vu Tran, is about a South Vietnamese soldier separated from his family while his children grow up. The narrative contains a stunning reminiscence of battle, but Vu Tran's tale explores the consequences of war in domestic terms. It's a story about the universal human reluctance to believe in events that take place in our absence, especially when it comes to our children.

"The Duchess of Albany" by Christine Schutt and "Mudder Tongue" by Brian Evenson are strikingly different stories about aging parents and children. In Schutt's story, a mother faces up to her widowhood by playing with language and image. Evenson's portrait of a deteriorating father's linguistic pathology evokes the reader's sympathetic frustration even as we wait for another fascinating mistake. Schutt's widow uses language as a way to avoid being meddled with as she mourns, and Evenson's misspeaking professor succeeds too well in concealing his loss of control over the spoken word. For both aging characters, language is a weapon against an increasingly alien world.

"A Stone House" by Bay Anapol and "In a Bear's Eye" by Yannick Murphy are testimony to the often-observed kinship between the short story and the poem. In "A Stone House" the narrator circles around her lover, who is chimerical even when he's within reach, and her memories of her dying mother. "In a Bear's Eye" observes the difference between adult grief and a child's literal understanding of loss. On the first reading, both of these lovely stories offer the pleasure of the language; a second reading reveals the force of their emotion.

It would be easy to categorize "City Visit" by Adam Haslett and "The Diarist" by Richard McCann as coming-out stories, but this sells both stories short. One of Richard McCann's gifts as a writer is the way he uses memory to wrestle experience into art. "The Diarist" begins with the narrator announcing, "Here's one thing I remember, from all the things I never wrote down in my diary the summer I was eleven, the summer before my father died." The narrator is impossibly different from his father and brother in ways he didn't then understand. At the triumphant end of the story it becomes clear that the narrator will find his way not only by recognizing his sexuality but also through writing.

The protagonist of Adam Haslett's "City Visit" believes that New York, where he arrives with his mother for a visit, holds the key to his secret identity and his freedom. What he doesn't notice, and the reader does, is that his mother knows his secret and is willing to step aside while he takes his risks away from her care.

Ariel Dorfman's "Gringos" and Sana Krasikov's "Companion" are stories of uneasy exile. In Dorfman's skillfully layered tale, an exiled Latin American couple who live in the United States pretend not to know Spanish, putting themselves in danger when they're abroad. "Gringos" is also the story of a long marriage; perhaps the marriage offers the couple their only secure citizenship. Ilona, the protagonist of "Companion," is a warm, sexy, cranky, lonely woman who's living in the United States, yet she thinks constantly of other places and other possibilities. Her struggle to improve her lot undercuts her existence. The story poses the question of whether Ilona's helpless, predatory stance is part of every immigrant's condition or simply Ilona's character.

In writing "The View from Castle Rock," Alice Munro used a diary from her own family, though the story as a whole is convincingly imagined. It's long been Munro's special gift to make vivid the historical surroundings of her characters. In this case, their desires and hopefulness seem especially dramatic and important, as Munro brings to life the promise and the price the obscure immigrants pay when they leave for a new world.

Eddie Chuculate's "Galveston Bay, 1826" takes the reader on an adventure over land and out of time as a group of Cheyennes cross the Red River and travel as far south as they can. Chuculate's characters are deftly portrayed, and the reader feels, along with them, their joy and terror about what they discover.

"The Scent of Cinnamon" by Charles Lambert is set in the nineteenth-century American West and begins with an exchange of letters between an American farmer and an English widow. As the two strangers move closer to becoming man and wife, the story takes another turn altogether, leaving the reader to decide what happened and what didn't, what was real and what wasn't. The Western pioneer setting, with its keen details of clothing, furniture, and horseflesh, makes an appropriate backdrop for a story about longing and loneliness.

Though "El Ojo de Agua" by Susan Straight takes place in contemporary Rio Seco, California, its heart is in another time and place altogether, the flood of 1927 in segregated Bayou Becasse, Louisiana. That nightmare time had a profound effect on the intertwined families in Susan Straight's story, so much so that the story's present-day tragedies echo the depredations of the past.

When Rebecca Curtis's narrator describes the sisters in her "Summer, with Twins," she is measuring them: "They weren't strikingly beautiful, and they weren't especially kind. But everything they did they did with enthusiasm . . . Their enthusiasm made me angry, because it seemed false, but then I became included in it and realized it was genuine." The narrator's desire to be included is her downfall. She's too dense to understand the selfishness and meanness of the twins, but the ambiguous reward of her summer—and the story—is an understanding of the power of money. Rebecca Curtis insists on confronting the confused morality of the twins.

Appropriate social behavior has gone missing in "Djamilla," Tony D'Souza's story of a young American in love with Africa. Disillusioned with the tribe he's living with, he flirts with a beautiful unmarried woman from another tribe. However much he sees himself as part of a community, because he's an outsider, he doesn't suffer the consequences of his actions. The interplay of desire, role playing, and carelessness makes "Djamilla" an intense exploration of how different people living in close proximity can be.

In Jan Ellison's "The Company of Men," Catherine, the young narrator, is deliciously naïve. In New Zealand she meets two young men, Jimmy and Ray, and the three settle temporarily in Sydney, Australia. They're all young and uncommitted: "There was the promise of some new knowledge—the shape of an ear, the smell of musk—or a shift in one's view of oneself in the world." They never become sexually entangled but she's seduced nonetheless, and in a way that shifts her view of her own sensuality.

"A New Kind of Gravity" by Andrew Foster Altschul takes place in a shelter populated by women and children who've suffered from violence, but its male narrator is the story's true subject. He works at the shelter, guarding the women from their abusive husbands and boyfriends. As his involvement with them becomes more complicated, the story grows more tense. He's trying hard to understand the women. We believe he's the good guy. Yet his secret flaw makes the story—and its subject—far more complicated than a tale of right and wrong, good and bad.

Once again, the stories in *The O. Henry Prize Stories* come from the three most important commercial publications for fiction—*The New Yorker*, *The Atlantic Monthly*, and *Harper's*—and from a variety of small magazines. The role of the commercial magazines in supporting and publishing new and established writers has never been so important. *The Atlantic's* decision to stop publishing a story per issue and to offer all its fiction in one annual issue raised distress signals among the community of writers, editors, and readers who care about literature.

Yet if the commercial magazines reach more readers than any of the others, the little magazines are the greatest evidence of our vibrant literary world. It's true that some of them fold when they lose university or private support, but heartening new magazines always arise in their place. For the second year in a row, an O. Henry Prize story comes from *One Story*, the innovative and successful dream of two young women. Another story is from *Noon*, an annual whose imaginative writing isn't widely known to the reading public. Two stories in our collection come from *Mānoa*, an especially handsome quarterly, which for two decades has engaged in cross-cultural publication of writers from Asia and North America.

Literary magazines and writers need an active readership. If you admire the writers in this year's *O. Henry*, please keep an eye out for their future work.

Laura Furman
Austin, Texas

The O. Henry Prize Stories 2007

William Trevor

The Room

D O YOU know why you are doing this?" he asked, and Katherine hesitated, then shook her head, although she did know.

Nine years had almost healed a soreness, each day made a little easier,
until the balm of work was taken from her and in her scratchy idleness the
healing ceased. She was here because of that, there was no other reason she
could think of, but she didn't say it.

"And you?" she asked instead.

He was at once forthcoming. He said he'd been attracted by her
at a time when he'd brought loneliness upon himself by quarrelling
once too often with the wife who had borne his children and had cared
for him.

"I'm sorry about the room," he said.

His belongings were piled up, books and cardboard boxes, suitcases
open, not yet unpacked. A word processor had not been plugged in, its
cables trailing on the floor. Clothes on hangers cluttered the back of the
door; an anatomical study of an elephant decorated one of the walls, with
arrows indicating where certain organs were beneath the leathery skin.
This gray picture wasn't his, he'd said when Katherine asked; it came with
the room, which was all he had been able to find in a hurry. A sink was in
the same corner as a washbasin, an electric kettle and a gas ring on a shelf,
a green plastic curtain not drawn across.

"It's all a bit more special now that you're here," he said, sounding as if he meant it.

When she got up to put on her clothes, Katherine could tell he didn't want her to go. Yet he, not she, was the one who had to; she could have stayed all afternoon. Buttoning a sleeve of her dress, she remarked that at least she knew now what it felt like to deceive.

"What it had felt like for Phair," she said.

She pulled the edge of the curtain back a little more so that the light fell more directly on the room's single looking glass. She tidied her hair, still brown, no gray in it yet. Her mother's hadn't gone gray at all, and her grandmother's only when she was very old, which was something Katherine hoped she wouldn't have to be; she was forty-seven now. Her dark eyes gazed back at her from her reflection, her lipstick smudged, an emptiness in her features that had not to do with the need to renew her makeup. Her beauty was ebbing—but slowly, and there was beauty left.

"You were curious about that?" he asked, his own dressing complete. "Deception?"

"Yes, I was curious."

"And shall you be again?"

Still settling the disturbances in her face, Katherine didn't answer at once. Then she said, "If you would like me to."

Outside, the afternoon was warm, the street where the room was— above a betting shop—seemed brighter and more gracious than Katherine had noticed when she'd walked the length of it earlier. There was an afternoon tranquillity about it in spite of shops and cars. The tables were unoccupied outside the Prince and Dog, hanging baskets of petunias on either side of its regal figure, and a Dalmatian with a foot raised. There was a Costa Coffee next to a Pret a Manger and Katherine crossed to it. "Latte," she ordered from the girls who were operating the Gaggia machines and picked out a florentine from the glass case on the counter while she waited for it.

She hardly knew the man she'd slept with. He'd danced with her at a party she'd gone to alone, and then he'd danced with her again, holding her closer, asking her her name and giving his. Phair didn't accompany her to parties these days and she didn't go often herself. But she'd known what she intended, going to this one.

The few tables were all taken. She found a stool at the bar that ran along one of the walls. "TEENAGER'S CURFEW!" a headline in someone else's evening paper protested, a note of indignation implied, and for a few moments she wondered what all that was about and then lost interest.

Phair would be quietly at his desk, in shirtsleeves, the blue-flecked shirt she'd ironed the day before yesterday, his crinkly, gingerish hair as it had been that morning when he left the house, his agreeable smile welcoming anyone who approached him. In spite of what had happened nine years ago, Phair had not been made redundant, that useful euphemism for being sacked. That he'd been kept on was a tribute to his success in the past, and of course it wasn't done to destroy a man when he was down. "We should go away," she'd said and remembered saying it now, but he hadn't wanted to, because running away was something that wasn't done, either. He would have called it running away; in fact, he had.

This evening, he would tell her about his day, and she would say about hers and would have to lie. And in turn they'd listen while she brought various dishes to the dining table, and he would pour her wine. None for himself because he didn't drink anymore, unless someone pressed him, and then only in order not to seem ungracious. "My marriage is breaking up," the man who'd made love to her in his temporary accommodation had confided when, as strangers, they had danced together. "And yours?" he'd asked, and she'd hesitated and then said no, not breaking up. There'd never been talk of that. And when they danced the second time, after they'd had a drink together and then a few more, he asked her if she had children and she said she hadn't. That she was not able to had been known before the marriage and then became part of it—as her employment at the Charterhouse Institute had been until six weeks ago, when the Institute had decided to close itself down.

"Idleness is upsetting," she had said while they danced, and had asked her future lover if he had ever heard of Sharon Ritchie. People often thought they hadn't and then remembered. He shook his head and the name was still unfamiliar to him when she told him why he might have heard of it. "Sharon Ritchie was murdered," she'd said, and wouldn't have without the few drinks. "My husband was accused."

She blew on the surface of her coffee, but it was still too hot. She tipped sugar out of its paper spill into her teaspoon and watched the sugar darkening when the coffee soaked it. She loved the taste of that, as much a pleasure as anything there'd been this afternoon. "Oh, suffocated," she'd said when she'd been asked how the person called Sharon Ritchie had died. "She was suffocated with a cushion." Sharon Ritchie had had a squalid life, living grandly at a good address, visited by many men.

Katherine sat a while longer, staring at the crumbs of her florentine, her coffee drunk. "We live with it," she had said when they left the party together, he to return to the wife he didn't get on with, she to the husband whose deceiving of her had ended with a death. Fascinated by that, an hour ago in the room that was his temporary accommodation her afternoon lover had wanted to know everything.

On the Tube, she kept seeing the room: the picture of the elephant, the suitcases, the trailing cables, the clothes on the back of the door. Their echoed voices, his curiosity, her evasions and then telling a little more because, after all, she owed him something. "He paid her with a check once—oh, ages ago. That was how they brought him into things. And when they talked to the old woman in the flat across the landing from Sharon Ritchie's she recognized him in the photograph she was shown. Oh, yes, we live with it."

Her ticket wouldn't operate the turnstile when she tried to leave the Tube station, and she remembered that she had guessed how much the fare should be and must have got it wrong. The Indian who was there to deal with such errors was inclined to be severe. Her journey had been different earlier, she tried to explain; she'd got things muddled. "Well, these things happen," the Indian said, and she realized his severity had not been meant. When she smiled, he didn't notice. That is his way, too, she thought.

She bought two chicken breasts, free-range, organic; and courgettes and fruit. She hadn't made a list as she usually did, and wondered if this had to do with the kind of afternoon it had been and thought it probably had. She tried to remember which breakfast cereals needed to be replenished but couldn't. And then remembered Normandy butter and tomatoes. It was just before five o'clock when she let herself into the flat. The telephone was ringing and Phair said he'd be a bit late, not by much, maybe twenty minutes. She ran a bath.

The tips of his fingers stroked the arm that was close to him. He said he thought he loved her. Katherine shook her head.

"Tell me," he said.

"I have, though."

He didn't press it. They lay in silence for a while.

Then Katherine said, "I love him more, now that I feel so sorry for him, too. He pitied me when I knew I was to be deprived of the children we both wanted. Love makes the most of pity, don't you think?"

"Yes. I do."

She told him more, and realized she wanted to, which she hadn't known before. When the two policemen had come in the early morning, she had not been dressed. Phair was making coffee. "Phair Alexander Warburton," one of them had said. She'd heard him from the bedroom, her bathwater still gurgling out. She'd thought they'd come to report a death, as policemen sometimes have to: her mother or Phair's aunt, his next of kin. When she went downstairs, they were talking about the death of someone whose name she did not know. "Who?" she asked, and the taller of the two policemen said Sharon Ritchie, and Phair said nothing. "Your husband has explained," the other man said, "that you didn't know Miss Ritchie." On a Thursday night, the eighth, two weeks ago, they said. What time—could she remember—had her husband come in?

She'd faltered, lost in all this. "But who's this person? Why are you here?" And the taller policeman said there were a few loose ends. "Sit down, Madam," his colleague put in, and she was asked again what time her husband had come in. A worse delay than usual on the Underground, he'd said that night, the Thursday before last. He'd given up waiting and had gone away, as everyone else was doing. And then it wasn't easy to get a taxi because of the rain. "You remember, Madam?" the taller policeman prompted, and something made her say Phair had come back at the usual time. She couldn't think; she couldn't because she was trying to remember if Phair had ever mentioned Sharon Ritchie. "Your husband visited Miss Ritchie," the same policeman said, and the other man's pager sounded and he took it to the window, turning his back to them. "No, we're talking to him now," he mumbled into it, keeping his voice low, but she could hear. "Your husband has explained it was the day before," his colleague said. "And earlier—in his lunchtime—that his last visit to Miss Ritchie was."

Remembering, Katherine wanted to stay here, in the room. She wanted to sleep, to be aware of the man she did not know well beside her, to have him waiting for her when she woke up. Because of the heat wave that had begun a week ago, he had turned the air-conditioning on, an old-fashioned contraption at the window.

"I have to go," he said.

"Of course. I won't be long."

Below them, another horse race had come to its exciting stage, the radio commentary faintly reaching them as they dressed. They went together down uncarpeted, narrow stairs, past the open door of the betting shop.

"Shall you come again?" he asked.

"Yes."

And they arranged an afternoon, ten days away, because he could not always just walk out of the office where he worked.

"Don't let me talk about it," she said before they parted. "Don't ask, don't let me tell."

"If you don't want to."

"It's all so done with. And it's a bore for you, or will be soon."

He began to say it wasn't, that was what the trouble was. She knew he began to say it because she could see it in his face before he changed his mind. And of course he was right; he wasn't a fool. Curiosity couldn't be just stifled.

They didn't embrace before he hurried off, for they had done all that. When she watched him go, it felt like a habit already, and she wondered as she crossed the street to the Costa café if, with repetition, her afternoons here would acquire some variation of the order and patterns of the work she missed so.

"Oh, none at all," she'd said when she'd been asked if there were prospects yet of something else. And wondered now if she would ever again make her morning journey across London, skillful in the over-crowded Tube stations, squeezing onto trains that were crowded also. It was unlikely that there'd be, somewhere, her own small office again, her position of importance, and generous colleagues who made up for a bleak-ness and kept at bay its ghosts. She hadn't known until Phair said, not long ago, that routine, for him, often felt like an antidote to dementia.

She should not have told so much this afternoon, Katherine said to herself, sitting where she had sat before. She had never, to anyone else, told anything at all, or talked about what had happened to people who knew. I am unsettled, she thought, and, outside, rain came suddenly, with distant thunder, ending the heat that had become excessive.

When she'd finished her coffee, Katherine didn't leave the café because she didn't have an umbrella. There had been rain in London that night, too. Rain came into it because the elderly woman in the flat across the landing had looked out when it was just beginning, the six o'clock news on the radio just beginning, too. The woman had remembered that earlier she had passed the wide-open window half a flight down the communal stairway and went immediately to close it before, yet again, the carpet was drenched. It was while she was doing so that she heard the downstairs hall door opening and footsteps beginning on the stairs. When she reached her own door, the man had reached the landing. "No, I never thought anything untoward," she had later stated, apparently. Not anything untoward about the girl who occupied the flat across the landing, about the men who came visiting her. "I didn't pry," she said. She had turned round as she reached her own front door and had caught a glimpse of the man who'd come that night. She'd seen him before, the way he stood waiting for the girl to let him in, his clothes, his hair, even his footfall on the stairs: there was no doubt at all.

The café filled up, the doorway crowded with people sheltering, others queuing at the counter. Katherine heard the staccato summons of her mobile phone, a sound she hated, although originally she'd chosen it herself. A voice that might have been a child's said something she couldn't understand and then repeated it, and then the line went dead. So many voices were like a child's these days, she thought, returning the phone to her handbag. "A fashion, that baby telephone voice," Phair had said. "Odd as it might seem."

She nibbled the edge of her florentine, then opened the spill of sugar. The light outside had darkened and now was brightening again. The people in the doorway began to move away. It had rained all night the other time.

"Nothing again?" Phair always inquired when he came in. He was concerned about what had been so arbitrarily and unexpectedly imposed upon her, had once or twice brought back hearsay of vacancies. But even at his most solicitous, and his gentlest, he had himself to think about. It was worse for Phair and always would be, that stood to reason.

Her mobile telephone rang again and his voice said that in his lunch hour he'd bought asparagus because he'd noticed it on a stall, looking good and not expensive. They'd mentioned asparagus yesterday, realizing it was the season; she would have bought some if he hadn't rung. "On the way out of the cinema," she said, having already said that she'd just seen *La Strada* again. He'd tried for her an hour ago, he said, but her phone had been switched off. "Well, yes, of course," he said.

Six months was the length of an affair that took place because something else was wrong: the man she met in the afternoons said that, knowing more about affairs than Katherine did. And, as if he had always been aware that he would, when a little longer than six months had passed he returned to his wife. Since then, he had retained the room while this reunion settled—or perhaps in case it didn't—but his belongings were no longer there. To Katherine, the room looked bigger, yet dingier, without them.

"Why do you love your husband, Katherine? After all this—what he has put you through?"

"No one can answer that."

"You hide from one another, you and he."

"Yes."

"Are you afraid, Katherine?"

"Yes. Both of us are afraid. We dream of her, we see her dead. And we know in the morning if the other one has. We know and do not say."

"You shouldn't be afraid."

They did not ever argue in the room, not even mildly, but disagreed without pursuing their disagreements. Or failed to understand and left that, too. Katherine did not ask if a marriage could be shored up while this room was still theirs for a purpose. Her casual lover did not press her to reveal what she still withheld.

"I can't imagine him," he said, but Katherine did not attempt to describe her husband, only commented that his first name suited him. A family name, she said.

"You're fairly remarkable, you know. To love him so deeply still."

"And yet I'm here."

"Perhaps I mean that."

"More often than not, people don't know why they do things."

"I envy you your seriousness. It's that I'd love you for."

Once, when again he had to go, she stayed behind. He was in a hurry that day; she wasn't quite ready. "Just bang the door," he said.

She listened to his footsteps clattering on the boards of the stairs and was reminded of the old woman saying she had recognized Phair's. Phair's lawyer would have asked in court if she was certain about that and would have wondered how she could be, since to have heard them on previous occasions she would each time have had to be on the landing, which surely was unlikely. He would have suggested that she appeared to spend more time on the communal landing than in her flat. He would have wondered that a passing stranger had left behind so clear an impression of his features, since any encounter there had been would have lasted hardly more than an instant.

Alone in the room, not wanting to leave it yet, Katherine crept back into the bed she'd left only minutes ago. She pulled the bedclothes up although it wasn't cold. The window curtains hadn't been drawn back and she was glad they hadn't. "I didn't much care for that girl," Phair said when the two policemen had gone. "But I was fond of her in a different kind of way. I have to say that, Katherine. I'm sorry." He had brought her coffee and made her sit there, where she was. Some men were like that, he said. "We only talked. She told me things." A girl like that took chances every time she answered her doorbell, he said; and when he cried Katherine knew it was for the girl, not for himself. "Oh, yes, I understand," she said. "Of course I do." A sleazy relationship with a classy tart was what she understood, as he had understood when she told him she could not have children, when he'd said it didn't matter, although she knew it did. "I've risked what was precious," her husband whispered in his shame, and then confessed that deceiving her had been an excitement, too. Risk came into it, Katherine realized then; risk was part of it, the secrecy of concealment, stealth. And risk had claimed its due.

The same policemen came back later. "You're sure about that detail, Madam?" they asked, and afterward, countless times, asked her that again, repeating the date and hearing her repeat that ten to seven was the usual time. Phair hadn't wanted to know—and didn't still—why she had answered as she had, why she continued to confirm that he'd returned ninety minutes sooner than he had. She couldn't have told anyone why, except to say that something like instinct came into it, and that she knew Phair as intimately as she knew herself, that it was impossible to imagine his taking the life of a girl no matter what his relationship with her had been. There was, of course—she would have said if she'd been asked—the pain of that relationship, of he and the girl being together, even if only for conversation. "You quarrelled, sir?" the tall policeman inquired. You could see there'd been a quarrel, he insisted, no way you could say there hadn't been a disagreement that got out of hand. But Phair was not the quarrelling sort. He shook his head. In all his answers, he hadn't disputed much except responsibility for the death. He had not denied he'd been a visitor to the flat. He gave the details of his visits as he remembered them. He accepted that his fingerprints were there, while they accepted nothing. "You're sure, Madam?" they asked again, and her instinct hardened, touched with apprehension, even though their implications were ridiculous. Yes, she was sure, she said. They said their spiel and then arrested him.

Katherine slept and when she woke did not know where she was. But only minutes had passed, less than ten. She washed at the basin in the corner, and slowly dressed. When he was taken from her, in custody until the trial's outcome, it was suggested at the institute that they could manage without her for a while. "No, no," she had insisted. "I would rather come." And in the hiatus that followed—long and silent—she had not known that doubt began to spread in the frail memory of the elderly woman, who in time would be called upon to testify to her statements on oath. She had not known that beneath the weight of importance the old woman was no longer certain that the man she'd seen on that wet evening—already shadowy—was a man she'd seen before. With coaching and encouragement, she would regain her confidence, it must have been believed by those for whom her evidence was essential: the prosecution case rested on identification, on little else. But the long delay had taken a toll, the witness had been wearied by preparation, and did not, in court, conceal her worries. When the first morning of the trial was about to end, the judge calmed his anger to declare that in his opinion there was no case to answer. In the afternoon, the jury was dismissed.

Katherine pulled back the curtains, settled her makeup, made the bed. Blame was there somewhere—in faulty recollection, in the carelessness of policemen, in a prosecution's ill-founded confidence—yet its attribution was hardly a source of satisfaction. Chance and circumstance had brought about a nightmare, and left it to a judge to deplore the bringing of a case that did not stand up. In dismissing it, his comments were stern, but neither that nor his perfect clarity was quite enough: too much was left behind. No other man was ever charged, although of course there was another man.

She banged the door behind her, as she'd been told to. They had not said good-bye, yet as she went downstairs, hearing again the muffled gabble of the racecourse commentator, she knew it was for the last time. The room was finished with. This afternoon, she had felt that, even if it had not been said.

She did not have coffee and walked by the Prince and Dog without noticing it. In her kitchen, she would cook the food she'd bought and they would sit together and talk about the day. She would look across the table at the husband she loved and see a shadow there. They would speak of little things.

She wandered, going nowhere, leaving the bustling street that was gracious also, walking by terraced houses, lace-curtained windows. Her afternoon lover would mend the marriage that had failed, would piece by piece repair the damage because damage was not destruction and was not meant to be. To quarrel often was not too terrible; nor, without love, to be unfaithful. They would agree that they were up to this, and friendly time would do the rest, not asked to do too much. "And she?" his wife one day might wonder, and he would say his other woman was a footnote to what had happened in their marriage. Perhaps that, no more.

Katherine came to the canal, where there were seats along the water. This evening, she would lie, and they would speak again of little things. She would not say she was afraid, and nor would he. But fear was there, for her the nag of doubt, infecting him in ways she did not know about. She walked on past the seats, past children with a nurse. A barge with barrels went by, painted roses on its prow.

A wasteland, it seemed like where she walked, made so not by itself but by her mood. She felt an anonymity, a solitude here where she did not belong, and something came with that which she could not identify. Oh, but it's over, she told herself, as if in answer to this mild bewilderment, bewildering herself further and asking herself how she knew what she seemed to know. Thought was no good: all this was feeling. So, walking on, she did not think.

She sensed, without a reason, the dispersal of restraint. And yes, of course, for all nine years there'd been restraint. There'd been no asking to be told, no asking for promises that the truth was what she heard. There'd been no asking about the girl, how she'd dressed, her voice, her face, and if she only sat there talking, no more than that. There'd been no asking about a worse day than usual on the Underground, and the waiting for a taxi in the rain. For all nine years, there had been silence in their ordinary exchanges, in conversation, in making love, in weekend walks and summer trips abroad. For all nine years, love had been there, and more than just a comforter, too intense for that. Was stealth an excitement still? That was not asked, and Katherine, pausing to watch another barge approaching, knew it never would be now. The flat was entered, and Sharon Ritchie lay suffocated on her sofa. Had she been the victim kind? That, too, was locked away.

Katherine turned to walk back the way she'd come. It wouldn't be a shock, nor even a surprise. He expected no more of her than what she'd given him, and she would choose her moment to say that she must go. He would understand; she would not have to tell him. The best that love could do was not enough, and he would know that also.

Charles Lambert

The Scent of Cinnamon

D*EAR M*RS. *PAYNE,*
I have been given your name by the Reverend Ware, vicar of the English community here. I am a blunt man, and I shall come straight to the point. Ware tells me that you have recently lost your husband and are without means. He has suggested to me that you may be interested in marriage with a man who can provide you with the security and affection you require. He has indicated to me that I may be such a man. I have every reason to trust Ware's judgment in these matters, above all because he knew you as an unmarried girl and speaks highly of your breeding, modesty and intelligence. For my part, I offer you a man of thirty-seven years, of which nineteen have been passed outside his own country. I have a farm that would comfortably contain an English county. I am fit, healthy and, if Ware is to be trusted also in this matter, of sufficiently pleasing appearance to make my appeal for your hand appropriate and possessing of some possibility of success.

I enclose a photograph. The dog's name is Jasper.
I look forward to receiving your reply.
Yours sincerely,
Joseph Broderick

It would do, he thought. He looked at the photograph for a moment and saw a man, a liver-spotted dog, a house, then folded the sheet of paper around it and slid them both into the envelope. Miriam Payne, he murmured, writing these words in his small clear forward-sloping hand, and beneath them an address in Cornwall, a county he had never seen. Miriam Payne, he repeated in a stronger voice, then: Miriam Broderick. Yes. It would do.

The reply arrived six weeks later and was brief.

> Dear Mr. Broderick,
> Thank you for your letter and the photograph enclosed, both of which have given me much food for thought. I shall say at once that I am prepared to consider your offer. However, before doing so, I too shall be frank. I would like you to answer me one question, which may appear impertinent but is, I believe, quite the opposite. Dear Mr. Broderick, have you ever been in love?
> I also enclose a photograph. As you see, I have no dog. I am not sure that I like dogs, nor that dogs like me.
> Yours sincerely,
> Miriam Payne

The woman in the photograph was younger than Joseph had expected. Her hair was long, caught up on one side by a clip of some kind and loose at the other to hang across her shoulder. He couldn't tell its color but imagined it deep and dark and heavy, a lustrous red. Her eyes and eyelashes were also dark. Although she wasn't smiling, the set of her mouth suggested that smiling was its purpose; even solemn, its owner had small dimples in both cheeks. She was dressed in widow's weeds, which made her form hard to decipher, but she appeared to be slender and even elegant. Her hands, crossed on her lap, were small but strong. He closed his eyes and she was still sufficiently there for him to move her and place her beside him, on the other side from Jasper, in front of the house he had built for himself and a wife he had never had. He saw them together and felt his heart beat faster, as though he had chased a runaway sheep across a field. He replied that same day.

Dear Mrs. Payne,

Thank you for your letter and photograph, both of which considerably eased my mind. The fact that you are prepared to consider my offer fills me with hope and, if I may admit such a feeling, trepidation. As to your question, which is more than pertinent, I can answer without shame that I have never been fortunate enough to have known love, convinced though I am that I possess the faculty for it.

I look forward with some anxiety to your reply.
Yours sincerely,
Joseph Broderick

Another six weeks passed. Broderick began to see the house he had built with his own hands through other eyes, through the dark and deep-set eyes of the woman in the photograph. The tamped earth floors, shiny with wear as if waxed, the stone and whitewashed walls, the bareness of the shuttered uncurtained windows, which before he hadn't noticed or had maybe thought appropriate to his single life, as hard and bare as his surroundings, now distressed and embarrassed him. The straight-backed chairs became uncomfortable, unyielding. How could a lady sit on them? How could a lady live in a house so male and austere and unadorned?

He would have asked another woman what could be done to make his house acceptable, but there was no married woman in the neighborhood he could trust to take him seriously. There was no one with the taste required; the women around had neither breeding nor education. Besides, he would look ridiculous if Miriam decided not to marry him, a single middle-aged man, alone in a house full of frills and ribbons. He could have asked Reverend Ware, who had an eye for such things, but didn't.

And what would she bring herself, if she did decide to come, he wondered. Paintings, embroidery, cushions perhaps. A musical instrument of some kind. Perhaps the wisest choice would be to wait in the bare house and allow her to mold it into the place she could most comfortably consider her own, her new married home in her new world. And then he imagined her trunks stacked neatly beside her on the quay, a dozen ironbound trunks, his cart weighed down with them. Sometimes the vision of her was so vivid it seemed that she was already there beside him and he would shake his head until she had gone, and then feel desolate.

When her second letter arrived, his hand began to tremble. Jasper barked and clawed at his waist. "It's all right, lad," Broderick said. "It's all right."

And it was.

The day that Miriam Payne was due to arrive on the spice boat, Joseph Broderick hitched his best horse to the cart and set off before dawn. He was wearing a stiff white collar and the brown serge suit he had bought for the funeral of his first and only friend, a Welshman who had helped him stake out and fence and stock the farm before dying of pleurisy twelve years before. Six years later Broderick had given the dead man's name, Jasper, to his dog, who now sat beside him as the cart jolted over farm tracks towards the road that would take them down to the harbor. The suit was too hot and tight around the waist; he had put on weight since the funeral.

By the time the sun was up he was sweating. By early morning he had stripped down to his vest and braces, and unbuttoned his trousers at the waist. He rode on, feeling sweat dry against his skin. The pleurisy that killed Jasper Preece had begun like this, it occurred to him, and he pulled over to the side to put on his shirt and jacket, his stiff white collar and carefully knotted tie. We all die one way or another, he thought, as the heat sank into his bones, from fire or ice. From passion or the lack of it.

When a back wheel of the cart slipped into a rut and refused to budge, he swore beneath his breath and jumped down to the dusty road, taking off his jacket once more and placing it, folded, on the seat, sliding his braces from his shoulders. He heaved the cart backwards and forwards, shouting at the horse to move. It took almost half an hour before it was back on the road. Overcome by sudden weakness, he sat down on the verge beside the cart. His left arm had begun to ache, strained, he supposed, by the heaving. A moment later, the ache grew worse, a sharp stabbing pain that rose from his wrist to his shoulder. He felt the tightness move over to the heart. His hand went up to his collar, to loosen it and allow him to breathe.

He opened his eyes to see Jasper bound away from him, bark from the far side of the road. The sun was higher; he must have fallen asleep. The rest had done him good, he found; he felt stronger than before. He spurred the horse on, the dog following at a distance. The road became easier on the approach to the town; perhaps he would not be as late as he had thought.

But she was the only person waiting when he reached the harbor. Even the spice boat that had brought her the last leg of her journey had gone to the next port along the coast. She was standing in a grey and white dress, beside a pair of large brown leather suitcases, and when she saw him she raised an arm and waved. It was almost noon. She was quite alone on the waterfront of the otherwise empty harbor. Her hair was redder than he had dared imagine. In the late morning light it looked like a beacon. He jumped down from the cart and almost ran towards her, Jasper barking behind him. She held out her hand as he pulled up, oddly shy; she smiled and nodded, a brief but certain nod, and he understood that he would do. He took her hand in his and stood there like a fool as she stepped so close he could feel the warmth of her body on his own; she kissed his cheek, first one and then the other, like a Frenchwoman. "Joseph Broderick," she said, her head on one side. "Miriam Payne," he answered. "I shall call you Joseph," she said, and smiled. "And I shall call you Miriam."

He was shivering, from fever or fear or excitement he couldn't tell, as he swung the two suitcases into the cart and gave her his arm, thrilled to see how easily she took it, as though she had known him all her life; as though they were already married. She had no gloves; her hands were colored by the sun. He noticed this and thought, She will like the farm. She belongs here.

Only Jasper seemed discontent. He had halted a yard or two away from them both and sat down suddenly on his haunches, his tongue lolling out at the side, his head cocked. "Come on then, get a move on," Joseph shouted across to the dog as soon as he and Miriam were seated together, the cases in the space behind them. Jasper stood up and sidled towards the cart, the hair on the base of his spine raised up in a brush, then scrambled up over the side, curling into a tight ring at the back, shucked down in the farthest corner, his muzzle beneath his tail.

"You'll need to wear a hat," Joseph said, half turning to Miriam. "You aren't used to this kind of sun in Cornwall." But the thought that she might cover her head distressed him as he spoke. He fancied he could smell the spices she had traveled with, the scent of cinnamon and cloves, in her clothes and hair. "Oh no," she said, "I love the sun. I can't believe the sun will do me harm."

He knew then that he had been right not to adorn the house with curtains and rugs. She would take him as he was, the bareness and the hard-trodden earth.

It was late afternoon when they reached the farm. He had expected they would talk, but she seemed content to sit beside him, her hand occasionally at rest on his arm, the other hand brushing her hair from her face as the breeze displaced it. She wore no jewels, he noticed, and was glad. She asked him once for water and he reached behind for the flask. As she drank, he watched her throat, the life in it. When she gave him back the flask he drank from it hungrily without wiping the neck, his blood rushing. She had taken the cork from his hand; she closed the flask with a swift firm gesture and returned it to its place behind their seat as though she had done this all her life. Miriam Broderick, he thought. Together, they rode on in silence, refreshed, until the house was in sight on the skyline.

He raised his arm and pointed. "That's where I live," he said, without any sense of breaking the silence, because what he had said was needed.

"Where we live," she corrected him.

She allowed him to help her from the cart, placing her hands on his as he circled her waist and lifted her up and then down to the ground. How light she was! He thought she would wait beside him while he stepped up on the wheel to take her suitcases, but she walked across to the house, her hands lifting her hair from her neck in two great waves of red, and opened the door. She seemed to shimmer in the heat against the whitewashed wall of the house, more like a flame than a living person. He saw her pause for a second, then step inside, into the darkness. He put the suitcases down beside the cart and, releasing the horse, was about to lead it to the trough to drink. First the horse, he thought, then us. But the horse shied away. Jasper had jumped from the cart and was edging towards him, almost on his belly, as though afraid of a beating. Joseph bent down and cradled the dog's head in his hands, startled when the dog bared its teeth and pulled away. He was putting it off, he knew that; he was putting off the moment when he and Miriam would be alone together in the house. He was scared of both of them and of what they might do.

But he was wrong to worry. As soon as he had entered the room, she walked across and took both his hands in hers and stared into his eyes.

"We are man and wife from this moment on," she said. "We are Miriam and Joseph."

"Miriam," he repeated in a voice so quiet he wondered how she could have heard. She kissed his mouth.

"I am God's gift to you," she said. "That's what Miriam means, did you know that? God's gift."

"I don't believe in God," he said.

The next morning, Jasper had gone. While Miriam dressed, Joseph walked round and then behind the house, calling the dog's name. He shouldn't have been worried; Jasper had often disappeared for a day or two, even three. He shouldn't have cared about the dog at all, with the memory of the skin of Miriam against his own, her lips on his; more than a memory, as he bore the woman's scent on his hands and in his hair, both utterly new and known, familiar to him. He tasted her, sweet and acrid, in his mouth like some strange flavor he had only heard of, some preserving spice that warded off death. Yet, after the dog's behavior the day before, he was worried. He hadn't liked the way the animal had cringed and snarled, nor the brush of raised fur above its tail. He called and called, without result. Finally, he went back to the house. In the kitchen, Miriam was setting the table for two.

"He'll come back," he said. "Dogs can be jealous."

"I told you dogs didn't like me," she said.

That morning Joseph showed her around the farm. He took her from barn to dipping trough to shearing house in a delirium of passion he had never imagined possible, as though he had died and been reborn in a place without hardship or solitude, where he was precious to someone else. Often, she stopped his chattering by laying a finger on his mouth, and then her lips. They leaned against the back wall of one of the outbuildings and made love, her skirt lifted up. Her hair was in his mouth, her fingers laced behind his head, her low moans in his ear.

The first day passed like this, and the second too, and there was still no sign of Jasper. At the end of a week, when the dog had not returned,

Joseph said: "I should go down into the town, to see what news there is." He didn't mention Jasper. They were sitting together outside the house, beneath a sort of canopy Joseph had made from wood, covered by Miriam with fine sheets the warm breeze lifted and furled.

"You mustn't worry about him," she said.

Joseph paused. "I suppose I ought to speak to Reverend Ware as well," he said, "about our marriage."

"Oh, that can wait," she said. She leaned back in her chair and lifted her arms. She was wearing a loose smock and the sleeves fell back so that he could see the soft pale skin of the underside of her upper arms. He knelt beside her and buried his face in her lap.

Almost a month passed before Joseph rode into town. He had begged her to come, but Miriam had refused; she had too much to do at home. She hadn't wanted him to go at all; and really there was no need, apart from a sense of restlessness, almost unease, that Joseph had begun to feel. It seemed to him that the work of the farm took no time at all. Each afternoon was as warm and sunny as the one before, each morning cool and fresh. His days and nights were devoted to Miriam, yet walking around the house and the nearest fields, as they did each evening, there was no sign of neglect, no fence in disrepair, no animal in need. He must be getting up and working in his sleep, Joseph thought.

In the end she said it would do them good to spend a few hours apart. She wrote him a list of items she needed for her dressmaking and mending, silk thread, buttons, elastic; he would have to go to shops he had never been into before. He would show them the list, he decided, rather than say the words, which struck him as shameful although he couldn't say why. And then he would go to the reverend, who would have heard of Miriam's arrival by now and must have wondered where they were.

He hadn't mounted the horse since Miriam's arrival. It snorted and bucked as he walked towards it with the saddle in his arms, as though it had never been ridden before. Not until it was cornered against the fence did it allow the saddle to be slung across its back.

He was three or four miles from the farm when he saw Jasper, sniffing at the broken wheel of an abandoned cart. He didn't recognize the dog at first, but it must have known him because it staggered away from the cart towards the ditch and stood there, staring at Joseph, before moving off. The ribs and haunches of the dog jutted out from beneath the skin, which was covered with dust, an almost uniform grey-brown, and burrs. One of the ears was torn and bleeding, the wound coated with flies. The dog panted in the heat, reeling slightly as it walked beside the road, heading in the same direction as the horse. Joseph called out, but the force of his voice was broken by distress and the dog appeared not to hear. It was only when Joseph drew level and leapt from the saddle no more than a yard away that Jasper reacted. The dog sank down on its belly, its front legs stretched out, its teeth bared. As Joseph approached it made a long slow growl, increasing in pitch to an anguished whine from the back of the throat. "Jasper," the man coaxed, trembling, his hand held out. "Jasper." The dog backed away, wriggling off without raising itself from the dust of the road, its belly dragging, the whine in the throat like the slow turning of a ratchet. It shook its head and the swarm of flies rose from the wound on the ear and resettled.

Joseph straightened up, shaking his head, then stood there and watched as the dog slunk off. He waited until the dog had gone a dozen yards before calling his name once more. At that, the dog turned back and stared at him, and Joseph turned his eyes away, abashed. Finally, with a heavy heart, he remounted his horse, which pulled away from him as he swung his leg across the saddle. He glanced at the broken cart behind him, left to rust and rot. It must have been close to here that his own cart had got stuck in the rut, he thought, and his hand rose to his heart.

The harbor town seemed as empty as it had the day of Miriam's arrival. The air was heavy with the scent of cardamom and ginger, cinnamon and cloves; he looked across the water for the spice boat, his vision blurred by images of Miriam, because there was nothing to be seen but her, his fingers in her hair, his hands around her waist; the air was filled with her. He was wandering towards the row of traders' shops, intoxicated, when a notice posted on a wall attracted his attention and he walked across to read it. It spoke of a shipwreck that had taken place in those waters a month before; there had been no survivors. His eyes skimmed down the list of the dead, out of habit. The whole world might be dead, he thought, for all it mattered, as long as Miriam and he were alive.

And then he saw her name.

Ten minutes later he stood before the Reverend Ware, shouting and waving his arms. The man was talking to a group of old women about the weather, how it had turned for the worse in the past few days, such terrible storms they had had. Joseph grabbed at the cloth of the vicar's sleeve, but his cold hand made no purchase. He might as well not have been there. Only once, the vicar turned his eyes in Joseph's direction and flinched, as though he had seen a ghost.

Justine Dymond

Cherubs

W HEN THE cook heard the American tanks and motor cars rumbling up the muddy road from the west, she ran out of the kitchen, through the courtyard, and past the barn, waving her apron, surrendering in delight.

This is what Béatrice tells us. In this moment that she tells us, we fear revealing any pride—those *Americans*, those Americans not unlike us, except separated by fifty-some years.

We think, Americans saved this house, St. Urbain, a mansion really. Tall ceilings, long hallways of rooms, a stone veranda with dancing cherubs atop its posts. A stretch of lawn that tumbles down to a pond and woods beyond. An estate. We think, the Americans—yes, the Americans!—saved the grandmother, the cook, and the maid, who stayed throughout the German occupation, *la grand-mère* who refused to leave the house, even when arrangements were made for all the children—Béatrice was nine at the time—to stay in Nancy. And the cook, forced to make meals for those stinking Germans—except the Austrian officer, always polite, always respectful of *la famille*—the cook now gloriously freed from her servitude to men who didn't even understand wine, who ate *coq au vin* as though they were animals thrown raw meat, with no appreciation for subtlety of sauce, the impeccable timing that renders the flesh tender.

We hesitate to smile at this. We do anyway—we know it's not us, *we* didn't personally save St. Urbain from the Germans, but Béatrice speaks as though those American soldiers, marching up the road, tired, hungry, scared, were our kin.

Béatrice says, The cook ran into the road, waving her apron at the American soldiers. See, *Maman* knew the Germans were gone. It had been a full night and into the next morning with no sounds of boots stomping overhead or voices shouting down the cellar stairs—those German voices that provoked shudders and tears in the maid as she and *Maman* huddled in the cellar. The silence was all they needed to know. The Germans had evacuated. Something else was coming.

When the cook ran out into the road waving her makeshift flag of surrender, the Americans shot at her.

This is what we feared—even if only in that smallest part of our consciousness that says, Don't get carried away, chauvinistic pride is always easily deflated.

Béatrice laughs at this point in her story.

We laugh, too, but a different kind of laughter, the kind that expresses embarrassment, horror, shame at our own sense—however hesitant—of national pride. The Americans shot at the cook!

Then Béatrice is abruptly interrupted in her story by one of the cousin bridesmaids reminding her of something urgent, something we can't quite make out, but something to do with the banquet arrangements, musicians who need something, and Béatrice is whisked away, leaving us to absorb this shocking change in events—the saviors, the Americans, who shot at the cook.

Was she hurt? we wonder.

We look around us, at the cousins and uncles and aunts running around, preparing for the wedding, the reason everyone has gathered for the weekend, for Claudine and Max's nuptials. And we consider—in our despair about a story cut short—should we stop one of the other aunts rushing by? Who's she? Isn't that Claudine's cousin Bette? Would she know what happened to the cook?

We have to know what happened to the cook, and not just out of curiosity, not just to know the ending. It's a matter of national pride; we say this jokingly, of course.

Well, there *is* the grandmother, Béatrice's *maman*, Claudine's *grand-mère*, who is alive, who is here at the wedding, the matriarch of St. Urbain. She didn't die, wasn't shot by Americans. There is that. We must console ourselves with this thought for now, at least until Béatrice returns or we find someone else to finish the story for us.

Everyone looks busy now. Bette is arranging the flowers on the tables outside one of the parlors where there will be dancing after dinner. The other parlor, across the marble entranceway, is where *Grand-mère* entertained *les américains* for coffee earlier that afternoon. She asked us polite questions. Where were we from? Did we like the goat cheese made in the local region? We sat on the edge of beautiful chairs, not elaborate, a bit worn actually, but nonetheless expressing a certain aristocratic class. We sipped the strong coffee as inconspicuously as possible. We smiled and wrapped our loose lips around pointed French words, inwardly grimacing at the sounds that emerged from our mouths.

The night before, Claudine's father, Jean-Paul, showed us the original Diderot encyclopedia owned by the family. Excitedly we watched as he took down a large volume from the bookcase in the parlor. Shouldn't it be kept in a temperature-regulated room? we thought, frowning, but not daring to say it aloud, remembering that we had to hide our gauche American ways, our obsession with the *right* way to do things, much like our obsessions with refrigeration, statistics, and showering.

Jean-Paul opened the encyclopedia and we flinched at the sound of the spine cracking. But we brushed this aside and oohed and aahed over the simplistic maps of Africa and America, the vast sweeps of earth Europeans thought of as savage lands, unpeopled, unsettled. We admired the columns of careful French cursive, the compiling of knowledge as though a thing of fragile beauty, vulnerable to thieves and natural disasters. We wanted to caress the pages with our hands, though we repressed this urge and merely nodded in agreement to everything Jean-Paul said, even when we didn't understand.

We took all that knowledge to bed with us that night, tucked in with us in the narrow, sagging mattress, our room an old servant's *chambre* above the barn. It looked as though the room hadn't been occupied since World War Two, but that's okay, we tell each other, it was nice of Claudine's family to arrange accommodations. Maybe this is where the cook slept! Over the barn, planning the meals for German officers, grimacing at the thought of wasting precious hens and pigs and goats on the swine. Béatrice had said that the cook, though she could speak German—indeed, her father was German—refused to speak their language to the occupiers, forcing them to rely on the shaky French of one young assistant to the commandant. But she understood everything they said, as she stirred soup in the kitchen, spitting and stirring, adding cod liver oil and rotting tomatoes. The next morning she watched from the dining room window, while she laid out bread and butter. The officers ran to the pine bushes lining the driveway. She cackled. She didn't care. Let them kill her, after they shit out their bowels. She'd be happy to die for poisoning Germans.

But the Germans didn't kill her. The *Americans* shot at the cook!

We wander toward the hallway, watch through the window as the caterer's helpers set up chairs and tables in the barn, where the reception will be held. There's a makeshift stage and flowers strewn along the tables. There are candles and white tablecloths. Earlier that morning we helped sweep the barn and the courtyard, move furniture and wash the windows—what they really needed was a new coat of paint. We did our part. We joined in and made ourselves useful. Now we feel a bit in the way, without a task, without purpose. Except to hear the end of the story. We head toward the stairway, hesitate a moment, hoping for a glance of Béatrice through the open kitchen door. We see an army of people chopping and stirring food, but no Béatrice.

Under the stairway is the door to *Grand-mère*'s rooms. She is resting now, we've been told, saving her energy for the church ceremony. We climb the stairs, curving up and around to the second floor, a wide hallway with windows to one side, looking down on the courtyard, and rooms on the other side. We hear the murmur of activity behind the bride's door. We wish we could be there, to be one of the "chosen" to spend the few hours before the ceremony with the bride and groom, helping to pin dresses and rouge cheeks, to keep track of corsages and run the myriad last-minute errands that always need doing.

But we are guests, we are *les américains*. We've been told to relax, to enjoy ourselves, to take advantage of the countryside and the early summer air. Instead, we turn at the top of the stairs and navigate the narrow hallway filled with bookcases and bric-a-brac and cross the wooden planks to our room. We decide to take a nap. We lie down, face to face, nose to nose, on the narrow mattress, huddling for warmth—it's chilly in the servants' quarters!—and smile, knowing we won't sleep, impossible to sleep with all the activity around us, knowing that a dozen people are working below us, and with the mattress so sagged, so bowed, that in minutes we are fidgety, our backs ache.

We are too soft, too accustomed to the comforts of the New World, too coddled. We laugh at our own fragility. How do the French do it? How do they stay so focused on what matters—love, life, ideas—when their mattresses sag and their rooms are dusty? We are clearly weaker, inflexible, unable to adapt. We don't admit it, but we could die right now for wall-to-wall carpeting and big, fluffy pillows.

What did this room look like when the cook lived here? We imagine a small dresser with a shrine to the Virgin, the cook waking early before sunrise, lighting a candle and saying a short prayer. She would have worn solid, leather boots, the kind that laced up, and she probably only had two changes of clothes. She would have used the kitchen sink to wash her face and then brew coffee. She'd have to feed the animals on her own, take care of all the barnyard chores since the stable hands had left to join the Resistance.

Yes, the Resistance! The cook longed to join the Resistance, but she knew that she must stay to help the family. In a way, she was a part of the Resistance, she would think to herself. She prepared *le petit déjeuner* for Madame and her maid, first. She knocked on the cellar door before clomping down the narrow stairs. She recounted to Madame what the Germans had been saying. They sound worried, she said. They say *die Amerikaner* often. They seemed to always be studying maps, rolling them up quickly when she entered the parlor with bread and coffee (just a little dirt added).

We think of the grandmother, so petite and frail now, her delicate ways. But to think she refused to leave the house while the Germans were here. She was brave! She was young and so brave! What would we have done? And with seven children, finally taken to Nancy, arranged by the Austrian officer, the one who was very proper and correct with the children, the cook almost regretted having poisoned his soup too. But what could she do?

We are restless. We need to know what happened to the cook. And where is the maid now?

Though it's still a couple hours until the ceremony, we decide to dress. We've laid out our things, a dress, a pair of stockings, a once-pressed pair of pants, now a bit wrinkled from travel, a clean shirt. We dress, slowly, carefully, savoring the feel of clean, fancy clothes, the act of dressing, as though the entire day depended on it. We continue the story, reminding ourselves of what Béatrice has already said, trying to find a clue somewhere of what happened next.

The French had occupied the house before the Germans came. They were proper, very proper, with *la famille*. Most of the French officers camped in tents on the lawn, waking early to the sound of cows baying, udders engorged. The family confined themselves to the upper rooms and the kitchen, while the officers used the parlors for their headquarters. The family made a game of it, telling the youngest children that they were safe because the soldiers were with them.

When evacuation orders came, the commanding officer told Béatrice's father to leave, to get to Paris, to Nancy even. The Germans were coming. The father pleaded with *Maman*—now *Grand-mère*—but she refused. It was her family's house after all, and she could not abandon it. She thought of the banquets and balls her parents had hosted, when she was just a little girl before the First World War. She thought of her own coming out on the eve of that war, the shells that fell in the garden, the east wing conservatory one morning imploded by a German bomber. The family didn't leave then. They slept in the cellar then, the family and the servants who stayed. How could she leave now?

And so the family waited. The French had left, clearing camp as carefully as possible, leaving behind only holes from their tent pegs in the lawn. The family waited. They went about their usual business. Then one day there was a peculiar silence in the countryside. The children were sent to the cellar, where they huddled with Father. *Maman* sat in her parlor, very still, very patient, and waited. The cook got down on her knees and scrubbed the kitchen floor. Again. She wanted to have this to do, she couldn't bear the waiting. The maid wept in her room above the barn.

Maman sat, listening to the sound of the brush's bristles against the stone floor, and beyond that, silence. With dusk came the first growl of engines.

We stand in the narrow passage between our room and the main hall, telling ourselves this story. On the bookshelf is a hodgepodge of things—

board games, tools, broken ceramic, and a helmet. We are shocked. We've passed by this bookshelf already a dozen times at least since the morning. Why hadn't we seen it before? It is heavy, smaller than we imagined a helmet to be—more like a cap. Its greenness reminds us of algae, of another war, of swamps. Inside in thick black ink: Johnson. An American name. We imagine a black American soldier, on his first tour of duty, his first time out of the U.S.—heck! his first time out of Georgia. A hero.

Except, we must remember, the Americans shot at the cook.

Someone is coming up the stairs. We hear footsteps and then gradually a head of short, black-and-gray hair appears. We can't believe our luck! It's Béatrice.

As she reaches the second floor, she sees us standing in the passageway with the helmet. We sort of gesture at her with it, a kind of wave with the helmet. We are saying, Look, here is proof, here is what war leaves behind, what stories leave behind.

Béatrice nods and smiles, showing us what she has in her hands, a bridesmaid's dress made of light green organza. She is delivering it to the room where the bride is sequestered. But Béatrice's nod promises us she will return.

We are delirious with anticipation. We turn the helmet over and over. We try it on, its heaviness pressing down on the skull like memory. Like history. We laugh at our own profundity. We are Americans after all. We are supposed to scoff at the shackles of history. We can slough off history like a snake sheds its skin, leave it behind for others to worry about.

And yet, here it is in our hands, solid, weighty, and green.

Béatrice gently takes the helmet from our hands, turns it over, and says aloud, Johnson. We loved the American soldiers, she says. It meant coming back home with Father. It meant chocolate and chewing gum. We'd never had chewing gum before.

We think about chewing gum as though it were a brand new idea. We remember chewing it as children, swallowing countless lumps of gum hardened by endless chewing, and the fear that we would never digest it.

Yes, yes, we say, but what about the cook? What happened to her?

Béatrice flaps her hand and laughs. Oh, nothing. When the Americans were coming, they were scared and they shot at everything that moved. But once they got closer and saw it was just a lady with an apron, they stopped shooting.

We are certainly relieved—those scared American soldiers!—they didn't hurt the cook. But there is a small part of us that feels disappointed, the drama turned to comedy, to farce. Is it better that the Americans were scared, rather than fierce?

Why did this helmet get left behind?

That, I do not know, Béatrice says and turns, heads down the stairs.

We hastily replace the helmet and follow her, not wanting her to leave us once again in midstory.

What happened to the maid and *Grand-mère*? Did they stay with the Americans?

Oh, yes. And the children, we all came back with Father. The American soldiers taught us baseball. I think, actually, they were quite bored.

And with that Béatrice scurries into the kitchen, leaving us at the bottom of the stairs. We consider the kitchen, but now that we've dressed we don't want to risk spills and stains. We turn the other way and walk toward the veranda. The sunlight dapples the marble hallway and children burst suddenly from doors and around corners, chased by older cousins or frazzled mothers. We smile in our distraction, hoping we will be stopped and spoken to, but no one approaches and we pass through the hall and the doors to the veranda.

The veranda stretches across the front of the house. At its center, where we stand now, stairs lead to a gravel driveway and then to the lawn. Stone cherubs twist and frolic along the veranda railing, frozen in movement. We touch their faces, chipped and pockmarked by weather and wear, their stone skin warmed under the sun.

It's a beautiful day for a wedding, we say to each other and skip down the stairs, holding hands, feeling ourselves young again, like children, escaped from adult concerns and tasks. We run across the driveway, gravel flying out behind our shoes, and across the lawn, down down down to the edge of the pond.

Out of breath, we stop and turn around, look back at the mansion, now spread out against the sky like a patient etherized . . . yes, yes, we could be in an earlier era, when people drank champagne out of shoes and Americans flocked to Europe. If you squint your right eye, we say, to erase the car parked at the side of the house, it could be just as it was then. We could imagine buggies and horse-drawn carriages coming through the gates and across the driveway, stopping at the veranda stairs, discharging their well-heeled passengers for tea, for dinner, for a ball.

From where we stand on the lawn, hands, like a military salute, shielding our eyes from the sun, we see a flutter of movement behind a second-story window. The bride and her bridesmaids. The groom and his groomsmen. The preparations continue, time continues. We can look back, squinting into the sun, but what can we see, blinded, the story half known, our desire, like children, fierce and fickle?

After the ceremony, we are driven back by a kind cousin and his wife. Scrunched in the backseat of the car, we listen to them exclaim about the wedding and we contribute what we can. Claudine was magnificent, so beautiful and serene. Max—Max in a tuxedo! What a laugh! Who would have guessed we'd ever see the day? And *Grand-mère*, in the front pew of the church—the huge, austere church with its stone arches reaching so far above us that voices got lost and never returned from that spacious heaven. *Grand-mère* so tiny and in her element. And the grandchildren— in costumes! they made their own costumes!—when they were called to the altar, they came marching like a parade of jesters and merry pranksters. Such formal elegance, such irreverent fun at the same time.

As we offer these observations and listen to the cousin and his wife, the car turns in to the long private road, shaded by poplars, leading to St. Urbain. Up ahead we can see the stone gates, but not the house, so thick are the woods and so long is the road. It's as though we were approaching again for the first time. When we pass through the gates and St. Urbain appears close and large, we feel the coolness of the poplars' shade, and a surge in the stomach that can only be described as love. Everyone is silent in the car, only the crunch of rubber tires on gravel, and then, slowly, the faint, ethereal sound of a piano playing somewhere in the house.

Everyone gathers on the veranda stairs, with champagne flutes and snippets of food—bruschetta and stuffed mushrooms. We stand and chew, murmur things like What a day! How beautiful they were! Do you remember when . . . ? We wait for the newly nuptialed to arrive, and after about an hour, as the sun starts to move farther west, cutting a sharp line of shadow across the driveway, we hear the sounds of laughter and wheels coming through the gates.

They arrive in a horse-drawn carriage, and we exclaim at how it is exactly as we had imagined it in another era. Small children, children of cousins, are lifted up and into the carriage with the couple. Everyone wants a turn. Everyone wants to be like the bride and groom, at the center, at the focus of attention, or at least to be in the viewing range of such royalty.

Someone hands the bride and groom glasses of champagne while they are still in the carriage. The best man presents a toast. He is in a wheelchair that has to be lifted up and down the stone steps. He will tell us later that he was in a car accident, paralyzed from the waist down.

The toast said, we raise our glasses and sip our wine. From behind us there comes a sound like a wave crashing onto a rocky shore, and then fluttering whiteness bursts around our heads. First there are shrieks, and then laughter and murmurings, as the doves fly above us, bank and turn as a group, and then circle around the house out of sight.

The champagne tingles now inside our heads, and after the releasing of the doves, we are ready to witness anything. What's next? Will there be elephants and tap dancers? Acrobatics? Fire eaters? We would be very impressed by sword swallowers, we agree. Yes, anything that involved ingesting fire or weaponry. Wouldn't it be great if more weddings were like circuses? Bride and groom would undergo intense trapeze training before declaring *I do* in the air. Now *that* would be devotion, not merely spectacle.

We follow the other guests as they follow the couple up the veranda stairs and through the house to the courtyard. We are going in for dinner. There will be more wine. There will be a long buffet table of food, deli meats displayed in the form of a peacock—yes, a peacock!—and cheeses and salads and, of course, long batons of bread, hard crusty baguettes that we will devour as though we have never eaten before. There are speeches and skits, singing, jokes, more speeches, voices slurred. And then, as we are imbibing another glass of wine—no use counting anymore, we lost count a while ago—we hear the strains of familiar music and a warm prickly sensation creeps up our backs, the body's knowledge, before the brain, that we are being watched. The music's familiarity wakes us from our gluttony before we consciously recognize the tune, and when we look up everyone is grinning at us. They are playing "The Star Spangled Banner." Flushed with embarrassment, we grin back and then affect little waves, like Miss America on her float, acknowledging the loyalty of the masses.

It's not *spankled* banner. *Spangled* banner.

The couple next to us argues in English tinged with French vowels. And with that distraction comes relief. The music fades and everyone is invited back to the buffet table for fruit and more cheese and chocolate.

Outside the barn, it's now dark. We've been eating and drinking for hours. We feel properly medieval in our dedication to feasting. Guests are speaking and laughing louder, as they meander through the courtyard. Someone has started playing music in the house and candles are lit all along the walkway and into the house. But the air feels marvelously fresh and we linger outside, wobbling around the side of the barn.

We walk up to the road behind the barn, where the cook ran, waving her white apron. There is a tree just there, across the road, magnificently fat, its leaves rustling like a Victorian lady's underskirts. We turn toward the west. Fireflies blink across the dark. We can barely make out the reach of the road, we strain to see its horizon. The cook would have seen the soldiers coming, an indistinguishable mass of men, and then, here—we point to the tree—she would have fallen flat at the crack of gunfire. Would she have yelled? Would she have called out, *Nous sommes les français!* Or would she have lain still, just waiting, her heart pounding, until the soldiers came so close that she could smell their sweat and hear their breathing? She would have heard the harsh nasal of an American soldier ordering her to stand up. And then once on her feet, her apron flung forgotten on the ground, she would have smiled and kissed the first soldier she saw. In her machine-gun French, she would have scolded them for shooting at her and taking so long to save them. The soldiers would relax, pull out cigarettes and slump into the grass beside the road, thankful for a moment's rest. A lieutenant who studied French in high school would be pushed forward to speak with the cook, and studiously she would listen to his questions, his confusion of words, his youthful fear as he asks, Where are we? Only, to the cook's amusement, he is asking her, *Qui sommes-nous?* Who are we?

The cook would clap him on the shoulder and laugh, saying, *Mais, bien sûr, vous êtes les américains!*

There is a sharp whistling sound and then a crack. We turn pale—what is that? A moment of nonsound, as though the air were sucked away, and then a fountain-spray of colorful light beyond the house. We head back across the road and through the courtyard. Everyone else is moving toward the house. More fireworks shoot off, one twirling and twisting like a snake, and then crack crack crack as they explode above the house.

Guests crowd on the veranda, the bride and groom, too, standing in the middle of the group like queen bees surrounded by worker bees. We are all looking up, our necks stretched up to the sky, its infinite backdrop. Our eyes reflect in miniature the streams and bouquets and twinklings of fireworks. We are hushed, we are awestruck, we are humbled by this god's display of power.

It is like July Fourth, is it not? Béatrice says. She is next to us, looking up into the sky.

It is, we agree, but we don't want it to be. We want it instead to be like this, like a wedding, like champagne and chocolate, deli meats shaped into peacocks, cooks who refuse to speak German, *mamans* braving occupation, and the faces of each other in the light of sky.

Béatrice beckons us over to the far end of the veranda. She puts her hand on a stone cherub's head, her thumb tracing a concavity.

She speaks and we push closer, tilting our heads to hear her better.

Vous voyez? You see these missing pieces? The American soldiers were so bored, she says. They had nothing to do all day but wait and wait.

We are stunned. We are speechless. Then there is a rush of popping and whistling, and the fireworks burst in a grand finale of noise and color. We look up and up and ooh and aah.

When we look down again, the guests are moving back into the house. There will be music and dancing well into the dawn, the bride and groom will slip quietly away to sleep, also the *grand-mère* and her memories. Only the drunken few who deny the end of things will linger, clinging to each other, smiling wearily, picking at the ravaged buffet.

We won't want to give up either. And so we will stroll along the gravel driveway in the misty sunrise. Beside us, the bullet-ridden cheeks and arms and legs of the cherubs will stay frozen in their postures of flight, enduring beyond even this.

Eddie Chuculate

Galveston Bay, 1826

O N THEIR second day, Old Bull's party began to see many wolves and coyotes in the distance, slung low to the ground, throwing backward glances. The animals appeared in the midafternoon as mirages through a heat-wave gauze that rose off the plain and made things shimmer and seem not as they were. One stopped and sat on his haunches and looked behind him. He licked his chops, then looked right at Old Bull before slinking away. Something extraordinary was happening, plainly, but Old Bull was unconcerned. There were many days to cover before reaching this Great Lake he had heard so much of. They were Old Bull, Red Moon, Sandman, and Whiteshield. Other than strips of dried meat wrapped in skins and an extra horse each on a side rope, they carried no excess baggage. Their horses were lean and muscled and born to run. But this wasn't a war party or a scouting trip. This was plain-and-simple joyriding, an adventure, and who wants to be bogged down on an adventure? Privately, Old Bull thought the stories were exaggerated: days and days of water in either direction? The absolute end of the Earth? If this was true, this would surely be the very origin of their existence, he thought.

The water was very low in the Red River, and they let the horses drink after they crossed. Toward evening the antelope came—sand-brown like the terrain and splotched with white—first one, then in twos and threes. Soon, Old Bull's party was surrounded front and back by the usually very skittish animals. They stopped their horses and looked in all directions. Old Bull liked the way the antelope sprang in long, graceful arcs, one after the other, like they were playing children's games. But Sandman drew and shot an arrow into one's neck right at the top of its jump. It fell on its two front legs and lay quivering in the grass. He got down and pulled out his arrow, then slit its neck with a quick jerk. He did all this calmly. Old Bull shook his head. Red Moon laughed. That damned Sandman.

Later on, Whiteshield was almost thrown from his horse when it nearly stepped on a rattlesnake. The horse dipped suddenly and reared up, but Whiteshield brought him down and calmed him, scratching the side of his neck. Old Bull told him he'd better watch where he was going next time. They splashed through a small creek, and on the top of the next rise a grasshopper flew into Old Bull's face. He felt its scratchy little legs on his cheek and tried to flick it off, but it leapt away. Sandman pointed. Old Bull looked and saw waves of insects flying toward them, heard their wings fluttering. There were locusts, grasshoppers, crickets. The riders hid their faces against the sides of their horses and galloped through the cloud of bugs. Once past, they slowed to a lope. The horses smelled smoke, raising their heads and flaring their nostrils. Old Bull's horse sneezed sharply. Then Old Bull himself smelled it. At the top of the hill, where they could see for miles all around, they saw a fire to the west. It rose up like the bluffs of a red canyon, its flame lapping and advancing. Animals fled as it progressed—more animals than Old Bull had ever seen at one time. That night, they dozed on their pallets in a cottonwood grove, the remnants of antelope fat spitting and sizzling on embers. A strand of Red Moon's hair was caught in his lips. It went in and out as he snored. Breezes came and went, rustling leaves and making music.

The fire now behind them, they left at sunup. Sometimes they rode in a lazy zigzag, taking it easy, or abreast in an easy lope. Sandman's horse would always begin to gallop when it smelled water, and Sandman had to check him. After two days they came to hilly, elevated country, and had to dismount and lead their horses around granite boulders and rocks and under clumps of juniper and pine. This landscape came upon them unexpectedly, protruding from the wildflower- and grass-whipped prairie like a miniature mountain range. They made camp near the top, which had a wide-open view of the plains to the south. Taking a leak, Red Moon saw a line of three or four schooner wagons, crawling insectlike into the sunset. He joked with Old Bull that they better not tell Sandman. No telling what he'd do.

Two days later, their horses began to smell water, raising and dipping their heads, wild eyed, snorting, difficult to control. They were on marshy low-land, and salt grass and wispy cane had taken the place of wild cotton and tumbleweeds. A sudden gale slung Old Bull's hair forward, and he traced the wind ahead of him, its current visible as it curled through stands of Johnsongrass and willow. Soon there was water everywhere: low-lying lakes, bayous, and swamps. The men stopped and surveyed. Nearby, geese and cranes covered a shallow pond, and more were dropping down, falling with outstretched wings and extended feet, settling with soft splashes. The birds bobbed upon the water, their mild puttering and clucking remind-ing Old Bull of a flock of wild turkeys he once spied up north. He was mildly disappointed, though. There was a lot of water, but this couldn't be the Great Lake. There were many lakes like this up north. Whiteshield said that they would probably have to cross here to make it farther south because soon the water would be too deep. With a yell, Sandman whipped his horse suddenly into the backwater, and his piercing scream, the splash-ing and frantic hollering of the geese, began to fill the universe. One by one, the entire raft of wildfowl rose up and blotted out the sky, and Old Bull felt the wind from their wings on his skin.

They started out before sunrise, and as they rode, the stars paled and the sky turned deep, clear blue. Red Moon halted and pointed out the Indian. A figure, apparently smeared in clay, knelt at the edge of a lagoon with a dark surface clear as a mirror. The men stroked and whispered to their horses, keeping them silent. The Indian rose and carried water up and over a hill, out of sight. They untied their spare horses, then secured them and quietly followed him, steam trailing from the horses' nostrils. When they topped the hill, about a dozen Indians faced them with bows drawn. Sandman reached for his bow, but Old Bull grabbed his arm and with his other arm waved back and forth in a friendly way. He told the others to do the same. They did, but an arrow flew by Whiteshield's ear and slammed into the riverbank, buried to the feather. They whirled around and galloped down to where their spare horses were waiting behind a cottonwood stand. Old Bull tried it again when the Indians appeared on the rise. Waving, gesturing. *No weapons. Friendly.* Red Moon and Whiteshield had their bows out but were hidden behind the trees. Sandman rubbed his knife, making sure it was there. Old Bull walked out farther into the open, arms up. He tried to signal that they had come from *the north*, were trying to go *that way*, to the *big water*, they meant *no harm*. His arms were wide open. They could have shot him through the heart. Then Sandman came out on his horse, followed by Red Moon and Whiteshield. They flanked Old Bull, showed *no weapons. Came in peace*. The Indians lowered their bows and began to approach. Old Bull said, Come on, meet them halfway. These Indians were odd, very odd, Old Bull thought, unlike any other he had seen. They were smeared in some sort of grease, half their faces clay red and half black, their nipples pierced with slivers of cane. The bows they held were as tall as they were. Red Moon untied his spare horse, the palomino, and went up to the man Old Bull was trying to talk to. He assumed this was the headman and offered him the horse. That seemed to ease tensions. The group began to yell and chant and retreat. The headman signaled to *come*. As they were untying their spare horses, Old Bull said that this Great Lake had better be worth it.

All night until dawn, the Indians gave a big dance for them, the craziest dance Old Bull had ever seen. The women shook rattles made of snapping-turtle shells tied on sticks with leather straps, and some of the men played little flutes made of reeds. The birdlike sounds made Red Moon smile. There were drummers and chanters, some of whom blew low, mournful sounds from pinkish-colored shells. Of course, none of it made sense to the Cheyennes, but it seemed to make their hosts happy. The dancers contorted around a big fire, bending backward or spinning sideways, seemingly without design or purpose, sometimes leaping through the flames. Some of them wore the strangest rainbow-colored feathers and necklaces of teeth. A spark flew into a dancer's hair, and he jumped and yelped and slapped himself on the head as he continued around the fire. The Cheyennes assumed it was part of the dance. Platters of roasted scallops, shrimp, and oysters were passed to the guests. The headman showed them how to shuck out the meat with a wooden, spoon-like device and dab it on sea salt that had crystallized in a depression in a stone slab. Sandman believed he had never tasted anything as fine and ate so much that his stomach protruded. The Indian they had seen getting water that morning came up to Sandman and signaled that it was *him* getting *a drink*, and that he *saw them* in the *reflection of the water*. Sandman told the others, and they had a big laugh while the dancing and music played on.

The next day, the headman and three others dragged out four canoes and they all set off: Old Bull and the headman in one canoe; Sandman, Red Moon, and Whiteshield and their guides in the other three. They traveled down a canal to a narrow stretch, then into a broad bay, which they crossed. Once on the opposite shore, each pair swung their canoes over their heads and followed a well-worn path through palmetto and saw grass. When they came upon a wide tributary, they got in the canoes once more. While Old Bull paddled, the headman untangled a limber net con-structed of vine and let it unfurl in the water. When they reached the opposite shore and hauled it out, the net held three big fish and dozens of fat, long-whiskered shrimp. They pulled the boats inland and flipped them upside down. While their hosts set about making a fire and gutting the fish, the Cheyennes hacked through sugarcane into a clearing, and there spread before them was a startling expanse of blue and white, roar of surf, glimmer of sand. Old Bull showed no expression, but his heart leapt. They walked together along the beach, saw gulls whirl and dip. Sandman picked up a shell and blew through it loudly. Almost immediately, one of the Indians came trotting out of the thicket to investigate, then retreated. Old Bull walked to the edge of the water. He liked the way the little stick-legged shorebirds followed the water as it flowed back out to sea, then tip-toed madly back as the surf came in again. That's how you run, he joked to Whiteshield. Sandman threw down the shell, stripped off his leggings, and sprinted into the ocean, screaming and scattering birds. He ran until he was up to his chest, then dove into the next incoming wave. He sur-faced, swinging the hair from his face, and spat out a mouthful of water. Salty, he yelled. They all laughed. It was true, Old Bull thought, water as far as you could see. Absolute end of the Earth. The sun was sinking, a fat globe that laid down an orange stairway on the waves. The Johnsongrass and saw grass cuts stung when Old Bull entered the water, but he figured it was good for them. He tasted the water first on his palm, then took a small drink. A little salt is good for you, he thought. The water was warm near shore but cooled farther out and was shockingly cold when he dove and touched the sandy bottom. Surfacing, he saw Sandman showing Red Moon and Whiteshield a trick. When a wave curled in, creamy and white, Sandman would float on his back and let the wave carry him close to shore. They were all yelling and having a good time. Old Bull bobbed in the water, wondering from what direction the white men had come and how many more would follow. How big were their countries, and how far away? On what type of boats would they sail? How many days did it take? He carefully scanned the horizon for boats but saw none, blinded momentarily by a crescent of sun.

They ate boiled shrimp and roasted snapper around a fire on the sand and slept on grass mats their hosts set out. Sandman braided his hair, looking into his little mirror occasionally. The Indians were fascinated by it, taking turns looking at themselves, but Sandman wasn't about to give it up. In the morning, the sky was mottled purple and strong winds had turned the surf rough. They all took wake-up dips, then set off.

Back at the camp, a crowd had gathered around two boys who had shot a big fish. Old Bull had never seen anything like the creature. With slick-looking leathery skin instead of scales, the fish was taller than either of the boys. An arrow protruded through the fish's back and out the stomach. Its eyes were wide open, and one of the boys knelt down and pulled its jaws apart. It's got teeth like a bear! Red Moon shouted. Old Bull thought that it looked fierce with its slanted eyes and rows of curving teeth. One of the boys signaled that the fish normally lives in the *big water*, but came up through *the canal* and got *trapped*. They could see its *fin poking above* the shallow water, so they *shot it*.

Old Bull told the headman that *he and his friends* would be *leaving today*, that their journey would take *seven days*, that they *appreciated* everything and would be *their brothers*. Old Bull went to his horse and got a heavy knife with a sparkling beaded handle and gave it to the headman, and the headman took off the tooth necklace he was wearing and gave it to Old Bull. The headman pointed at his mouth, then at the fish the boys were dragging off to the canal to clean. Soon, the dancing and singing began again, and the children rode the palomino around the perimeter of the camp. If we don't leave now, Old Bull said to Red Moon, we'll never get out of here. They'll dance all night. The Indians were dancing and singing even as the party rode off, four abreast, their spare horses trailing. The headman and a few others stood on the top of a small hill and watched them, their hands raised in farewell.

After a while, the sound of the Indians' drums faded and blended with far-off thunder. Southerly winds picked up and brought gentle rain that dissipated the pressing humidity and ushered in cool air. Fat drops peppered Old Bull's back. Flocks of honking geese flew north in staggered V-formations. Looking behind them, Red Moon said it looked like storms, but that they'd probably blow over in an hour. The men found shelter in a thick cypress grove. Whiteshield passed around dried buffalo, delicious after their recent diet of seafood. After an hour, though, the rain intensified and the treetops were bending north from a steady gale. The men were getting soaked, but there was nothing to do but wait. When it grew dark, they drew their horses in a circle and huddled inside them. Blue lightning illuminated the horses briefly; their heads were lowered and eyes shut, as if to sleep through it all. The horizontal rain, the spooky howl of the wind reminded Old Bull of a tornado he had experienced as a young man, but at that time, the wind and rain had passed quickly, albeit ferociously. This storm had more stamina. He heard leaves being stripped from their branches, then a big limb snapped with a wicked *crack!* As if on cue, the rain slowed to a trickle and the trees returned to their original shape. The clouds broke to reveal a pure-blue circle in which gulls and terns swirled. After the din of the storm, their cries came to Old Bull slowly, then with startling clarity. Rain dripped steadily from overhead branches. They untied their horses and remounted, anxious to make up for lost time and find high ground.

Pools of water lay all around, mirrorlike in the bright light. It seemed to Old Bull that the sun shattered off every drop of the splashes Red Moon's galloping horse made. To their backs, spinning clouds and sheets of rain were swallowing the blue sky. The party rode all-out for the cover of an adobe structure rising forlornly near the edge of a bayou. It reminded

Old Bull of some houses he had seen out west, on the other side of the mountains, while on a trading trip several autumns ago. White men in robes had lived in them. The party squeezed into an archway, and Old Bull was amazed to see that there was no roof. Fat mottled clouds raced overhead in the purplish twilight, so close Old Bull wished they could rope one and fly home. The adobe walls had already crumbled to the ground. All that remained was the façade, but it shielded them from the wind and rain, which were on them again. Gusts gathered into steady gales, the rain tilted sideways, darkness descended. For hours the rain and wind assaulted the mud bricks. Slowly, they began to melt from the top, red streams flowing down the sides and collecting in gullies around their feet. A chunk of mud and straw fell on Whiteshield's horse, causing it to bellow and rise. It kicked hard with its hind legs, slamming the building solidly, and the entire east side caved in. Bewildered, the horse turned in nervous circles, this way and that, until Whiteshield spoke to it and rubbed its neck, calming it. The Cheyennes huddled with their backs against the west wall, their horses turned away from the rain and their heads lowered. Then the winds lessened, and the rain suddenly quit. The men looked south. The sky was an electric pink. A blast of cold air delivered a hard spray of sleet, and, glancing at the white pellets, Old Bull saw they were up to their ankles in water from the overflowing lagoon. Lightning popped over their heads, and the horses jumped. Sandman's pinto pony, ears twitching, heard the whistle first, distant but growing louder. Again, lightning cracked the air above them. Again, the horses jumped. The whistle turned into a roar. They looked all around, up at the low ceiling of sky, out over the lagoon. They all pointed at once. Skinny dancing ropes, three of them, had dropped from the bruised clouds hovering over a big tree. The tree began to lean backward slowly, bending as if pulled magnetically. When its tops began to brush the ground, the trunk exploded and stark-white chunks as big as clubs splintered free, whirled, and speared the mud wall. Ride! Red Moon yelled.

They jumped the south wall. Behind them the three ropes had meshed into a fat snout, which whined and skipped along the ground. They were showered with mud and rocks. Old Bull kicked and whipped his horse to catch up with the others; a tree limb sailed overhead. Red Moon, Whiteshield, and Sandman plunged into the bay, intent on crossing at a narrow inlet. It was too deep, and the horses lost footing, listed sideways, and tried to swim. Instantly it grew dark again, a shadow enveloped the earth. Old Bull yelled, but the wind snatched away his voice. He felt himself being lifted from his horse, rather had the sensation he *and* his horse were rising. Then suddenly, his horse wasn't there and Sandman was twirling above him, mouth open in a silent scream, his face a dazed mask. They reached for each other but were repelled. Three arrows pointing upward floated past Old Bull at eye level, followed by a limp swamp rat and Red Moon's appaloosa, upside down. Old Bull felt himself turn a flip, one slow revolution as he pawed at the air, and then he was dunked underwater. He opened his eyes briefly, saw midnight. Deeper and deeper he sank until hitting his back against the muddy bottom. He paused a moment, stunned, before realizing he was out of breath. In a sudden panic he sprung off the bayou floor and shot up, kicking his legs and fanning his arms. He rose and rose, and just when he thought he couldn't hold his breath any longer, he broke through, gasping and spewing water, arms flailing. The sky was dark, but from nightfall. He grabbed a tree trunk bobbing past him in the roiling current. At first he floated swiftly between what appeared to be bluffs; then the water lessened, then stopped, and he was beached on the floor of a small canyon. He stumbled to his feet, slipping in mud. It was still and quiet. A silver spray of stars pulsed in the bleached sky. He began to walk, northward he hoped. He yelled once, Anybody out there? But his words only echoed back to him: out there, out there, out there . . .

He never saw Sandman, Red Moon, or Whiteshield again but dreamt of them often, even as an old man. It took him ten days to reach home, riding the final two nights on a horse coaxed from the fringe of a camp in the black of night. When he was certain he was in his own territory, he relaxed, nearly hallucinating, and drifted in and out of sleep. That was how his people found him when he arrived: riding but slouched over, his face buried in the horse's mane. He was shirtless and shoeless and wore a strange necklace of teeth that clicked softly when they pulled him off the horse. Eventually, he recuperated on corn soup and antelope meat. He didn't speak of the trip for some time, but eventually told his wife and fellow chiefs all that had happened. There were dances for Sandman, Red Moon, and Whiteshield late every fall. Gradually the trip assumed a dreamlike quality in his mind, and children and grandchildren loved to hear the stories of turquoise-colored fish, screaming pigs with tusks, birds that talked and had yellow and blue feathers and orange beaks. He embellished things when talking to the children, who were awestruck to hear of white men from different worlds who rode on big ships with billowing sails and wore brown robes and lived in mud houses, of giant fish with big, sharp teeth like a bear's. He would hold up his necklace as evidence.

Old Bull dreamed of these things—not entirely unconvinced himself.

Vu Tran

The Gift of Years

W HEN HIS daughter was twelve years old, Nguyen Van Lam began noticing in her a strange taste for violence. Until then she had given him little reason to worry or to think her any less traditional a daughter than her three older sisters. He often figured she was normal for what she was not: not dumb, not mopish, not devious or rebellious, not even tomboyish for that matter. She would become, many years later, both a wife and a widow before he understood how feeble this logic was, for at the time he could only say that fatherhood had its limitations. A decade in the war had separated him from the family, and upon returning home for good, he realized how little he knew about his five children, particularly this daughter, named Nguyen Tram-Mai—the youngest, the prettiest, and for him the most beloved.

She was twelve when her only brother was beaten one day by two neighborhood boys. The row began on the way home from school, in the deserted square outside the church. She alone stayed behind while her sisters rushed home to call their father. When Lam arrived, he found her seated on an old tree stump with her hands in her lap, drawing blind circles in the dirt with a toe and watching the two boys land blow after blow to her brother's body, his cries muffled and the kicked-up dust clinging to his bloodied face, as he lay pinned and writhing on the ground. Lam chased and cursed the boys away and in his bewilderment forgot about Mai's presence in the faint shadow of the church, forgot even later on, as a neighbor drove them to the hospital, that he had left her by herself in the square. Not until after his son was taken home and lying in bed, with his arm in a cast and thirteen stitches on his face, did Lam finally remember that his daughter had been there and had witnessed everything. He noticed that while everyone was gathered around the son's bed, Mai was alone at the other end of the house, curled upon the couch with her hands between her thighs, fast asleep.

Months later, this image of her on the couch would invade his mind at moments when he loved her most. Those tranquil cheekbones, the mouth slightly ajar, a forehead as smooth as porcelain: that expression of blissful childish indifference would return to him and make her acts of kindness seem more complicated than they should be; so that when she bought him cigarettes without being asked, or fanned her mother to sleep during the hot afternoon, or hushed the neighbor's colicky baby in her arms, Lam—who once spent three days on the jungle floor calmly waiting for enemy footsteps—found himself distracted by vague feelings of doubt.

Over the years, there were other moments of odd behavior: a look, a gesture, an incident made severe in memory. And although they were rare enough for him to believe he was overreacting, although he had faith in the notion that men need not show their fears unnecessarily, his love for the girl kept him privately wary.

More so than anyone he knew, Nguyen Van Lam was paranoid about forgetting the important things. When he was young, his father had said that "what was easily forgettable was worth remembering the most," and though Lam did not believe this was true of everything, his father's solemn voice lingered in his mind. Once he became a husband, a father, the protector of his own family, he decided that everything had its ounce of importance. He made a point of remembering the weather on the days his children were born, the exact dates of their baptisms, the fact that his wife prayed with her eyes open, that his son had a fear of dogs, that his oldest daughter never went to bed without using the bathroom at least twice. Remembering details helped him heed his father's words, helped him suffer the doubts and uncertainties of fatherhood.

But with Mai, it was different. At her uncle's funeral, when she was two years old, she cried during the ceremony and did not stop until he placed his army beret on her head. Then, as if struck by some strange giddiness, she began laughing and dancing at his feet with the oversized cap balanced on her head, tipped over her eyes, giddy still when it came Lam's turn to cast his handful of dirt upon her uncle's coffin. Ever since then, he bought her hats on special occasions—on his visits home from the war, when she graduated from school, when she became engaged. But attached as he was to this memory of her, it would not come to help him forget the day she sat on an old tree stump and watched two boys nearly beat her brother unconscious. If anything, the two memories merged, one an amorphous shadow of the other.

So when, decades later, Mai's husband of ten years was found drowned in the river one summer morning, Lam was horrified but not shocked. Inside, perhaps without knowing it, he had been awaiting this moment for years.

They found him floating on his stomach. At dawn his body appeared along the far banks of the east river, undulating against the early morning swells near a block of bungalows and shacks, one sandal still clinging to his toes and his legs entwined in rotten banana leaves. It was hard to spot him at first with all the trash and broken water coconuts strewn along the bank, some in the water, some in the mud. They said there was a half-empty bottle of rice wine bobbing in the water twenty feet away from him with the cap still firmly attached. It could have been anyone's.

When they told her the news, she did not cry. When the body was brought to the house, she crossed her arms, stared at it momentarily, then withdrew to her room. At the funeral, flanked in the pew by her eight- and nine-year-old daughters, she sat stiff-backed and expressionless, like some unhappy queen too dignified to accept consolation. Friends and relatives attended out of respect for her and the family, but had they been complete strangers, they'd have had no way of knowing who the widow was or whether she was there at all.

As he sat beside her and the children, Lam watched the solemn faces in the congregation and tried his best to share their sympathy. He saw what they saw: the wife of a man taken in morbid death, a young widow perhaps too grief-stricken to show emotion. He even believed, as they did, the possible deeper truth, that she had fallen out of love with a husband who, sooner or later, would have drunk himself into another grave. Indeed, this was the same man who pissed on their front porch after a night of drinking, the same man who sometimes forgot his children's names when asked, a man not seen on Sunday morning in years, whom they knew would surely have done her no good alive.

But Lam could not help his suspicions. *Drowned in a dark river of mud and feces*, he imagined, and his prayers buoyed up his son-in-law's bloated, floating carcass. Was this wrong, Mai's husband lying pale and unrecognizable in a casket before her while others wept and she sat quietly with a face of grim content?

Lam closed his eyes for the rest of the funeral. His lips moved but his prayers were feigned, for in his mind he was conjuring up memories of his youngest daughter that no one else had. There was another reason why he never forgot her odd behavior as a child. Mai only acted that way in his presence, and it seemed to Lam she would awaken this dormant personality for him and him alone.

From the day she was born, she had always clung to him. As a baby, she stopped crying only in his arms and at night slept by his side. Growing up, she never disobeyed him, followed him everywhere he went, and often hummed songs she heard him sing. He left for the war the year she turned two and for the next decade he saw her only two or three times a year. But during those visits home, his wife would tell him how differently Mai behaved with him around. "She argues less with her brothers and sisters and sleeps better at night," his wife would say, "and with you here, it's like she forgets to talk back to me."

Lam usually came home in those days to find his children quiet and timid, as though a stranger had arrived to stay at their house. It would take a day or two for them to talk and laugh with more abandon, to argue with each other again, to eat with ease at the dinner table. With the exception of his wife, Mai was the only person who seemed comforted by his return to the household. She asked him about his life away from the city, from home—why, for instance, he fought in the country, to which he could only say that the city was too busy and crowded for the business of fighting. She often sat by his side in the afternoons and recounted stories he had missed while he was away: the new family across the street, the girl her brother was in love with at school, the time it rained for three days straight and flooded the front room. The other children spoke to Lam and sometimes even joked with him, but it was Mai who kept him company without being asked. Once, when she was eight years old, Lam came home after a four-month absence to find that she had preserved a game of checkers left unfinished between them from his last visit. She had made a drawing of their positions on paper, and before he left that same week, they resumed the game, and he tried his best to let her win.

When Mai turned fifteen (a few years after a mine explosion shattered Lam's ankle and sent him home for good), her name had become well known in the neighborhood. She won many honors and awards at school, which was no surprise considering her talent at home of winning card games, arguments, and the wary respect of her mother, from whom she had inherited her dislike for losing. Her sisters loved her, of course, but Lam figured they nested a little envy inside. Her oldest sister was married that year, and at the wedding Mai sang songs for everyone and even charmed the priest into dancing with her at the reception. "Whoever ends up marrying her," the priest would say afterward, "if he's a jealous man, he'll never stop worrying, and if he's a lazy man, he'll regret it." The other guests agreed, and so did Lam. He noticed that Mai received more attention that day than her sister. By the end of the night, he realized he had not only lost his oldest daughter to marriage, but would probably lose his youngest one sooner than he thought.

But in Lam's mind, his daughters were all sculpted from the same stone, the older teaching the younger what their mother taught them, what all women should know. His oldest was a seamstress and married now at twenty, to a math teacher oddly enough, though she'd always hated math in school; the one below her, at eighteen, worked as a clerk at the hospital, where she pined for a new doctor every month; and his middle child, a meek and plain seventeen-year-old, whiled her days away writing poetry and helping her mother with household duties her older sisters could no longer do. Lam insisted to himself that the only difference between these three girls and their youngest sister was that Mai was the brightest and, incidentally, the prettiest ("Like my very own Japanese daughter," his wife used to say), and that anything beyond that was a mere difference in personality. But now and then Mai made him change his mind.

She came home from school one afternoon and calmly marched into the kitchen without greeting or looking at him. He saw her face from the corner of his eye and wondered, as he continued reading the newspaper, if what he saw had actually been blood. It was common in those days to see his son this way, but never his daughters. As soon as he heard his wife's cry from the kitchen, his first thought was who had done it.

"Phuc did," she replied, averting her eyes.

"Why?" he asked her. There was a half-inch cut on her upper lip, a flower of red across her check.

"Ông Binh's daughter?" cried his wife. "What did that girl do to you?"

"We were arguing outside her house, and she got mad and cursed at me and said I was stupid and weak. So I pushed her and she tripped and fell. Then Ông Binh came out and slapped me."

"Slapped you?" Lam said. "Enough to make you bleed?" Already he felt his fists clenching, his fingernails digging into his palms. Mai was about to say something else, but he did not stay to hear it.

When he arrived at the house a few blocks away, Binh's wife dropped her broom on the porch and began shaking her head and hands at him. "No, Ành Lam," she said, "Please—there is no fight for you here!" She spoke as if out of breath. "My husband has no fight with you!"

But Lam was not looking at her. The front doors were open, and from where he stood below the porch steps, he could make out a figure cowering in the darkness of the house. Directed at the wife, his words came out in a growl: "Tell that boy to come out here." The figure shifted in the shadows.

"Please go home, Ành Lam—" Binh's wife said. She had noticed the brass knuckles on his right hand. "Please, Ành Lam."

Lam raised his voice: "Tell him, if he doesn't come out now, I'll go in and get him myself."

Binh appeared then at the doorway and stepped gingerly out onto the porch. He stood hunched as though there were weights on his back.

Lam moved as if to mount the porch steps, sending Binh and his wife retreating toward the wall, but then he stopped, was silent for a moment. He pointed a finger up at Binh and spoke in the calmest voice he could muster: "If you ever touch my daughter again, I'll come and beat you like a child."

Binh was about to speak, but his wife waved her hands in his face to shut him up.

A small crowd of people, mostly young boys, had gathered nearby to watch. Lam paid them no attention. As he walked away (his limp by then hardly noticeable to most people), he flung his brass knuckles on the street and heard the boys scramble behind him to snatch it. His mind wandered momentarily before he realized that he had taken the wrong way back home. His rage returned and made him regret abandoning a worthy fight. He could have easily leapt onto that porch and struck Binh where he stood, floored him with a single blow. But what stopped him was the slight figure of Binh's daughter behind him in the doorway, her face visible enough in the afternoon light for Lam to see the gash on her brow and her dark, bruised eye, swollen shut.

That night, when everyone had gone to bed and Lam sat smoking on his front porch, Mai wandered out of the house and knelt by his side. She leaned in closer, and in the arc of pale light that flooded half the porch, her face looked like a pearl.

"Father," she whispered. "After she fell, I kicked her. That's why Ông Binh slapped me. Please don't tell anyone."

(There was another time, much earlier, and perhaps he thought nothing of it then. Mai was eight or nine years old and had accidentally broken her mother's statuette of Saint Joseph, given as a gift by her deceased grandmother and blessed by the priest at church. They were alone in the front room, her sweeping the floor and him smoking on the sofa, when he heard the statuette shatter on the floor. She yelped and he turned to see her eyes well up with tears, her face ashen and strained. He called her name three or four times, but she did not hear him. She remained frozen on her knees until he approached her and squeezed her elbow. He thought she was crying out of fear—the certain whipping she would get from her mother. But as she knelt on the floor and held the shards of china in both hands, some inexplicable grief seemed to seize her, as though she had just destroyed something precious beyond mere material or sentimental worth, destroyed St. Joseph himself, in porcelain flesh, his once smooth and lustrous body now in pieces, that destruction irrevocable. Lam swept up the mess and quietly scolded her for crying. And then he promised to tell her mother that he had broken the figurine.)

The police said Mai's husband was indeed intoxicated when he died, that most likely he must have stumbled drunk into the river and lost himself in the deep waters of the night. For the family and the neighborhood, this news only confirmed what had been assumed all along. Two young men reported seeing him at a café drinking with friends the night before. The woman who owned the late-night *banh bao* stand near the café said he lumbered by and pestered some of her customers. There were also two children who swore to their parents that they had heard him singing outside their window. Lam had no reason to doubt what people were saying, and in the months following the funeral, when he was reminded of what he used to tell his children, what his own father had told him, that "everything has its ordered place," he felt inclined to believe the death was both accidental and inevitable.

He had never liked his son-in-law. He gave his blessing back then because Mai was in love and, with the stubborn romanticism of all young women, could not imagine herself with any other man. The boy was handsome and mild, some said charming, but over the years he became skinny and shiftless from his vices. He reminded Lam of those soldiers in the war who were neither cowardly nor brave, whom the war had only made lazy, because, once they returned home, no one, not even their loved ones, saw any value or threat in them. They were not smart enough to be endearing, not strong enough to be bullies. Their mediocrity doomed them to indifference, and like them, Lam's son-in-law was a failure—a harmless fool who failed at being a father and a husband, who once forgot his five-year-old daughter at the market, who once gave his wife stolen flowers to apologize for losing three months' salary in a card game, who once went to his daughter's first Communion drunk and fell asleep on the pew, in a suit he borrowed from a friend. His death did not sadden Lam; once the shock of it faded, his only concern was what had led up to it.

Months before the drowning, Lam came to visit his grandchildren one afternoon, and as he turned in to the small alley that bordered their house, he saw Mai and her husband arguing loudly outside. He stopped where he was and veered out of sight, watching the scene behind a grove of chestnut trees.

Her husband appeared sober, his voice sharp and animated, as were his hand gestures, stabbing the air in front of Mai's face. But angry as he looked, Mai spoke to him without flinching or giving ground. Their voices grew louder still, but Lam was too far away to hear what they were saying. A few neighbors walked by, glanced at them, and went on their way, apparently familiar with these spats. Mai began interrupting and shouting at her husband when he abruptly reached out and slapped her across the face. Lam lurched forward, scratching his cheek against a tree branch, on the verge of barking out their names. But then he saw Mai swing her arm and strike her husband's face with the back of her hand and, whether from the force or the shock, stagger him back a few steps. Regaining himself, he could only stare at her with what from a distance looked like dumbfounded grief, as though it had been a child and not his wife who had just struck him. Mai walked into the house and left him standing there holding his jaw. A minute later, he wandered away down the alley.

Lam tried following him but soon decided it was best to leave things alone. The family had long known about Mai's marital problems, and he was not one to interfere. "If he hurts her, I'll kill him," he once told his wife, "but beyond that, their business is their business." And to himself, he'd also say that to know as little as possible about their business was the best and only way to avert his eyes. Lam was of the mind that fathers not only give away their daughters to marriage, they relinquish them, and that the husband's job thereafter was to protect and provide—the job of the father only to love and keep his distance.

Lam returned home and kept silent about what had happened. His wife already knew too well about Mai's marriage, and the news would only worry her more. And as for Mai, there was no use in confronting her, for as it was, Lam could still not decide on the importance of what he had seen, whether he could even help her if she needed it.

He invited himself to dinner at her house that night. Mai's husband was not at home, and though Lam waited for her to bring up his name, to recount the argument that afternoon, she remained silent during most of the meal. He lingered at the house, watching television with the children until their father finally sauntered home, greeted him with a nod and a weary smile, and went immediately to bed. Mai sat there with her arms crossed and ignored the box of sugared prunes he had left on the table beside her. Only then did Lam say good night.

A few days later, as he was fixing the wooden balustrade on his front porch, Mai wandered up from the dusty road and slowly mounted the porch. Without a word, she kneeled next to him and held up one of the balusters.

Minutes of silence passed between them, punctuated by his brief directions. The metal roof overhanging the porch sheltered them from the hot sun. He could tell by her flushed forehead that she had been walking out-side all day.

She finally spoke, in a voice she would have used to remark on the weather: "I don't know what to do about him, Father."

Lam began hammering a baluster to the frame of the balustrade, but the large nail buckled and refused to drive in cleanly. He pulled it out, bent and useless, tried again with two other nails, and failed both times. He spat away from his daughter as the third ruined nail fell to the ground, bouncing metallic against the concrete. He motioned for her to let go of the baluster. She now knelt there with her hands wedged between her thighs, watching people and traffic pass by on the narrow road that bordered the house.

"He does nothing for the children, ever," she continued, as though talking to herself, that casual sawdust voice unchanged. "Doesn't even make an effort to scold them when they misbehave. And he drinks every day, wanders home for an hour to eat or nap, then spends all his evenings at the bars and billiard halls." She picked up the bent nails and held them in her palm. "At night, when he does come home, I can hardly stand the smell of him, and I have to push him out of bed to go take a bath. If he even hears me, he'll go and pass out on the couch, in clothes he's worn sometimes for days."

"Is he still working?" Lam finally asked, calmly, still facing his work.

"Yes, at his brother's garage, but I see hardly any of the money. And I don't want to imagine some of the things he wastes it on."

Lam set down the hammer to do more measurements. The baluster did not quite reach the handrail. Mai took up his hammer, laid the bent nails on the ground, and began hammering them straight.

"A few weeks ago," she said, "he came home late one night and said he was hungry. I ignored him, so he sat at the dining table and began scraping the dried bottom of the rice pan. He scraped and scraped with that damned spoon—it so infuriated me and the children." Her voice swelled now with each hard blow of the hammer. "And when I still refused to go see to him, he went over to the girls' bed and poured water over their feet. They were probably more annoyed than scared. If he's at home during the day, I go to Lien's house to get away from him." She paused. In the distance, children were laughing and yelling in the street.

"He humiliates the children, Father," she said. "They just humor him. He humiliates himself. And me."

Lam ran his fingers across the handrail and realized it was warped. A loud curse escaped him. He peered at Mai's downcast face as he held the baluster dumbly in his hands. It was rare nowadays for her to wear makeup. She used to share her sisters' love for clothes and had a habit of wearing blue blouses, but for the last year or so, she hardly dressed up for church on Sundays, and usually went alone.

He noticed she had hammered the nails perfectly back into shape. Even with his strong hands he'd never been able or patient enough to do that. He coughed gruffly and said, "When I was his age, I had three children I never saw and a wife who gave birth to two of them without me. I was hundreds of miles away, yet none of you ever went without food or clothes or behaved like these kids around here. I made sure of that when I came home, and your mother kept it that way while I was gone." He grabbed the handrail and tried bending it straight. "Your sisters—I thank God their husbands are doing what they're supposed to. Even Lien's husband, given to gambling as he is."

"He's not nearly as bad—"

"Please, no more about that husband of yours."

Mai bowed her head as she had done as a child when scolded. Lam let go of the rail, regretted his sharp tone of voice. He waved a fly away from her hair, and wished then that easing her problems was as easy as taking her husband aside and scolding him—slap him a few times to give him sense.

"Why are you telling me all this?" he said. "There's nothing I can say to help you. Go talk to your mother or your sisters—I know nothing of this business."

"But Mother will only tell me how she didn't want me marrying him in the first place. And Lien and Huong have their own problems—they already know mine well enough. I just wanted to tell you—"

He looked at her.

"Yesterday afternoon, I saw him pissing in the street, in full view of everyone in the neighborhood—" She gasped as if to catch her breath. "Some days I wish he were dead, Father," she said, staring at her hands. "I wish I could just make him disappear."

She placed the three straightened nails by his feet and descended the porch. Lam watched her hesitate in the street and look up at the sky, as if to gauge the heat of the sun, as if to decide whether defiance was enough to bear her burdens, then watched the quiet weariness of her gait as she meandered through the crowd of noon pedestrians and weaving bicycles that soon engulfed her.

During Lam's years as a soldier, Mai was the one child who asked outright about his killing others in the war. It was a question she directed at him with the quiet vigilance of a priest, coming out the first time as "Have you ever killed anyone in the war, Father?", progressing to "How many people have you killed, Father?", and culminating in "How did you kill them, Father?" And in some form or the other, the brief inquiry usually ended in the same way:

"Silly child—we're forced to kill in war. And what does a young girl want with knowing how I killed people?"

"You won't tell me?"

"None of you children need to know. Not from me or anyone."

He expected this response to silence her from further questions, but suspected, too, that her interest would return on his next visit. She was a curious girl, though it seemed her curiosity was not inherent of some need for understanding, but was simply impulsive, as spontaneous as a nervous tic or a ludicrous dream. They might be walking together in a crowded marketplace or sitting alone on the porch, and abruptly she would ask him such questions as though they were part of a game she and Lam were playing, an exchange of secrets that would make up for their time apart.

Perhaps it was his absence that inspired her curiosity, but Lam felt it odd that he, in turn, hardly ever thought of her or anyone in his family while he was away. Out in the jungle, consumed by the fear of death and the vacuous passage of time, his mind did not wander to his wife, his children, or his home. He thought of less complicated things, like smoking on a cool rainy Saigon night, that tingle in his breath. Or eating a bowl of *pho*, steaming hot with fresh basil leaves and lime, the raw beef submerged in the broth, curling pink then grey. And inevitably his thoughts veered not to his family but to where he actually was: a mass of crumpled, hot earth overlain by trees and brush and vines and human bones, a verdurous place that could not bury the violence and the terror but only mute them.

It seemed this precarious world had no place or patience for thoughts of home—it was a world entirely separate from the one inhabited by his family, and in some irrational way, he was never able to believe in both at the same time.

Which was what bemused Lam when the war followed him home. There were times when he returned from being gone six months and found her sitting on the front porch with an expression that saw him unchanged since last they met, an expression no different had he been her father three hundred and sixty-five days out of the year and just returned then from a brief walk. But after a day or two of him being home, in a moment of sudden curiosity, or perhaps unease, she would ask him one of those questions.

In his mind, it was the same recurring moment: she and he walking through the neighborhood, the city, her hand latched to his, passing the palisade of buildings that flanked the streets, passing houses thrown open for anyone to come eat at or shop at or perhaps drop by for some tea and conversation, passing through the bustle of traffic and pedestrians and vendors and vagrants, passing the church and from there the cemetery where the colorful graves of his family and friends resided—when out of nowhere she would ask the question, and a memory like this one would return to him—

—where one day he and his troops came upon a village burning within a clearing of jungle, smoke billowing into the napalm-tinged air like ribbons and they all creeping among the abandoned interior of the village, stepping over bodies—some with charred flesh, some cowled thick with dried blood, and still others peacefully dead as though asleep. There was one young soldier who, at the sudden sound of voices or cries, lunged at a hut that had just caught fire. This same soldier only days before had wept for his mother. Lam remembered his slight build, his neck from behind resembling a woman's, his voice timid as he refused his meals, and those dull eyes as he quietly cried to himself and clenched his fists to his chest. Those same eyes glared at the entrance to the thatched hut now engulfed in a spiraling welter of flames. His shoulders hunched, his rifle punching the air in front of him, the boy soldier leaned away from the leaping flames and kept his eyes on the doorway of the hut. As if falling from the sky into sound, a feral cry rang out, and then out of the dark column of smoke fuming from the doorway, the fiery body of some animal materialized. The boy floundered a few steps back as the animal contorted its body and flailed its legs, giving a series of ferocious yelps. It was a dog, nearly as tall as the boy's waist, its color now obscured by the serpentine wave of fire jumping along its back and legs. The boy appeared momentarily awestruck by the sight, not so much scared as delighted. But the dog suddenly leaped awkwardly at him and he kicked it in the head, staggering it back into the doorway as it still writhed maniacally and barked out the squeals of a pig. The boy kicked it again, even harder this time as if also to put out the flames scorching its flesh, but it only sent the dog reeling into the hut. Instantly the dog reappeared and again the boy kicked it in the chest, and it reared like a horse and fell back into the smoke. Each time the dog stumbled out of the hut, the boy would kick it back with more force, covering his mouth to keep from choking on the smoke, bowing his head to avoid the flames. It yelped each time he kicked at its ribs or its head, loudly at first and gradually weaker, until eventually it made no sound at all, tiring with each charge from the doorway before finally disappearing one last time into the black innards of the hut with a long, ululating bellow. The boy backed away from the hut as one wall caved in and sent a rush of black smoke and tangled fire toward the sky, stuttering sparks of ignited thatch into the air. Lam had been watching with equanimity, unsure if the pain lodged in his chest was caused by hunger, the pungent heat, or what he had just seen. He felt an urge to say something to the boy, console him, slap him. But before he could step forward, he saw the boy walk up again to the failing hut, and for reasons perhaps elusive even to himself, the boy began firing his rifle directly into the hut, firing into the smoke and flames of the falling doorway until he was empty and no one, not even Lam, could look at him—

—"No," Lam would always say to her, his daughter, as this memory faded, "I will not tell you how men kill and die in the war."

And he never did. Once he exited the war, Mai's curiosity faded and so he figured it must have been a childish whim, a young girl making fanciful leaps into the world of her elders as he had done when he was a boy. Nothing to bring about a clamor. It was not until her husband drowned those decades later that he again remembered her questions and realized how difficult it would be to ask her what she had once asked him.

He tried. In his mind he asked the question many times, in many ways, saving it perhaps for the finale to a long conversation they would have in a dark corner of his imagination—but when he finally approached her, the words did not seem right, could never seem right, and so he again acted as if nothing was wrong, as if those doubts in his mind were as normal for a father as moments of pride and adoration.

A year passed after the drowning. The family saw one another every day, shared meals together, continued doing those things they had done as a family before the death, though Mai's husband was rarely mentioned. At times it appeared to Lam that his daughter's silence was the repression of whatever grief she might have had; other times it seemed forgetting was a way of keeping the dead respectfully dead, of not revisiting the misery her husband had once caused. Mai moved back into Lam's house with her children since they no longer had enough money to live alone. With the sale of her house, it seemed all traces of her husband were left behind as well. Only the hushed knowledge of what had happened persisted.

But now and then, when suspicion drifted through his head, Lam would look for a sign of something withheld, a breach in the indifference Mai showed. He asked his wife and children if they ever saw her cry or heard her talk at all about her husband, but they had not and declared that they did not care to. "Cry for whom," his wife would say, "that worthless fool?" Lam even asked his granddaughters whether they felt their mother seemed the same to them, if she for any moment in the last year appeared extraordinarily happy or angry or sad. But they only shook their young heads vaguely, for it seemed they, too, had already accepted the convenient death of their father. Lam searched their faces and remembered the time when Mai spanked one girl badly for some petty reason and afterward held her and cried: mother and child in an awkward embrace, one crying because of the pain, the other for the pain that was given. "Your daughter will not cry for that man," Lam's wife would say, "and don't expect her to. If you were the same man, I wouldn't cry for you either."

Lam sometimes mentioned Mai's husband to see if a reaction would follow. "That husband of yours never ate enough meat," he might say during dinner; "Doesn't this shirt look like the one your husband used to wear?" he might ask when she was ironing his shirts. But each time Mai would only say yes or no and continue, unmoved, with what she was doing.

He decided at one point that if what he thought was, in fact, true, he would forgive her—it would remain *their* secret. He made up his mind that relieving himself of the curiosity was all that mattered and kept this firmly in mind when he approached her to ask the question outright.

But then always a certain laziness would set in, for by now he had conceived of the right words, only his mouth could not utter them; at once anxious and weary, he realized it was not curiosity that wanted relief, it was the uncertainty of his disappointment. The laziness was just one symptom of the fear, for though he would remind himself to try, the threat of an answer, of a finality terrific in its inevitability, made the uncertainty and self-denial already there a pain he preferred to bear, only so the alternative could never hurt him more—which was why the question could not come, and would not come. And then he would remember all those moments in her life when she revealed her strange nature to him and him alone, those aberrations of the person she normally was and, he wanted to believe, had always been: the fifteen-year-old waltzing with her priest, the eight-year-old buying him cigarettes, the two-year-old at a funeral wearing a beret too big for her head, laughing and dancing at his feet. He would reremember these images, hold them fast to his chest, then convince himself that meaning and connections conceived in memory were flimsy bridges and that to corrupt a good memory would be to corrupt them all. And so, selfishly, not because his suspicion might have been wrong but because it could have yielded the truth, he never asked her.

The next ten years went by in calm succession. Not counting his time away from home, it seemed Lam had lived three lives with his family—the life of his children's childhood, the life of his children's marriages, and now the life of his children's children—and that this last life so far was the least remarkable, and the easiest. He had eleven grandchildren who were all mostly healthy and happy, and in them, in the unfurling of their young lives, he was prepared to face the inevitable closing of his own. His wife often accused him of idleness, of "sitting on the boat and watching others swim," but he would only say that he was too old to get wet and that the view from the boat was a beautiful one. At times, he even fancied himself a fish underwater, heedless of what lay above the surface and what loomed in the depths; and though in reality he would never be able to ignore the past or what lay ahead, he had learned to be satisfied with the present so long as others around him were safe and, themselves, content. It was with this attitude that he helped himself suffer things one summer when he fell ill.

He lay in bed during much of the day with a thin blanket over his legs and an electric fan nearby. His wife glanced at him each time he coughed, and his children stopped by every other hour with feigned reasons for being there. It was true he'd never been this sick, but he knew and insisted to everyone that he'd be better in a week, at the most two. More than probably anything else, he had always been certain of his own health, had risked it too many times in his life to doubt it now, even in old age.

Mai came to visit him every day. She now lived with her second-oldest sister and that sister's family. In the foyer of their house, extending out onto the porch, the two sisters sold clothes they had bought cheaply at the shopping malls in Saigon. Mai went to Saigon twice a week and would purchase as much fabric and clothing as could be strapped to her moped. She spent the rest of the week, every day except Sunday, selling shoes, toothpaste, soap, and whatever else the two sisters could display in their limited space. She also helped with household chores and watched after her young niece and nephews. Her own children had recently married and left her for their new family, the youngest girl only days ago. Mai herself had never remarried, despite offers from various men over the years. Lam would have been happy had she taken another husband, but inside he found a certain sense of peace knowing she never did. Perhaps that was the one sign of her private mourning.

On his tenth day of illness, she came by with pictures from her daughter's wedding. Lam was half asleep in bed, but he could hear Mai talking to his wife in the next room. He was the only family member who did not attend the wedding, and he felt sharply reminded of this as he listened to their conversation.

"The pictures turned out wonderfully," Mai exclaimed, "but that photographer charges more than double now what he charged for Huong's wedding pictures! And he only does this as a hobby."

"That reminds me," Lam's wife said. Footsteps approached the room. Lam saw his wife enter the room and reach into the top drawer of the dresser, where she kept her purse. Mother and daughter stood in the doorway, whispering, unaware that Lam lay there watching them. "Take this," Lam's wife said, handing Mai some money.

"I didn't mean for you to pay for the pictures, Mother."

"Well, I intended to give you the money anyway. You've put enough into the wedding already." As his wife walked back to the front room, Lam saw Mai return the money to the top drawer. She followed her mother, and their voices became shrill again in the next room, mother and daughter sounding more alike with every year.

"I haven't told you what happened yesterday," Mai said, giggling. "This crazy little woman, she comes by and picks over our shoes like fruit for about ten minutes, then asks me if I have more in the house. I leave her there to go look, and when I come back out, I see her running down the street with a pair of our shoes clutched to her chest."

"She stole them?"

"Chi Loan saw her run off with them and even yelled at her son to chase after the woman, but the boy said he lost her a block away. No one in the neighborhood knows who she is. But the funny thing is that I went to the market in the afternoon, and there she was, walking towards me and wearing those shoes."

Lam's wife chuckled. "Was it really her?"

"The nerve of the woman! And they were definitely our shoes. I stepped in front of her, and when she recognized me, she froze. I thought she was going to run away again, but she only stood there—completely terrified. I told her I knew what she did and demanded that she pay me immediately. She asked me how much and when I told her, she said she didn't have enough. So I took what she had, plus the bundle of baguettes under her arm, and walked away." Mai guffawed. "I'd never seen anyone so afraid of me—the woman could barely speak."

"Be careful now," Lam's wife said. "They won't always be that weak and stupid." Lam heard his wife's sandals slapping the tile floor. "I'm stepping out to buy some coffee while you're here. Go show the pictures to your father."

"Is he asleep?"

"I don't think so."

"Is he feeling any better?"

Lam did not hear his wife reply. Her footsteps drifted out of the house.

Mai's head appeared in his doorway, and when she saw that he was awake, she smiled and approached the bed.

"I have the wedding pictures, Father," she said, almost in a whisper. She dragged a chair to his bedside and sat down level with him. He noticed that her head had more grey now than he had remembered. Her face, however, had aged very little, her ivory complexion still flawless. She slowly placed one picture after the other on his chest.

The first was of his granddaughter and her new husband standing outside a car with some wedding guests. She was dressed in a red *aó dài* and stood with her head tilted—a picture of her mother in youth. The next photograph showed them sitting in the car with palm fronds fanned across the back window. The groom was grinning awkwardly, and Lam's granddaughter, her red *aó dài* vivid against the white leather seats, was looking sadly into the camera as though she had been crying.

Lam studied each photograph and imagined the smells and sounds that day, what the sun must have felt like on the people's shoulders, the thoughts behind their smiles. When he reached the one where the bride and groom stood with their parents and grandparents, his hands fell.

"Did you get a good photographer like I told you?"

"Ba Lu's son took the pictures. A professional would have charged too much, you know that."

"But these pictures—some are too bright, and this one here is out of focus."

"They're just fine, Father."

"But I told you—" he said but then stopped when he realized how irritable he sounded. She noticed and did not say anything more.

He went through the pictures a second time but could feel her peering at him, as if looking for blemishes on his face. Her moments of silence and scrutiny lately had become noticeable and discomfiting. This was the third time this week that she had come alone to his bedside in this solemn manner, annoyingly akin at times to someone prepared to offer last rites.

He coughed and felt it burn in his chest. Another cough followed, and as they always seemed to do, each cough spurred on another more vigorous one. He held the stack of photographs to his throbbing chest.

"Father," Mai said. He swallowed to soothe his throat and expected her to fake an apology to him. "I must tell you something. I confessed it at confession years ago, but I feel now that I should confess it to you as well."

In her face, Lam suddenly saw the extent of his illness. Many years had passed since her voice last carried this serious tone, and the instant, inexplicable recognition of what she was about to say made him hold his breath. How long had it been since these thoughts had crossed his own mind? He could not decide then if he should refuse to listen, or resign himself to words he had long banished from his mind.

"It's been so many years," she said, her voice as dull as spoken prayer. "I'd like to tell you how Bao died. I want to tell you this," and she looked at him as if to ask for his approval to go on. He nodded with his silence.

"I came out to the cafés that night looking for him," she began but then stopped. She was staring at the stack of pictures on his chest. Her hesitation seemed a need for articulation, a need to say what she was about to say in a way that had perhaps been conceived differently in her mind. She continued slowly: "There was no particular reason that night for me to do so, except that I felt angrier than most nights. One of the café owners told me he saw Bao head toward the boat docks, and so I made my way over there. When I finally found him, he was standing on an empty pier at the end of the quay with a bottle in one hand, staring out at the water. My God, at that moment, I wanted to run over there and push him over the edge, show him how awful a man he was." Mai's face was calm though her hands now lay on Lam's bed in tight fists. "As I approached him, he turned and looked at me dumbly, like he didn't recognize me, and he began backing up awkwardly, and then he stumbled and fell into the water. I ran over to the edge and looked down at him holding on to a dock pile, and he was spitting water and flailing about like he didn't know where he was. He didn't say anything, scream anything, and I couldn't tell if he was able to or not. I looked around frantically for some way to get him out. I knew I couldn't jump in to save him and I thought about yelling for someone, anyone, to come help. But then he lost his grip on the dock leg and began drifting away. He went under and then came back up choking on water. For a moment it looked like he suddenly remembered how to swim and he began making awkward strokes in the water, but again he went under and as he came up, he let out a gurgled cry, and I yelled out his name. But then I just stood there and watched him, and I couldn't bring myself to call for help. He was moving about more slowly now, and I could hear him coughing and choking, and his short moans—"

Mai lowered her head to her knees, then sat up again. She was not crying, her face still composed. She breathed in deeply, and her voice fell to a whisper: "But I did not budge. I remember holding my breath, listening to him struggle in the water, then backing away from the edge so I could no longer see him. But then I looked again, and he was drifting farther away from the dock, and for an instant I thought he looked directly up at me. He disappeared into the darkness, so I turned around and ran home. I couldn't sleep that night. I couldn't talk at all the next day, and it was lucky that they found his body in the morning because then I had a reason to stay silent without people asking why."

She ceased. She was looking at Lam as though pleading with him. What she was pleading he did not quite know, but he found himself stricken by a cold and peaceful silence. All at once, the past ten years of his life felt illusory to him—artificial. He questioned how the truth would have changed things, whether ignorance had done his family or him any good. He could have doubted Mai's story, but the will to do so was no longer there. A lone image flowered in his mind: of himself long ago forcing his ten-year-old son to dive into a pool so that he would learn to swim. *I'll save you if you* . . . and he ended up jumping in to do just that, the boy so wearied afterward that his eyes did all the cursing—so that years later Lam imagined, as he did now, the cold water engulfing the boy, all his fears compressed into an instant and then bursting forthwith not in anger for his father—though that was there—but in silence.

"Father."

"Yes?"

"What do you think of this?"

"What do I think?" he murmured.

"I've told no one. I know it was horrible what I did. Unforgivable. But I also believe . . . I also believe that night was like something God gave me. As a gift." She spoke slowly, as if waiting for him to interrupt her. "Is that wrong?" she said. "Am I wrong to think that?"

"No," he replied vaguely.

He heard his wife's voice from out front calling back to her neighbor, laughing.

He looked again at the wedding pictures and murmured, "You really should have gotten a good photographer like I told you."

Mai bowed her head. A few of the pictures slid off his chest, and she slowly picked them up, one by one, and set them neatly on the bed.

Lam's wife entered the room. "I spoke to Chi Loan," she said to Mai, "and she told me about everything yesterday."

"Yes," Mai replied without looking up.

"Said her boy ran as fast as he could but that the woman outran him." Lam's wife laughed heartily. "I guess it's fitting that thieves have quicker legs." She walked into the kitchen, still laughing.

Mai leaned closer to Lam and said, "I'm sorry, but I would have regretted never telling you." He shook his head faintly, then coughed twice before Mai spoke again, as if entreating him for a better response, "Father?"

"Do you know," he began, and in the same instant another image flashed in his mind, perfectly distinct after years of being forgotten: his old army beret, dark brown and a perfect fit, emblazoned with a menacing tiger head and its exaggerated fangs. What had become of it, he thought? Was it lost? Did his wife burn it when Saigon fell? Buried it perhaps?

"Do you know," he said again, "that at your Uncle Phong's funeral years and years ago, when you were only two, you wore my beret on your head and laughed and did this silly little dance during the ceremony? You refused to take it off the rest of the day. You know that's the reason I bought you all those hats when you were younger."

Mai laughed suddenly, somewhat mournfully, then stopped. "But Father," she said, as though she wasn't sure it needed explanation, as though it were mere forgetfulness on his part. "Uncle Phong died before I was born. It must have been Lien or Huong you remember, not me."

Richard McCann

The Diarist

HERE'S ONE thing I remember, from all the things I never wrote down in my diary the summer I was eleven, the summer before my father died:

I was standing at the kitchen window, watching my brother, Davis, help our father load our station wagon with the gear we'd need to bring along—fishing rods and tackle boxes, canned foods and cooking pots, butterfly nets and BB rifles—when we left the next morning for Lumber Run, Pennsylvania, population 231. Lumber Run was paradise, my father said.

In fact, although Lumber Run had once been a boomtown, back when it still served the logging trains that once ran through there, from Williamsport to Wellsboro, it was now little more than a crossroads on Route 414, marked only by a general store, an abandoned Quonset hut, and a tar-papered tavern called the Wagon Wheel. But for two weeks each August, our father rented us a place there, an old farmhouse a former army buddy owned, wedged between the railway tracks and the banks of Pine Creek, where he liked to go fishing. He said Lumber Run reminded him of Bishop, the coal-mining town where he'd grown up, before his brakeman father was killed in a machine accident in a switching yard outside Altoona.

I knew I should have been helping my father, like Davis, as he packed our stuff into the storage space he'd created by folding down the station wagon's middle seat, so that everything was fitted neatly together. And I knew this: I didn't want to go to Lumber Run, not this time, now that I knew my mother wasn't coming with us, as she always had before. She'd already left the previous morning on the train from Silver Spring, Maryland, where we lived, to New York City, where she was going to visit her sister, who still lived in their family brownstone in Brooklyn. It was the same trip she'd taken at least monthly the year her mother was dying.

I dreaded my mother's departures, those Friday afternoons I came home from school to find her in her bedroom, packing her monogrammed train case—"I like to travel light," she said. I sat on the edge of her bed as she packed, watching her reflection in the small mirror secured to the satiny lining of the train case lid; together, we seemed one instrument, the mirror and I, catching the bright flutter of my mother's dress as she crossed the bedroom, back and forth, from her dresser to her closet to her vanity.

But this time she had packed the matching Samsonites she'd bought at Woodward & Lothrop a few weeks before—a splurge from her inheritance, she said. From where I stood in her doorway, I could see she wasn't traveling light. She asked if I'd please set her hatbox by the front door so she wouldn't forget it when the taxi came to take her to the station.

"I want to come with you," I told her.

She kept on packing as if she hadn't heard me.

"I've gone with you before," I urged. It was true. Once she had taken me with her for the weekend. We'd seen the Rockettes at Radio City Music Hall, and afterward we'd eaten at Schrafft's. "We'll be having the chicken à la king," she'd instructed the waitress without even consulting her menu. This proved she had once lived in New York City.

For a moment, she looked up. "No," she said. "You have to go with your father. He and I have already discussed that."

Then she resumed her work, folding her blouses into a suitcase, separating each layer with a sheet of white tissue.

At what point did I begin lying to my father, stammering nervous answers to whatever questions he asked me? "What are you doing?" he asked when he came in from packing the car to find me still standing in the kitchen.

"Making sandwiches," I told him. As I spoke, I wondered if he believed me, since he could see for himself that I hadn't done anything, at least not yet—I hadn't even taken the bread from the refrigerator. My mother had always made our sandwiches for car trips; she liked to cut them into quarters before wrapping them in waxed paper.

"I want you to go to Wheaton Plaza with Davis," he told me. He said he was giving us each an extra buck, so we could stock up on candy for the car ride.

Davis was waiting for me on the front stoop, holding the zippered change purse in which he stored his allowance. We headed for the plaza, through the woods behind the elementary school and across the divided highway. On the way, Davis told me our father had promised him he could sit in the front seat and navigate the whole way to Lumber Run.

"I don't believe you," I said.

"It's true," Davis answered.

When we got to Wheaton Plaza, we decided to separate, as we usually did. He went to Kahan's Hobby Shop to look at model cars; I went to S. S. Kresge to browse the bargain bins, where I sometimes found things, like scented bath salts or clip-on daisy earrings, that I could present to my mother.

It was there, standing near the bargain bins, that I first noticed the diary. It was bright pink and beautiful.

I lifted it from the rack to examine it. On its laminated cover, a teenage girl with a ponytail was lying on her back with her legs upraised, as if she were admiring the way she had her ankles crossed, while chatting on her blue Princess phone. She was wearing capri pants with a matching top. But because the picture included neither the bed she was supposedly lying on nor the wall on which her feet were supposedly propped, she appeared to be floating in space, in defiance of all gravity.

"That's a *girl's* diary," Davis said when he joined me at the S. S. Kresge lunch counter, where we'd agreed to meet, and where, having already ordered a glass of ice water, I now sat daubing a moistened paper napkin on the sticky blemish the price tag had left on the diary's plasticized cover. Having just spent ten minutes negotiating my purchase—lifting the diary casually from its display rack and saying loudly to no one in particular, "I'll bet my sister will *love* this," then presenting it to the cashier and asking if it could be gift wrapped—I was still rocketing through the ionosphere of my anxiety, light-headed from the deoxygenated air.

When Davis sat down, I felt something heavy and immutable settling beside me. I dropped the diary back into its paper sack and heard it land with a heavy thump, as if its cover girl had herself just fallen from orbit.

"It's the only kind they've got," I told him.

I couldn't tell if Davis knew that I was lying. I started to add that Mrs. Tucker, my sixth-grade teacher, had once advised our class that we should all keep diaries, especially now that we were entering junior high, so we could look back one day at all the interesting things that happened in our lives. But as soon as I started to say this, I regretted it, remembering how my father had once told me that it was easy to spot a liar, because a liar always said more than he needed to.

"Sure," Davis said. "Like you've got something to write about."

I didn't know what to say. It was true I seldom had the urge to write things down, except occasionally, when I was angry. Once I had scrawled "I HATE DAVIS" on the notepad my mother kept by the kitchen phone, though as soon as I realized that my parents would see it, I tore off the top page and ripped it into shreds, so that all that remained was the clean white page beneath, on which my secret words were still almost invisibly imprinted.

Walking back from Wheaton Plaza, I tried to think of a way to make Davis promise not to tell about the diary; I considered telling him our parents had confided in me that they were worried about the bad grades he kept getting in school—maybe that would shut him up. But when we got to our block, I realized I should be worrying even more about what I'd say to my father if he asked to see what was inside the paper bag I was carrying. All summer he'd been telling me that I needed to stop playing so much with the neighborhood girls, and once, when he overheard me gossiping on the extension phone with my best friend, Denny, he warned me, "You don't need to be a Chatty Cathy."

But I was in luck. As we got close to our house, I saw my father standing in our backyard, talking to a next-door neighbor. I went to my room and stashed the diary in my duffel bag, tucking it beneath my shorts and T-shirts. All night, I thought of it there, secured in its dark enclosure, while I lay awake, trying to imagine what I'd soon be writing on its lined pages. I tried for a long time; but I kept thinking instead of the diary my mother had kept in high school, the one she sometimes shared with me on rainy afternoons, lifting it carefully from the bottom drawer of her dresser, a small book bound in red tooled leather, with the word *Diary* filigreed in gold on its cover. It was made in Morocco, she'd once told me.

"Read to me," I asked as she thumbed through the diary's fragile onionskin pages, pausing occasionally to read a passage aloud. In one, she recounted a date with a boy from Brooklyn Prep with whom she'd seen *Their Own Desire*, with Norma Shearer; in another, she described her evening at the Emerald Ball in the Grand Ballroom of the Waldorf-Astoria, hosted by the Diocese of Brooklyn. She hadn't even made it across the Waldorf's lobby, she noted, before a half dozen suitors had filled her dance card. She had worn a polished satin gown, pale yellow, with an Empire waist.

The next day, Davis and I took turns as navigators, with one of us sitting in the front seat beside our father while the other sat in the rear. I sat in front first, plotting our route from home to Harrisburg, where we crossed the Susquehanna. The whole way, my father kept inventing games for him and me to play, like the one where we tried to tell which drivers were Catholics, like we were, by checking whether or not they had rosaries hanging from their rearview mirrors or plastic Virgins mounted on their dashboards, as we did. When we passed Burma Shave signs posted along the highway, we read them aloud together: NO LADY LIKES/TO DANCE OR DINE/ACCOMPANIED BY/A PORCUPINE/BURMA SHAVE/BURMA SHAVE. I knew even then, I suppose, that I belonged to my mother, just as Davis was our father's, but that morning, riding in the car beside him, I could remember times when I'd belonged to my father, too, sitting with him in the bathtub as a small child, while he rinsed my back with warm, soapy water, or leaning against him on the sofa on Saturday nights, watching *Have Gun— Will Travel*.

After lunch, Davis and I changed places. I sat in back, listening to my father play the same games with Davis he'd just played with me. After a while, I shut my eyes and tried to imagine what my mother was doing—perhaps she was sitting at the kitchen table in Brooklyn at that very moment, I thought, drinking sugared coffee with her sister. As soon as I pictured it, it seemed like something I might want to set down in my diary, although written from the perspective of my sitting at the table with them.

When I opened my eyes, I saw that we were passing through Sunbury, where we'd stopped the previous summer, at my insistence, to visit a snake farm I'd seen touted for miles on garish billboards. But as soon as the guide had shown us the first chicken-wire cage of timber rattlers massed horribly together, I'd gotten sick and had been forced to wait with my mother in the gift shop, looking at miniature souvenir teacups, while Davis completed the tour with our father.

After Sunbury, the road narrowed and the small towns grew smaller yet. I knelt on the backseat, looking out the rear window, so that I saw the names of towns only after we passed through them, catching sight of signs meant to welcome arriving travelers—Dewart, Duboistown, Larryville, Avis. All afternoon, we drove deeper and deeper into my father's world, through quick tableaux of thick-waisted women draping their laundry on porch rails and teenagers huddling on the roadsides, tossing rocks at telephone poles. I'd been to places like these, the times my father took us to Bishop, where his sister still lived with her husband on a truck farm at the edge of town, past the coal mines. To get there, we had to drive by the boney dumps, the worthless mounds of slate and low-grade coal that the mining companies had rejected as waste. People said the boney dumps were dangerous; they could combust from compression. If even a small fire went unseen in a mound of boney, my aunt once told me, the whole thing could explode without warning.

It was after dark when we got to Lumber Run. Our father trained the station wagon's high beams on the house so he could find his way across the front porch to undo the padlock that secured the door. Then Davis and I dragged our suitcases from the car to our rooms. "I'll heat a few cans of ravioli," our father told us.

My room was the smallest in the house, tucked behind the kitchen. I'd chosen it the first time we'd come to Lumber Run because my mother had told me it reminded her of the butler's pantry where she'd played dolls as a small girl in her family house in Brooklyn—not that *this* little house ever needed a *butler*, she added. But I had always liked my room, at least until now, with its austere furnishings and theatrical severity; I'd liked lying on the narrow bed in the late afternoons, with the door closed, studying the battered fiberboard dresser and the single small window whose green paper shade snapped up violently when touched. Sometimes I'd pretend I was staying in a room in a run-down boardinghouse or fleabag hotel, like the ones I'd seen in western movies. But now, as I stood there, picking at the flecks of ceiling plaster that had fallen onto the bedspread over the winter, the room seemed merely grim. It was nothing like my room at home, a room I'd taken to redecorating almost monthly, setting a kerosene lamp on my study desk to create a colonial effect, or hanging wooden wind chimes from the ceiling light to make the room look Japanese. This room would bear no changes; this was a room that was meant to change me.

I opened my suitcase and pulled the diary from beneath my shorts and T-shirts; then I sat down on the bed, holding it in my lap. For a while, I just stared at it, as if I were somehow expecting it to speak, although that was really stupid—I knew that. It was a diary; I was supposed to be speaking to it. But I could feel a muteness settling in my throat, as if something mangled were lodged there, and the longer I studied the diary, the more I could see how cheap it really looked, at least beneath the harsh, naked bulb of the ceiling light. For the first time, I saw how a few pages were already coming unglued from its binding, and how a crease had begun to deform the flimsy, plasticized cover. Even the cover girl looked sort of pathetic, now that I could see that the yellow of her ponytail had been printed somewhat out of register. It's not *my* fault, I wanted suddenly to explain to someone—it was the room's fault, or my father's, or my mother's, for not coming with us. Right then, I hated the diary. I wanted to hurl it to the floor and step on it.

"Time for supper!" I heard my father call out.

When I came into the kitchen, I saw that he looked happy, spooning ravioli onto paper plates. He was humming along to some song playing on the transistor radio propped on the windowsill.

"Hungry enough to eat a horse?" he asked me.

Then Davis came in and joined us. As we ate, our father kept telling us how he'd soon be catching plenty of blue trout for our suppers. "Me, too," Davis told him.

I was silent. It felt wrong, sitting there beside the empty seat that belonged to my mother. I wondered if maybe she was having her supper then, too, or if maybe she'd gone someplace, like to a movie with her sister. As I imagined her, I began feeling bad about having wanted to hurt my own diary.

As soon as my father finished his meal, he carried his paper plate across the kitchen and stuffed it into the garbage. "Let's have some fun," he said to Davis and me.

"Like what?" Davis asked him.

I looked at my father. I thought maybe he wanted to take us to the Wagon Wheel—he and our mother had often liked going there at night to drink beer, the two of them sitting on stools at the pine-paneled bar while Davis and I fed nickels to the jukebox, playing "The Wayward Wind" over and over, because our mother said she liked it. Or maybe he just wanted to take us out back to practice shooting tin cans with our Daisy BB rifles, as he'd taught us on a weekend camping trip a few months before. He'd gotten us the rifles for Christmas.

"I thought we'd head down to the railroad tracks," he said.

I liked walking to the tracks with my father. More than once he'd told Davis and me the tracks made him think of his father, who must have passed through Lumber Run at least a few times, or so he imagined, on freights hauling coal.

Davis and I went to change into our sneakers, then joined our father in the backyard, where he was waiting with his flashlight. We followed him across the cut grass and through a small arcade of trees, toward the watchman's shanty, where highway crews stored salt for winter roads, now that trains no longer stopped there.

"Quiet," he said when we got to the railway crossing. He bent down toward the tracks, as he did each time he brought us here, pretending to be listening for the distant sound of the freight train on which his father had long ago ridden.

"Can you hear it?" he asked.

Davis and I just stood there in silence, watching him. Nothing was coming. For a moment, I tried to imagine my father as he must have been as a boy growing up in Bishop, though it was hard to do so, since he spoke so seldom of his childhood, except to say he'd had to go to work when he was ten, sweeping out railway cars, and that when he was twelve, he'd been consigned for a year to the State Youth Sanitarium for Tuberculosis. Once he had told us that when he was a small boy, his father had called him "honey."

He stepped into the railway bed, almost slipping on the oily gravel. Davis and I moved toward him. I couldn't believe how dark it was, though when I looked up I saw the Dog Star quietly blazing above me. "It's called Sirius," my mother had once told me when we were sitting together in our backyard on a summer night a few years before.

"Here you go," our father said as he reached into one of his trouser pockets. He withdrew a fistful of coins, from which he counted out the pennies. Then Davis and I laid the pennies on the tracks, one by one, knowing that when we returned the next morning, we'd find them flattened and flung into the high weeds by night trains we'd neither seen nor heard as we slept.

The next morning, I watched my father head down the narrow path to Pine Creek, his fishing rod and tackle box in one hand, his creel slung over his shoulder, beating on his back as he walked. I was sitting on the front steps, eating my cereal.

"Don't you want to come?" he'd asked as he was leaving.

"Not right now," I'd told him. I'd said I'd try to catch up later, after I'd done the dishes.

I watched him walk away until he disappeared behind a stand of cattails; then I carried my bowl back to the house. I was relieved not to have gone with him to Pine Creek, where he would have once again instructed me how best to bait my hook. I hated touching the worms, with their greasy, quivering bodies, as I pulled them from the bait bucket, and I hated jabbing them onto the barbed hooks, making sure I'd stuck each of them onto the hook in at least two places, so it wouldn't fall off too quickly in the water.

The house was silent when I entered it. Davis had left earlier that morning; I didn't know where he'd gone. But that was all right. I liked being alone with no one around to see me. The whole past year, I'd begun feigning illness on school days so I could stay home by myself. Once my parents had left for work, I'd lie for hours on the basement sofa, slowly devouring the coffee cakes I made for myself from Bisquik, brown sugar, and margarine, until I could feel myself at long last dissolving—nameless, benumbed, unfettered—into the noise and canned laughter of the game shows I watched on TV.

But now I had something important to do. I went into my room and retrieved the diary from the drawer where I'd hidden it the night before. I was glad to see it looked a lot better by daylight; even the cover girl looked brighter and more cheerful. I carried it out to the front porch glider, along with a pencil I'd found in a kitchen drawer. If someone showed up, I figured, I could slip it quickly beneath a cushion.

But when I sat down and opened the diary—I was ready to inscribe my first entry—I was jarred by the emptiness of its white ruled pages. What was I supposed to write there? The only thing I could think of was the odd, throbbing absence of my mother, and how the previous summer I'd sat beside her on the very same glider, reading the *Reader's Digest* condensed books I'd found in the attic, while she flipped through back issues of fashion magazines, occasionally pausing to comment on a pair of shoes or a cocktail dress she particularly admired. But that wasn't something I could put in my diary. What would be the point of that? It was stupid—*case closed*.

Maybe if I just got a bite to eat, I thought, *I might calm down.* I went inside to get a piece of bread from the loaf I'd seen on the kitchen counter. I ate the bread quickly, standing there; then I ate another slice, and then another, and then another one yet. Then I saw how much bread I had eaten and worried that my father would be upset with me for eating so much, but that didn't stop me—I couldn't seem to help myself. I laid a slice on the counter and rolled it around until it turned back into dough, and then I ate that, too, because it was sweeter like that, almost like candy.

By the time I got back to the porch glider, I felt sluggish. I told myself I should lie down, since I felt too tired to write, even though I could feel something hard and insistent tugging inside me, telling me I should try to put at least something on paper, even if it was something I invented, since I wasn't sure I could think of anything true to say. I opened the diary to try again, but I felt even worse, just from holding it. Maybe I'd thrown away my money by buying it. Maybe I'd made a terrible mistake. What if I needed my money for something else?

That's when I heard Davis come into the house through the back door, laughing and talking with someone whose voice I didn't recognize. I hurriedly shoved the diary beneath one of the glider cushions, then went into the house.

"Dad's looking for you," Davis said when I came into the kitchen, where he was standing with his friend Frank, a local boy he'd met while fishing the previous summer. After their initial meeting, they'd gone out hiking together almost every afternoon, canteens strapped to their army surplus belts, while I went to country auctions in the car with my mother, who was trying to add to her collection of cut glass.

I could see Frank didn't much like me—or maybe he was just shy, as I'd once heard Davis telling our father. In any case, Frank barely looked in my direction as Davis told me all about the morning they'd spent together— how they'd gone to the tracks to gather the flattened pennies, as he and I had planned to do, and how they had walked to the remains of the old sawmill with BB rifles to shoot at some blacksnakes Frank's brother said he had seen there. Now they were packing a bag lunch, Davis said, to bring to our father.

I didn't need to ask if the BB rifle Frank had used had in fact been mine; I could see it sitting right there in the corner, propped against the wall.

"See you," Frank murmured in my direction as they left.

I was alone again, and I wasn't sure what to do with myself. I didn't want to resume my diary. I didn't want to read a book. There was nothing good to eat in the house except the loaf of bread, from which I'd already eaten too much. For a moment, I was sorry they hadn't asked me to come with them.

That's when I decided to follow them down the path toward Pine Creek. At first, I couldn't hear them ahead of me, not even when I stopped in the first clearing in the cattails, where people sometimes dumped their old tires. But by the time I got to the second clearing—someone had abandoned an old car there, I noticed, a broken-down junker with its running boards nearly rusted out—I could hear them laughing. I stepped into the cattails. From there, I could see them sitting side by side at the edge of Pine Creek, talking back and forth between themselves as they took off their shoes and socks and rolled up the legs of their blue jeans. They stepped into the water—neither seemed shocked by its sudden coldness—and began wading toward the rock where our father sat fishing.

Then I saw Davis start to slip on the creek's mossy stone bottom. I could see small whirlpools of white water clutching at his ankles, and a look of panic rising in his face. I wondered if Frank could see the panic, too.

For a moment, I thought to call out to warn my brother, suddenly remembering the times he and I had played there together, building small dams from branches and twigs and then coming back later to kick them apart.

But I stayed silent.

Davis slipped; Frank caught him. Frank laughed, and Davis splashed him with water. Then they continued wading toward our father, Davis holding the paper lunch sack above his head, the way a soldier carries his rifle through high water.

I stepped forward from the edge of the cattails. But when I emerged into the open, I saw that my father was watching me.

He waved. I waved, my hand stirring from the cattails a sudden updraft made visible by gnats. But I went no farther. I wasn't sure if I was waving hello or good-bye.

What might I have written about my father in my diary, had I been able to write down anything at all? That I felt afraid when he watched me too long or too closely? Or that the things he kept warning me to stop doing, like cutting out Winnie Winkle fashion paper dolls from the Sunday funnies or designing elaborate ball gowns for my favorite movie stars, were in fact the very things that came most naturally, unbidden, from my hand? *If thy right hand offend thee, cut it off.* Or maybe I would have simply written that I loved him, and missed him, and that I wanted him to call me "honey," too, as his father had called him.

In any case, I was unable to write even a word. Not one word the whole time.

Each morning for the next three days, as soon as I was alone in the house, I resumed my seat on the porch glider, my pencil poised, my diary opened on my lap, waiting for words to strike. One morning it occurred to me that I could address the whole diary to my mother, making her a record of all the things I'd done since I'd last seen her, though in my heart I knew I'd done nothing worth writing down. Another time, I decided I should save the diary to use later, after I'd begun what I hoped would one day become my real life, a life just like the one my mother described herself as once having had, catching a taxi to the Stork Club for cocktails before grabbing a late supper at Luchow's or Toots Shor's.

But for the most part, I just sat there until I felt too lonely to persist. Then I wandered over to the general store to buy red licorice and pretzel rods, counting and recounting my coins, worried that I was depleting my savings too quickly; or I walked the railroad tracks across the old wooden trestle, staring down into the depths below, which I could see through gaps in the cross ties. I carried the diary with me, tucked into my waistband and covered by my camp shirt. But the diary sometimes chafed me as I walked, and when this happened, I'd be seized by the sudden desire to throw it onto the tracks, even though that desire filled me at once with shame, as if I'd just caught myself wanting to kill something small and defenseless. Once, on my way home from one of my walks, I ran into Mrs. Purvis, a widow I'd met with my mother at an auction the previous summer. She invited me back to her house, where we sat on her porch, drinking sweet tea while she showed me an old scrapbook filled with photos of her and her dead husband. When I stood to leave, I decided I wanted to show her the diary, though I told her I'd just found it on the side of the road. "I don't know," she said as she examined it. "It looks mighty new to me."

As for my father: I knew he was upset with me. Each late afternoon, when he got home from fishing, he came to my room and stood in the doorway, as if there was something he wanted to say. But I just kept on reading, stretched out on my bed, its coarse woolen blanket tucked tight into army corners, as he had taught me. After he turned and walked away, I shut the book and listened to him as he crossed the kitchen to the sink. I could hear him turn on the tap, and I could hear the water rushing forward as he began to gut and clean whatever trout he'd caught that day.

But on the fourth afternoon, he got angry.

When I got home from walking the railroad tracks, I found him in the backyard, watering the lawn with a garden hose, as he sometimes did, so that he could come back later and hunt for night crawlers, which emerged when the soil was wet.

"I want you to tell me what's going on," he said as soon as he saw me.

"What do you mean?" I asked, worried that he'd somehow found the diary, even though I felt sure I had it with me, tucked into my waistband. I had to fight the urge to reassure myself by touching it.

"You haven't come fishing like I've asked," he said, looking at me directly.

"But I'm going to," I told him.

"Sure," he said. "When?"

"I will."

"So you say," he said.

I just stood there, shifting from foot to foot. Had he been like my mother, I might have distracted him by getting him to tell me some story about himself, but that didn't work with him.

Later, at supper, Davis started talking about an abandoned CCC camp he'd come across while hiking up a fire trail with Frank; they'd seen the remains of a few barracks and a tree growing through what they figured had once been the floor of the mess hall. Our father said the whole country should still be thanking FDR for the CCC and the New Deal, because without him no one would have gotten even an honest dollar for an honest day's work.

As soon as I had finished eating, I excused myself. I couldn't stop thinking about my diary. Even though I knew I'd returned it to its drawer the second I'd gotten back into the house, I needed to check to make sure it was there, the same way my mother sometimes had to turn the car around and drive home, worried that she'd left a cigarette burning and that it had already fallen onto the carpet.

But I was also nervous about going back into my room, since I didn't want to do anything that would call attention to myself. So I went out back to catch lightning bugs, just like normal. A few minutes later, Davis came out the kitchen door and settled himself in a chair beneath the back porch light, looking through a copy of *Boys' Life* he'd gotten from Frank. He and Frank liked reading *Boys' Life* together, mesmerizing themselves with stories of scouts who proved quick-minded in the midst of disaster, slashing open a snakebite puncture on a child's arm to suck the venom out or forming a human chain to rescue a skater who'd fallen through thin ice.

I liked catching lightning bugs; I liked collecting them in jars with lids I'd studded with air holes. At night, the jars made small, radiant galaxies that by morning would be dead.

I went to the honeysuckle bushes in the side yard, where the lightning bugs were flickering among the fragrant white and yellow flowers; I reached out a hand and grabbed one from where it hovered, flashing, in midair. Then I remembered a trick a girl had once told me about in school. If you pulled off a lightning bug's belly, she said, and stuck it on your finger, you could make a ring from it, because when a lightning bug died, its belly continued to glow.

I wasn't sure I could actually do it, but I gave it my full attention, first pulling the wings from the lightning bug's body, then setting its belly, still glowing, on my left ring finger. If I squinted, I realized, the lightning bug's luminescent belly looked almost like the yellow diamond solitaire my mother had inherited after her mother's death. But who would inherit the solitaire, I wondered, when my mother died? It would never go to a boy.

I look up and saw Davis still reading beneath the porch light. I walked across the yard toward him, holding out my left hand as steady as possible.

"Look," I said, showing him what I had made.

He looked up briefly from his magazine and gazed at my finger. "That's dumb," he said.

"No," I said. "It's beautiful."

Then I heard the screen door slam, and when I looked up, I saw my father coming out to the porch from the kitchen. I hurriedly turned my hand over, and the lightning bug's belly dropped into the grass. For a moment, I watched as it extinguished itself like a cigarette butt's dying ember.

"What are you doing?" my father asked.

"Getting the lightning bugs something to eat," I told him. To prove it, I bent over and yanked up a few handfuls of grass to stuff into one of the jars.

"I thought maybe you boys were telling ghost stories," he said. "That's what my brothers and I used to do after dark. Did you ever hear 'The Monkey's Paw'? We always liked 'The Monkey's Paw.'"

"We saw it on TV," I told him.

"Oh," he said. Then he stepped forward from the porch into the dark. "I want you boys to help me look for night crawlers," he told us.

He instructed Davis to go around to the front porch and fetch a few flashlights and the dirt-filled coffee can in which he kept his live bait. When Davis left, he turned toward me. "Maybe you won't mind helping with *this*," he said. "Since you can't seem to find it within yourself to come fishing, I mean."

"I want to help," I told him, though it wasn't true. I hated searching for night crawlers. I hated having to grasp them, damp and slick, as they first emerged from the ground, and I hated the way they tore into pieces if I got nervous and pulled at them too hard or quickly.

Davis came back around the side of the house, carrying the bait can, along with two flashlights, which he was toting in his pant pockets. He had switched on a third flashlight and was holding it under his chin as he walked, so that his illuminated face looked cadaverous and ghoulish. "Ooooohh," he was moaning like a ghost as he came toward us, "you've got three wishes on the monkey's paw . . ."

"Okay, that's enough," our father said. "Let's get down to business."

For a moment, I stood there without moving, as if Davis's words had cast some spell that had stilled me. I knew what my wish would be, if one wish were granted me: *Please let me seem, even if only for this hour, my father's son.* I knew the time had come. I knew I had to please him.

Then I heard my own voice speaking, a muffled sound, as if from a distance: "Dad," I was saying, "I'll go search in the compost."

I could see my father was surprised by what I'd said, just as I was. He knew I was afraid of the compost pile. It sat in the darkest and farthest part of the yard, near the stand of trees that separated our house from the Wagon Wheel's parking lot. Davis and Frank had once told me that rats went to feed there, drawn by the stench of decomposition; they said brown snakes liked to nest there, seeking the warmth that rises from decay. But it was also where night crawlers were most abundant. I knew that.

"Are you sure?" my father asked.

"It's not fair," Davis complained. "Dad said he wanted us to do this *together.*"

"Yes, I'm sure," I told my father.

"All right," he said.

He handed me a flashlight and I started to walk away.

"Wait," he said. He removed his fishing cap, the one to which he affixed his hand-tied flies, and set it on my head. "Walk softly," he told me. "Keep your eyes peeled."

I crossed the yard, walking softly. I kept my eyes peeled.

When I got to the compost, I stepped over the low chicken-wire fencing that enclosed it, sinking to my ankles in the soft mulch. I guided my flashlight's beam back and forth across the surface. Everywhere the light fell, I saw small, sudden motions: a wood spider struggling through the sticky albumen glazing an eggshell; pale grubs devouring wet leaves. Then I heard music, the faint sound of a song playing on the jukebox at the Wagon Wheel. It was hard not to think of my mother, to picture her sitting at the bar in her white sundress with the spaghetti straps, holding her beer glass aloft. "Meet my pretty wife," my father always said as he introduced her to his fisherman friends—"Meet my wife, pretty Maria."

I looked up. On the other side of the yard, my father was holding a flashlight for Davis, who was kneeling within the wide circumference of its beam. Davis was lowering his hand toward the ground and pulling up a night crawler.

I wanted my father to watch me. I knelt in the compost and reached down, and all at once, I saw at least a dozen night crawlers emerging simultaneously from their air holes, as if in response to a single command. I was just beginning to touch one, preparing to yank it out from its hole, when suddenly something fell toward me—a leaf?—and landed on my shoulder.

I turned to look: Its wings struck my face. Whatever it was, it was caught in the fabric of my shirt, straining to pull itself free. It jerked upward and rose briefly, only to catch itself again on my collar. I could feel the violence and terror of its movement at my throat, thrashing and thrashing.

"Get it off me!" I cried.

My father came running, his flashlight's beam swinging crazily through the dark, like an emergency.

"Get it off me!" I begged him. "Get it off!"

He pointed the flashlight at my collar, where the creature was struggling, its pale green wings furiously beating.

Through the flashlight's beam, I could see my father study me; I saw how I looked in his eyes.

"It's a luna moth," he said. He reached toward my collar and flicked it with his fingertips. Suddenly it seemed small and insufficient. It rose and flew away.

"I thought you'd been bitten by a snake," he said.

"Me, too," I said. "That's what I thought, too." We both knew I was lying.

"Just get inside," he muttered.

I switched off my flashlight and walked back across the yard. As I passed Davis, he whispered dramatically, "Oooohh, it's the curse of the monkey's paw."

I said nothing back. When I got to the porch, I didn't turn around to look at my father.

I simply opened the back door and stepped into the kitchen, flinching from the sudden brightness of the ceiling light. When my eyes adjusted, I saw it. I saw it lying right there on the kitchen table. My diary. Someone had found it and taken it from my dresser, and now it was lying there, just lying there, out in the open, beside the salt and pepper shakers.

That night, I didn't claim the diary by taking it back to my room; in fact, I didn't even want to touch it. I went right to bed and stayed there until late the next morning, when I heard my father drive off in the station wagon, headed to Slate Run, where he was planning to try his hand at fly-fishing with some men he'd met at the Wagon Wheel.

When I got up for breakfast, the diary was still sitting in the center of the table. I just sat there looking at it as I ate my cereal, imagining the things I might have written down had I gone to New York with my mother. Perhaps we would have had dinner at Michel's, my mother's favorite restaurant in Park Slope, or perhaps we would have taken in an early movie at the Rialto. Perhaps I would have been happy simply to sit in the Victorian room my grandmother had called her "boudoir," remembering the time she had invited me in to ask me questions for a personality quiz she'd prepared on a legal pad especially for me. "Whom do you prefer," she had asked, "Jayne Mansfield or Marilyn Monroe? Whom do you regard as the greater actress, Bette Davis or Greta Garbo? Which do you prefer, the plain Hershey bar or the Hershey with almonds?"

I sat at the kitchen table most of the morning, as if I were bidding the diary adieu. But I couldn't sit there forever. I had something to do, something I'd figured out the night before while lying awake in my room.

I waited until I finished lunch. Then I stacked my dishes in the sink and went to the broom closet, where my father stored our Daisy BB rifles, out of immediate reach. I took my rifle and carried it out to the front porch glider. Then I began to clean it, just as my father had taught me, first moistening a cleaning patch with a few drops of heavy oil, then inserting the patch directly into the muzzle on a long rod in order to swab the bore. When I was done, I opened the small paper cylinder of BBs and poured them into my palm; I fed the BBs slowly into the narrow loading tube affixed to the base of the barrel.

I carried the loaded rifle down the path toward Pine Creek, past the first clearing and through the cattails. At the second clearing, I stopped. I pulled hard on the cocking lever and raised the rifle straight, positioning the old junked car in its sight.

I fired. The first shot struck the junker's windshield. I pressed the trigger again so that a second shot struck the glass, and when I saw that my aim was right and good, I pulled the trigger over and over, until the windshield cracked into a silvery web and then shattered, raining small bits of glass across the dashboard. I liked the way it felt. I walked around to the driver's side and shot out those windows, too, and then I shot at the side panel until it was scored and dimpled, and then I walked around to the other side and did the whole thing over again. Finally, I took aim at the small winged ornament on the rusty hood. But I wasn't through.

I set the rifle down and walked back to the house empty-handed. Once there, I took the diary from the kitchen table and carried it back down to the clearing. I opened one of the car doors and set the diary on the front seat, and then backed up until I had the cover girl within my rifle's sight. I fired at her, too, again and again, until she and the diary were both obliterated, the pink plastic cover split from its cardboard backing, the blank pages shredded.

Later, I ate supper with Davis. We heated up a few more cans of ravioli, since our father had warned us he'd be late—he was stopping at the Wagon Wheel to drink some beer with his buddies. After supper, I went into the front room to wait on the musty horsehair sofa. I was eager to tell my father how I had practiced my marksmanship, as he had encouraged.

I heard him on the porch before he came in. From the way he grabbed at the screen door, I could tell he was angry. "Where are you?" he called out as he came into the house. He was calling my name.

I was scared. The room was dark. It was late. "I'm here," I finally said.

Suddenly my father was standing in the doorway. "What the hell did you think you were doing?" he demanded. "What the hell made you think you could destroy something that isn't even yours?"

I knew what I thought I was doing: I was trying to please him. Even now, looking back, I honestly believe that. But what could I have said to him then? That I had hoped to turn myself into a son he might love?

My silence made him angrier. "That damn car isn't yours!" he bellowed. He said the car belonged to one of the bartenders at the Wagon Wheel. It wasn't a junker. It ran just fine. He said he was just drinking a beer and minding his own damn business when some man he'd never even met before came into the bar and told him what I had done, how I'd been down at the creek shooting at a car until I'd destroyed it. "And just how the hell do you think you're going to pay that back?" he asked.

I could see he was trying to contain himself, even though he was furious. I just listened to him yell. After a while, he started to spend himself until, finally, he just stood there in silence. It wasn't until then that he noticed that the room he was standing in was dark. He reached over and switched on the table lamp.

"Do you have anything to say for yourself?" he asked.

"No," I said.

"Then I want you to get ready for bed," he said. "I'll go ahead and check you."

I knew what he meant: Each night in Lumber Run before Davis and I went to bed, we stood before him so he could check our bodies for ticks that we ourselves might not have spotted.

He unscrewed the shade from the table lamp next to the sofa and bent my head into the arc of light, parting my hair with his fingers as he inspected my scalp.

"Stand up," he said.

I stood. I began to undress, as I did each night: first my shoes and socks, then my pants, then my shirt, until I was standing there naked. He lifted the table lamp and moved it back and forth across my body, studying my chest, my back, my legs, my buttocks. I felt right then as if there were nothing about me that was not visible to him. I could feel the heat of the bulb on my skin.

I hate you, I thought. *I hate you, I hate you.*

In retrospect, I'm not sure who I was hating most right then, as I stood there—my father, my mother, or myself. That night I didn't know that my father would soon die suddenly of liver failure, or that it would be Davis who would one day explain to me that it was not he but Mrs. Purvis who had told my father that she had seen me with a diary, or that I had scarcely even begun what was to become my life of secrets.

I knew only the heat of the bulb as it passed over my naked body. *I hate you,* I thought, *I hate you.* I no longer had a diary. But for the first time I felt as if I actually needed one, a need that was at once acute and unfamiliar. It wasn't that I needed to speak to my mother in her absence; it wasn't that I wanted to make something up. For the first time, I wanted to write something down, something true, even if I had no idea what words I'd one day use in doing so.

Joan Silber

War Buddies

I ALWAYS LIKED getting lost in projects; I liked doing things on my own. I was a Navy Brat, moved from post to post as a kid, and I got used to occupying myself without company, with a surprising degree of contentment. Ernst was the one person I ever met who was better at this than I was; I was an amateur of aloneness compared to him.

I might have turned out more like Ernst. There was a spell in my life when I made an effort to. I admired him, and in many ways he was admirable. After I settled in Bangkok, I used to write to Ernst every year at Christmas. I wrote him summaries of what I was doing at work, what my wife and kids were up to. Ernst never wrote to me—he never wrote to anyone. Why would someone who hardly spoke in person get gabby on paper from thousands of miles away? It was hard to imagine him doing such a thing, but I wanted it even though I knew better.

We were both in our twenties when we met. Bydex was my first job, right out of engineering school, and Ernst had started a few years before me. The guy who hired me said he was putting me on a project with the company genius who was not a social butterfly, was I okay with that? When I walked into our shared office, Ernst raised an eyebrow and nodded while seeming to look over his shoulder. He shook hands, went back to whatever he was writing, and that was the end of our first meeting.

But he loved the work. Once he'd sized me up, he made a point of taking me across the hall to meet the guy who was designing the electronics for a laser rangefinder that measured the distance from an airplane to the ground for accurate bombing. He thought I'd just want to see the beauty of it. I did.

Almost everyone in the company was married except us. This was in the late sixties, in a sedate outpost of that era—we were in Phoenix, then a dusty town in the middle of nowhere. Ernst and I didn't know what to do with ourselves. We played Ping-Pong in our married friends' furnished basements, we played pinball in roadhouses off the highway, we drove for miles with nothing but static and Bobby Darin on the radio, we went to a shooting range and killed the shapes of ducks. No women worked on our project—we were devising tests for the guidance systems on military aircraft—or were anywhere outside the typing pool. I was so lonely I used to make surprise phone calls at noon to my high school girlfriend, who had a husband and a baby.

Ernst and I were summoned one day to a large inner office with ugly maroon drapes, where a project manager told us what everyone knew, that Bydex systems were letting planes go off course in Vietnam, a place you definitely didn't want to get lost over. And how would Ernst and I feel about seeing the world? Following the equipment into the field, being the company's tech reps over there? "We can't send mediocre drones on this," the manager said. "We need our best, which is you." I knew he was flattering us into believing it was a reward to be flown into a war zone, but I was immensely flattered anyway. I said I'd think about it, but Ernst knew right away. He tilted his head and gave his small crooked smile and murmured, *Why not?* It wasn't a jaunty question—it had in it his private satisfaction that as a rule situations were as crappy as he expected.

Saigon was not a combat zone. That was what I told my family, although they could see how jittery I was. It was a city near the bottom of a country at war—the ground fighting was mostly in the countryside (I hadn't yet heard anyone say *in-country*) around villages farther north or down in the Delta. It was true that the Vietcong had invaded Saigon during the Tet offensive some six months before, but they hadn't held it very long.

I don't know what Ernst told his family. He had one sister (who was out marching against the war, he said she'd always been an airhead), and he had a mother and father. His father owned a dry-cleaning plant. That was all I knew about them. He didn't act as if he needed a family or understood why anyone did.

When we changed planes in Anchorage, I called my folks from the airport, while Ernst sat reading a Nero Wolfe mystery. The cover had a drawing of a corpse bleeding onto a carpet. My mother got very emotional, and I knew it had been a mistake for me to call. I envied Ernst, absorbed in his book. Our flights were on commercial planes filled with soldiers, and on the long middle route to Japan there was a group of marines behind us, telling the world's dumbest dirty jokes. But Ernst slept like a baby. His sinuses made his breathing loud—this new intimacy did not please me.

Tan Son Nhut Air Force Base was teeming with soldiers. They looked very young, even to me, under their hats and helmets. As soon as we landed, I was looking for wounded ones on stretchers, or battle-weary groups covered in mud—I wasn't hungry for horror but I had prepared for these sights the way I'd tried to learn a few words of the language. *Cam on.* Thank you. *Phong tam o dau?* Where is the bathroom? And then I did see men loading heavy duffles onto a plane, and they moved with such focused deliberation that I understood these were body bags, and I stopped in my tracks. Ernst was behind me. "Just walk," he said.

Saigon was loud with traffic and smelled of exhaust fumes and hot asphalt and something faintly vegetal and pleasant. I did not see how our driver could make his way through the headlong flow of bicycles and cars. I hadn't understood that it was a real city, with broad avenues and big boxy modern buildings and pink French colonial palaces, at the same time that it was a sprawling bazaar with people in conical straw hats carrying sacks of rice on shoulder poles and hawking packs of cigarettes and magenta fruits.

Our car moved slowly and was like an oven. Since my dad was in the navy, I'd lived in some hot places in the U.S.—San Diego and Corpus Christi and Key West. Saigon was definitely muggier than any of them. Sweat was running down Ernst's face as if his pores were weeping.

"*They* look cool," Ernst said, looking through the window. The women on the street were all in long-sleeved tunics and shirts (for modesty, the driver said) and did not seem to be sweating much, standing over their piles of auto parts and bananas and steaming vats of soup. Every item of the first and third worlds was set out on the pavement for sale—Bic lighters, bottled beer, sugarcane. In the midst of this jumble of enterprise, the vendors' faces were distant and closed. I couldn't tell if they were resigned or infuriated or just exhausted. It was too soon to even guess. Some of the women were very beautiful. Not the men, who looked bony and fierce eyed to me. Even then I didn't know what to make of the men.

The government had bunked us into an old faded-glory hotel, a tiered white hulk with a soldier on guard outside. The lobby held a stiff arrangement of dark lacquered wood settees inlaid with mother of pearl, and we sat on these and waited with our luggage while someone checked us in. Across the marble floor, a man whose trouser was tucked where a leg had been cut off at the hip was crawling, begging from anyone who happened to be there. When he tapped my knee, I fished an American quarter out of my pocket to give him. One of his eyes was milky and vacant. Even Ernst gave him a dime.

Our rooms were not bad, with their big rattan headboards and the windows X'ed with duct tape to keep them from shattering. Over my bed was a woodblock print of a happy native paddling a boat under a willow tree. Where was *that* kingdom? It took about ten minutes for me to notice that nothing could make me cool in that room, not the ceiling fan, not the blinds drawn down, not mugs of ice brought up from the bar.

From the first morning on, we worked very long hours at the air base, and when we came back to the hotel after dark, I went upstairs and lay down on my bed and listened to the noise of the street. Some of it was our noise—convoys and trucks and boisterous American voices—and some of it was theirs, the shrill and glottal syllables. I knocked on Ernst's door to see if he wanted to go out. "You mean now?" he said, from behind the door. He didn't sound eager but he came out right away. At home he'd been like that too.

Once we were on the sidewalks, people kept calling out to us. Men's voices said in their half-swallowed English, "Where you going? I can take you cheap. Not safe to walk. You like young girls, how young? I can take you now, cheap for you." They didn't stop, no matter what we said or didn't say. They trailed us across the avenue, around the square. "I see you before, I know you," a girl of about fourteen said. "You looking for me?"

So we took a cyclo—our two big western bodies in a cart pushed by a skinny old man on a bike—to a bar that the corporal who was our driver had told us about. We walked into a dark basement lit by purple lights and full of soldiers and Vietnamese girls playing pool at a table in the center, with Mick Jagger singing "Under My Thumb" in the background. It took about a second to see that we were out of place in our seersucker suits and not welcome either.

So we walked back to the hotel bar, where we drank glasses of beer with American civilians who were older and richer than we were and we let them brag to us about what they knew. "Never trust anyone. First rule. Get it tattooed on your chest over your heart." This hackneyed lesson was intoned by a chemist who'd been setting up ice-cream factories for the troops. "But the French restaurants are good, I'll tell you which ones." A construction engineer who'd been in the country for years, carving up new harbors, kept trying to tell us about the huge motorcycle he'd bought for a song. He described every part of its mighty carcass, one of the few things likely to interest Ernst. I got a little jolly from the beers and the talk, but Ernst went silent, frozen (I later realized) in contempt. In the elevator I asked if he'd had a good time, and he said, "Not really. I'm not very crazy about profiteers."

I wiped, as my mother used to say, the smile off my face. Now I saw what he saw, how the men all looked oozing and overripe. Inflated and blustering.

There were plenty of other bars in other hotels, and our first nights were spent going from one to the other. And women found us, as it was their job to do. Two pretty teenagers asked us if seats at our table were taken. "You always so tall?" one of them said to Ernst. She was delicate and long waisted, with a rough voice. The softer, plainer one picked me. Mine could speak a little English but not a lot, and it unnerved me later that night to have her small, pliant feet above my shoulders and her scent all around me and have so few words of hers I could follow. What was she saying, was she saying anything? And I didn't even like, not really, the jolt of pleasure that arrived in the midst of my not wanting anymore to be there.

And where was Ernst? I'd last seen him led by his girl into one of the other rooms. There'd been a tiny, awkward smirk on his face. A man like other men, I'd thought.

Now he was waiting for me on the inner stairs of the building where they'd taken us. "Everything okay?" I asked.

"Hurry up," he said. "It's late."

"How was it?" I said. "You liked her?"

He didn't bother to answer.

Someone earlier that night, a man who was very drunk, had told me he knew Ernst was in the CIA. "He has that spook look," he said, "that expressionless look. I'd know it anywhere."

Certainly no one was better than Ernst at keeping things to himself. Before we left the States, a few people we worked with had pretty much voiced the same opinion. But what did the CIA do? It gathered information, didn't it? If this involved asking anyone questions, Ernst was not your man. He was notably incurious about other people and had no practice in exacting even a sentence. And CIA work would have required lying and disguise. Ernst hated even the small white lies of most social exchanges (*good job on that* or *nice house you've got*) and was famous for never uttering them. He had no tolerance for falsity. "Phonies," as he (like Holden Caulfield) called them, made him shudder in disgust. The widespread habit people had of humoring each other was why he mostly chose solitude.

We spent a lot of time at the airfield. Ernst's hearing had already been damaged at home by the roar of engines, so I wore ear protectors, which he laughed at. The soldiers also found me hilarious. We watched the planes take off and we rode with the pilots on practice runs. Everything we checked out worked fine. We spent a lot of time rerunning the checks. Ernst was methodical.

I was never very comfortable going up in those planes. I had enough sense to keep this sentiment to myself. Fear had settled in me as soon as we arrived. A week after we got there, a bomb went off in a nightclub in our part of town, a place I'd been to, with walls of mirrors that were now piles of slivered rubbish. My high school girlfriend, Betty, had started writing to me. "Please take very good care of yourself, Toby," she said. "All of us at home are thinking of you." I was thinking of me too.

The Air Force pilots hated us. They liked to tell us the grisliest stories they could—mutilated soldiers who'd screamed the whole trip back, deadly bamboo snakes in the cockpit, kids on bikes throwing satchel charges into American trucks—and said we should talk to the Infantry guys if we really wanted to hear stuff. G.I.s with necklaces of ears, eight-year-old girls luring men into ambushes, had we heard about those? I said, "Jesus. Holy Christ." I thought they were overdoing the list for me (these weren't wartime clichés yet) but Ernst didn't flinch.

"Planes go back out there into the thick of it every morning," the pilot said, "early, like when you're buying your croissants for breakfast."

"But we love our planes," the copilot said. "You love this one?"

"I do like these actually," Ernst said.

The two pilots gave each other a look, and we were swooping down nose first. Only our seat belts, digging into our bellies, kept us from being thrown into the cockpit. Even Ernst was yelling, "Fuck! Oh, fuck!"

And then we were gaining altitude too fast, our heads jerked back. The plane did a jarring, nauseating loop and then another lunge—the ride wouldn't stop. I was shouting, "Right now, cut it out!" which probably egged them on. I thought they were going to kill all of us—why would they do that? I managed to stop yelling *cut it out*. I sounded like a first-grade teacher. But why wouldn't they stop?

"Enjoy that?" the pilot said, when we were level again. "Either of you shit yourselves?"

We hadn't. Ernst was white and sweating. "Interesting," he said. "Very interesting."

I envied him. Everyone in Vietnam had to go through a process of hardening; even the civilians working for American contractors talked about how green they'd been in the beginning. But Ernst arrived with his own crust.

"Those guys are crazy," he did say, when we were back on the ground, having coffee (a beverage then thought to calm you) in one of the air base canteens.

"*Why* did we come here?" I said. "We didn't have to come."

I thought he was going to say there was a war on. We worked in the defense industry, it went without saying we believed in the necessity of wars generally. You could not allow certain people to get away with certain things. Ernst thought the world consisted largely of such people, but he especially hated the Communists. No one could tell him they had a few okay ideas. "They're bad news," he said.

"I wanted to travel," he said now. "When Bydex hired me, they said I would travel."

"This is travel?"

"You get to see people," he said.

He did? What people? It was true he walked around with a camera, a fancy, complicated number with extra lenses, and he used a light meter. But he mostly took pictures of buildings, as far as I'd seen—the post office, the opera house, the American embassy with its flank of giant flowerpots. The post office had been designed by the same guy who did the Eiffel Tower and it had a very handsome arched ceiling. So what?

And how many Vietnamese had I talked to? How many conversations had I had? My circle of local acquaintance was notably narrow. So far I had talked to the hooker who called herself Miss Mai, the bellhop, and the crippled beggar who came every night to the hotel, with his one sealed eye and his slurred speech.

Inside those long days, I was longing for Betty. And I was thrilled when she wrote, but her letters disappointed me. They reminded me not only that she was married but also what I hadn't liked about her in the beginning. She was nice but shallow and sometimes downright sappy. I had lied about this to myself when we were together—decided she had her own kind of intelligence or was sharper than her language showed—and it struck me now that this was the sort of lying Ernst was free of. His life seemed very free to me and very clean.

Ernst knew a lot of details about the war, for a guy who wasn't in the CIA—where exactly Prime Minister Diem had been murdered by his own generals, how long the DMZ actually was, and what Madame Nhu had really wanted. He said he just remembered what he read in the newspapers. Didn't I know what I saw on TV at least? His memory was pretty remarkable. He was famous at work for being able to recite the figures on any project without looking.

And he could describe every shop on a block he'd just walked through. At night, when we made our way back to the hotel, he was the one who kept me from turning down the wrong avenue and getting lost in a tangle of unmarked streets. He could always say which direction the river was in or how far we were from the brick Notre Dame Cathedral. He's more *here* than I am, I thought.

But I liked the country more than he did. I started to have more chats with Can, the bellhop who worked nights; he knew a little English and some French. He offered to sell us drugs, as did the laundress and every cyclo driver we met, but once we were off that topic, he let me ask him the names of all the plants in the courtyard. Of course, he only knew them in Vietnamese, and my attempts at repeating the tones reduced him to a very dignified form of high amusement; he cracked up without making a sound. I tried to describe Florida to him, and my mother's yard with its croton and yucca and allamanda. He probably had no interest whatsoever but he repeated the words. He had a noble politeness.

He had three kids, a boy and two girls. I asked how they liked school. "They like school, when there ever is school." I pantomimed eager students raising their hands, but he didn't understand me at first. Apparently, his kids were so good, they would never rush to answer—"Don't want to make mistake, and also don't want to brag." I was tickled by this idea of comportment and reported it to Ernst. It did make me think of myself. I had been timid and modest for an American boy, much to the dismay of my family.

Can wasn't at the hotel for a few days, and I asked at the desk if he was sick. "Gone," the day manager said.

"He's okay?"

"Gone," he said.

It was Ernst who told me he'd heard Can was one of those who'd planted a bomb in an ordinary blue-and-yellow Renault taxi, and it had blown up in front of another hotel and taken out the lobby and part of the bakery next door. "It was a humongous bloody mess," Ernst said. "Lot of people in that lobby."

I knew that lobby, with its mosaic floor. It was a nicer hotel than ours, where visiting brass sometimes stayed. I'd been there for drinks. Can might have killed me, he wanted to kill people like me. My Can.

"Wake up, Dorothy," Ernst said.

It was an old story, but it was fresh to me. I'd had no inkling, of course, what Can believed or how strongly he believed it or that he had any capacity for sacrifice. He seemed so mild and civil and wryly entertained by the world. And Can's cadre had been betrayed by someone else (it did not pay to think what duress led to that betrayal)—that was how Ernst knew the story.

"Can's gone," Ernst said, "as in dead."

Ernst had his own phrasing, different from a soldier's. Not so hideously comic (nothing about crispy critters), cooler and flatter. And he was not about to comfort me.

But I wanted to be like Ernst. I wrote home to Betty and to my mother—"Pilots took us for a roller coaster ride, doing loop-di-loops the other morning. Very *interesting*, I can tell you!" I leaned on Ernst, even more here than at home. An evening with anyone else—the other tech reps or the fat-cat contractors who hung out in the bars—always had its coarseness. At first I'd thought I was going to change in that direction; I wanted vividness, like anyone. But I wasn't a real drinker—some people just aren't—and after a while I didn't want to be out every night, with all the work we had. And I had my ambitions, unformed lump though I was. I'd chosen to be an engineer, a nerd with a slide rule, partly because I didn't like the world of business, where showing off was part of the code of conduct. I was sort of interested in being a genius (though I knew I was a dark horse for this category), so that people would respect me and leave me to my own methods. I wanted to be like Ernst; I wanted praise and my own corner, both at once.

We worked very hard in those weeks. New information kept coming in, data that contradicted itself, and we sat at our desks trying to resolve it. And I saw that I was glad to be indoors, though I had been so dazzled by the streets. The gap-toothed woman who sold pilfered American liquor and toothpaste at her stand, the shoeshine boy with his playful nasal pleading, the old man walking his bicycle loaded with rope bags of melons—they yelled at me to buy from them, to give them money. Why was I there if I was only going to walk along in my towering foreign fatness, my oblivious overfed height? Did I know they were there, did I know where I was, where was my money? I was becoming afraid of all of them. As I had reason to be.

And what was making the planes fuck up? While we were in Saigon, four planes that flew out from Da Nang got shot down over Dak To, where they weren't supposed to be. The officer who told us said, "This can't go on. It can't." And we were the assholes who'd let the pilots go down; gone as in dead. Or captured, which was not pleasant to think about. Why were we so slow, what was the matter with us? I looked at Ernst when they called us in. He shook his head, which meant *no good, no good.*

We stayed at the office all through the night, trying to make some glimmer of sense out of measurements and charts and maps and whatever we had of radio logs. There was a moment when I thought I was coming to an answer, but a second later I was lost again, dizzy and stupid over the figures. Ernst grunted to himself, as he did when he was concentrating. He made the sudden soft sounds people make in their sleep. He was the clearest-brained engineer I'd ever met and he should have been able to *get* this, if anyone could, the buried glitch, the needle in the haystack. It was a human error, it had to be solvable by a human.

We got word the next day that they needed to send us to the air base in Da Nang. We had to look at more of the planes. I wrote my mother a long, stupidly chipper letter; even she, who didn't know much, would recognize Da Nang as a place closer to the DMZ, a name repeated on TV in reports of heavy fighting, heavy losses.

"We're moving to a noisy neighborhood," Ernst said.

"Wasn't this just an office job?" I said. "They didn't mention any extra excursions back at Bydex." We couldn't exactly complain to the soldiers around us, since we were the pampered kittens of the war.

"*Au revoir,* Saigon," I said, when we were at the airport.

"See you later, alligator," Ernst said to the city.

Da Nang was a good-sized city too, it turned out, but we weren't really in it. Our new home was on the air base, off a dirt road near an airfield of yellow dust, with a long, low ridge of mountains in the distance. They had bunked us in what looked like a village of beach bungalows, two-story wooden huts lining the road on both sides, a jerry-built stage set.

Ernst came up with a fact while we were carrying our duffles into our rooms. "This airport in Da Nang, if you count everything in it," he said, "has the most traffic of any airport in the world."

"Big vacation spot," I said. "Wildly popular." On a garbage can next to our hootch someone had spray-painted "Not My Home, Just A Passing Thru."

But soldiers liked us better here. We were now consultants to the marines, not a group known for their sweet manners, but they were decent to us in the office where we worked. They had a standing joke about fixing up Ernst with a nymphomaniac nurse, a figure whose tastes for bizarre practices grew with each telling, and they liked to insult me about my wardrobe—had my mother picked it out and could they divvy up my shirts if I got shot? They called us the two brainiacs. Having come this far got us credit. We'd been issued flak jackets and helmets, we weren't just a couple of hot dogs hanging around a hotel pool sipping martinis.

We were not, of course, in the shit with them. We had by this time some inkling of what the shit was. Well, the whole world knows now, doesn't it, what we made soldiers do. Not that I ever saw any of those villages. Around us some of the landscape was charred from bombings, and I was doing my best to help our planes char it—that part was all right with me. But I got so I hated to see the men go out from the base. At all hours you could hear overhead the Medevac helicopters bringing back the wounded and the dead. We sent them in and then we plucked them out.

Ernst and I were working eighteen-hour days. If we couldn't find anything wrong in the guidance systems, maybe the bug was in the navigation systems or even in the control systems that moved the planes around. Ernst, who had never been one to let go of a problem, would hardly leave his office even to eat, and he was a big eater. I got someone to drive me to the settlement of shacks the Vietnamese had built up, west of the base on the road to the beach. Ernst wasn't much of a gourmet but he liked the beef noodle soup one woman made, with the green herbs and the lime juice you threw in as you ate. Their shantytown was quite something, with its hodgepodge of boards and patched roofs, its crowing roosters. Someone had named it Dogpatch, after Li'l Abner's hillbilly town in the funnies. The soup woman had a sister who sometimes laundered my famous shirts.

I watched Ernst slurping down the noodles at his desk, and I was glad he had me to look after him. He was probably glad too, in his way. "Thanks for the nourishment," he said, which was a wild burst of expressive fervor from him. And he shared a government chocolate bar with me for our dessert. We had our comforts, our spots of mellowness. He had bought a cassette recorder at the PX (cassettes were pretty new on the market then), and we listened to a tape of Ella Fitzgerald singing while we worked. The sound was thin and hoarse and miraculous.

The next morning at six, when we got to our office, a lieutenant colonel was waiting outside for us in the misty brightness. "New development," he said. "There could be a reason two smart jerk-offs like you can't find anything." A Vietnamese worker had been located on the airfield where he wasn't supposed to be. He was asleep under one of our planes. Maybe sabotage was the answer here to the big mystery. Maybe monkey business had been going on all along.

I was flooded with relief—that was my first response—it wasn't my fault, it had never been my fault. Those pilots hadn't gone down just because I was an idiot. The lieutenant colonel said we might as well keep working, but they would be questioning this individual and would get back to us with what they learned.

And then for a week nobody said a word to us. Ernst kept working as if this new wrinkle hadn't turned up. I thought he just wanted to occupy himself. We heard from the enlisted men around the office that the guy they'd nabbed was the one called Chu Nam, which meant Fifth Uncle. He was supposed to be the soup lady's uncle. Maybe they were all related, we didn't know.

She disappeared too, and you couldn't blame her for making herself scarce. It was a very creepy week. When Ernst and I walked back from the office at night, I jumped at any noise, and the night was full of noises. If that guy had managed to get out on the airfield, anyone could be right next to us. "They always could," Ernst said. He was scornful of my jumpiness. "Keep cool," he said. I was thinking, not for the first time, that Bydex had picked us to send because we were the unmarried ones. I was very lonely. I hadn't known I was that lonely.

By Monday, though we never actually heard anything official, the grapevine gave us as much as we needed. The prisoner had not been cooperative. The lieutenant colonel, who had sent his own good pilots off in those planes, had not been able to get the prisoner to answer and had thrown the man out of a helicopter. The marine who told us the story made the sort of grim joke marines made—"He got a free ride back down to his village, express." I started coughing when I heard this—horror was choking me—I didn't know what to do in front of the others. Ernst's eyes had gone blank—I supposed the report fell into a well of darkness Ernst had in him always.

And why were we so fucking shocked? Didn't we know what kind of war this was? We knew now. I was angry that the marine had told us. You always heard that certain things were kept secret. I had come as a consultant, not to be *in* the war. I was furious with the marine while I coughed.

We kept working. Ernst liked best to be lost in work, and I wanted to be walled up in that thicket with him. He had devised some new calculations, which we went over together and which suggested a new, purely mechanical solution. Ernst wanted to look inside the plane again. It took two days to get one of the men to take apart the inertial guidance system for him; any personnel who could do that were busy fixing damaged aircraft, not hanging around loose to serve our whims. When some overworked, bare-chested guy in shorts finally showed up, Ernst followed him into the cockpit while I stood outside. I wanted to stand by to shout suggestions, hot though it was in the hangar. I was about to go back to the office just when the two of them climbed out.

"Eureka," Ernst said, flatly and maybe bitterly. In his fingers was a half-corroded screw that had been in the gimbal of a gyroscope, about to cause it to split and throw the whole navigation system off. Simple as that. He held it out to me in disgust. "Cheap crap," he said. "Somebody gave the lowest bid. All the gimbals have these lame-ass screws."

And we were heroes that night—Ernst especially, though I got some of the glory, despite my disclaimers. I supposed I had helped a little. The lieutenant colonel and two other officers took us out to celebrate at a seafood restaurant along the river in downtown Da Nang. We had hardly been off the base before and kept saying how much better the waitresses looked than the jarheads who usually fed us. The murky waters of the Han River glinted outside the windows. We were toasted with bottles of beer and a speech about how no one ever thought two dorks like us could come up with anything. The thanks were sincere. "A fucking bright spot for a change," the youngest officer said.

"Just doing our jobs," I heard myself say. The two of us were as stiff and remote as they always figured we were.

"The goddamn truth is that Ernst is more of a fucking genius than any-one even *knows*," I said. "If the marines had any sense, they'd give him a fat, fat bonus for the kind of work he did."

"You got to die to get a bonus," a sergeant said. He was not laughing.

Ernst, who didn't eat seafood, picked at his barbecued beef without looking up. He was in a rage about how someone had cut corners to save money on the screws, how the shoddiness and sloppiness and lying crud-diness of mankind had turned up yet again. He hated the whole armed services for this, everyone at the table.

The lieutenant colonel was discussing the build on one of the wait-ressess. How much soup would you have to feed her till she grew breasts?

I was thinking that if we had found the trouble earlier, Fifth Uncle would still be alive. What had taken us so long? I couldn't get past that line of thought. I don't know that I ever have.

"They'll send us home now," I said to Ernst, at the end of the evening, when we were walking to the row of huts where our hootch was. We'd both had a lot of beer.

"Send us what?" he said. His hearing was never perfect.

"A return ticket from Adventureland here," I said.

But my voice was drowned out by a sudden clap of thunder. "Now it's going to rain," I said. "I hate this country."

There were more loud claps, one right after another, flashes of orange light, and a bunch of crackling, whistling noises—what a dope I was—they were the trails of rockets. Not a storm. We were in a fucking rocket attack. Streaks of flame were landing somewhere behind us. I looked back at the burning trees and I ran.

Ernst wasn't running with me. When I turned my head, I saw that he was standing completely still, a dumb civilian ghost in the dark. *Ernst!* I shouted at him, and then I dashed back into the smoking night and grabbed his arm and pulled him with me—*You have to move!* Ahead of us some other men were yelling. He was too heavy to drag, he was much big-ger than I was. I wanted to leave him, I didn't want to die helping him. And then he began to run, he seemed to remember how all of a sudden.

I thought we were okay once we got in our building, which was barricaded with sandbags on one side. Ernst at least knew to put on his flak jacket and helmet right away. His face was clenched and blank. We were supposed to go into the bunker but it seemed a better idea to stay put. I looked around for cover and I pulled a mattress down over us. We stank together under that hood.

"You okay?" I kept saying. "You okay?"

"Fine," he said.

I wondered if the kapok in the mattress was flammable. Every one of my organs was pulsing, thudding under the skin. And the other, unmoving body with me—Ernst's body—heaved in and out to get air. Ernst looked, in his sweating blankness, like a staring animal, like a bear sullenly waiting out its panic.

It unraveled me to see him as he was now. I had never thought of him as pitiable before, though other people did. I couldn't exactly stand it.

"You comfortable?" I said. I was trying to make a joke.

"Fine," he said.

People died all the time around us—I didn't know why I'd thought we were any safer. I felt like a fool, like the most naïve person in the country. I was a fool in a hole with a bear.

"If we stay here long enough," I said, "we'll be around for Christmas when Bob Hope comes to visit."

Ernst wasn't doing any smiling yet.

"Maybe Ella's coming. You think she would?"

I wasn't glad to be the one asking these questions. Why wasn't Ernst asking me? Who in the whole world did I have to lean on? Soldiers had each other in a war, but I didn't have shit.

He shook his head. His helmet nudged the mattress.

"Does she have views about the war? You know anything about her views?"

I didn't give a fuck about Ella's politics, if she had any, and the USO always had girlie shows anyway, not middle-aged black singers with glasses.

"Did she have a contract dispute with Verve?" I said. "I thought her manager owned it. Why did she leave them?"

The noises outside had stopped. We sat waiting for more.

"After ten years with one record company," I said.

I was talking to myself. What did I expect? I was the one who knew not to expect Ernst to be different.

"I hate Capitol," I said. "Why she'd go to Capitol?"

How long had it been quiet? I didn't trust the quiet.

"Money," he said.

It was a small victory for me when I heard his voice. Training my attention on Ernst, trying to bore a hole in his wall of silence, took me out of myself just a bit, and gave me some relief. It occurred to me that Ernst never felt that kind of relief. Not ever.

The noise of firing had been worst to the east of us, on the other side of the airfield. "You know Ella was only twenty when she recorded 'A Tisket, a Tasket'?" I said. I pulled the mattress off of us—we were going to suffocate if we didn't get blown up.

"Twenty is young," I said. Ernst, in his helmet and vest, unfolded himself and stood up. Then he was walking toward his own room.

"Leaving so soon?" I said. "Leaving me to my own post here?"

He murmured, "Good night," with his back turned. I was the one who knew not to expect him to be different. But I was angry at him for not being more human. Just this once, this time of all times, couldn't he have fucking managed it?

Early the next morning, when the first haze of light was showing through the window, I heard Ernst talking, through the wall. Either he was talking to himself or he was praying. Anything was possible. *". . . fine,"* he said. There was a whirr behind him. *"It's pretty hot and the rainy season is starting, which doesn't really cool things off."* He was making a tape. *"The food is not too bad. I haven't been writing so I decided to send a tape. Maybe Susan has a cassette recorder or you can buy one to hear this. We can send tapes back and forth. Last night we had to get our protective gear out because there was a rocket attack in our area. You have the address. Signing off now. Bye."*

He probably hadn't written to his family in years. One of the little-known facts about him was that he had trouble writing—he was a terrible speller and his sentences were always short and childish. He must have been shaken to the bone to send them a tape now—to remember them, to have them land in his imagination as an audience. His family would be glad and scared to get the tape.

I didn't think we were going to be there long enough for anyone to answer him, but they kept us in Da Nang another three weeks. The roads on the base turned to mud when it rained, and I slipped into a crater left by a rocket and I banged up my leg—the last straw, I thought. And Ernst and I were arguing every night, when we were alone, about the war. I hadn't actually stopped being afraid of Communists—no, I was more afraid, I was properly scared of almost everything now—but I'd stopped seeing the point, I thought the point had been lost. At great, great cost. I said we were spreading evil instead of containing it. "What does *that* mean?" Ernst said. He talked about the Red Chinese and the Soviet Russians, did I know how many people Stalin had killed in the gulags? Seven million disappeared in just four years of the purges. "What does that have to do with it?" I said. We went round and round. He held (I knew) to his principles. Nothing I said about Fifth Uncle softened him. He said I was too emotional. It was hard to argue with someone who ruled out the claims of feelings. He must have thought he'd won every time.

When Ernst got an envelope from his parents, he waited until night to play the tape, and I lay in my bunk and listened as the voices came through the wall. *"Wonderful surprise to hear from you,"* his mother said. *"Very glad you're enjoying your work,"* his father said. *"The dog is getting so fat,"* his sister said. You could hear they were very careful around him.

Every time I asked Ernst if he'd answered them yet, he shook his head, but he played the tape night after night. Through the flimsy wall, I got so I recognized the sequence of their voices, the different pitches in order.

Before we went back to the States, we got flown to Bangkok for two weeks of R & R. We didn't know whose idea that was, but we landed in Thailand in a state of amazement. What a palmy, good-natured city it seemed to us. The streets were every bit as hot and fetid as Vietnam, maybe hotter, but the crowds seemed wonderfully gentle and sunny. Nobody hated us, as far as we could tell. I couldn't get over it. It made me feel light and crazy just to walk around.

Our hotel had a small garden in the courtyard, and Ernst liked to sit out and drink the sweet Thai coffee they made with condensed milk. He could knock off a few hours just reading the *Bangkok Post* and the *Herald Tribune*. He wasn't up for photographing any gilt-encrusted temples or schoolchildren in uniforms—"No new data" he said—but I was restless, I wanted to wander.

It was all quite dreamlike. I got lost in the streets, I rode a ferry on the river, I fed myself on snacks of grilled bananas and seared noodles. On the third day, my leg that I'd gashed and scraped falling into a rocket crater in Da Nang began to throb and feel swollen, and I had the nasty sense that Vietnam was still claiming me. Was I a little feverish? Maybe I was. I sat down on a bench in Lumpini Park and drew up my pants leg. There was an old gauze bandage on my shin, and when I lifted a corner, the skin was oozing and gave out an odor. Why did I think I could forget the place that fast?

I was so interested in my revolting little wound that I didn't see the two youngish Thai women coming toward my bench until they called out, "You all right? We don't think you all right." I was embarrassed to be caught baring my hairy Western leg; my manners were worse here. "You hurting?" one of the women said. They did not look like hookers—they were dressed more like office workers, in crisp little blouses and narrow skirts.

"We nurses," one said. "Is okay we look? We don't hurt you."

They lifted the bandage and clucked and muttered—what a mess I was. They were quite sure that they should take me back to the hospital they had just left. "No trouble," they said. "No problem." I rode in a *tuk-tuk* next to their smooth-skinned, smiling selves. One of them was Bua, a girl who'd come down from the north to study here, and the other was Toon, who lived on Thanon Wisut Kasat with her family and who later became my wife.

On the ride to the hospital, when I got a better look at Toon, I was thinking what a very fine day I was having. I thought the two women were going to just drop me off at the hospital, but I'd at least have the imprint of Toon to keep, like a good wish for my future relationships in the States. *Though I did but see her passing by, / Still I love her till I die.* We'd sung that in school. I had the traveler's idea that something fleeting was blessing me.

It was more complicated that that. My family thought I was nuts when I came home to America just to quit my job and turn around and go back to Bangkok. They thought that the war had done something to me, which it had. Hadn't my nice girlfriend Betty always tried to get me to settle down, but I was Mr. Too-Cool, Mr. Don't-Fence-Me-In? But now I wanted to nest.

It was true that Vietnam moved me toward Toon. Constant fear can make you see the real drawbacks to going through life alone. Though I wouldn't say Ernst especially took that lesson from it. He said, "If that's what you want," when I told him about my engagement, and he thought well of Toon too.

It hasn't all been an idyll, of course, my marriage and my life on another continent. It's had its hills and valleys. My job difficulties have strained us and we've had problems with our son. During one of my worst times, I was seeing a therapist, a fairly smart guy from Chicago, who happened to say I was an unusually private person, which made me wonder if I was like Ernst after all. I spent some time explaining Ernst to the therapist (on my nickel) and he told me that, as far as he could tell, Ernst sounded like someone with Asperger's Syndrome. A neurobiological disorder—like having a pinch of autism. Many people probably had it. "Well," I said, "there are all sorts of ways of being human, aren't there?" I wondered how Ernst would have felt about his personality having a material cause— perhaps he would have been affronted, though he did prefer the measurable world.

There are people who say Einstein had Asperger's. I'm not sure I believe in geniuses anymore—in a superspecies of mental giants—but I think Ernst was probably brilliant. In our last days in Vietnam, we had to file reports about the defective screws (God knows what became of these reports), and Ernst wrote a few lines of tirade in capital letters against the fraud of the manufacturers. LETHAL CHEAPNESS, GREED KILLS. Bydex, who'd bought the screws for cheap, would not have been pleased. What a pure, unsullied life Ernst led, in his way.

I had a very nice wedding in Bangkok, not big but flowery and pretty, and I sent a set of photos to Ernst, who was back at Bydex in Phoenix. I don't know if he ever received them, since he didn't send any word back. I picked the ones in which Toon looked especially wonderful and I didn't look too geeky. He didn't envy me, I knew that, but I wanted him to see.

"Behold the giddy American," I wrote. *What is that sucker doing?* Ernst must have thought when he looked at them, at me surrounded by the smiling strangers who were my in-laws, by the unheard lilt and spit of all of them talking. I imagined him shaking his head over the smeary mess of a future I insisted on wanting. How stubborn he was. Always when I thought of him a kind of envy spread through me. In spite of everything, it just did.

Tony D'Souza

Djamilla

S HORTLY AFTER Khadija's death, Mamadou brought me a sack of mandarins from his father's orchard. I wasn't much in a mood to be with
the Worodougou after what had happened, and each morning when the
families would set out for their fields, a wife or husband would salute me
as I sat on my stool. "Not going to the fields with us today, Adama?" they'd
ask. I'd wave them off with my hand, hold my side, and say, *"Djekwadjo."*
Malaria.

I was often down with malaria, everyone in the village was now and
again, but this time it was something more serious, a sickness of the heart.
In my early months there, I had romanticized the Worodougou, made
them out to myself to be better than they were. But I now understood that
they were as flawed as anyone.

It was nice to be alone in the village those days, everyone gone to the
fields but a few scattered old women tending to their families' hearths. I
ate mandarins and watched the clouds scud across the sky.

One morning, the village empty and quiet, a Peul girl came in her fancy
wraps and silver anklets, a wide calabash of milk on her head, trading ladles
of it for yams from hut to hut. The Peul were nomadic cattle herders from
Mali, and a family of them lived on the village's far western edge, near
where they corralled their herd at night. Aside from trading milk, they did
not bother with the Worodougou, nor the Worodougou with them. The

Peul considered themselves a superior race because they did not work the soil, and the Worodougou thought them contemptible for the same reason. Despite this, Peul girls had the reputation of being the most desirable in the region. Perhaps it had to do with their mystical desert roots, the pride of their tall carriage, their shyness, their exotic language and culture. But perhaps, too, it was because of their fantastic beauty.

The girl stopped in her tracks, surprised to see me. I had never before been alone in the village in this way: in the daytime, the time when the village belonged to women. She was tall and slender, with old colonial coins hammered into a necklace that hung over her collarbones and strings of amber beads hanging from her long earlobes. Her lips were tattooed around with black ink, and her hair was woven into tight plaits, coins arranged again in them. Of course I knew who she was: Djamilla, the Peul patriarch's unmarried daughter. She would have been considered beautiful anywhere.

Djamilla looked at me in a defiant way, set her hands on her hips. Maybe she didn't like being surprised; maybe again it was because she was used to the village men calling lewd slogans at her for everyone to hear. She was far enough away that if I wanted to say something, I'd have had to shout. Instead, as though propelled by a force other than myself, I rolled a mandarin to her. It crawled over the dust as though time itself had slowed, came to rest between her bare feet. Her eyes lined with kohl made her seem dangerous. The heavy calabash on her head made her seem taller than she was. I wondered what she would do, why I had rolled the fruit to her in the first place, why I cared. Then, like a wading bird, she ducked and picked the mandarin up.

"I know your name," I called to her.

"I don't speak Worodougou, white man," she said back at me fluently in that language.

"Dja-mil-la," I called, the syllables rolling off my tongue like a song.

"Who are you to say my name, you dirty Worodougou farmer. Aren't your fingernails covered in soil and filth? Don't you know I'm a Peul?"

"I'm not a Worodougou," I told her and grinned, "and your name is in the village for all to know, as pretty as the moon and stars."

"I'll tell my father!"

"I'll tell him myself."

"Then tell him. See what I care."

"I'll come tonight."

"I'll hide in my hut."

"You'll hear my voice."

"I'll plug my ears with cotton."

"You'll know in your heart that I've come."

"I'll cut my heart out, feed it to the dogs."

"Then I'll pet those dogs, because they've eaten your heart."

"Then those dogs will bite you, because they have my heart inside of them."

"Djamilla, put down your milk. Come inside my hut. I want to show you pictures from my country. I want to show you a picture of my mother."

"You have pictures to show to me? Show them to my father. You will see what he says. Then you won't roll mandarins at me like a Worodougou monkey."

"And then you won't pick them up."

Djamilla looked at the fruit in her hand, as though understanding what it meant. For an instant, I thought she would throw it at me, but instead she folded it into her wrap. She said, as she turned and left, "My father likes to eat them, so what?"

The funk I had been feeling dissipated into the air. I stood in my morning wrap as she receded, my chest bare, and struck a pose as vivid as I suddenly felt. Then a stooped old woman came by—the witch doctor's mother—chasing a duck away from her compound with a scrap of blue cloth tied to a stick, which is what old women used to chase away ducks, and she saw me, the parting Djamilla, understood something, and straightened. "Adama! Get in your hut," she said and poked me in the ribs with the stick. "That you are white is bad enough. But you are also hairy! Cover up! If you let Djamilla see how ugly you are, then she may not marry you."

Usually after dinner, I'd sit with Mamadou under his mother's mango tree, where we ate, and talk late into the night about life. As a third son, Mamadou didn't have any other options but staying in the village and helping his father work in the fields. But his dreams were vast: he wanted to go to Abidjan to look for work like his older brothers had. He wanted to own an Ajax soccer jersey and leather shoes and a cell phone, and, one day, a car. I'd try to extol the pleasures of a traditional and honest life in the village to him, but he wouldn't hear it. The lights of Abidjan called to him, France and America after that.

"I'll work in a cloth factory like my brother, I'll tend a big field for a rich man. I will send some money here to my father, save the rest, and then I will open a kiosk and sell omelets and Nescafé. I'll buy a stereo so my customers can have music. You will visit me, I will visit you in Chicago, America. We'll be big men together. I will drive you in my car, a Citroën—"

There wasn't much else to do at night but talk. People were talking at the hundred hearths of the village. Voices droned on in this way, simple worn laments for rain, for love, for money. I stood, brushed off the seat of my *boubous*, and Mamadou was startled out of his reverie. He said, "Hey? Where are you going so late?"

"For a walk. To salute some people," I said vaguely and waved at the dark.

"I'll come with you—"

"Stay here. Spend some time with your *go*. Isn't it time you had another child anyway?"

"Adama, where are you going? Where is there to go? Adama, are you feeling unwell?"

"Unwell?"

"You are behaving strangely. When you behave strangely, it means you are getting sick. If you get sick, I will have trouble with the chief. Tell me where you are going so late. If you don't, I will follow you."

"I'm going to salute Bukari."

"Bukari? The Peul?" he said and shook his head. "The only time we salute the Peul is when there is a business of milk or meat. Do you want to eat meat, Adama? I will tell my father to send them some yams and we will eat meat tomorrow."

"I want both milk and meat, Mamadou," I said in a low voice.

"We will send for them."

"You can't buy this milk and meat with yams."

"Milk and meat that you can't buy with yams? Adama, why are you talking in riddles? The moon is not full. Why are you behaving mysteriously?"

"Every night I listen to you, little brother. Has it ever occurred to you that I might have a few dreams of my own?"

"Dreams, Adama?"

"Desires. I'm going to see Djamilla."

Mamadou lifted his eyebrows, then grinned and rubbed his knees. "I thought you were sick, white man. But you are not sick. You are a goat. Many men turn into goats when they see Djamilla. Go and try your luck. Soon enough, you will be my friend again."

Bukari wasn't in his hammock, as I expected an old man such as he was to be, but cross-legged on his mat, sipping mint tea under the stars. He had a long Arabic beard streaked through with gray, and his flowing blue robe made him seem as foreign as he was. The fire burned low in the circle of stones beyond him, and nobody else was around. He had a second glass waiting on the small steel tray as though he'd known I was coming. "Oh, Adama, come and sit," he said in his Fulani lilt, patting the mat beside him. "Too long it has been that you have not saluted me. Let us drink tea. I want to know all about life in America."

I sat with Bukari a long time as the crescent moon carved its way across the sky. I talked about Chicago, about snow; he wanted to know how cattle were raised there. From the dark hut behind us, I heard giggles now and again. Once I heard a slap, and a child's voice cried out in protest. Then it was quiet again.

"What is this 'cowboy'?" Bukari asked me. I explained as best I could. Bukari reclined back on his elbow, said, "But what does one need with a horse? To know cattle, one must walk with them. Your Peul do not seem very strong to me, Adama. We drive our cattle by foot from Bamako to San Pedro. We sleep in the grass, move them slowly so they do not thin. It takes many months, and we are alone in the bush with our herds and Allah. This is how we are Peul."

"I'd like to know cattle as I know planting," I told him. "If you invite me, I'll come and visit your herds."

"Oh, Adama, this is good. But what about your Worodougou people? Will they not be jealous to see their white man drinking tea with a Peul?"

"I've had enough of the Worodougou. Too many genies. Too much digging in the soil like moles."

"Ah, Adama, this is good. Tomorrow, come before the sun and we will take the cattle to graze."

Bukari offered me his hand good night, and I shook it and bowed low in their way. I felt distant Mali calling me—the land of cattle and true Islam, of the Sahel and stars, as embodied in that calm old man—and for a last thing as I stepped off into the dark, loud peals of girls' laughter emptied from the hut where they'd been gathering all through my visit.

It began first thing in the morning. As I walked across the village through the morning mist that would soon burn off, women set their long pestles on their shoulders, hitched their wraps higher on their hips, and called to me in laughter, *"Anisogoma Fla ché, oh! I be i muso chulla?"* Good morning, Mr. Peul! Are you off to salute your wife?

At Bukari's compound, Djamilla pounded corn for flour while her younger sisters tended the fire. She blushed when she saw me, dropped her pestle to the dirt, hurried into the hut, and shut the door. The sisters sat on their stools and hid their faces in their hands. Their shoulders trembled as they fought their laughter, they snorted and choked, the coins in their hair rang like chimes. Bukari was on his mat, praying. The Peul were real Muslims, while the Worodougou guessed at it. The language of Bukari's prayer was Arabic.

When he finished, he sat a moment looking at the morning sky as though meditating, then rose, smiled, and took my hands in his. He had a clear and open face beyond his beard, was as tall as I was, though thinner. He said, "Adama, so early you have come. Like a son. This is how sons come to their fathers in Mali."

At the corral, Bukari leaped over the barring pole in his robe, and then I did. The long-horned and humped Brahmans stamped and lowed like prehistoric creatures, larger in the mist than they really were. It was warm among them, there were flies and dung piles everywhere. I waved flies from my face while Bukari separated calves from their dams with his staff. The calves cried and the cows lowed, but none of the beasts made a move at him. He tied the dozen calves to the piled brush that made the fence, and while they strained at the ropes like dogs on leashes, Bukari milked the cows into a great calabash one by one. He nickered to calm them in an ancient language of man and kine, and though they could have easily thrown a hoof or horn, he petted their shanks and they didn't. It was a fine art, gentle. Bukari lifted the gourd over the gate pole to the head of one of his young girls who had come, and she bowed beneath its weight, found her legs, straightened, and set off into the mist for the village. Then Bukari raised the pole, and the cattle filed out in a long and dusty train toward the brush, their hips shifting like women's.

We followed the cattle for miles to where the forest opened into thick savanna, sitting and chatting now and again in the grass as the herd grazed, sometimes sleeping, only to awaken with the hundred head lowing calmly in the distance like wild buffalo at ease in the world. Bukari talked to me about Allah, about how every blessing of his life—his cattle, his daughters—came to him from God, and I asked him to tell me Peul words, which I recorded phonetically in Roman letters in the notebook I'd brought. For lunch, I climbed a wild guava and he made a basket with his robe to catch the fruit I tossed down to him, and then Bukari bent water lily leaves from a pond into wide cups, milked the cows into them, and we drank the hot liquid, thick as cream, like princes. When the cattle crossed a stream, we waded across with them. When they came to a Worodougou rice field, Bukari ran ahead, warding them away from the golden crop with whistles and clicks. Not once did he hit or curse them in any way. They were his children and he knew each one's name. It was a long and tiring day, pleasant in the walking, and when the sun began to sink, the cattle turned around as though on instinct. By the settling of evening, the forest was a dark wall before us again on the plain, and I was whistling and clicking at them too, patting their high haunches as if they were old friends. My notebook was full of Peul words: sun and moon and grass and water and stars. The cattle entered the corral, lowing as though glad to be home, and when Bukari untied the calves, they rushed to their mothers, found their teats, and began to suckle vigorously.

"Now we pray to Allah, Adama," Bukari said, and cleared a patch in the corral with his staff like wiping a trowel across wet cement. He took my hand and led me down to my knees. "Like this, Adama. Follow," he said, and genuflected toward the earth, touched his forehead to it. He said the Arabic words, and I knew them too from hearing the Worodougou say them every day. But with the Worodougou, the words were rounded, slurred. Bukari knew the words as they were meant to be pronounced.

"Now you, Adama," Bukari said, and he sat on his heels and smiled at me. I lowered my forehead to the dirt, and the coolness, the softness of it, calmed me. Arabic was like singing. I felt happy when I rose again.

Bukari held my hand on the way back to his compound, and I felt close to him. The women had dinner waiting—corn *toh* and peanut sauce—and

Djamilla sat on a nearby stool and smiled off into the night. Something was happening now. Bukari squeezed my hand and said, "All day together. Like a son."

Mamadou came and found me outside my hut that night. We sat on stools and smoked cigarettes and enjoyed the stars, the last sliver of the moon. He said, "Eh, Adama? How was your day with the Peul?"

"My day was fine."

"Ah, that is good. And did you make progress with Djamilla?"

"Maybe," I said and shrugged.

He was quiet awhile, considering. It was a cool evening and at the witch doctor's hearth, his sons huddled over the fire against the chill, the fire standing up between their shapes. Then, like giving up, Mamadou said, "So you are a *Fla ché* now. That is as it will be. It is as the ancestors say: 'When food is plentiful, the dog will wander. When he feels the pinch of hunger, he will crawl to the fire with his tail low.'"

"You're jealous of the Peul."

"Jealous? No, Adama. It is only a proverb. It is good to tell proverbs. It is good to talk and make our hearts known. Adama, what has been troubling you these past days?"

I wanted to say nothing, to go on as we had all been as though nothing had happened. But something had, and I was tired of carrying it around. "I don't like what happened to Bébé's wife."

"No one liked that here."

"Why couldn't the village just let her go home to her mother?"

Mamadou looked at his hands. He said, "Khadija killed her child. What precious thing do we have if not children? Her life ended when the baby disappeared. Even her own mother would have poisoned her. Adama, can I tell a story? Two stories."

Mamadou had told me a hundred stories over the past year, proverbs by the dozen.

"One dry season when my father's father was a young man, three boys went into the forest and found a beehive in a stump. For a moment, they thought to come back to the village and tell the honey collector, but instead they decided to poke sticks down into the hive. The first two boys ran forward, put their sticks into the stump, then dashed back onto the path. Then it was the third boy's turn. The sound of the bees caused him to lose his courage, but the other two teased him. So he ran forth with his stick, put it into the hive, and the bees rose out in a black and angry swarm.

"They ran through the forest. If they'd been wearing sandals, they lost them. They ran so fast that perhaps even their clothes fell off. Behind them came the bees, the sound of them angry. When they reached the clearing before the village, the boys began to shout, 'Bees are coming! Angry bees are coming behind us!'

"Everything ran for shelter; the goats and ducks for the tall grass, the old women for their huts. The boys dashed into their mothers' huts, shut the doors. All through the village, the angry bees circled like smoke. At one hearth, a mother had stayed home from field work to rest, her small children with her. Back and forth she ran, picking up as many of her children as she could, taking them inside the hut. Then the bees arrived. There was nothing she could do but shut the door. She watched through a crack as the bees descended and stung her infant daughter to death. Do you see, Adama?"

Then Mamadou told me this story: His uncle, Mustafa, had a bitch dog that was a good tracker. She was such a fine dog that Mamadou's uncle fed her meat from time to time. The dog loved the uncle, and if anyone would approach the old man, the dog would lift up off her haunches and growl.

"Why don't you kill that mean bitch before she bites someone?" the people would argue at his hut.

But the old man would say, "She is a fine hunter. The best in the village. I'll tend to her odd ways."

The old man fell sick and was bedridden. His dog began to wander in his absence, became pregnant. All around, people watched the old man's hut for signs of recovery. He had been a hard worker in his life; with his cotton profits he had managed to purchase things people desired: a portable radio, a Dutch wax *boubous*, a number of well-formed calabashes that could be used for many purposes. When he died, the dog guarded the door to his hut with such a fury that no one could get past her to claim his possessions in the night. Then his son came from a neighboring village, Somina, gathered up what was his, and buried his father.

The hut was empty and no one bothered to feed the dog. If anyone dared approach the hut, she would rise up and growl. A wave of rage swept through the village dogs, and she caught it too. When the witch doctor went through the village killing the dogs with his machete, he found that the old man's bitch had given birth to a litter of six. Somehow, she had managed to wean them. Many people of the village, out of curiosity, followed the witch doctor about as he chopped the sick dogs to pieces. They followed him to the old man's hut, and the bitch dog came out from her place in the bushes, growling, foaming at the mouth. With a quick blow to her neck, the witch doctor killed her. The puppies hid themselves in the bushes and he went home.

After a few days, the puppies came out again. They growled and barked like grown dogs, their fur bristling. They also had the rage. The witch doctor went to kill them, but all the people said, "No. What can they do? They are small."

For a week, people would go to the old man's hut and the rabid puppies would come out of the bushes on their short legs, growling and foaming at the mouth like angry, full-grown dogs. Imagine, such small creatures acting as though they were greater than they were? No one had seen such small angry dogs. Everyone laughed about it. Then the puppies thinned and died on their own.

"Do you see, Adama?" Mamadou asked me as he finished his story. He stood and brushed off his *boubous* as though the storytelling had taken something out of him. "I am not jealous of the Peul. I know that your life here is difficult. But know that ours is difficult as well. Wander now. But do not circle about like bees if you don't intend to sting. Do not foam at the mouth if you don't have the teeth to bite. Good night, Adama. Sleep and dream of Djamilla. Make progress. I will be pleased when you come back."

The Worodougou did not make it easy on me. Everywhere I went over the coming days, it was, "Good morning, Mr. Peul," and, "How is your lovely Peul wife?" I went to Bukari's and we grazed the cattle. Djamilla seemed to inch her stool closer to us every night.

I can't say that Djamilla entered my dreams the way true love should, but she was beautiful and I enjoyed the tension. I also enjoyed being with the Peul. The food they ate, the soft lilt of their language, even praying to Allah with Bukari in the corral was like escaping the Worodougou world I lived in.

Every night as she sat closer to us, Djamilla seemed more at ease. Would I really marry her, stay in Africa with her as my wife? Would I take her home to America, return to the village in a long car with her and our children, bearing gifts for everyone? Wrestling the calves and following the herd was hard work, as demanding as any. I begged off one morning, told Bukari that I needed a rest loudly enough for Djamilla to hear where she stood pounding corn. I hoped that she hadn't closed her ears to me as she had once promised she would.

I sat on my stool outside my hut in the empty village, waiting for Djamilla. Soon, she came. If I had thought she would rush into my arms behind her father's back, I was wrong. She stood across the courtyard the way she had before, the wide calabash on her head, her hands on her hips. I rolled a mandarin to her and she picked it up. She peeled it, ate it, spit out the seeds. Then she said, "Why are you always at my hut, white man?"

"The moon and stars," I said in Peul. She blushed despite herself. For an instant, her kohl-lined eyes looked less like a raptor's than a doe's.

"My mother lives in Mankono, you know. We are only here while there is grass for the cattle."

"Are there moon and stars where your mother lives?"

"Adama, enough. Don't you understand? With us, it is the mother one must speak to after one has spoken to the father."

"Mankono is far. I don't even know where Mankono is."

"Eh? Then why have you done all of this? Forget it, white man. I must sell my milk."

I let her start to walk away, and then I called after her, "Moon and stars, I will even go to Bamako, if that is where your mother lives." I rolled another mandarin to her feet. She looked at it, at me, narrowed her eyes.

"Why do you tease me?"

"Dja-mil-la," I said.

"Why do you say my name like that?"

"Dja-mil-la."

"Stop! It makes my ears itch."

"Djamilla, come here. I want to show you something. A picture of my mother. If I must go to see yours, then you must come and look at mine." I went into the dark of my hut, waited, and my heart began to pound. Soon, again she came, the mandarin in her hand. She lowered the calabash from her head to the ground, and I could see flies sucking moisture from the cheesecloth, covering the milk like black jewels. She peered under the thatch of my doorway and said, "Show me here."

"Not there," I said from the shadows of my hut, "here. These are only for you to see. I want to show you here."

She glanced about the deserted courtyard, bit her lip, ducked her head under the thatch, came in. I offered her a stool, and she sat on it. Her feet were powdered with dust, and she seemed smaller somehow now close to me. She glanced all about without turning her face, and I saw my hut through her eyes: a worn raffia mat, a mosquito net hanging over it from the thatching, my trunk where I kept my few Western things: T-shirts and jeans, vials of malaria pills, notebooks; then my machete and short-handled hoe, my field clothes, my ceramic cistern of water, my shotgun and shells, my bathing bucket. If she had hoped to see something in there to reveal my soul to her, she was disappointed. I had less than most of the Worodougou did. I rummaged through the metal trunk, came to her with a short stack of photos. She looked at me warily, and I kneeled and offered her the photos.

She took the first one up carefully, as though she was afraid of damaging it. It was my mother and sister in Hawaii, where they'd gone together after my father died. They were trying to smile, though the sun was in their eyes. They were on a deck somewhere, piña coladas in their hands, pink cocktail umbrellas in the drinks. My mother had a yellow flower behind her ear. My sister looked pale and tired.

"Your mother is fat!"

"Not that fat."

"Is this your wife, Adama?"

"My sister."

"Is this your village?"

"More or less."

"What is all this water?"

"That's the ocean."

"Your mother's hair is the color of ripe rice."

"She put the color in it."

"But henna makes things dark, Adama."

"It's another kind of henna."

Djamilla accepted the pictures one by one, studied them closely as though trying to enter America through them: the house I grew up in covered with snow, my sister beside some boyfriend or other in his new Camaro, my mother at her retirement party, me in my black coat on Michigan Avenue, snowflakes on my shoulders.

"What does snow feel like?"

"Cold like the moon."

"Where is the grass?"

"Far from where we live."

"Who do these pigeons belong to?"

"To no one. They live like that. Nobody eats them. Old women whose children have left like to feed them peanuts and talk to them."

"Is it a good place to live?"

"Sometimes."

"You must be very rich, to have pigeons you do not eat, to let old women throw away the harvest to them."

Without realizing it, we were sitting close together on the floor. Our fingers touched again and again as I passed pictures to her, as she pointed things in them out to me: the red boots of a girl in a background, a woman wearing green mittens. Djamilla smelled faintly of cream and butter, the amber beads of her earrings familiar to me now, the tattoos around her lips as though all women had them.

"What is this? A dog in a bed? Is America so rich that even the dogs sleep in beds?"

It was my sister's rottweiler, Daisy, up on her bed when she'd been a puppy. I held the picture and smiled. "Sometimes they do," I said.

"How could I live in such a filthy country? Where dogs sleep in beds?" Djamilla said, leaning against me as she laughed. Her body was warm, almost heavy. All around us on the floor now were pictures of a faraway place, the people in them looking back up at us from gray landscapes of concrete and snow. Djamilla touched a picture of my mother with the back of her hand, as though trying to feel the curve of my mother's cheek. I held Djamilla close to me as she did.

"Your mother won't accept me because I am black."

"My mother will accept anyone I choose."

"I will pound corn *toh* and peanut sauce for her."

"She might like that."

"I will make it so your mother will never touch a pot the rest of her life."

"I don't think my mother has done that for a long time."

"And how can I honor your sister?"

"You can plait her hair."

A shadow darkened the doorway. It was the old woman, her stick in her hand for chasing away ducks. She peered in, let her eyes adjust. "*Fla muso*, come out of Adama's hut. Take up your milk before it curdles. Go to your father's house," she said in a low voice, stern but not angry. Djamilla went out, and the old woman helped her lift the calabash to her head. Then I went out too, to watch Djamilla walk away.

"Adama," the old woman said to me, "don't you have women where you come from?"

"We do, mother."

"Then why do you trouble this girl?"

"I'm not troubling her, mother."

"Adama," she said and poked me with her stick, "is this all that you are? A man? Another man to trouble a girl? Go to the fields and work, you lazy goat. 'The white man this, the white man that.' Since I was small, people have said it. Ah, Adama, if your mother was here, she would scold you. Go to the fields now before I beat you with this stick. *Toog gbenna aug gbenna, konani of la whella*." In the forest or fields, the duiker is the duiker. "What a disappointment!"

Did I love Djamilla? I loved Africa, loved being in the fields with Bukari and his cattle, the tender hands he laid on their haunches. I loved the sound of the children singing at night, the long drape of the stars. I loved the forest and being in it. I loved it when it rained and the air was so clean it was like there wasn't any air at all.

After a long day with Bukari, the herd corralled and lowing, I'd say good night to him, salute a few hearths here and there, and then Djamilla would find me in the dark. We'd walk the paths in the tall grass along the edge of the village like lovers from an older time, the moon waxing above us. She worried that she'd be cold in America and I promised her that I'd buy her a coat to keep her warm. I teased her that she could sell milk in those steel labyrinths she'd seen in the pictures, that she could trap those pigeons that belonged to nobody and sell them too. She'd laugh and slap my hands, this tattooed girl from Mali.

As we reclined and sipped tea one night, the moon finally full, Bukari said to me, "You are truly like my son, Adama. Anything you desire, ask and it shall be yours."

I went to Mamadou's. I'd neglected him a long time, but he still brushed off a stool for me. He smiled and said, "Ah, Mr. *Fla ché!* Long time. Are the cattle well?"

"I think I want to marry Djamilla."

Mamadou's smile faded. He looked at me in earnest. The night was dark, the hearth fires glowing in it. He said, "Djamilla is very beautiful. She is calm and works hard. Any man would desire her for a wife."

"I need you to talk to Bukari for me."

"Does it mean that you would always be near me?"

"Perhaps."

"And are you certain that this would make you happy?"

I nodded.

After a day alone hunting francolin in the forest, I felt sure of my love for Djamilla, and I came home to the village and told Mamadou to visit the old man. I looked at the stars from under his mother's mango tree and smoked cigarettes as I waited. Here it was, my life. When Mamadou came back, he sat down beside me and sighed as though spent. He said, "Adama, Bukari accepted almost as soon as I stepped into his courtyard."

"What happens now?"

"We wait. He will send word to Mankono, and the mother will decide. That is their way."

The days became long. I avoided Djamilla's compound as was the custom, and she avoided me. A hush ran through the village. I could tell from the long looks people cast at me that they knew. What they thought of it, I couldn't tell. But they didn't call me "Mr. Peul" any longer, as it wasn't any longer a joke. Many nights lying awake in the dark of my hut, I felt that I'd made a terrible mistake that I couldn't now undo. Then I'd see Djamilla in her beads and wraps and coins across the village, bent at the waist and drawing water from a well, and I'd think to myself, *That is my woman.*

I went to work in the fields with my neighbors to pass the time. For some reason, I was glad now to be with the Worodougou again, singing the field songs, and back in that familiar rhythm. I looked at pictures of my mother and sister now and then in my hut. They felt like people I had never known. A young and somber Peul came from Mankono on foot.

Word had finally arrived. A buzz ran through the village. I waited under the stars with Mamadou for the messenger to present himself at my hut, to tell me which way my life would turn.

He was tall and lean. His *boubous* was green satin with gold filigree embroidered about the neck. He stood before us like a desert prince. Mamadou offered him a stool, but he refused. He said, "If the white man wants Bukari's daughter, then Bukari's daughter is his. That is the word of her mother. It is finished."

The young man asked leave, and I heard Mamadou give it to him. Then Mamadou shook my shoulder. He said, "Rejoice, Adama! What you have desired is delivered. *Allahu Akbar!* You are to be married!"

But I wasn't married to Djamilla that time or any other. In the morning, I jumped on a logging truck to Séguéla, stayed in the city a week, two. When I went back to the village, Djamilla had gone. I didn't explain myself to Bukari, was too embarrassed. Also, he was a Peul and I didn't have to.

For weeks, no one said anything to me about it. Then one night as we lit cigarettes and leaned back against the mango tree after dinner, Mamadou said to me, "Milk or meat, Adama. Those are the only times we deal with the Peul."

I nodded, smoked my cigarette, considered the stars.

A wandering bead trader came through some days later with a story. I was in the fields and didn't see him. A beautiful Peul girl in Mankono had fallen in love with a white man, and had been scorned. For some days, she had been very ill, and then she was well again. Now she was becoming famous for giving alms of milk to the albino beggars in the Mankono market. When people asked her why she did, she told them it was because the albinos reminded her of the man she loved. The villagers found the story hilarious. They would stop me now and again over the coming years to recount it, laughing hard to remind me that it wasn't a funny story at all.

Yannick Murphy

In a Bear's Eye

S HE HEARD the bear. It hooted like an owl, only lower, sounding like an owl far down in a well or in a cave. She looked out the window. There it was, in the field above the pond on its hind legs. It shook the apples from the apple tree. Her boy did not look up at the bear in the field. He was by the pond. The bear was not so close but neither was he far away. If the bear had wanted to, the bear could run to the boy and the bear could be on her boy in no time at all, in the time it took an apple to fall from the branch and onto the field.

She ran outside with her gun.

Her boy had brown hair that over summer had turned almost blond. In the light of the setting sun she imagined how her boy's hair would look golden, how when he moved about, as he never kept still, how the color of his hair would surely catch anyone's eye, even a bear's.

When she was a girl she wanted her hair to turn that color. She cut lemon wedges and folded them around the strands of hair and pulled down on the lemon wedges, all the way to the ends. She would then lie down and bathe in the sun. She spread her hair out behind her on the towel. The strands were sticky. There was lemon pulp clinging to them in places. Bees flew close to her hair. The color stayed a light brown.

The gun was heavier than she had remembered. There was probably some muscle in her arm that was once stronger when she had carried the gun with her husband through the woods. They had hunted grouse every season. Now the muscle was weak. To get to her boy she knew that she would have to first crouch behind the rock wall and then, like a soldier, she would have to run and hide behind trees. She would have to be in some way like a snake. Serpentine, her pattern. Isn't that what a soldier would say? Serpentine, she would have to run down the line of trees that bordered the field for a few hundred feet. She did not think she could do it. She would eventually be seen. The bear would stop shaking the apple tree and look around, sniffing the air. The bear might come at her.

Her husband was the one who always shot the grouse. He was a good shot. She always aimed too high. Her husband, while she was aiming, would put his hand on top of her gun, to lower it down, but still she never shot a grouse.

The boy took some small rocks from the pond's shoreline. He stood up and threw them into the water.

"Sit down," she said out loud in a whisper that didn't sound to her like her own voice.

The boy was not doing well in school. He liked to read during class. Beneath the desk he would hold an open book. A book about beavers or silk moths or spiders. The teacher sent him home with notes for his mother. The notes said the boy must pay attention. Her boy would sometimes read to her from his books while they ate dinner. There were things she had never learned as a girl. A silkworm female moth is born without a mouth. It does not live long enough to eat. It only lives long enough to mate and lay its eggs before it dies. Her boy would stop and show her the pictures. She would shake her head. She was amazed at how much she had never learned as a girl her boy's age. Was she just too busy squeezing lemon wedges onto her hair? Her boy never said he was sad that his father, her husband, had died. But she knew he was sad. Her husband was like a book that could talk. At the dinner table he would tell their boy about science and math. He talked about zero. "Zero scared the ancients," her husband said. "No one wanted to believe that there could be nothing."

He walked into the ocean one day and he did not stop walking. She liked to think he was still walking under the water. Skates stirred up sand and rose to the surface as he walked by them. Water entered his shirt cuffs and his shirt back ballooned. She and her boy sometimes talked about it. Her boy said how the hair on his head must be floating up and wavering like the long leaves of sea plants. Her boy said how his father must be reaching out to the puffer fish, wanting to see them change into prickly balls. His father must be touching everything as he walks, the craggy sides of mouths of caves where groupers lurk and roll their eyes, the white gilled undersides of manta rays casting shadow clouds above him. "My father must be in China by now," the boy said to his mother.

China because after he had died and the boy and the mother cleared out the father's drawers, they found a travel brochure for China. They had no idea the father was interested in going to China, but the words "See the wall" were written on the outside of the brochure.

The mother now saw how the sun was going behind the hillside. Its last rays hit the black steel of her gun and it hit the very top of her boy's hair before it sunk down. The bear was finished. It had knocked almost all the apples to the ground. He began to eat them. The mother thought how the boy would be safe now, the bear would eat and then leave and she would not have to run closer to the bear, going from tree to tree, looking for a shot she would probably miss because her husband was not there to put his hand on her gun, pushing down, keeping her from aiming too high.

Not long ago the boy's teacher had come to see her. She held open the screen door for the teacher and told her to come in. They sat in the kitchen and the teacher asked the boy if she could speak with his mother alone. The boy nodded and slid a book off the kitchen table and left the room. The mother could hear the boy walk up the stairs and close the door to his room.

"Your boy is a smart boy," the teacher said. "The death of his father must have come as a shock. But still," the teacher said, "there is school."

She looked into her refrigerator to offer the teacher something. There wasn't much. She hadn't been to the store in days. She opened the bottom bin and found two lemons. She took them out and put them on the table, where they rolled for a moment. The mother got her wooden chopping board and placed the lemons on it and cut each lemon in four. She pushed the chopping board toward the teacher. "Please, have some."

The teacher did not say anything. After a while the teacher said, "I'm sorry. I'll come back another day to talk about your son." When the teacher left, the mother went upstairs to her boy. He was reading a book about spiders. Together they lay on his bed and looked at the pictures.

She would take her boy on a trip. They would go to China. They would see the wall. They would look for signs of him. She had yet to tell the teacher how her boy would miss days of school, even weeks.

Now, at the pond, the boy thought he would try it. He walked in slowly. The brown water filled his tennis shoes. It was cold. The boy knew from his books that beavers had flaps of skin behind their front teeth. They could shut the flaps when underwater, sealing the water out of their mouths and lungs. When the water came above the boy's eyes and finally over his head, the boy imagined he had these flaps. He opened his eyes underwater. The darkness was like four walls all around him. Maybe he could reach out and touch them.

The bear stopped eating. It sniffed the air and lifted its head. It went toward the pond. When it walked it looked like a man who was sauntering. She did not know before how bears hooted like owls, how they sauntered like men. She followed it. She did not run from tree to tree. She ran in a straight line. "No, no, you'll never shoot anything running at it like that," she could hear her husband say. Where was her boy? Where was her husband?

She saw ripples in the pond where her boy had gone in and then she noticed that the bear was looking at her. Its upper lip was curled. It had white on its chest, the shape of a diamond, but not perfect, a diamond being stretched, a diamond melting. She let the gun drop. She ran fast through the milkweed. The butterflies flew ahead of her. She ran past the bear. She dove into the water on top of the ripples made by her boy. She wanted to save him. She wanted to tell him he did not have to drown. She swam down, wishing she could call to him underwater, wishing she could see through the black silt. She had not taken a breath before she went down and she could not believe she did not need one. She thought for a moment how everyone must be wrong, there was no need to hold your breath underwater. She now knew it. She thought her boy knew it too. They had both found out a secret. She could stop thrashing about in the water now, looking for her boy. He would come up and out when he was ready. When she came to the surface she realized the pond was shallow. She was standing with the water only coming to her hip.

Her boy was on the other side of the pond. He was sitting on a large flat rock on the shore. He was holding something in his hand. The bear was watching them, his lip no longer curled. She walked to her boy while still in the water. It dragged her shirtsleeves and her pantlegs behind her. She moved her hair away from her eyes.

The boy had mud in his hand that he had scooped from the bottom of the pond.

"What's that?" she said.

"Maybe some gold," the boy said, moving the mud around and poking at it in his palm.

"Look over there," the mother said, pointing to the bear. The bear turned and sauntered away.

"Yes," said her boy. "I saw him ages ago. He likes the apples from our apple tree."

That night she told the boy that maybe they had better not go on their trip to China after all. There was school to think about. The boy nodded. "All right," he said.

She thought how she missed her husband. She thought how she would now miss him the way other women must miss their dead husbands. She would wear his shirts. Isn't that what other women did? They took long walks and thought about their husbands and when they sweat the smell that came up to them was not the smell of themselves but the smell of their dead men?

Rebecca Curtis

Summer, with Twins

THAT SUMMER I lived with the Serrano twins in their parents' summer house. I'd met the twins at college, and even though the university was large, everyone knew them and just called them the twins. There were other twins, like Hami and Hamid, two Iranian guys who smiled at, greeted, and bowed their heads to everyone they'd ever met as they walked across the campus, but none of them mattered. The twins were two girls, five foot eight, with long, straight brown hair that fell exactly halfway down their backs. They were athletic, high school soccer stars, with faces you'd never notice if there weren't two of them, oval and a little indignant-looking—they had full lips, dark brown eyes, and chins that jutted out when they talked. When I first met them, I wondered what all the fuss was about, because they seemed stupid. They got C's in their economics classes, even though that was their major. They thought Singapore was a city in China, and once they'd spent an hour looking for Persia on a map. They weren't strikingly beautiful, and they weren't especially kind. But everything they did they did with enthusiasm: if they ate a bite of food, the food was delicious; if they kissed a boy, the kiss was long and deep; and if they went to sleep, the sleep was dreamless and divine. Their enthusiasm made me angry, because it seemed false but then I became included in it and realized it was genuine.

After a few weeks, I'd learned to tell them apart: Jean's eyebrows were darker, thicker, and closer to her eyes, and Jessica's lips were larger and her cheeks were fat, a beautiful bedroom face, as if made as a place for a hand or another face to rest. She was three minutes younger, sweeter, quicker to anger and quicker to forgive. Later, after our friendship ended, maybe their interests diverged, but when I knew them they took the same classes, spent all their time together, argued over their shared clothes, and as far as politics, they were in agreement, and as far as I could tell, would always be: they favored self-starters, a free economy, and zero government intervention.

Their father was a banker, and they planned to be bankers, too, and dropped financial phrases into everything they said.

The twins knew I needed money for college, and had told me this town where their parents had a summer house was chock-full of expensive restaurants. We would all waitress at one of them, they said, and over the summer make a killing. In high school the restaurant I'd bussed tables at served only sandwiches, so I said yes. I'd been surprised when the twins and I became friends, because in terms of the college, I didn't exist; but they thought I was funny. The first day we met, we went out to lunch. At lunch, they watched me squeeze my lemon into my water. Then they watched me open one pink fake sweetener and one blue one, pour them in the water, and stir the drink with my straw. Jessica asked to try a sip. She proclaimed it delicious. A minute later, Jean tried a sip. Her eyes went wide with delight.

It's poor man's lemonade! she said.

Then she squeezed her own lemon into her own water, and added one blue sweetener and one pink. You're so funny! she said. I love it!

From then on, every time we went out to lunch we all drank poor man's lemonade. I had to come stay for the summer, they said, because they were lonely with each other, and they always got along better if someone else was around.

When I arrived, I was thrilled. The twins' parents' summer house wasn't the nicest one on the lake, but it was two stories, of white brick, and had a large back deck and a backyard that dropped down to a beach. The windows of the house let sun in all day long, the lake was deep and clear and had a sandy bottom, and in the garage was an ancient red Fiat the twins said could do one-twenty on the straightaways of the town.

The restaurant the twins had picked was the Christmas Inn, which was on the main route, by the waterfront. One long rectangular room in front was the dining room, and a narrow, rather trapezoidal space behind it was the bar. Both rooms had green shag rugs and a lot of green linen tablecloths. It wasn't a prepossessing place. But it served seafood and steak, and the menu was overpriced. After filling out our applications, we met Boris, the owner and head cook, a man with a huge stomach and longish silver curls on his head. He had merry blue eyes, a bulbous mauve nose, and cracked pink lips. He was wearing a white T-shirt, tan shorts, and a bloody half-apron. His arms were thick, his posture erect, and his gut sailed before him like a flock of decapitated geese. He glanced at our applications, saw we had no experience, and said they looked good. The restaurant, he said, could use pretty girls. Then he looked at the woman who was moving through the dining room, setting tables for dinner. She was maybe forty-five and had short black hair, olive skin, and droopy, off-kilter eyes.

Of course we have Dina, he said. We've had Dina for what, how long now, ten years?

The woman said something without turning around. Boris gave us a look. Then he called her over and told her to show us the restaurant.

Thanks for showing us everything, Jean said, when she was done.

Don't thank me, Dina said. I was doing my job.

Well, thank you anyway, Jean said.

Just what we need, Dina said. Three girls with no experience.

When the twins and I got home we went for an evening swim in the lake and then sat in the living room, eating buttered popcorn and watching TV.

We got a job, Jean said.

Dina's skanky, Jessica said.

Waitresses are like that when they're older, Jean said. It's from waitressing too long. They get a hardened, slutty look. She turned to me. Know what I mean?

I didn't really. But I really wanted to seem like I did, so I nodded and said, You mean she looks like a wench.

What's a wench? Jean said.

It's like a hardened slut, I said.

Oh, Jean said. Then yeah. That's exactly what I meant.

. . .

We worked for two weeks under Dina's tutelage. Each night, at Dina's direction, we brought Dina's tables their drinks, served her tables' food, and cleared her tables' dirty dishes, then set the tables back up and handed her the tips. She would take the money, fold the bills, and put them in her apron. By the time our legs were numb, our bodies salty with sweat, and our hair oiled with it, Dina would be dressed in her coat, thin, black, with a tattered fringe edge. She'd wait for us by the door. Then she'd thank us, say she was sorry it wasn't much, and give us each a few bucks.

What a wench, the twins said, on the way home, the first time it happened.

We're having our last fun summer, Jessica said. Her hair flapped over the front seat of the car, and jasmine strands struck my face. Beyond the road, enormous pines bowed toward each other and bulbous lamps glowed on granite blocks. When we're investment bankers, Jessica said, we won't ever take charity, and we'll give ten bucks to homeless men.

I would die, Jean said, if I were in my forties and a waitress. Did you see the huge veins on her legs?

It's worse if you carry trays, Jessica said. We don't carry trays. And we're just doing it for one summer. Next summer we have our internships.

Her veins are gross, Jean said.

I feel bad for her, I said. She has two kids.

She could have had two abortions, Jean said.

Jean! Jessica said. Don't say that!

Jean rolled her eyes. Kidding, she said.

When we got home, we drank tea and watched a few shows, as we did every night, before bed. When we woke up in the morning, we drank juice-water—we consumed nothing but juice-water all morning, for our health—and then we rested for hours on the white beach by the house, splashing occasionally into the lake.

At first Dina earned the most money, but soon the twins were each earning double and triple what Dina or I did. Dina didn't seem to notice; she didn't seem to notice much. She was a better waitress than the twins, but the twins had a secret weapon—their sameness. Halfway through a meal, a man would reach out a fat arm, cup a shoulder in his moist hand, and say, Honey? Jean? And Jessica would say, I'm Jessica. But I can get something for you. What do you need?

The man's eyelashes would flutter, his mouth corners twitch, his lips press together and make a raspberry sound. Then he'd say: Are you twins?

Jessica would nod.

He'd nudge the others in the party, mostly doctors, lawyers, and dentists who'd grown little beards and come up from Massachusetts on motorcycles for the weekend. Twins, he'd say. Our waitresses are twins!

I knew it, another man would say modestly. I've been watching them.

Jessica would wait, in these moments infinitely patient, balancing empty plates in one hand, holding an empty wineglass in the other. Then the first man, patting a tender, sun-charred face, would say, Are you identical?

By the night's end, half the table would be able to tell Jean and Jessica apart, because they would have been served by both, and they would have pulled the tale of the twins' aspirations from them. They would have handed the twins their phone numbers, shocked that the twins also liked golf, also liked boating, and also liked to water-ski; and made the twins promise to call them, so they could do these things together, and those in the party who'd been able to distinguish—that one's bigger, that one's got slightly larger lips—would lord it over the others, saying, It's obvious, if you know where to look, and then they'd leave the twins an enormous tip.

The twins serviced all their tables together and pooled their tips; they called it their mutual funds, their honey pot, and the fruit of their sweat. At each night's end, when Dina was cleaning the kitchen, they'd count up loudly in the hall nearby.

It wasn't long before Dina pulled us aside. She said we needed to start getting to work on time. She'd been doing all the prep work. Also, were we stupid?

Because we'd been taking her parties' dinners and serving them to ours, whenever ours had ordered the same thing, and so her parties got their dinners late.

She's just jealous, Jessica said, in the car on the way home. Because she gets shitty tips.

I'd give her a shitty tip, too, Jean said. I'd tip her zero dollars.

I wouldn't, Jessica said. I'd never tip any waitress less than twenty percent. Because waitresses work hard.

All I know is this, Jean said: Dina has no right to yell at us.

She had a point though, I said, about us taking her dinners.

I'm sorry, Jessica said, but I don't think getting your dinner late is a big deal. Whenever I have to wait for my food, it tastes more delicious!

Dina was divorced and had two kids, a boy and a girl. The boy was sick. I didn't find out with what, because I didn't ask. I just knew the boy was in the hospital, had been there a few months. One night when we were in the kitchen chopping vegetables, she dragged her wallet out. The kids were maybe eight and ten. The boy was chubby, had stringy brown hair, and was wearing a blue velour shirt. He was missing a tooth. The girl's hair was gray, and her right eye was rolled toward her nose. I wanted to ask Dina why her daughter had gray hair. Instead I said they were cute. Dina got an olive glow on her face and said she thought so, too. Then she put the wallet back. She might have liked them, but she couldn't have hung out with them much, because some days she worked lunch then dinner, and other days she worked dinner and cocktailed after in the bar and lounge. When she cocktailed she wore a red bow in her hair. She'd take her last table in the dining room around eight. Then she'd do her sidework, find the twins, and ask them if they needed anything else, and after she did the five or six things they wanted her to do, she'd put on some lipstick, stick the red bow on, and go in the bar.

When I thought about Dina and her kids, I felt sad. But I only thought about them when I spoke to her, and luckily we didn't talk much.

In June my tuition bill arrived, and I put it in my tip box. I was worried about money, mostly because I was not a good waitress. I tried—I'd chant, Redhead wants prime rib w/pilaf, blondie gets rib w/potato, dickwad gets teriyaki w/potato, nice guy veal w/pilaf; but by the time I got to the kitchen, everything was jumbled in my head. As soon as I had six parties, I was swamped. A few times I asked the twins to help. They each said I should ask the other. The twins were never flustered, because they worked together and because they had a strategy: sacrifice. Whenever they had too many tables, they picked the party they thought would tip least and ignored them until they'd taken care of everyone else. Later they'd explain to the sacrifice how busy they'd been, and the sacrifice would forgive them. I saw the strategy's merits but lacked the resolve to do it myself, and as a result I was flustered a lot.

By the end of June, Boris said things had to change. Did I know how many complaints he had had about me? Did I want to guess?

I don't know, I said. Three?

Keep guessing, he said.

I don't want to, I said.

Then consider this your warning, he said.

One weekend the twins' parents showed up at the house and held a barbecue for their friends. I met the twins' parents in the kitchen, where I'd come to get a snack. They hugged me, welcomed me, and told me to help myself to whatever was in the fridge. The door to the wide deck was open and I could see the friends outside, playing croquet on the lawn. I was about to thank the twins' parents, when Mrs. Serrano turned and said that while they were here, why didn't we settle up on the rent?

I must have looked confused, because Mr. and Mrs. Serrano said, more or less simultaneously: the summer's rent. Mr. Serrano named an amount. Then he put his hand on my shoulder. He seemed embarrassed for me. It's a modest rent, he said.

It wasn't. But I went up to my room, got my tip box, and piled up my tips. When nothing was left, I brought the pile down. Mr. Serrano stared at the pile and said he'd been expecting a check. Then he said he'd make do. He took the pile and went back to the sunroom, where he'd been eating a peach cobbler, to count. I walked down to the beach. The twins were resting on it. Their long brown bodies were shimmering on one huge purple towel, and the gold ends of their dark hair were flicking at their chins. I sat down and stuck my hands in the sand. I said I hadn't known I was paying rent.

You weren't, Jean said. I mean, we didn't want you to. But when we were presenting the idea to our parents, of you living with us, we threw it in, like to sweeten the pot.

Jessica's eyes were wide. To make the pot a little sweeter, she said.

They must have seen a sour look on my face. Not only would I not make a killing, I realized, I might not break even. And then I realized something that shocked me: the twins would become investment bankers after all. They would be good at it.

Jean touched my shoulder. You would have paid rent anywhere else, she said.

So, Jean said. Do you want us to help you a little bit, with the rent?

We didn't know it would be a problem, Jessica said.

Jean poured some oil on her stomach and rubbed it in. Maybe we can talk to our parents, she said. To get them to lower the rate a bit, for the second half. She looked at me. How about that? she said.

I started working lunch shifts in addition to dinner ones. This meant I spent my days with Dina. I didn't mind working lunch, because Dina refilled my customers' waters and bussed my tables. I told her not to, but she did it anyway. I'd realized she wore the same shorts every day. They were black and said "Tiger Wear" in a big red logo on the back and had pleats in the front that made them look skirtlike and accentuated her hips. But I didn't feel bad for her, because she liked her job and was good at it. She had a lot of regulars, old people who tipped her ten percent. Her favorite was a Swedish couple. They must have been seventy-five, but they came in every day at noon, ordered six scotches and two prime ribs with pilaf, and ate the whole thing. They left Dina five dollars no matter what. I thought that was good, until I found out what their bill was. Then I thought it sucked.

Dina shrugged. They're old, she said.

But they drive a Mercedes, I said.

She stared at me. They're my customers, she said.

The next day Dina called in sick. I served all the regulars. They all seemed to know Dina well, and they all made me stand at their table while they talked about her: how she was so nice, how her son was sick, and how she had huge hospital bills because she didn't have health insurance. The Swedish couple gave me a lecture about America that ended with the conclusion that Sweden was better because in Sweden the streets were sparkling clean and everyone had health insurance, and I nodded because I thought if I did they'd tip me well. They left me three dollars and fifty cents.

I was worried about money, but my waitressing did not improve. No matter how fast I ran through the restaurant, I couldn't manage to get my parties what they needed when they needed it. One night Boris said he wanted to talk to me in the bar after work. In the bar he made me a drink. Then he said I was no good in the restaurant.

I told him I'd do better. I said I'd been memorizing the menu. But he shook his head. He said some people didn't have the brains to waitress. He said his restaurant was a dining establishment. He said he himself had seen me hold up a steak dinner and ask a table of twelve to hand it down to the person who'd ordered it.

Okay, I said. I'll stop doing that.

He shook his head again. He put his arm around my back. I like you, he said. He had a habit of smiling like he'd just heard a secret. He was smiling now, and his teeth were narrow and long. I think his gums had receded.

I like you too, I said.

The twins, he said—they're brats. Spoiled rotten. I don't even want them here next summer in fact.

I said I thought they had some internships lined up.

He didn't seem to hear what I'd said. He said the twins were vicious girls. Then he squeezed my shoulder hard and said that the twins had started life on third base and no one would ever look at me twice, the way people looked at them.

Maybe if there were two of me, I said. I was kidding, but I guess he didn't realize that, because he said No, they still wouldn't. Then he said he needed a cocktail waitress. Dina had been doing it. Between me and him, she was better in the dining room. He finished his beer. God love her, he said, but she's too old to wear a bow in her hair.

I said I didn't want to take Dina's job. Boris stared. He said I wasn't taking her job, because he was giving it to me. Then he said I was lucky to have a job, the way I sucked in the dining room, and that Dina wasn't my concern, she was his.

Anyway, he said, she needs to spend time with her kids.

In the bar I did well. It was easy—all I had to do was write down the drink orders, carry the drinks over, collect the empties, and get my tips. The bar's triptych of glass walls faced the lake, its dark expanse and the pine-studded islands in its gray distance, and even though I often arrived before the sun had set, somehow the bar was always dim, and I moved through it with the buoyancy and power of dreams. When I got home the first night, it was two A.M., and the twins were watching TV.

I wouldn't want to cocktail waitress, Jessica said.

No offense, Jean said.

He asked us if we'd work in the bar, you know, Jessica said. But it seems gross.

Anyway, Jean said, we knew *you* needed it.

The next night I saw Dina in the bathroom at the restaurant. It was nine o'clock, time for me to start work and for her to go home, but she wasn't dressed to go home. She was wearing a shiny purple shirt and a tight black skirt, and was leaning across the counter and putting on purple lipstick. I thought maybe no one had told her she'd been fired from the bar. I felt embarrassed. Before I could back out, she waved me in.

The purple lipstick was smeared above her lip, and her right hand was shaking a bit. She said she had a date—her first in eight years. She said the guy wore silver chains on his neck and worked at the dog track, but that other than that, he seemed nice. He'd told her she looked a bit like this Italian film star, one people used to tell her she looked like sometimes. She brushed a hand through her hair and repeated the star's name. I'd never heard it before. Then she added that the woman had been in a very famous western with Charles Bronson once, and I pretended to know who Charles Bronson was.

Good luck on the date, I said.

She thanked me. Then she shoved her stuff in her purse and asked me if I was working in the bar. I said I was. Whatever Boris had told me, she said, it wasn't true. I apologized, but before I could finish, she said to forget it. I was just a kid, she said, anyway, and I didn't decide shit.

Without any shifts in common, the twins and I barely talked. I wandered through their house during dinner hours, when the twins were at the restaurant, feeling like a thief or a guest. I looked through their closets, tried on their clothes, and ate tiny bites of their food. Then I smoked cigarettes and watched TV, until it was time for me to leave for the restaurant and for them to come home and watch TV.

In mid-July the twins drove to the mall in the southern part of the state, near the college, and spent a few thousand dollars on clothes for the fall. When they got home, they brought the clothes to their room, laid them out on their bed, and told me to come see. I particularly admired one sweater, a gray cashmere one with a soft turtleneck, and I was rubbing the fabric between my fingers, pretending the sweater was about to go over my head, when I saw the price tag.

I said something stupid.

Jean looked annoyed. She explained that the clothes were an investment because they could wear them to work at their internships. She added that it was worth it to spend money on clothes you loved. If you wear a two-hundred-dollar sweater twenty times, Jean said, that's ten bucks a wear. But if you buy a crappy sweater for forty dollars and you only wear it once, that's forty bucks a wear. So expensive sweaters are cheaper than crappy ones.

I fingered the sweater. Its incredible loveliness reminded me I didn't have tuition money for the fall. I wasn't good at college—the social part, the academic part, any of it—but I wanted to go back.

Hey, I said. Did you ever ask your dad about reducing the rent?

The twins looked at each other.

Now is not a good time, Jean said.

Timing is everything, Jessica said.

We didn't want to tell you this, Jean said, but our dad's stocks are not doing well.

He got bum advice.

That's why he didn't stay up here this summer, because he really needs to concentrate on his stocks.

Nothing is certain, Jessica said.

We're not getting our new car this summer, Jean said. That's certain.

We've been cutting corners, Jessica said.

We're working hard, Jean said. We're really shopping for bargains.

Jessica took the sweater from me and held it against her breasts. Worrying about money is awful. I can't wait until we're bankers! We're going to help people invest!

Jean tapped my shoulder. There's no better way to help people, she said, than to help them invest.

I asked Boris to give me more shifts, and he said that as a favor, he'd let me work dinners again. One night dinner was slow, and the twins, Dina, and I spent most of the night on the back step smoking cigarettes. We worked up a good feeling talking about how hard the work at the restaurant was. When the good feeling wore out, the twins stared pensively into the dark. Then Jessica touched Dina's hair.

I can't believe you've been waitressing fifteen years, she said.

Dina said it wasn't bad.

It's kind of bad, Jessica said. I mean, we only get two dollars and twenty-five cents an hour.

Plus tips, Dina said.

Yeah, Jean said. But we have to sing happy birthday to doofuses, and the benefits suck.

There are no benefits, Jessica said.

Dina shrugged. Once I got a Christmas bonus, she said.

How much? Jessica said. Jean poked her.

Ow, Jessica said.

Dina's elbows were on her knees, and she was staring at the ground. It was generous, she said.

Later that night, when the twins and I were watching TV, I told the twins about Dina's kid being sick. I told them about her hospital bills and how she'd been angry when I'd taken her place in the bar.

I'm sorry, Jean said, but if someone wants health benefits, they should really work at Vollman's Mart, because Vollman's Mart gives health benefits.

I like Dina a lot, Jessica said, but no one's forcing her to be a waitress.

What do they get paid at Vollman's Mart? I said. Don't they get like five dollars an hour?

Jessica changed the channel to the late show.

Everyone has to start somewhere, Jean said.

I'd been working in the bar a few weeks when Boris said he wanted to talk to me after work. The carpet had needed vacuuming that night, and I wasn't done until 2:30. When I was done I was tired and hoped he'd forgotten about our talk, but he came in once I finished and sat at the bar.

I've been thinking, he said.

He sat down next to me.

What I thought is this, he said. He put his hand on my leg. You could spend the night on my boat with me, he said, tomorrow night. Then he said, looking away from me, that it wouldn't have to be a big deal. It would be a relaxed time, and he'd bring champagne. He looked at me. His white curls were damp, and his face was a hot shade of pink. I could use the company, he said. And I'd give you something for it. I know you could use extra cash.

I don't know, I said. What I meant was, no. The glass in my hand felt slippery. I wanted extra cash, but I didn't think I could do it.

I'll pay you a thousand dollars, he said.

Oh, I said. The money was staggering. But there was no way I would do it.

All right, I said.

The next night at ten o'clock I was folding napkins in the waitress station when Boris came up behind me, pressed his stomach against my back, and wrapped his arms around my chest. It seemed unfair, as we weren't on the boat. The twins had left to go home—I'd told them I had a date with a guy I'd met, and they'd stared, and then shrugged, and left—but Dina was in the kitchen, cleaning all the machines that the twins had supposedly cleaned. Boris whispered something about us both having a really good time. When he whispered, I turned around and saw the white hairs tufted on the pads of fat beneath his chin. He was smiling gently, his mouth half open. His breath smelled like peppermints and soured milk.

Excuse me, I said. I walked to the bathroom. I locked the door and sat on the toilet. On the toilet I tried to think about the thousand dollars. Thousand dollars, I thought, thousand dollars. But it didn't work. I didn't want to go on his boat. I knew I was behaving badly. I'd been taught not to back out of commitments. I wasn't sure why I'd said yes in the first place. It seemed stupid. If I didn't go back to school this fall, I could go back the next. I bit my nails. I recounted the tips I'd made at dinner. I counted three times. It wasn't much. But I felt sure I was getting better as a waitress. I put my tips in my apron and went out to the dining room. Boris was sitting at a table.

I said I didn't think I could make it.

He was angry. He stood up and yelled in the empty dining room that I'd wasted his night but that he wouldn't let me waste his night. Then he said some other things, about how he'd brought champagne from home and bought a new radio. He was swaying, and there was beer spilled on his shirt. I said I was sorry. He said he didn't care if I was sorry or not. I went back to the bathroom. I stayed there a while. I counted my tips a few more times. Then I went into the kitchen to ask Dina for a ride. It was late, and I'd thought perhaps she would have been gone, but she was there. She had her black coat on, and all her things were in a bag. When I asked her for the ride, she stared. Her black hair was pulled back, her face looked gaunt, and she had the purple lipstick on. She didn't answer right away. When she did she just said, Call a cab.

The next morning when I came downstairs, Jean was eating a muffin at the kitchen table and Jessica was making tea. They said, in gentle voices, that they were glad I'd come home. Then they said that I should probably live somewhere else.

But the day was bright, and by our third hour on the beach together, they'd hugged me, forgiven me, and told me they didn't want me to leave.

We're not stupid, you know, Jessica said. Especially when it seems like someone gross asked you to do something gross, and it seems like you said yes, and then it seems like you changed your mind.

I knew you wouldn't do it, Jean said. I was just mad you considered it. And I wasn't mad, it was more I was concerned for your health.

Your mental health, Jessica said.

Not to mention your soul, Jean said.

Sometimes times are hard, Jessica said. But you still have to play the game right.

I nodded. Then I lay down on one of their towels, drank a bottle of their juice-water, and put some of their suntan lotion on.

At three o'clock, Jean went up to the house, and when she came back, she was yelling, Yahoo! Yahoo!

Jessica wriggled up onto her elbows and shaded her eyes. My sister's lost her mind, she said.

Jean yelled, Our dad's stocks are healthy again!

Yahoo! Jessica said.

Healthier than they've ever been!

Jessica turned to me. He was really worried, she said. He was so worried he could barely do number two.

And we're getting our car! Jean said.

Jessica's hands shot up. Yahoo, she yelled. Yahoo!

And, Jean said, I saved the best for last. She looked at me. Are you ready?

I nodded.

He reduced the second half of the summer's rent! He cut it right in half and then he cut it in half again!

That's terrific, I said.

Jean touched my arm. I told you not to worry, she said.

That night, at four fifty-five, we arrived late to the restaurant. Dina was setting the tables for dinner, and her white shirt had the same patch of dried grenadine on the pocket that it had had on it the night before. She was walking funny, taking tiny steps around the room, walking without moving her hips. Also, it looked like someone had punched her in the mouth.

In the kitchen, Jessica's eyes went wide. Wow, she said.

Jean nodded. I don't feel bad for her, she whispered.

Jessica put a hand on Jean's.

That night Dina was slow serving customers, and she got stiffed twice. Boris stayed in the kitchen, and he didn't get drunk while he cooked or yell at us for not picking up our meals right away. He mostly stayed in the back, chopping things.

The next day I came down with the flu. I was sick for a week. When I recovered, the twins told me that while I was absent the Swedish couple had come in to eat lunch at the restaurant and Dina had told them to get out. According to the dishwasher, the Swedish couple had simply walked into the restaurant, and Dina had told them to get out. She'd also said other things. Boris, who'd been listening from the kitchen, came in and made Dina take the rest of the day off. Then he served the Swedish couple their meals himself and gave them their drinks for free. The dishwasher, who'd listened from the hall, said the Swedish couple hadn't been angry at Dina, and that they'd even argued on Dina's behalf—they'd said a child's illness could make anyone crazy, and that they'd gone crazy several times themselves, for less compelling reasons, and that therefore Dina should be forgiven. Boris had told them not to think about it.

Soon after Dina was let go from the restaurant, Boris took me aside. The twins had gone back to the college, I'd stayed on alone to finish the season's last few weeks, and the restaurant seemed different without them—familial. Boris said a lot of things had happened that summer, and that he hoped he and I were okay with each other. I nodded. He said Dina had wanted to leave the restaurant. I nodded again. He thrust an envelope into my hand. The envelope had some paper in it, but I couldn't tell if it was money or a long letter. Boris wished me well at college. His T-shirt had hardened yellow armpits, and he looked tired. But he smiled. I hope you also know, he said, that whatever happens at school, you can always come back here. He put his arm around me and squeezed. He said, We'll make a place.

Brian Evenson

Mudder Tongue

I.

T HERE CAME a certain point, in his speech, in his confrontation with others, in his smattering with the world, that Hecker realized something was wrong. Language was starting to slip in his mouth, words substituting themselves for one another, and while his own thoughts remained lucid as ever, sometimes they could only be made manifest on his tongue if they were wrung out or twisted or set with false eyes. False eyes? Something like that. His sense of language had always been slightly fluid; it had always been easy for him, when distracted, to substitute one word for another based on sound or rhythm or association or analogy, which was why people thought him absentminded. But this was different. Then, when distracted, he hadn't known when he misspoke, had only been cued by the expression on the faces of those around him to backtrack and correct. Now, he *heard* himself say the wrong word, knew it to be wrong even while he was saying it, but was powerless to correct it. There was something seriously wrong with him, something broken. He could grasp that, but could not understand where it was taking him.

The first time it happened, the look on his face had been one of appalled wonder—or so he guessed from the look of glee his daughter offered in return.

"Oh, Daddy," she said, for even though she was mostly grown she still called him Daddy for reasons he neither understood nor encouraged. "It's not gravy you mean, but fishing."

Gravy? he thought. *Fishing?* There was too far a gap between the two terms to leap from one to the other by any logic available to him. He had heard his voice say *gravy* while his mind was busy transmitting *fishing* to his tongue. He was amazed by what he heard coming out of his mouth, didn't understand why it didn't have some relation to his thoughts. But to his daughter he was merely the same old father: absentminded, distracted.

"Oh," he said. "Of course. Termite." And was amazed again. But to his daughter he was only playing a game, taunting her. And then, a moment later, he was fine. He could say *fishing* again when he meant fishing. He alone knew something was seriously wrong. When would his daughter realize? he wondered. What, he wondered, was happening?

There were days. They kept coming and going. He opened his mouth and he closed his mouth. Mostly what he heard form on his tongue made sense, but sometimes not. When not, he entered into an elaborate and oblique process of trying to convey what he had in fact intended. In the best of circumstances the person or persons came up with the words themselves and offered them to him. Nodding, not speaking, he accepted them, hoping that when he next opened his mouth his brain and tongue would have realigned.

He quickly acquired a dread of meetings, of speaking in front of his colleagues. Once, his language collapsed in the middle of articulating a complaint against his chair, colleagues touching their glasses or faces and staring at him and waiting for him to go on. Fear-stricken enough to improvise, he stood, speechless and shaking his head, and walked out. Some of them later congratulated him on his courageous gesture, but others shied away.

His daughter began to notice a tentativeness to him, though that was not how she would have phrased it. But he could see her watching him, slightly puzzled. His past personal behavior had been eccentric enough, he discovered, that she was willing to give him an alibi for almost anything. And yet, she still sensed something was wrong. At night, after she claimed to have gone to bed, he would sometimes hear her sliding through the halls. He would shift in his cushion on the sofa to find her behind, in the doorway, staring at the back of his head.

"Why do you melba?" he said to her. "Pronto."

She looked at him seriously, as if she understood, and then, nodding, returned to bed.

The dog began acting strangely, panting heavily around him, keeping a distance when he tried to approach, creeping slowly off with its tail flattened out. *Am I the same person?* he wondered. Perhaps that was it, he thought, perhaps he was not. Or perhaps he was only part of himself, and whoever else he also was had never learned to speak properly.

He tried to make friends with the dog again, offering it treats, which sometimes it took gingerly with its teeth, careful not to touch his hand.

In the classroom, where before he had been sure of himself, aggressive even, he became jittery, always waiting for the moment when the smooth surface of his language would be perforated. He took to dividing his students into small groups, speaking to them as little as possible. He tried, mornings before a class, to practice what he was going to say to propel them into their groups as quickly as possible, how to deflect or quickly answer any potential questions. But however many times he uttered his spiel perfectly beforehand, the actual moment of recitation was always up for grabs.

He instead began practicing alternatives for each sentence: on the first moment of collapse he would switch, attempting to get the same thing across with a different sentence pattern, entirely different words. But if a sentence crumbled, which it did one or twice per class—often enough in any case that the students, like his dog, like his daughter, like his colleagues, seemed now always to be looking at him oddly—the alternative usually crumbled away as well. But if a third variant did not hold, the fourth usually did, if there had to be a fourth, for by that time his mind had cycled around to a track that allowed it direct contact with his tongue again.

And thus it took a number of weeks before he found himself standing at the front of the class with all his options exhausted in the gravest misspeakings, each more outrageous than the last, so much so that he was afraid to say another word. The class, a carefully wrapped part of him noted, was more uniformly attentive than they had been at any other time in the semester, peculiarly primed to receive knowledge. But he had nothing to offer them. So instead he turned, wrote something banal on the board. *Nature of evil. Consider and discuss.* And then, suddenly, he could speak again.

For a time it seemed that writing would be his salvation. In the classroom, whenever his words started to come out maddened or stippled or gargled he would turn to the board and write what he had actually meant. This worked fine up to a point, though he had to admit it sometimes looked odd when he suddenly stopped speaking and began to write. But still it could be dismissed by students as mere eccentricity, or as an attempt to avoid having to repeat something twice.

At home, such a strategy was more fraught, fraughter. Any time he tried it with his daughter he found her turning away before he could find a pen, she perhaps believing that he had decided to ignore her. Elsewhere too, it didn't seem to work. At a restaurant, one could point at an item on the menu but this wasn't well received, and the one time he tried this in a social situation it was thought he was making fun of the deaf.

But there were other places it did work. He could talk to his colleagues by note or by e-mail as long as he wasn't physically present. He also tried leaving his daughter scrawled messages, but she chose to ignore them or pretended she hadn't seen them. Once, when he asked her about one, whether she had seen it, she looked at him fixedly for some time before finally rolling her eyes and saying, "Yes, Daddy."

"Well?" he said.

"Well, what?"

"What's your answer?"

She shook her head. "No answer."

"But," he said. "Corfu?"

"Corfu?" she said. "In Greece? What are you talking about? Don't play games with me, Daddy."

"Sandwich," he said and covered his mouth.

"Here I am, Daddy," she said, angry. "Right here. I'm usually right here. I'm not going to let you mess with me. If you want to ask me something you can just open your mouth and ask me."

But he couldn't just open his mouth, he realized. He didn't dare. *Sandwich?* he thought. He sat staring at her, hand over mouth, trying to gather the courage to speak, to misspeak, until, fuming, she gave a little cry and marched out of the room.

II.

As his condition worsened, he stayed silent for hours. His daughter rallied, sometimes referring to him raillingly as "the recluse," as in *How's the old recluse this morning?*, at other times merely accusing him of becoming *pensive in his dotage*. Where, he wondered, had she picked up the word *dotage*? The frequency of his misspeakings grew until finally he felt he could no longer meet his class; the last few weeks of the term he phoned in sick nearly every day, or rather had his daughter phone in for him. He sent his lesson plans in by e-mail, got a colleague to fill in for him, finally wrote a letter to the department chair requesting early retirement.

"You're lonely," his daughter said to him one evening. "You need to get out more."

He shook his head no.

"You need to date," she said. "Do you want me to set you up with someone?"

He shook his head emphatically no.

"All right," she said. "A date it is. I'll see what I can do."

She began to bring home brochures from dating services, and left the *women seeking men* page of the city's weekly out with a few choice ads circled. Was he *adventuresome*? No, he thought, reading the ads, he was not. Did he like long walks and a romantic dinner for two on the beach? No, he did not care for sand in his food. *Bookish*? Well, yes, but this woman's idea of high lit, as it turned out later in the ad, was John Irving. Unless the Irving referred to was Washington Irving of Sleepy Hollow fame. Was that any better?

And what would he put in his own ad? *SWM, well past prime, losing ability to speak, looks for special companionship that goes beyond words*? He groaned and arranged everything in a neat little stack at the back of his desk.

A few days later, e-mail messages began showing up addressed to "Silver Fox" or "the silver fox" or, in one case, "Mr. F. Silver." They were all women who claimed to have seen his "posting" and who were "interested." They wanted, they all said in different but equally banal ways, to *get to know him better*.

He dragged his daughter in and pointed at the screen. "Already?" she said.

He nodded. He had begun to write something admonitory down for her to read but she was ignoring him, had taken over his chair, was scrolling through each woman's message.

"No," he said. "I don't—"

"And this one," she was saying, "what's wrong with this one?"

"But I don't," he said. "Any of them, no."

"No?" she said. "But why not? Daddy, you *said* you wanted to go on a date. I asked you, *Daddy*, and *you* said yes."

No, he thought, that was not what he had said. He had said nothing. He opened his mouth. "Doctorate," he said.

"Doctor?" she said, and looked at him sharply, her eyes narrowing. "Are you all right?"

That was not what he had meant his mouth to say, not that at all.

"You prefer the one that's a doctor?" his daughter said, clicking open each message in turn as she talked. "But I don't think any of them are."

But what was he to do? he wondered. First of all nobody would listen, and second of all, even if they did listen, he himself did not know, from moment to moment, what, if anything, he was actually going to say.

She was there, chattering away in front of him, hardly even hearing what she herself was saying. Why not tell her, he wondered, that something was seriously wrong with him? What was there to be afraid of?

But no, he thought, the way people looked at him already, it was almost more than he could bear, and if it came tinged with pity he would no longer feel human. Better to keep it to himself, hold it to himself as long as possible. And then he would still be, at least in part, human.

In the end he took her by the shoulders and, while she protested, silently pushed her out of the room. His head had started to ache, the pain pooling in his right eye. He closed his door and then returned to the computer, deleting the messages one after another. They were all, he saw, carefully constructed, with each woman trying to present herself as unique or original or witty but each doing so by employing the same syntactical gestures, the same rhetorical strategies, sometimes even the exact same phrase, as the others. *This is what it means to be immersed in language*, he thought, *to lose one's ability to think. To speak other people's words. But the only alternative is not to speak at all. Or was it? Nature of evil*, he thought. *Define and discuss.*

Depressed, he glanced through the last three messages. God, his head hurt. The first message was addressed to "silver fox" with three exclamation points following *fox*. It was from someone who had adopted the moniker *2hot2handel. Music lover or bad speller?* he wondered. He deleted it. The second to the last one was to "F. Silver," from "OldiebutGoodie." *Oh, God*, he thought, and deleted it. The pain made his eye feel like a knife was being pushed through it. The eye was beginning to water. He clenched it shut as tight as he could and covered it with his hand. He stood, tipping his chair over, and stumbled about the room, knocking into what must have been walls.

Someone was knocking on the door. "Daddy," someone was calling, "are you all right?" Somewhere a dog was growling. He looked up through his good eye and saw, framed in the doorway, a girl.

"Tights," he said, "cardboard boxes," and collapsed.

III.

He awoke to a buzzing noise, saw it was coming from an electric light, fluorescent, inset in the ceiling directly above his head. His daughter was there beside him, looking at his face.

He opened his mouth, then closed it again.

"No," she said. "Just rest."

He nodded. He was in a bed, he saw, not his bed. There was a rail to either side of him, to hold him in.

"I'm going to get the doctor," she claimed. "Don't move."

Then she was gone. He closed his eyes, swallowed. The pain in his head was still there, but subdued now and no longer sharpened into a hard point. He rolled his head to one side and back again, pleased that he could still do so.

His daughter returned, the doctor beside her, a smallish tanned man hardly bigger than her.

"Mr. Hecker?" the doctor said, setting down a folder and snapping on latex gloves. "How are we feeling?"

"Groin," he said. *Goddamn*, he thought.

"Your groin hurts? It's your head we're concerned about, but I'll look at the groin too if you'd like."

Hecker shook his head. "No? Well, then," said the doctor. "No to the groin, then." He clicked on a penlight, peered into first one eye then the other. "Any headaches, Mr. Hecker?"

He hesitated, nodded.

"Head operations in your youth? Surgeries of the head? Cortisone treatments? Bad motorcycle wrecks? Untreated skull injuries?"

Hecker shook his head.

"And how are we feeling now?" he asked.

Hecker nodded. *Good*, he thought, *good enough*. He opened his mouth. The word *good* came out.

The doctor nodded. He stripped the gloves off his hands and dropped them into the trash. He came back and sat on the bed.

"I've looked at your X-rays," he said.

Hecker nodded.

"We should chat," the doctor said. "Would you like your daughter to stay for this?"

"Of course I can be here for this," his daughter said. "I'm legally an adult. Be here for what?" she asked.

Hecker shook his head.

"No?" said the doctor. He turned to Hecker's daughter. "Please wait in the hall," he said.

His daughter looked at the doctor and then opened her mouth to speak, and then gave a little inarticulate cry and went out. The doctor came closer and sat on the edge of the bed.

"Your X-rays," said the doctor. "I don't mean to frighten you but, well, I'd like to run some tests." He took the folder from the bedside table and took the X-rays out, held them above Hecker, in the light. "This cloudiness," he said. "Do you see it? I'm concerned."

Hecker looked. The dark area, as far as he could tell, ran all the way from one side of his skull to the other.

"We'll have to run some tests," said the doctor. "Do you want to let your daughter know?"

Hecker hesitated. Did he want to tell her? No, he thought, but he wasn't certain why. Did he want to shield her or simply shield himself from her reaction? Or was it simply that he didn't trust words anymore, at least not when they came out of his own mouth? Maybe someone else could tell her. Maybe he would figure out what to do when he had to.

"Perhaps no need to frighten her until the results are back," said the doctor, watching him closely. "There's no reason to panic yet," he said. He turned and began to write on his chart. "Any difficulties? Loss of motor skills? Speech problems? Anything out of the ordinary?"

Hecker hesitated. Was there any point trying to explain? "Speech," he finally tried to say, but nothing came out. *Why nothing?* he wondered. Before, there had at least always been something, even if it was the wrong thing. Frustrated, he shook his head.

The doctor took it to mean something. He smiled. "That's good, then," he said. "Very good indeed."

A few days later, waiting for the results of the tests, he began to panic. *First*, he thought, *I will lose all language, then I will lose control of my body, then I will die.*

He tried to push them out of his head, such thoughts, with little success. Now, having resigned from teaching, he didn't know what to do with himself. He sat around the house, read, watched his daughter out of the corner of his eye. He had a hard time getting himself to do anything productive. He felt more and more useless, furtive. She was oblivious, he thought, she had no idea that she would watch him first lose the remainder of his speech, then slowly fall apart, wasting away. Having to live through that, she would probably pray for his death long before it actually arrived.

And so will I, he thought.

Better to die quickly, he told himself, *smoothly, and save both yourself and those close to you. More dignified.*

He pushed the thought down. It kept rising.

His daughter was trying to hand him the telephone. It was the doctor calling with the test results. "Standish," Hecker said into the receiver. But the doctor was too worried about what he had to say, about saying it right, in the kindest way possible, in the most neutral words imaginable, to notice.

The tests, the doctor claimed, had *amplified his concern*. What he wanted to do was to recommend a specialist to Hecker, a brain surgeon, a good one, one of the best. He would open Mr. Hecker's skull at a certain optimal spot, take a look at what was really going on in there, and make an assessment of whether it could be cut out, if there was any point in—

"I didn't mean that," said the doctor nervously. "There's always a point. I'm saying it wrong." The proper terminology to describe this was *exploratory surgery*. Did he understand?

"Yes," Hecker managed. "Was fish guillotine sedentary?"

"Hmmm? Necessary? I'm afraid so, Mr. Hecker."

How soon, he wanted to know, could Mr. Hecker put his affairs in order? Not that there was any serious immediate risk, but better safe than sorry. When, he wanted to know, was Mr. Hecker able to schedule the exploratory surgery? Did he have any concerns? Were there any questions that remained to be answered?

Hecker opened his mouth to speak but felt already that anything he said would be wrong, perhaps in several ways at once. So he hung up the telephone.

"What did he say?" his daughter was asking him.

"Nobody," he said. "Wrong finger."

IV.

First, he thought over and over, *I will lose all language, then I will not be able to control my body. Then I will die.*

All he could clearly picture when he thought about this was his daughter, her life crippled for months, perhaps years, by his slow, gradual death. He owed it to her to die quickly. But perhaps, he thought, his daughter's suffering was all he could think about because his own was harder to face. Even as he was now, stripped only partly of language, life was nearly unbearable.

First, he thought. *And then. And then.*

He remembered, he hadn't thought about it for years, his own father's death, a gradual move into paralysis, until the man was little more than a rattling windpipe in a hospital bed and a pair of eyes that were seldom open and, when they were, were thick with fear.

Like father, like son, he thought.

First, he thought. *Then. Then.*

He lay in bed staring up at the ceiling. When it was very late and his daughter was asleep, he got up out of bed and climbed up to the attic and took his shotgun out of its case and cleaned it and loaded it. He carried it back downstairs and slid it under his bed.

No, he thought, *No first, no thens.*

He was in bed again, staring, thinking. The character of the room seemed to have changed. He could not bear to kill himself with his daughter in the house, he realized. That would be terrible for her, much more terrible than watching him die slowly. And too horrible for him to think about. No, that wouldn't do. He had to get her out.

But ever since he had been to the hospital, she had been sticking near him, never far away, observing him. She kept asking him what exactly was wrong with him, what had the doctor told him, why hadn't she been allowed to hear? And then, what had the doctor said on the telephone? She was always giving him cups of soup, which he took a few sips from and then left to scum over on the bookshelves, the fireplace mantel, the windowsills. It wasn't fair, she said, she had only him, they only had each other, but the way he was acting now she didn't even feel like she had him. What had the doctor said? What exactly was wrong with him? Why wouldn't he tell her? Why wouldn't he speak? All he had to do, she told him, was to open his mouth.

But no, that wasn't all. No, it wasn't as simple as that. And yes, he knew he should tell her but he didn't know what to say or if he *could* say it. And he didn't want her pity—he wanted only to be what he had always been for her, her father, not an old dying man.

But she wouldn't let up. She was making him insane. If she wanted a fight, he would fight. He turned on her and said, utterly fluent, "Don't you have someplace to be?"

"Yes," she said fiercely. "Here."

"Fat cats," he misspoke, and, suddenly helpless again, turned away.

He made a grocery list, a long one, and offered it to her. She glanced at it.

"Groceries, Daddy?" she said. "Since when did you have anything to do with groceries?"

He shrugged.

"Besides," she said, "we have half this stuff already. Did you even open the cupboards?"

He was beginning to have trouble with one of his fingers. It kept curling and uncurling of its own accord, as if no longer part of his body. He hid it from his daughter under his thigh when he was seated, felt it wriggling there like a half-dead worm. He and his daughter glared at each other from sofa and armchair respectively, she continuing to hector him with her questions, he remaining silent, sullen.

He ate holding his utensils awkwardly, to hide the rogue finger from her. She took this as an act of provocation, accused him of acting like a child.

It went on for three or four days, both of them at an impasse, until finally she screamed at him and, when he refused to scream back, left the house. He watched the door clack shut behind her. How long would she be gone? Long enough, he hoped.

He got the shotgun out from under the bed and leaned it against the sofa. He dialed 911.

"What's your emergency?" a woman's voice responded.

"I've just killed myself," he told her. "Hurry, please. Cover the body before my daughter gets home."

But it didn't come out like that. It was only what his mind was saying, his tongue uttering something else entirely.

"Excuse me?" said the operator.

He tried again, his voice straining with urgency.

"Is this a prank call?" the operator said. "This isn't funny."

He fell silent, tried to gather himself.

"Sir?" said the operator. "Hello?"

He looked desperately around the room. The dog was now regarding him intently, ears perked. He picked up the shotgun, held it one-handed near the receiver, and fired it into the wall behind the sofa. The kickback hurt his wrist and made him drop the weapon. The dog skittered out of the room, yelping.

He put the receiver to his ear again. The operator was talking more urgently now. He hung up the telephone.

Picking up the gun again, he sat down on the sofa. He hoped they would come soon, and that it would be soon enough, before his daughter's return. He leaned back and closed his eyes, trying to gather himself.

When he was calm again, he braced the shotgun's stock between the insoles of his feet and brought the barrels to his face. Carefully, he slipped the ends of the barrels into his mouth.

It was then that his daughter chose to return. He heard her open the front door and then she came into the room, her face pale. It was clear she had been crying. She came in and saw him and stopped dead, then stood there, her face draining of blood. They stayed there like that, staring, neither caring to be the first to look away.

He waited, wondering what words he could use, what he could possibly say to her. How could he ever talk his way out of this one?

"Daddy?" she said finally. "What are you doing?"

And then the words came to him.

He lifted his mouth off the barrels and licked his lips. "Insect," he explained as tenderly as he possibly could. "Grunion. Tentpole motioning."

Sana Krasikov

Companion

S INCE SHE'D arrived in America and got divorced, Ilona Siegal had
been set up three times. The first man was not an ordinary man but a
Ph.D. from Moscow, the friend who'd arranged the date said. When Ilona
opened her door, she'd found the Ph.D. standing on her front steps in a
pair of paper-sheer yellow jogging shorts. He was thin, in the famished
way of grazing animals and endurance athletes, with folds of skin around
his kneecaps and wiry rabbit muscles braiding into his inner thighs. Under
his arm he held what, in a moment of brief confusion, Ilona took for a
wine bottle. But when he stepped inside she saw that it was only a liter of
water he'd brought along for himself. Their plan had been to take a walk
around a nearby park and then go out to lunch. But the Ph.D. had already
been to the park. It wasn't anything special, he said. He'd just gone jogging
there. He didn't like to miss his jogs, and since he'd driven an hour and a
half out of his way to meet her he'd got in a run first. Ilona poured him a
glass of grapefruit juice and listened to him talk about his work at Bell
Labs. He reclined in his chair, his knees apart, unaware that one of his tes-
ticles was inching out of the inner lining of his shorts. Ilona stared at his
face, trying not to look down.

The second man was American, somebody's coworker, brought along
to a party to meet her. He had graying red hair and his light lashes were
coated with dandrufflike flakes. He took Ilona to an outdoor concert at

the local community college. Afterward, she waited while he searched the cabinets of his kitchen, finally producing a tray of crackers and a dry triangle of Brie. All she remembered now of the man's small apartment was the blinding light of his empty refrigerator.

The last man was too young for her and obviously gay. He'd agreed to meet Ilona because he had the impression that she was an illegal who needed to marry to stay in the country. As soon as they sat down at an outdoor table at a café, the man told her that he wouldn't normally consider such an offer but his mother had fallen ill and he needed to pay for her treatment. Ilona nodded in sympathy and asked the young man to repeat himself more slowly. She understood that her case had been shoved so far into the recesses of her acquaintanceships that the people who now gave out her phone number no longer knew who she was or what she wanted.

It had not always been this way. There had been happier times, when she'd had both a husband and a lover; when she and her husband had thrown parties in their Tbilisi apartment that went late into the night, with longer and longer rounds of toasts and the smell of sweat and sharp cologne overpowering even the odor of cigarettes. Nothing fed Ilona's spirits more than the company of men. She loved the sound of their hoarse voices, the amateur authority with which they spoke about world affairs and other matters they had absolutely no effect on. But most of all she loved the flattering light of their attention. After the last female guest had said good night, and she had found herself in the thrilling half-susceptible state of being the only woman at the party, was when modesty came most easily to her. It lent coherence to her whole character, so that she could finally be her most humorous and disarming self. But all that had been a world ago and she tried to think about it as little as possible, now that she came home to an apartment that was not hers, and to a man who was neither a spouse nor a lover but who seemed to demand more of her than either possibly could.

"Have you met Thomaz?" Taia said. "He's outside."

"The Georgian?" Ilona went to the sink to rinse off her hands. "I hope you didn't invite him here for me." Her fingers were grainy with the watermelon she'd been slicing. She ran them under the tap and felt around on the counter for her rings.

"I didn't invite him at all. He came with the Gureviches."

"He's a bit young, no?" Ilona slipped on the bigger of the three rings first, a teardrop diamond in a five-prong setting.

"If you're comparing him with your roommate," said Taia, who almost never referred to Earl by name. "Don't lose those." She glanced down at the rings. "One day you'll take one off and it'll fall down a drain. Some women don't even wear the jewelry they own. They have copies made."

"So maybe I should tear off a piece of tinfoil and wrap that around my finger instead?"

"Do what you want," Taia said.

There was no point, Ilona decided, in reminding Taia that before Felix started making money she'd been so cheap she'd gutted empty tubes of Crest, scraping the toothpaste from the creases. No matter how tough her life got, Ilona thought, she'd never lower herself to something so miserly. At least she made use of the nice things she owned. Unlike Taia, whose kitchen had floor-to-ceiling pantries, brushed stainless-steel *everything*, and polished granite counters that she touched only when she was throwing a party.

"Did you put new low lights in the ceiling?" Ilona said.

"It was Felix's idea," Taia said, tipping her head back. "He thought we'd get more for the house if the kitchen was brighter."

"You're selling it?"

"Not right away. It usually takes a year."

"You didn't tell me."

"We haven't really told anyone. Except the Kogans, and the Weinbergs, in case anyone knew of anyone who was looking. It isn't a secret."

There were plenty of things that Taia forgot to tell her—but selling a house? Was that just another bit of information exchanged between people with money, like a stock tip?

"Oh, don't be upset. A year's a long time. You can still come here whenever you need to get away from that man. Come this weekend. We're going to Providence for Parents' Day. You could drop in and water the plants, feed the cat." Taia laid down her paring knife and stood up. "Let me find you a key."

"I still have the key from last time," Ilona said. She couldn't tell if Taia was offering her a favor or asking for one, just as she couldn't judge if her friends kept things to themselves to protect her feelings or because they found her irrelevant. She knew they gossiped. A year ago, she used to bring up Earl in conversation all the time—told her friends stories about his two favorite activities, researching his genealogy and organizing his video collection; and mimicked him mercilessly even if he was in the next room, or precisely *because* he was in the next room and didn't understand a word of Russian. She was staying with him so she could save up for her own apartment. But lately she'd started to realize that unless she wanted to move north into Putnam County or south into the Bronx, and either way end up an hour's drive from her job, her sojourn would have to drag on for at least another year.

She stepped outside and into the sun. The clouds were coasting slowly in the sky, forming metallic reflections in the second-story windows. The air was smoky from the grill. On the patio, two men were lamenting the loss of jobs to Bangalore. Ilona walked past the Kogans and the Ulitskys, past the women reclining in white lounge chairs. It was mid-September, but already she felt a kick of cold in the air. She wore a silk blouse, while the others had come in cotton sweaters. She set her cup on the refreshments table and bent down to refill it with seltzer. A few dead leaves had fallen on the grass. They were the weakest leaves, the lemon-lime color of early fall.

When she turned around she found Felix standing behind her. "Where is your friend today?" he said, and surveyed the people scattered around the lawn.

"When I left, he was still sleeping in front of his sixty-inch television."

"So Earl fell asleep and you snuck out?"

"Do I need Earl's permission to see my friends?"

"No. But I thought you'd extend the invitation to him."

"And what makes you think I didn't?"

"I don't think he would have missed an opportunity to be seen with you."

She was too tired to play this game today. Every time Felix tried to make her feel better he only made her feel worse. It was his diplomacy that was the worst of it, his awareness that every comment could be taken as a potential insult. The old contrite song, not for their affair of eleven years ago—which, thankfully, no one had learned about—but for all the other disappointments in her life.

"Earl couldn't come because he isn't feeling well. He's still weak from his bypass." It was a lie, an obvious one, because five months had passed since Earl's surgery. But who was going to argue? She picked up a plate. "I'm going to get something to eat."

"Please do." Felix stepped back a pace and returned her evasiveness with a delicate smile.

It was her fault for allowing Earl to meet her friends in the first place. She'd brought him along to the Fourth of July party a year ago and introduced him to everyone as her "roommate." As though this would explain anything. He was seventy, she was forty-five. She may as well have called him her chef or her architect—it would have sounded more plausible. The minute she left him alone, he'd drifted off into an empty hallway. She'd discovered him an hour later in the foyer, talking to Felix about Hiroshima. Laughter from the party floated in from the yard while Earl went on about the Japanese who had jumped into the Motoyasu River only to be scalded alive by boiling water.

She felt her heels sinking into the lawn as she walked. Most of the other guests were wearing loafers or sneakers. A few had gathered around the grill to listen to the Georgian, the man Taia had mentioned. It was hard to tell if he was handsome or not; Ilona had seen him on the way into the party and had noted the light-gray eyes and crooked lower teeth, a combination that stirred an almost queasy sympathy in her. He looked younger than the men around him, possibly as young as thirty-five, yet he appeared to be on the brink of a decline that might be rapid, so that, when he finally did age, he would do so overnight.

"They told me they were guarding a base," the Georgian said, as the men parted to make room for Ilona. "They said that their friend had been shot in the hand and needed drugs to relieve the pain. I offered antibiotics, but they wanted morphine." She had no idea which war he was speaking of. It could have been Abkhazia or South Ossetia. She'd left Georgia three years before the republic had split from Russia, and its new problems—which autonomous province wanted independence next—had little impact on her. She'd heard of addicts in Tbilisi raiding hospitals even in peacetime. Perhaps it was the snobbery of distance: nothing would ever change there.

"I wanted to get out," he went on. "But when I stood up one of them was pointing a rifle in my face."

"But you had a gun!" one of the men interrupted. "You should have shot him in the mouth!"

"Which mouth?" another said. "There were two of them!"

"I did something more dangerous than that," the Georgian continued. "I began to curse. I called them every name I could think of, hoping to alert someone who might overhear me. But I was running out of profanities."

He paused, glancing at Ilona. He looked surprised by the silent attention he had drawn.

"Aren't you going to tell us if you survived?" Ilona asked.

"Thank you," he said, nodding. "I did survive." He had a long jaw with a dimpled chin; it was the only feature that lent any merriment to his face. "I heard a vehicle drive into the hospital yard. The addicts thought it was a carload of soldiers. But it was only a man with an attack of pancreatitis."

"Pancreatitis? He must have been an alcoholic," Ilona said.

The Georgian acknowledged her mutely with his brows. He waited for the people around him to disperse into smaller groups. "He was. You work in an alcohol clinic?"

"No, a urologist's office. But I was a nurse in Tbilisi," she said.

"And what do you do now?"

"Catheters, rectal exams. Technically, I am only a receptionist, so I also pick up the phone. But that's the only *legal* thing I do."

"Then your work is closer to medicine than mine," he said. "During the day I lay carpet."

"And at night?"

"At night I clean supermarkets."

"Then I wish you luck finding something more suited to your skills."

The man's eyes flitted across her face, as if they couldn't decide which part to examine first. "That may be hard for me to do without a work permit. My visa expires in a month."

"And after that?"

He shrugged. "We'll see. I am Thomaz," he said, offering his hand.

She squeezed it lightly. "Ilona."

He held on to her fingers. "In my life I have met only two Ilonas, and both of you are very beautiful."

She felt heat rising in her face. So he is this kind of man, she thought. He was standing close, and she had to look up to speak to him. "You live in the city?" she said.

Thomaz aimed his dimpled chin at a heavyset man with a short, square beard. "Yosif is a cousin of my friend in Chiatura. He and his wife are letting me stay in their apartment in Brooklyn. Their son is at college and I'm taking his bed. It is awkward sometimes. I help buy food. If I have to use the bathroom at night, I tiptoe. But I'm not complaining." He touched his hand to his heart. "I am grateful. I feel as though I need to lose three limbs and an eye before I can be sorry for myself."

An illegal who cleaned supermarkets . . . She smiled to herself. This was all they could find for her? And yet she suspected he knew his appeal to women, and that in the worst of times he could still rely on it.

"It is a nice place here," he continued, looking around the property. Ilona followed his gaze down to the small rectangular pond. A dog was barking in a distant yard. "All this space," he said, shaking his head. "I am inside all the time now. It has been too long since I've seen woods, nature. The spirit starts to forget."

"This is hardly nature," she said. "But if you want to see nature you should come back and walk the trails. I could pick you up at the station. The trains run every hour." Her voice had slipped into the perfect fluency of half-truth. When was the last time she had gone hiking? The sun and the mosquitoes bothered her.

"You live nearby?" he said.

"Not far."

"In a house like this?"

"An apartment." He was staring at her fingers. "I share with a room-mate," she added clumsily.

"You are not married, then?"

Ilona gave a bland, cheerful laugh. "Not anymore."

"Your rings. I didn't know . . ."

She straightened her fingers and examined her hand at a distance. "Some might say they are extravagant. But I invest in living."

"Who knows here?" He laughed. "There is a ring for everything. For university, for fiancé, for boyfriend."

"Well, some of them *were* gifts," she said. "But not contractual ones."

By the time Ilona got home it was dark. The dog was at her feet as soon as she unlocked the door. "Quiet, Elsa," she whispered, and knelt down to let the dog lap at her palm. On its short dachshund legs it followed Ilona down the darkened hallway, where she slipped off her shoes and set them on a shoe rack next to Earl's. Heel to toe, their feet were practically the same size. It seemed perverse that, given all the things in the world they *didn't* have in common, shoe size would be something they shared. She walked barefoot across the carpet to where Earl lay dozing on the couch. A plaid throw hugged his hard ridge of stomach. The air was stale with the yeasty scent of bread. Earl had probably spent the afternoon grilling cheese sandwiches, buttering the pan to get a good, deep fry. Ilona leaned over the couch and tugged a creased newspaper out from under Earl's knees, then picked up his bottle of hypertension pills from the coffee table. A glass of water had left a bloated white stain on the wood. Ilona lifted it and rubbed at the polish, but that made it worse. She carried the pills and the glass into the kitchen, which was separated from the living room only by the switch from carpet to tile. "Like mopping up a child's ass," she said to the dog, which waddled in after her.

The room she slept in had once been Earl's office. He'd cleared it out for her when she moved in, and now tall file cabinets and a gray plastic computer desk occupied one side of the living room. She'd asked him to get rid of them, but he said he needed to have all his old files available in case someone from the insurance office called. Six *years* the man had been retired.

Ilona rolled up her sleeves and lowered her hands into the sink. Earl was muttering something in his sleep and turning over on his side. A growth of silver stubble had sprouted on his cheeks. He barked a cough and opened his eyes. "What time is it, Luna?" he said, slowly rotating himself into a sitting position. He squinted at the clock on the VCR. "Seven thirty? That can't be right." He found his glasses, adjusted the pads, and pressed them to his nose. He had a thick nose, German and retroussé, the kind glasses easily slid off.

"You told me you were coming home at six. Didn't we have plans tonight, Luna?"

"Did we?"

"It's *Saturday*, Luna. I had to call Delmonico's twice so they'd hold our table."

She ignored him and continued rinsing. When had going to Delmonico's become one of her duties? Now that the maître d' greeted them as Mr. and Mrs. Brauer, Earl didn't like to miss a Saturday night. She dumped out a teacup and began to untwine the wet string from the handle.

"It's a good thing I called," he said, and raised his heavy body off the couch.

Ilona tossed the tea bag into the trash. "Call or don't call. They *always* say they'll hold our table, Earl. Because there's nothing *to* hold. Every time we go to that restaurant, it's half empty."

"You don't like Delmonico's now?"

"I don't care, Earl." She rinsed a plate and crammed it into the drying rack. "Does it matter what restaurant we go to this week? Can I just finish these dishes?"

His lower lip hung open as he searched for a thought.

"Earl."

"What?" He looked up, a white hair from his brow drooping into his eye.

"We have to trim your eyebrows."

His eyes scrolled up. He licked his thumb, then smoothed it over each brow. When he finished, he took a few silent steps toward his room. Ilona waited until he had closed the door, then wiped her hands on a hanging apron and went into her room.

She could hear him moving around on the other side of the wall. She knelt down beside the old-fashioned trunk that doubled as her night table. There was barely enough room in the tiny closet for all of her things. On good days, she tried to imagine that the office she lived in was a cabin on a ship and that she was in the middle of a journey across the Atlantic of another century. Kneeling, she removed the densely packed sweaters and beaded scarves one by one until she found a flesh-pink cashmere sweater. It was finely combed and as thin as lambskin; she had thought about saving it for a more interesting occasion. But now she bit through the plastic line of the tag and snapped it off. There would be other items for other occasions. She allowed her new clothes periods of latency that could last weeks or even months. This way, when she finally did take off the tags it was with the satisfaction of unsealing a ripe bottle of brandy. And if some people thought she was extravagant she was only preparing herself for a future that was far more uncertain than theirs. Would Earl ever have knocked on her door if she had looked any different? Would he have asked her to join him for a neighborly cup of coffee the very week she'd decided to move out of her apartment, three doors down? Would he have given her the sewing machine she'd admired? Or a fur coat two weeks later? And while she'd had to decline the fur (it smelled like naphthalene and had obviously belonged to his dead wife), she'd got something better. Very politely, she had told him that she had no room for it now, because she was planning to move out of the neighborhood. It had become too expensive for her to live here—with her credit-card debts, car payments, and the money she'd paid in advance for nursing classes she discovered she had no time to attend. She spoke undramatically, but, like the best actresses, she had an instinct for timing. "But Mrs. Siegal," Earl had said, "a woman like you should never have to worry about money." And that was when he'd offered her his old office. She could stay as long as she needed to, as long as it took her to get her finances in order. That had been a year and a half ago.

She could hear Earl padding around the hallway now. She pulled off her shirt and slipped on the sweater. Her eyes looked tired in the mirror. Her hair seemed a shade closer to purple than to the burgundy she'd dyed it two weeks ago. She pulled it up from the nape of her neck and fixed it with a large lacquered pin. *Right this way, Mr. Brauer, Mrs. Brauer.* That's how the waiters would greet them at Delmonico's. Did she really look old enough to pass for his wife? Or were they playing the game, too? Well, it didn't matter to her what these people believed, whether they thought she was his wife or his girlfriend or his mistress. She was happy to cooperate with whatever public fantasy he had planned. Earl was outside the door, knocking.

"I'll be a second!" Ilona called.

What was she supposed to tell people—that even if Earl *did* want to he had his hypertension and his arrhythmia to worry about? Not to mention his prostate surgery four years earlier. For all she knew he was impotent, and it was more of a relief to him than a disappointment if she rebuffed his attentions.

He knocked again.

"Yes!" she said, opening the door.

Earl's striped shirt was buttoned almost to his chin. He stood in the doorway wearing his slacks and slippers. In his hand was a pair of manicure scissors.

"Let's do this quickly," Ilona said.

She let him watch her while she unfolded a sheet of newspaper in the bathroom sink. "Lean over, Aristotle Onassis." Earl closed his eyes and tipped his face toward the mirror. "Here's our friend," she said, finding the errant hair and snipping it. She trimmed the rest, and then with the back of her hand brushed the clippings from his moist face onto the newspaper.

When he opened his eyes again, he stood up straight. "Luna, you're my angel," he said, meeting her reflected eyes.

Delmonico's always made Ilona think of a hotel restaurant. The trellis-patterned carpet, the mirrored walls, the sense that its patrons were dining there only because they were too tired to search for something more interesting. But it was expensive, and for this reason Earl always seemed to enjoy it. She watched him hitch up his sleeves and open the leatherbound menu. He took to the business of ordering with an almost proprietary seriousness.

"You can't fool me," she said, smiling. "I know you're looking at the calf's liver."

"Nah, I wasn't, angel."

"Look at this, the steak comes with bacon. How can we keep coming here after what your doctor said?"

"I've been good, Luna."

"You've been good? Is that why the apartment smelled like grilled cheese when I came in?"

"I made those for Lawrence. He came by today with Lucinda."

"Your son just dropped in?"

"They asked where you were. I said you were visiting your friends. Nothing wrong with that."

Ilona stared at him. "Is something *supposed* to be wrong with it?"

"You know, they always have their own ideas."

Ilona folded her menu and placed it to the side of her plate. "What ideas?"

"They worry, you know. After the surgery. They think I ought to get an aide, just someone to come and check on me once in a while."

It was possible that he was making it up, she thought, as revenge for her not having taken him to the party.

"They think a professional can take better care of you than me?"

Earl didn't lift his head. "I told them I was fine."

"It's strange the idea didn't cross their minds when you had pneumonia and I took a week off work." She sipped her glass of water.

"I told them it was silly. I'm fine. I don't need anyone."

She could see that he regretted telling her. He'd started sweating, and she felt sorry for him. Ilona took a deep breath and slid her hand across the tablecloth to pet his. "I'll always take the best care of you," she said. They sat like that until the waiter approached. Ilona looked up at the young man and smiled. "I will have the tagliatelle pasta," she told him.

"And sir?"

"He will have fish," she answered.

Thomaz was arriving on the six-twenty. She left the clinic at five-forty and drove straight to the train station. By the time she joined the snaking line of cars at the platform, her windshield was speckled with rain. She gazed at the children twisting in the backseat of the car ahead, bouncing and looking out the windows every few minutes for the silver flash of train. Finally, it came, with a high squealing of brakes, and Ilona watched the crowd disappear under the covered stairwell and spill out again on the rain-slicked street. When she saw Thomaz, her stomach tightened. He was standing on the sidewalk, shielding his head with his hand. He wore an orange-and-coffee Windbreaker that was too large for him. Her guess was that he'd picked it out of a charity bin. He spotted her car, and she had no choice but to lift her fingers in a weak wave before she reached over to unlock the passenger door.

He got in and laid his wet backpack on his lap, then pressed his head against the window and looked at the sky, which had dimmed to a bruised purple.

"I'm sorry," she said, turning on the radio. "I should have checked the weather."

"Maybe it will stop in an hour," he said optimistically.

But it didn't. It continued as they drove down the parkway, the heavy drops pounding the windshield and the radio bridging the silence between them. It continued as Ilona steered the car up Taia and Felix's narrow driveway, paved now with fallen leaves.

They ran inside the house and took off their shoes and turned on the heat. Ilona told Thomaz to make himself comfortable on the leather couch, while she disappeared into the kitchen and fed the cat its supper from a tin can. When she returned to the living room, he was holding a small parcel wrapped in coarse tissue paper. "A souvenir from Tbilisi," he said, handing it to her. "It's only silver, but I thought you might like it."

It was a bracelet: stones set in twisted wire like flower petals. She molded it around her wrist and leaned in to kiss his cheek. "Thank you," she said, and went back into the kitchen to make tea. It was half past seven, and Earl was probably waiting for her. She thought of taking the walk she had promised Thomaz once the rain stopped. But it was too dark now, and already she knew that she would not be driving him back to the station tonight.

She heard the TV in the background when Earl picked up.

"What are you doing?" she said.

"I'm watching *Schindler's List*."

"Can you lower the volume?"

The background voices died down. "I got the movie because you wanted to see it."

"I'm staying at Taia's tonight. Did you eat dinner?"

"Yeah, I made some canned beans."

"I left you real food in the refrigerator."

"I looked. Couldn't find anything."

"Earl, I left you chicken. And the steamed vegetables are in the glass container."

"I ate those yesterday."

"I made them for *both* days."

"You didn't tell me anything about it." The TV voices got louder again.

She listened silently for a moment, until she could hear his strained breathing.

"Are you still there?" she asked.

"Where am I going?"

"Did you take your pills?"

"I took them. They never do anything."

He was just being difficult now. "What is it, Earl?"

He coughed into the phone. "I've got chest pressure."

"Is it in your chest or your upper abdomen?"

"I don't know. Just . . . general."

"It's very different."

He didn't answer.

"It could be the beans," she said. "I promised Taia, but do you want me to come home?"

"No." It was a halfhearted reply. "Maybe I'll call Lawrence."

"Lawrence? If you *aren't* sick . . ." She stopped herself. "I'll come home if you want," she said again.

"I'll be fine."

The teakettle whistled.

"I'll call you later," she said, hanging up. She found a dish towel and poured the boiling water into two porcelain cups on a carved metal tray that she'd taken from one of Taia's display shelves. She carried it into the living room, where Thomaz had stood up. He was running his fingers over the leaded glass of a Deco lamp. "It must be nice to live in a home like this," he said.

Ilona set down the tray. "I don't envy anyone."

It was hard to tell if he was smiling or sneering. His face seemed to say, "Yes, this is also an answer, but not to the question I asked."

She had imagined she'd take great pleasure in showing off Taia's house. And she was happy that he seemed impressed, as much by the high sloping ceiling as by the heavy art books in the built-in bookcases, and even the bird's nest retrieved from the backyard, which spoke to a kind of collecting pleasure that transcended mere attainment. She wanted him to feel the character behind these things. And yet it was not *her* character, and she had to repress the urge to say that she might have done the room differently, that she would have placed the furniture closer to the windows or painted the walls a brighter color, a color she could wrap herself in. Thomaz circled the couch and lowered himself into the overstuffed armchair.

"I look around here and everything is clean, nice," he said. "People work, they do well."

She knelt on the rug by the glass table and dipped a tea bag into her cup. "Not everyone. Some people fold, they lose themselves here."

Thomaz watched her. "Like your husband?"

"Maybe if he had got an earlier start, but . . ." She shrugged.

"But?"

"To make it here, you have to *want* to be here."

"I see. He did not want to come to America?"

"We had a good life in Tbilisi," she said, watching a ribbon of color spread in her cup. "Good job, good apartment."

"Then why did *you* leave?"

"Everybody was leaving, all our friends. I didn't want to be in the last wagon on the train."

How else would she explain it, she thought? Could she say that she had followed a man who was not her husband to America? A man whose wife was her closest friend and who had become involved with her only because he was leaving the country soon and thought that she would stay behind? Or that she'd stayed with her husband because she'd been too scared to make the long journey alone? She had been thirty-two then, and without children, not young, perhaps, but young enough for her choices to seem reversible.

"My husband was an administrator at an electronics institute," she said. "You know what that means: he knew how to tell a joke, how much to slip in someone's palm. He was a smart dog. He knew when to bark and when to lick. But none of that helped him here. He tried programming, like everyone else. But it only gave him ulcers."

Her husband's whole being had recoiled from survival the way a half-asleep person recoils from the light. She had felt responsible for a while, but then war, the upheavals of independence in Georgia, had absolved her. The friends who had stayed began to write letters full of horror stories: demonstrations stopped by troops armed with shovels and clubs, backed by tanks, spraying tear gas and chloropicrin in people's faces. Then the electronics institute had closed, bankrupt without the contracts that had come from Russia. The Russian families they knew were fleeing and set-tling in remote towns where the government in Moscow had given them asylum and a bit of land. Even if her husband had wanted to return, there would have been nothing to return to.

"He isn't doing badly now," she said to Thomaz. "He went to San Antonio to work at his cousin's furniture store."

Thomaz leaned over the table and picked up his teacup. "Your hus-band's weakness irritated you?" The question seemed aimed more at him-self than at her.

She answered automatically, "No. We were not a good match from the beginning."

"When a man can't support his family . . ." He was leaning back in his chair, shaking his head. "In my town, the men are all dying younger. They have heart attacks, strokes. But really it is because they've lost their pur-pose."

Ilona looked up at him from the floor. "Have you?"

"No, because I am here." He sipped his tea and set the cup down. "When I returned from Abkhazia, I could find no work. Then a clinic gave me a job. But no one paid us, at least not with money. And now people don't go to doctors at all."

"What do they do?"

"They die at home."

Ilona rested her palm on his fingers. "I'm sorry," he said. "All these sad stories." He parted his lips to add something more, then shut them on his thought. She took his hand. The skin of his knuckles was as smooth and tough as a walnut shell. He interlaced his fingers with hers, and before she could feel her sweat or pulse he was lifting her up, as a person would pull someone out of water, until her body was again doing what it knew and sinking deeply into the saddle of his lap.

She allowed him to kiss first her hands and then her face. She kept her eyes closed while Thomaz kissed the line of her jaw and the curve of her neck. When his lips moved down, she pressed her face into his hair and inhaled the smell of the weather he had brought inside with him.

Upstairs, he was only a flicking shadow, the taut muscles of a back and the scratchiness of a cheek. He moved his weight over her with slow concentration, the two of them conscientious to avoid clumsiness, not testing each other, careful not to trample whatever small force they'd generated. Afterward, they lay together in silence. When the air became too warm, she asked Thomaz to open a window.

"Tell me something," she said when he returned to the crumpled bed. She rolled onto her stomach and ran her fingers over the straight ridges of his forehead and nose, down to the stubbled cleft of his chin.

"You were too young to have been a doctor during Abkhazia."

"I was twenty-five. I had finished medical school. I did not consider myself young. The soldiers were younger. Nobody taught them anything. They didn't even know how to part with the dead." He tugged a sheet over his shoulder, for the room had got cool. "One night, three boys brought in a fourth. I could see as soon as they carried him in that there was nothing left to do for him. They shouted at me to rescue him. One fired a bullet into the ceiling. I forced fluid into his body so his heart would have something to beat. I kept going in front of his friends. I pumped his chest, just for show. It was worse than anything I had done to a living person." He turned away from her toward the wall. His body was still stiff a few minutes later, and she knew he hadn't fallen asleep.

"Do you have children?" she asked, finally.

Thomaz rolled onto his back and breathed in the room's chill air. "I have a son. He will be twelve next month."

"And your wife . . ."

"He and my wife are with my mother in Chiatura. My parents have a house there. I will probably also stay there when I go back."

She found the crook of his arm and curled her head into it. "It's good to have a place to go back to," she said.

They awoke at noon, to the sun leaking through the blinds. On the way back to the station, she drove him through the well-laid-out neighborhoods of Tarrytown—down the tree-lined streets, through the park, and past the tennis courts that gleamed in the sun. "Maybe next time I can see your home?" he said as she pulled up to the station. She smiled and planted a dry kiss on his lips.

In a diner across the road, she drank a cup of coffee. She considered the menu and put it aside. The coffee was strong enough to quench her hunger, and soon she would return home to cook Earl's supper. She felt as if her body had taken a long, full breath. She'd forgotten the way sex could sweep the clutter from the mind, and now she wanted to sit and inhabit this emptiness awhile longer.

Elsa was yapping when Ilona opened the door. The air inside was cold, laced with the bitter scent of carbon, the smell of oil that had burned and then cooled.

"Earl?" she called into the living room. She walked into his bedroom and found the bed made. "Earl?" she called again, louder.

She'd left the heavy front door open and now someone was knocking scratchily on the screen door.

"Hello?" Ilona said, stepping halfway into the hall.

"Mr. Brauer?" It was the woman from next door. Her name might have been Martha, but Ilona had never asked.

"Do you need something?" Ilona looked the woman up and down. She was in a sweatshirt and her thighs bulged under black leggings.

"I just wanted to see if Mr. Brauer was back." The woman cocked her head for a better look inside.

"Back from?"

"I guess you weren't here this morning, then, when the ambulance came? It was pretty early. Woke me up." The woman rested her eyes on Ilona's sweater, her handbag and shoes.

"He isn't back," Ilona answered. "Now, please excuse me. I was picking up a few things to take to the hospital for him."

"Weren't you just calling him?" the woman asked.

"I was speaking to the dog," Ilona answered.

The receptionist at Phelps Memorial would tell her only that Earl had been taken to the cardiac ward at 9:30 A.M. Was she an immediate relative?

"No," Ilona said. "I am his . . ." She threw a glance down the hall and saw Lawrence stepping out of the large steel elevator with his wife, Lucinda. "Just a second," she said to the girl. She slipped her rings into her palm and dropped them into her purse. "I am his companion," she said, turning back.

"Companion," the receptionist repeated to herself and searched her monitor. Ilona stepped away from the desk and threw Lucinda a sympathetic smile that was ignored. When Lawrence looked at her, his face was reproachful, but not, thank God, pained with grief. If they still had energy left for civilized hostility, she thought, Earl was certainly all right.

"How is he?" she said, approaching.

"Fine," Lawrence said. "He's fine." He seemed disappointed not to be able to tell something worse.

The doctors had told them that it was an anxiety attack, but with a patient who'd already had one myocardial infarction they had to take all complaints seriously. They were still doing blood work, Lawrence said. They would finish the serial cardiograms this afternoon.

"In that case, I will stay with him today," she said.

Lawrence threw a glance at Lucinda. "We don't think that's a good idea," he said. Like his father, he was not tall. His hair curled in a single wave on top of his head. "He will be staying with us at our house for a day or two."

"He likes his apartment . . ." Ilona stared at both of them, confused. "This is what he wants?"

"It doesn't matter what he wants," Lucinda said. "What matters is his health."

"We like you, Ilona," Lawrence said. "But wouldn't it be better for you to be in the company of a more . . . energetic person? My father is weak. He has his illusions. But they can damage him." He seemed to be memorizing his shoes. "You can stay at the apartment for a little while," he said.

She did not ask him how long "a little while" meant. Like anyone else, Lawrence would be gracious until the time came to be cruel. Back at the apartment, she set a frying pan on the stove and poured in some oil. Through the window she could see the trees turning dark under the softening evening sky. At her feet, Elsa nibbled a few squares of salami. Ilona cracked two eggs and whisked them, then poured the mixture into the pan and watched it spread on the surface of the oil. If she left, she would take the dog with her. Earl wouldn't challenge her on that. Her plans struck her with the kind of certainty that overtakes the mind after a day of hunger. She could fly to Alaska, where the men were as plentiful as salmon. Or she could rent a cheap basement apartment in Ossining and invite Thomaz for the weekend. She laughed at the thought of them, in a windowless white-painted brick basement, refusing to feel sorry for themselves because neither of them had lost three limbs or an eye. He believed that his hardships had galvanized him, but she knew that anyone could be fearless as long as there was no other option. In her case, it wouldn't be so easy. As soon as Earl walked in the door and saw her boxes spread out on the floor, he would ask her where she thought she was going. He'd tell her to drop it all and offer to take her shopping, and if she resisted he'd beg her to stay. How good giving in would feel. Tomorrow, she would begin to pack. She tipped her omelette onto a thin dinner plate, chopped the chives on the cutting board, and sprinkled them over the top. A little garnish always made it taste better.

Bay Anapol

A Stone House

FOR J.M.A.

N OW THAT her mother is dying—will, in fact, die very soon—Kit manages most of the time to forget her. She types her dissertation. She weeds the garden. But her mother creeps in anyway: unannounced, unwanted. Kit imagines 1938, the year her mother's parents rented a stone beach house on the unfashionable edge of Cannes. They took their daughters out of the heat of Paris as if they were any other middle-class French family. Kit imagines the stone house as small, gray, and perfectly square, the kitchen stocked with ingredients for croque monsieur, buttered croissants, chocolate pieces tucked in baguettes. Kit's mother, Solange, is perfectly calm, like all French schoolchildren, the part in her hair not the slightest bit crooked. She strokes each stone of the house with her little hands. She is smiling. She does not know what Kit knows: that in less than a year, the war will take over her life, and she will lose her father, her sister, everything. But now—in this last wonderful summer—Solange sheds her clothes, her city skin, and runs down to the water slapping the white sand cold and pure, far from the smelly streets of Paris. It is only 1938. She dips a clean toe into the sea.

This may or may not be the real story, but Kit adds details to the one she tells Jon. She adds a German boy swimming with a blonde girl very close to the stone beach house, so close her mother's heartbeat stops and starts again at the words: *Werner, nein. Nein.* Kit adds a broken-down train on the way back to Paris, her grandfather searched and taken to Auschwitz, never to return. In the true story, Solange returned to Paris and to school, and the terror, the important things happened later. But Kit cannot help twisting her mother's fate for effect. She's been with Jon for more than a hundred nights, but every night, she spins a tale to capture his attention once again. Her ordinariness is like a birthmark—how can Jon not see it? There is no other dramatic incident to share with him, so she makes the most of what she has.

Kit continues to curl up in the bed, under her mother's old silver comforter. It's true that the stories she tells Jon come from her grandmother, second-hand. Her mother said almost nothing of her life before the war, before she left France, before she married a dull American who called her So. There are many stories Kit doesn't know about her mother: her first kiss, her first love, what it was like sailing into Ellis Island. *I don't remember*, her mother says, brushing aside all her questions. *It isn't important.* Her mother was strong. She had willed her past to evaporate as completely as clear water in a jar.

"That was the last time she felt safe" is the way Kit ends the story of the stone house. Jon is not listening. He comes into her bedroom with carefully washed strawberries and whipped cream in a small blue bowl. It's like a movie scene, Kit thinks, a perfect movie scene of passion. In a movie, however, the stems from the strawberries and the red stains on the sheets would magically disappear.

Jon smiles, but his smile is faraway. "Organic berries are the best." Kit understands this is not the first time he has eaten strawberries in a woman's bed. She feels for her heart's relentless pound, buried under clothing and skin, refusing to halt.

There is another story she could tell him, but what would it help? In this story, it is Kit who is nine and at a beach house with her parents. The beach house is in America, not France; it is made of pink stucco instead of stone. Florida, where the sun shrieks all day and the cars are white and turquoise, the color of wind-up toys. Her mother is standing by the doorway, calling for her, unsmiling, impatient. Kit is always late. For the beach? What does it matter? Her mother's graying hair is pulled back with an old barrette. The other mothers have bright-colored hair, magically afloat above well-fed faces. Solange doesn't dye her hair blonde or puff it up with hair spray. She doesn't shellac it to her shoulders.

The beach is crowded with other mothers, the kind Kit yearns for: younger mothers in tight bathing suits cutting red marks in their jowly thighs, mothers playing mahjong with bits of damp tile, mothers lighting cigarettes and smoothing chalky cream on peeling red noses. Kit's mother would never play mahjong on the beach or talk to the others in their coarse, singsong New York accents. The other mothers are thick branches, bending to everyone's demands. Their children eat hot dogs and swim without waiting an hour. It's vacation, the mothers say to each other. Who has the energy to fight?

And Kit is afraid of all that sand, the drying starfish, the water retreating and invading in sudden bursts at her feet. She turns around to run back to her mother. Here the memory stops. Where is her mother?

Kit slides out of bed and dumps the remaining sticky berries in the disposal. She enjoys the grinding noise of their disappearance. She almost wants to make Jon disappear as easily. Jon, who has lived in dirty rooms in Afghanistan and Lisbon, furnished but without running water, without a current passport, or a ticket home. He walked through Spain with only a tiny backpack and five dollars in American money. He stayed six months, then ten. His sandy-haired girlfriend back home waited while a dark-eyed Spanish woman took him in and fed him rich, strange stews the color of blood. She loved him, but he left for Pamplona.

The day Kit told Jon about her mother's illness, he held her face and traced her wet eyes with his fingers. Now Kit cannot possibly tell him the truth: that she is not crying for her mother. She is crying because he is a man who has lived in too many places, and none of them was home. Her mother is dying and all she feels is relief. She has wanted her mother to disappear since she was a child; she has willed this final illness. Now she crawls back into bed. She places Jon's hands on her, on the narrow curves between her hips and breasts. His hands are astonishingly warm.

"I like the way you use the word *just*," Jon says suddenly. "Most women use it to slice down their demands: like *I* just *want you to tell me about your day*; *I* just *want you to love me as much as I love you*. You don't demand like that."

"I don't need anything," Kit says.

"It's a wonderful thing about you. I love that about you."

Oh, the great lie of this. It is Jon who needs nothing, who wants nothing. He is an air fern. But Kit is aware of how very much she wants. She wants a stone house and a cocker spaniel and a child. She wants to look at Jon each and every morning of her life. She wants to immerse herself in the odd junctions of his face, the tiny quirks of expression, the way his nose bends slightly to the left, the high lift of his cheekbones. She wants to press him to her, to crawl between his arms, to be as necessary to him as water. She can mete out these desires carefully, but in the end he will realize that they add up to the same catalogue of wants, the same amount of yearning. For now, she can hide in the crevices of his body, in his hard skin. She can cover him like a secret. She can wrap her ankles around his, which always seem to be moving, to be running from her, running, even in sleep.

It is frozen in her memory: the day she was alone without warning on a crowded, noisy beach. How could this be? Her mother was always there, picking her up from school when other little girls rode the bus or waiting for her after her ballet class, watching through the big glass window as Kit practiced third position and later calling her "my little elephant." She says this as if Kit is yet another burden put on her life, a child so bulky, so lacking in grace, that even a leotard and pink stockings will not lift her from her American shortcomings. French children are not fat, she tells Kit, saying it with so much authority that the summer they visit Paris, Kit looks everywhere for excess weight. But the French children are wispy. They fly through the winding streets and down the subway halls, leaving Kit with nothing to do but count the endless Dubonnet advertisements as they speed through the metro tunnel.

On the day Kit can't forget, she is looking frantically for the beach chair and her mother standing in front of it, dressed in a plain white top, dark-blue slacks. Solange is French, but she is not glamorous. She wears no makeup, not even lipstick. Kit has done something bad to make her leave. *Kitty, when I count to ten, you better be in this house*. Solange likes to use American expressions. When Kit loses toys by not picking them up, she says, *The way you make your bed is the way you'll sleep in it*. When Kit makes fun of an ugly red burn down a little boy's back, her mother snaps, *People who live in glass houses shouldn't throw stones*.

When her mother is angry, there are tight lines around her eyes. Kit squints until she imagines her mother is with her, then far away, a tiny speck of white and blue. She puts a shell to her ear, a shell she has saved from the tide, but it is her mother's voice that she hears. *Come back here.*

Why won't she remember being found?

Kit keeps the shells of that summer. She layers them in tissue and buries them carefully in a tiny cedar crate. Jon loves this about her: her passion for keepsakes. He loves the photo albums with their dateless, disordered progressions. He loves her overflowing jewelry boxes, the tangles of silver charms and gold chains, the tiny suitcases filled with French coins and old receipts.

He tells her that he saw her standing in front of a clothing store she had always admired but never shopped in and that he watched as she began to laugh, laughing at the unbelievable expense of hoping for nice things—the way it spoils you for what is possible—and decided then to approach her. He touched her arm gently so as not to scare her and said, *I just wanted to tell you how happy you look. I've never seen anyone look so happy.* What Kit hides is how very unhappy she is; she is broke, her mother says she will amount to nothing, and Kit sees quite clearly even then the terrible price of wanting anything as beautiful as Jon. But when he touches her arm, Kit is suddenly, magically happy, and later too, when they wait for the store to open and she tries on all the expensive clothes, the linens forming to her skin, the silk folding and unfolding above her head, parachutes of silver and gold. She buys nothing, she can buy nothing, but she is speechless at how soft the fabrics feel when she dares to touch them. And later, when she moans, he slides against her body like an expensive dress. It is not until much later that she wonders how often he has touched down like this into other women's lives, how often he has opened them and sprung away without leaving a trace.

"How old are you here?" Jon asks, flipping through the photo album she has pulled out and dusted off. He points to a photograph of a small girl standing barefoot, hidden by trees. He is waiting for a phone call from a "friend." He will claim it is a magazine sending him on a travel assignment. The girl's stare in the photo is solemn.

"That isn't me," Kit says. "It's my mother."

"It can't be, it's in color."

Kit looks again. The photo is of her, Kit, with her mother's pointy fox expression. She has so much from her mother after all. The lessons in the value of expensive silk scarves with tiny names scripted onto the corners. How to layer her perfume in stages so it lasts: first the soap, then the powder, then the touch at the wrist, the temples. Now her mother's hair is gone from the chemotherapy, and large Xs are marked on the sides of her bald head where the radiation strikes. I love you, Kit said to her in the beginning, six months ago, sweetly, falsely, I've always loved you.

You never said that before, her mother answered, raspy voiced, chicken headed, unforgiving to the last. You never said that when I was *alive*. She pulled away from Kit's hand with her last ounce of strength. She would remind her that loving anyone is like invading a country: no matter how far you get across the borders, you remain a foreigner.

"Where was it taken?" Jon asks idly. The photograph. He is holding the phone now, tapping it against his thigh. Perhaps he is having an affair with a famous actress, someone who changes her name and number every week, who registers at a fancy hotel under the name Dorothy Parker. Or, more likely, Wilma Flintstone.

"Pennsylvania," Kit says. It was in a park in Amish country. She was ashamed to be a tourist in a place where people wore serious black clothes in the summer heat and traveled in buggies instead of cars. Jon thinks there are things she won't share, he thinks her charming in her inaccessibility. But this is a lie. There are simply things not in her interest to share, which is entirely different.

In 1942, when Solange was thirteen, she stood in front of a German, an SS soldier. It was only her and her mother then; her father was already gone to the camps, her sister lost in the stream of lost children. They did not wear the yellow stars on their arms. The stars, the ones that say *Jude*, are at the bottom of a brown leather bag. They run from Paris and hide with a Christian family not too far from the stone house, an hour or two north. Solange averts her eyes as they pass near the turnoff; she is too old for games and beaches. They have a car, a miracle, and Solange wills herself to drive, although she is not quite sure how to. She knows, however, that when the car sputters to a stop, the problem is gas. Gas is not easy to come by. The two women wait in silence for an hour, then two. Finally, a jeep with German soldiers. It is Solange who waves them down. *Vas nicht?* they ask. *Vas nicht?* Solange is very pretty when she smiles, and she smiles at the soldiers. She looks into their faces without fear. *We need gas*, she responds in perfect German.

When Kit tells Jon this story, she fills in the details, what cannot be explained. For example: how did her mother know German? And more disturbing: why do the soldiers give them the precious gas? Why do they leave Solange and her mother alone?

Back in bed, the silver comforter is like a frame for Jon's golden skin. He flickers next to her in the dimming light. His ear is cocked toward the phone. Kit is only the background. She will always be the background. She imagines Solange dead and calling to her from the grave: *Why did you dress me in the blue for the funeral? I wanted the red. I told you the red. Kit, you never concentrate.*

Kit is out of stories. Jon knows everything of any interest. Even the true thing: that her mother will die. He thinks Kit will be brave about it, but she won't be brave. He will be gone. She will want him so badly she'll weep.

But she knows he will soon fade away like Solange, who was practiced at ghostly silence. She could punish Kit with it. Silence even as the other children on the beach make sand castles to show their mothers and scatter potato chips in all directions. Her mother leaves the beach, leaves her alone, the sand forming scary shapes in the late-afternoon sun, the sky darkening. *I survived*, the silence says clearly to Kit, *and now I have an American child who demands Barbie dolls and rubber rafting toys*. Does she wish for her mother to go away, to have never arrived, to have remained in Paris, where she belonged? The soldiers taking her. The white shutters of her grandmother's empty apartment swinging like ghosts or angel wings, high above the noisy Rue du Chemin Rouge.

"I'll probably be sent to Barcelona again," Jon says, as if it is a fate worse than death to spend time in that beautiful Spanish city. Kit realizes she has never actually seen any of the travel articles Jon has written.

"You might as well go," Kit says dryly. They stare at each other for a moment. Then he shuts his eyes and dreams, she thinks, of galloping horses. She wants to laugh at him, she knows she should laugh at his horses and bowls of red soup, but she can't. She never will.

When the phone call comes, Jon packs up. She is not home. The magazine has given him an assignment, he writes on a tiny note stuck to the refrigerator. He wants to spare her, or himself, a scene. He does not add where he is going. She finds an old shirt on the bedpost, but no explanation. It is possible that there is no explanation. People leave because they simply want to leave. His memory fades slowly, like old clothing too often laundered. He becomes as much a ghost as Solange.

So it is amazing, truly amazing, when Jon is long gone and her mother, of course, is dead, that Kit snaps awake one morning with one clear and final memory.

Her mother did not leave her. Her mother is there on the beach, and she is not angry. She went to get lunch, and she is hurrying back, laughing, carrying cool red slivers of watermelon, curled slices of cheese on bright-yellow plates. And Kit is frantic because she loves her mother so much that she cannot bear for her to be out of sight, not even for a moment. The beach shines like polished ivory under Kit's little feet, and she picks up a starfish and is not afraid. And when Solange comes close, she smells wonderfully of Arpège and strokes Kit's hair and calls her *monkey, my little monkey*. Oh, she is hers, she is hers after all. *Watch me*, Kit cries to her mother, *watch me*, and she cartwheels until her mother reaches out and brings her close, so close Kit is sure in that moment she could dive right into her skin and swim that warm red stream directly to her heart.

Jan Ellison

The Company of Men

FOR A few years I had in my possession two rain slickers that smelled of whiskey and cigarettes and aftershave. They were cherry-red and lined with fleece, and I kept them in a cardboard box on a shelf above the toilet in the tiny apartment where I lived alone. Then when I was about to be married and I wanted to be rid of so many failings, so many unhelpful habits and longings, when I believed the past could no longer inform me, I threw the slickers into the Goodwill pile and lost them forever. Now what is left is a single photo I return to now and then, of two young men in bright red coats hitchhiking under a darkened sky.

I met them first on my last full day in New Zealand, after I'd rented a bike and ridden three miles up a dirt path to touch my fingers to a glacier. It began to rain, and by midmorning when I got back down to the village, I was soaked through to my bra. My bus for Christchurch wasn't leaving until one, and across from the bus depot was a pub. Inside there was a fire in the fireplace and two young men—Jimmy and Ray—standing at the bar in their rain slickers drinking martinis. Ray was stocky and dark, with a sunken torso, small eyes, and a huge, humped nose. His hair was thin and black above a high, smooth forehead, and all his features seemed bunched up in the middle of his face. Jimmy was taller and fair, with square shoulders and fine blue eyes. His hair curled at his ears and at the nape of his sunburned neck. There was something loopy, almost acciden-tal about the way Jimmy stood in his frame, as if he were blind to the effect his size and good looks might have—the effect they were having—on a wet girl standing in the doorway of a bar seven thousand miles from home.

I'd been traveling alone for a year, since I finished college, through Europe and India and Southeast Asia, and I'd just spent a month at the northernmost tip of the North Island picking tomatoes in the sun for minimum wage, eating cheese sandwiches, and sleeping alone in a pitch-black room of empty bunks. It came to me suddenly as I stood in the doorway of the bar that I was sick of the struggle in it—sick of crouching in the sun, sick of taking it all in, of making notes on yellow legal pads, of stumping across rock and snow in my boots and across sand and kelp and coral and wet grass in my worn-down Tevas. It was not exactly loneliness I wanted to banish as I crossed the bar toward them but a kind of self-imposed austerity, a compulsion to justify the experience, to tear meaning from it, to bring something home. It was the days of weighty, maturing experiences strung together one after another in what seemed to me then a long stretch without a flirtation, a debate, a convergence—a blackout drunk.

Jimmy and Ray had just graduated from the University of North Car-olina and they were on a tour of New Zealand and Australia and maybe Bali or Kathmandu. Under their rain slickers, they dressed the way they must have dressed back home, in jeans and leather loafers and button-down shirts, and they drawled when they talked. They addressed me as *y'all*, which made me feel oddly important, as if I carried with me the authority of a secret entourage. We drank five fast rounds together while the rain beat the window and the mud slid off the hill outside into a great brown puddle. In the distance were the white tips of the glacier rising up out of a black mass of cloud. While we drank, Jimmy rested his hand against the small of my back and Ray told me about his girl back home—a redhead who'd stolen his money and broken his heart.

When it was time for me to go—when the exhaust was shooting from the back of the bus and the faces of passengers began to appear in the win-dows behind the drenching rain—the wish to stay had hardened into longing. But I had a half-price ticket to Sydney in the morning and my tourist visa was about to expire.

"Y'all need to stay and drink with us," Jimmy said, as I stood and dropped a twenty on the bar. He picked it up and stuck it in the back pocket of my jeans. He downed his martini, put the toothpick between his teeth, and leaned in toward me, so close I could feel his boozy breath in my eyelashes. I slipped off the olive and held it between my teeth, then passed it back to him in an almost-kiss.

"You're still wet," he said. He slipped off his rain slicker.

"Don't give her that, you loser," Ray said.

"Easy, boy," Jimmy said. Then he shrugged and slipped the coat back over his own shoulders. I stuck my tongue out at Ray and walked from the bar into the rain and got on the bus.

Everywhere in Sydney I saw people I knew. I'd step out of an underground station into the sun, and there would be a girl from my freshman dorm, sitting at a bus stop, or the married man I'd been with in London the year before, ducking into a cab. My arm would shoot into the air to flag them down, then when they turned toward me, the people I knew vanished into the puzzled faces of strangers. The idea of going home was always with me, but there were good reasons not to. My father had moved out again, before I'd left, and I suspected this time it was for good. "At some point things have to be admitted," was what he'd said, not to my mother but to me. I knew I was making it easy for him, staying away, giving up the cause, but the time and distance had muted my sense of responsibility. It had lulled me into believing my mother might be only heartsick and sad, not despairing, not desperate.

I moved into a flat with three German girls who'd been backpacking around the world together for a year. They hardly spoke English and that made it easy; there was no pretending we would take up as friends. I signed up at a temp agency—one that didn't check work visas and paid in cash every Friday. The agency found me a six-month assignment, typing for an insurance company in the city. The work was dull but the money was good and I buckled into it. In my spare time I renewed my longstanding self-improvement campaign. I quit smoking and stayed out of the bars; I worked on my typing speed; I wrote down words I didn't know on yellow legal pads and looked them up in the dictionary in the library on my way home. From the library I'd walk through the park, past the pub at Woolloomooloo and up over the hill to King's Cross. I'd buy myself a falafel and sit at the fountain in the square, watching the hookers in the doorways, the backpackers and tourists and solitary businessmen moving in and out of the strip joints and clubs, the restaurants and shops and seedy bars.

I was taken up in the change of seasons, the shift from the misty rains of May into the flat gray cold of what was summer back home. Then the holidays approached and the days began to lengthen and grow hot and expectant. On the last day of my typing job, I took the long way home through the park and stopped at the railing overlooking Sydney Harbor. The opera house glowed white and magnificent in the distance, the water glistened, and a full blue moon floated low in the sky. I was filled up with a vast emptiness, a glorious freedom, and as always I was careful to stay there and treasure it, to take it all in. But what can you do with a feeling like that? It was like other solitary moments during those years of traveling—it was the Himalayas at dusk after a cold day walking alone, it was the deck of a freighter on the Adriatic Sea at sunrise, it was Paris under a velvet snowfall. It was manufactured and overly private and tiresome. The other murkier moments meant more, finally, the dramas that began for the most part in bars, when the swirling motion of the evening would straighten itself and alight on a human form and there was suddenly the possibility not just of desire, and of being desired, but of a story of poverty or addiction or betrayal. There was the promise of some new knowledge—the shape of an ear, the smell of musk—or a shift in one's view of oneself in the world.

I started walking again, fast now through the park, and when I got to the bar at Woolloomooloo I went right in, sat down on an empty stool, and ordered myself a pint. Bob Dylan was on the jukebox. I sang along to "Like a Rolling Stone" and ran my hands over the smooth wood of the bar. I thought I heard my name, but I was done with phantoms and I kept my head steady. I cupped my beer between my hands. Then there was the heat of a body behind me, and sudden hands on my shoulders, and I turned and it was Jimmy.

"Hey, Catherine," he said. He took the seat on one side of me and Ray took the seat on the other. I turned toward Ray. He looked at me deadpan and stuck out his tongue. I stuck out mine and we both laughed, as if this was the way we'd greeted each other every Friday night for a decade. It encouraged me, Ray's laughter, but it unnerved me, too. He was so ugly, so private, until his face was thrown open with that laugh. Then he was all teeth and bright eyes, his forehead wrinkling like linen. What I learned, though, was that he could close down again in an instant and make me wonder what I'd done.

Jimmy opened a tab on Ray's dad's card and ordered us all martinis, and we started drinking hard and fast. Ray began to talk.

"So this girl, Jasmine, back in Raleigh. The reason we're here?" He said it like a question. "Her house was next to mine growing up. Jimmy's was three doors down. She was just punky, a tomboy. Then she lets her hair grow out and she has these green eyes that look like contacts. Junior year in high school, she gets a '67 Mustang convertible for her birthday and we paint it up for her. Yellow like she asked for. 'Yellow like a lady slipper,' was what she said."

"She was into flowers and shit," Jimmy said.

"Yeah, but only yellow," Ray said. "She planted up her whole front yard with them—roses and tulips and whatever. They even wrote it up in the paper, with her picture and all in a yellow dress. Then she went off to Brown and her mom sold the house and we didn't see her for a while. Until bingo. She turns up last summer on the Cape, and she's still got the car. Jimmy was down in Miami working on a boat so it was just me and Jasmine, staying up all night doing coke, driving around in the Mustang. And in the backseat she's got all these pots she made on a potting wheel in school, like dozens of them, all planted up with yellow flowers."

Ray stared straight ahead as he talked, at the orderly rows of bottles lined up on the bar. He paused and took a swig of his martini.

"So what happened?" I said.

"Well so she transfers to Carolina, right, for senior year? And we spend the whole year pretty much together, and we're talking about moving to New York after graduation. I was dealing, so I knew I could get us an apartment and everything. Then right after finals, she takes five thousand bucks out of the stash in my room and splits. She just drives her car out to California and hooks up with some professor dude—he's ancient, like forty, and he's gotten a job out there—and the way I find out about the whole deal is she sends me a postcard."

"My God, there must have been signs," I said to Ray. "To just take off and leave like that."

"Maybe. But I never had times like that with anybody," Ray said.

"Except me," Jimmy said.

"Even you, Jimmy my boy."

I'd been listening to Ray with my elbows up on the bar and my chin in my hand, with the intensity that can come over you when you've had a lot to drink. His story seemed strange and sad and unforgettable. While Ray talked, Jimmy kept the drinks coming and he let the back of his hand fall against my arm on the bar. He let his thigh rub against my knee beneath it. This seemed to be the arrangement. With the drinks and the roving hands and the sweet eyes and the good looks, Jimmy's role was to draw people to the two of them, and Ray's—with his stories and his mournful eyes—was to keep them there. He would keep us there until finally we could not bear to hear the story again, then Jimmy would rescue us, with a drink or a song or a wild run in the dark through the park.

"Fucking A!" Jimmy said now from the jukebox. He slapped his hands against the glass and dropped in some coins. Neil Young's "Sugar Moun-tain" came on and he came and sat close beside me and Ray stopped talk-ing while Jimmy and I sang. The song was suddenly something that was ours alone—we both knew every single line—and Ray would not join in. When we pressed him he said, "I don't sing," as if singing were a habit he'd long since outgrown.

Jimmy and I sang it over and over, and after a while Ray and his story seemed to recede until there was only Jimmy and me and those lyrics and the smoky blue glory of the bar. My final memory of that first night is of standing at the jukebox at last call, trying hard to fit a quarter into the slot so we could sing that song one last time.

The next morning, I woke up fully dressed under the covers with my shoes placed neatly next to the bed. There was no obvious evidence of inti-macy—no chafing or fluids or foreign smells. There wasn't a phone num-ber either, nothing inked on my palm or scribbled on a napkin and tucked into my sock. I spent the day sleeping off my hangover and waking from time to time to wonder how I might track them down—Jimmy and Ray—I didn't know their last names. When I finally got up and showered, it was late afternoon, and the German girls were watching TV. I started a letter to my mother. I wrote things I knew she'd like: I'd saved some money, I was getting along with my roommates, I was enjoying the neighborhood—all the shops, the square, the outdoor cafés. She didn't need to know that it was the seedy heart of the red light district, that the streets were lined with drug dealers and prostitutes and strip joints and bars. I started a letter to my father and crumpled it up and threw it away. It was the first of many letters to him that I started and never finished, or finished and never sent. I was afraid to lose the closeness we'd had, but contact with him seemed duplicitous—an encouragement or even a betrayal.

At six o'clock, Jimmy lumbered in through the open door of the apartment with a tall potted plant held against his chest. The trunk was flung over his shoulder and the branches swept along the carpet behind him. He dropped the plant to the ground, spilling potting soil onto the worn white shag. His eyes were closed to half slits and there was a look of deep concentration on his face. He seemed especially large in the narrow white room and his cheeks were full of color beside the pale German girls, who carefully moved their eyes from the television set to him.

"What are you doing there, sir?" I said.

"Liverin' you a *gif*," he said, and he walked out the door. I went to the window and watched him. He staggered across the street into the lobby of the old Rex Hotel and emerged again with a plant under each arm. Then he was back in the apartment to deliver them, and still the Germans said nothing. When he left again, they began to murmur amongst themselves, and when he returned with two more plants, they smiled at him and then at me and they actually laughed.

He made a dozen trips, each time pinching a plant or two without anyone seeming to notice and dropping them heavily in the center of our living room floor. Finally he sat down hard on a bare patch of carpet, crossed his legs Indian style, and gave me a triumphant grin made up of perfect white teeth. Then he closed his eyes and his body tipped backward and his head landed on the ground with a thump.

He was too heavy to move. All we could do was straighten his legs and lay his arms over his chest. Later, when the German girls had gone to sleep, I brought out a pillow and blanket and lay down next to him. His shirt was pulled up out of his jeans and I put my palm on his stomach and touched the fuzzy blond hairs around his belly button. His stomach was not exactly fat, but it was not so firm as to suggest vanity or self-discipline, two qualities that at that time I found unpleasant in a man. I ran the back of my hand over his sunburned cheek. He smelled of booze and smoke and the kind of aftershave frat boys wore in college. It was a smell that reminded me of fast, haphazard sex.

I curled into him, into the sheer size of his body. There was heat in the places where our bodies touched and the moment seemed simple and absolutely complete. It stayed that way between us. I never knew what he thought about most things, whether he had grave opinions about the economy or the nature of men or the existence of God. The things he knew about—football, sailboats, the business of manufacturing heavy equipment—couldn't power a conversation between us. We were rarely alone and we were almost always drunk, so there was never a requirement to get to know each other in an essential way; there was no imagined future. We were free of the heaviness I had so much of in college and later, when you announce to yourself and the world that you've met someone special and then you must stay the course. You must whisper into the night and you must embrace his terrible flaws—the dandruff at his temples, his tendency to speak rudely to waitresses, his inclination to over-dress.

With Jimmy it was simply about putting "Sugar Mountain" on the jukebox and letting our thighs touch under the bar. It was about talking to Ray and drinking and letting time pass without clutching it or measuring it. It wasn't about ideas; it was about the weight and heat of a body against your own. I felt something like it again when I held my firstborn in my arms. The simple physical fact of her moved me—her button chin and the fleshy lobe of ear, her head smooth and blond as sand, her milky breath against my face.

After that first night, the Germans moved the plants onto the balcony of the apartment, and with muted hand gestures and apologetic smiles, made it clear they'd prefer it if Jimmy didn't make a habit of passing out on our living room floor. So we took to passing out at the flat just off the square that Jimmy shared with Ray and a half-dozen other backpackers—mostly Kiwis on summer holidays—who came and went. I was happy in that scrappy flat—the stained green sofa, the tiny kitchenette stocked with beer and tomatoes and sometimes an avocado or a lime, the walk-in closet where Jimmy and Ray slept on bare mattresses that, laid end-to-end, reached the entire length of the room. There was a collection of empty whiskey bottles in one corner, two fishing poles in the other, and their open backpacks in the center, overflowing with clothes. Taped to the wall over Jimmy's bed were photos of their trip so far; Jimmy and Ray in wet underwear beside a lake in the sun, Jimmy and Ray climbing a mountain trail in their loafers, Jimmy and Ray in their rain slickers, hitchhiking under a darkened sky.

We got drunk every night, mostly in the Cross, sometimes down at Woolloomooloo or The Rocks. We'd sleep until noon and then head out for lunch and start drinking all over again. I had enough money saved that I could have picked up a round or two from time to time, but they never once let me. The drinks were charged to one of their fathers' cards, and the bills were taken care of back home.

Jimmy was a drinker without angst or moderation. He always said yes to the next one, and I was the same. It was not exactly that we set out to get drunk. It was that there was always the idea of that first drink in our minds, and when that one was gone, there was the idea of the next. Later it would work that way for me with babies, so that despite the burdens in it—the chaos and worry, the sleeplessness, the unqualified loss of freedom—when one child was weaned I was ready for the next, for the sweetness of a small hot body against my chest.

Ray was different. He got drunk when he set out to, did not when he did not intend to, and was often sober enough to remember the night and report back in the morning.

"Jesus, you puked on my fucking shoes," he'd say to Jimmy, or "You hit the bartender in the eye with a paper airplane."

"Did I?" Jimmy would ask me, grinning.

"Not that I remember," I'd say, which was most always true.

When I was drunkest, Jimmy would get me onto the mattress, cover me in a blue sheet, and tuck it tight around me. He knew something about being kind to women. He opened doors for me, he held my hair out of my face when I threw up, he made me drink a glass of milk before bed. And when Jimmy was first to get bad at the bars, Ray and I would each take an arm over our shoulders and drag him home. He'd stand on the mattress with his shoulder propped against the wall and yell, "I wanna get drunk."

"Lay down," Ray would order. "You're already drunk."

"Am I?" Jimmy would say. Then he'd sink down and close his bloodshot eyes and sleep for fourteen hours straight. It was a routine they knew by heart, and I sensed that Ray took a deep pleasure in keeping Jimmy safe in the world.

I never asked Jimmy what he studied in college, or what he planned to do when the trip was over, or whether he'd ever been in love. It was Ray I wanted to understand. Ray lived right on the edge of ugly but to talk to him was to want to heal him or win him. At the bars, sometimes he ignored me, or coldly put up with me as if I were a wart he might someday burn away. Other times he sat up close and talked to me about Jasmine, telling me the same stories over and over again. For years I carried around a picture in my head of Jasmine driving fast along a coast road in her yellow convertible, her red hair flying out behind her, her backseat filled with flowers. It was a picture that could bring on a tightness in my chest, a vague longing to be an original, a girl who could win love absolutely and then walk away. When Ray spoke of her it was with reverence and regret; he had not forgiven her but he had not given her up either. Something about that made me want to make him see other women in the world; it made me want to make him see me.

On Christmas Day we planned a picnic on the beach. We took the ferry over to Manly early in the morning when the beach was empty and the air was still damp. Ray went off to the boardwalk and came back with three-dozen clams in a bucket and a gallon jug of red wine. He opened the clams with his pocketknife and we ate them one after another, washing them down with wine straight from the bottle. By noon the beach was packed and it was so hot you couldn't walk on the sand. Ray went off again and came back with bread and cheese, peaches, pistachios, and a case of Victoria Bitter. Later, the German girls came by, pale and strong in their one-piece suits, and the Kiwis arrived with another case of beer. We assembled for a game of football—gridiron, the Kiwis called it—American style.

I can still feel myself in that day, my stomach flat and brown in an orange bikini, my hair wet down my back, the way I could sense my own ribs under my skin. The sun was hot on my head as I bent for the snap, ready to sprint after the ball. I didn't catch a single pass, and Ray traded me for one of the German girls who caught one and scored. But I didn't care. With every drink I became more beautiful in my own mind and the day grew more perfect. Later I would throw up over the railing of the ferry in the wind. I would pass out on the couch in the flat with a cigarette in my hand and burn a hole in the upholstery, and I would find, in the morning, dark spots of sunburn high on my cheeks that took years of creams and gels to take away. But in the place in my memory where that day lives on, nothing was damaged. Nothing was lost.

By dusk everyone else had gone and I sat between Jimmy and Ray under the changing sky and watched the water go from green to indigo to an oily black. In the half-dark, we staggered into the huge surf. I dove, stayed low to the sand and let the waves beat in my ears and sweep over me. I went through every wave, and I never ran out of breath. I might have been afraid out there in the waves, but I wasn't. That whole time was like that; I might have been worried about my health or my reputation or my safety but I never was. I was protected and drunk and happy, and if there is room for regret it is not for the time we wasted but that it ended too soon.

In February, when the Kiwis were leaving Sydney to go back home, Jimmy and Ray threw them a going-away party in the flat. I imagined later that it was the night I lost them, the night that the trip around Australia in the green van—up through Queensland and the Gold Coast to the hot wastelands of Darwin and the white beaches of Perth—became a journey that would take place without me.

What I remember about that night is Jimmy with a threadbare undershirt over his square shoulders and how we ripped it, not in a rage or a passion but because there'd been a tiny hole above the right nipple, and I began to tear and everyone joined in and then someone poured a beer over our heads. At some point in the night the German girls came by—three steady girls with thick calves, short skirts, and high heels. I remember that when they arrived I had a paper bag over my head; someone had cut holes in it so I could see and breathe.

When almost everyone had gone and I was edging toward a blackout, I found myself in the walk-in closet on the wrong side of the room on the wrong mattress—with Ray. We were sitting cross-legged, facing each other, our knees touching, and Ray was holding a fishing pole across his lap. Then he was reaching his fingers out toward me and as I raised mine to meet them, he looked right at me, he leaned in toward me, and we were caught up in a kiss. It was gentle at first, almost a question, then it grew more urgent, until his lips against mine were hard and necessary.

Jimmy was suddenly standing over us. *Hey!* he said, laughing at first like it was a joke he might have been in on. Then *hey!* again, then *hey!* a third time, loudly, with his hand pressing the ball of my shoulder away from Ray. So we stopped. Ray whispered something to me as we pulled away from each other, some words that I understood and cherished and then forgot—and that I can never get back.

I woke the next day on the mattress next to Jimmy. The afternoon sun filtered in through the doorway and fell on his face. The circles under his eyes were purple as dusk, and he seemed impossibly dear, the more so because I was afraid I'd lost him. At the same time, there was a small, stubborn part of me that wanted Ray to acknowledge the thing that had happened between us, that wanted him to make it happen again. It was a part of me I had not yet begun to understand—the part in the habit of expecting attention from men under the most extraordinary circumstances. Not just the first glow of desire, of glossy hair and full lips, but the whole messy miracle of love. It was not that I wanted the entrapments that come along with love, or that I would promise to offer it in return. It was that I believed that once a man knew me, he would see how different I was from an everyday girl—how forthright and clever and secretly kind—and he would find me indispensable.

It was a habit that persisted through heartbreak and havoc, through years of evidence to the contrary. Then I was married, and there were glimmers of it sometimes—at the pool where my son takes his swimming lessons, at the grocery store when a bag boy pushed my extra cart to the car—but for the most part I became convinced I'd outgrown it. Then on a hot night in August we threw a dinner party for friends. The kids were at my in-laws' for a long-awaited overnight, and afterward, when the wives had kissed me and thanked me and gone home to relieve babysitters, and the other husbands—three men I'd known for a decade—had assembled for a game of poker, I sat down in the chair left empty by my husband, who had promptly passed out on the couch. One arm was flung across his face and the other hung over the back of the sofa, so that from where I sat I could see his long fingers dangling there, I could see his clean, clipped nails.

The game progressed. There was bluffing and folding. There was whiskey and chain-smoking and there were outrageous bets scribbled onto cocktail napkins. There were forearms—handsome, hairy, manly extremities brushing against mine on the tabletop as we handled the cards. Then all at once there was a knee pressed purposefully against my thigh beneath the table. There were brown eyes intent on my face and breath hot against my ear. And beyond that, where my husband's arm had been, was only the back of the couch. There was no sign of the formidable wrist, the sturdy thumb, the callused, well-loved palm. There was no further sign of my husband in the room at all. I was on my own in the company of men with the makings of a straight in my hand, aces high. Desire was thumping in my chest and the instinct to win, to go forward with abandon, was shooting through me, across the back of my neck and down between my legs.

At the same time—reaching me through the fog of scotch and cards and sex—was the power of my own house. There was the china waiting to be put back in the hutch. There was the cabinet door threatening to come off its hinge and a stack of catalogues to sort and toss. There was the phone, the bulletin board, the family calendar—the command center of our domestic life. Down the hall were my children's rooms, their mattresses and pillows encased in special covers to keep the dust mites at bay. Those rooms where each night I checked breathing and the temperatures of foreheads, where I kissed the gentle dip between cheeks and ears.

The question that persists, that pursues me even now, is whether it was only the card I was dealt—the seven of spades—that saved me. That freed me to shift my legs into open space, to lay my cards down on the table in a fold, and with an unlikely pinch of resolve, take my leave.

Jimmy got a two-week job down at Rushcutters Bay scraping the underside of a yacht. When he was working that first week, I imagined him there, drinking a Coke in the sun. On Friday, I bought two sandwiches and a six-pack and made my way down to the boatyard. The day was warm and bright and the bay was dotted with sails. Jimmy was there and so was Ray. They were fishing. They weren't sitting close to each other and they weren't talking, but there was something between them, something silent and male, both a history and a future, and I almost turned around and left.

"Hey," Jimmy said, when he saw me. He glanced at Ray.

"I brought beers," I said.

"We never drink when we fish," Ray said. There was a silence. Then he laughed and took two beers. He popped one open for Jimmy and one for himself. "They're biting today. That's damned sure," he said.

I opened myself a beer and sat down on the dock next to Jimmy. The wood was gray and splintered, the water green with moss. We sat in silence for a while and then Ray's line began to move. I stood up as they did, as Ray reeled in his line, a fish slick and panicked at the end of it. Jimmy picked the pliers out of the bait box and worked the hook out, while Ray held the fish and then dropped it in the bucket with three others. There was nothing for me to do but stand and watch.

They finished their beers and began to pack up their fishing gear.

"That Kiwi band's playing at Woolloomooloo a week from Saturday," I said to Ray.

Ray looked at Jimmy then, and something passed between them, something that had already been decided.

"We're gonna be heading north, actually," Jimmy said. "We got a van and all." His face was soft with apology as he said it, and I might imagine now that he touched my cheek or took my hand in his. But he did not. He knocked his elbow against mine and punched me gently in the arm. We were like that together sober—clumsy and halting and overtaken by silences it was Ray's job to fill. But Ray had already turned and was walking up the hill home.

The day they left, the sky came down low and dark. They had their rain slickers on. I was coatless and cold. Ray loaded the arsenal of booze they'd assembled for the trip into the back of the van while Jimmy and I stood on the sidewalk and watched.

"I could sleep in the front seat," I said finally.

"No fucking way," Ray said from the back of the van.

"Ah, c'mon, Cath," Jimmy said. He cocked his head to the side and turned his lips down in a pout. Then he took off his slicker and laid it over my shoulders. It had started to rain.

Ray came and stood next to Jimmy. For one long minute, he looked right at me and the lines of his face softened. My nose began to tingle with emotion and I had to look away. He walked toward me, slipped his rain slicker off his shoulders and laid it over me, so that I was wearing both coats, one on top of the other. I didn't know then what he meant by it, and I don't know now, but I hope he meant that I was forgiven—for my secret greed, for wanting to be so universally loved.

When they'd heaved their backpacks into the van and closed the doors and waved and were gone, I stood alone for a moment on the sidewalk in the rain, excessively dry under two rain slickers—cherry-red and lined with fleece. Then I walked up to the flat and let myself in and surveyed the closet that had been their room. They'd left the photos behind and I peeled one off the wall, slipped it into my pocket, and headed out into the rain. I started walking in the opposite direction of home, in and out of weather, into parts of the city I'd never been before, with my hands first in the pockets of one coat, then in the pockets of the other. As I walked, I thought about them hard—Jimmy and Ray—going over each episode in my mind, weighing and measuring, considering cause and effect. Not in an effort to shed the loss but to savor it, to shape it, to give it permanence.

Adam Haslett

City Visit

A s they rose onto the bridge, Brendan leaned against the taxi window, gazing into the towers lit against the night sky, just as they are in the beginning of all the Miramax films, or the shots from the blimp when they show evening games at the U.S. Open—only now he could see the red-and-white streams of car lights rushing along the river's edge, beacons on the prows of ships jetting down the waterway, a helicopter's taillights cruising down the glittering shore. His hand tightened on the wallet in his pocket, the $300 he'd saved from afternoon shifts at OfficeMax secured in the inner fold. This must be what it's like, he thought, for diplomats and stars—Roddick returning from another victory at Flushing, an actor weary from a foreign shoot, night travelers longing for the comfort of lovers and apartments back in the gilded city.

"I hope this man doesn't get us lost," his mother whispered across the backseat.

"Jesus, Mom. Like he's never been to the Plaza."

"What do you know about the Plaza Hotel?"

"I know what everyone else in the world knows, which is that it's at Fifty-ninth and Park Avenue, and it used to be owned by Donald Trump."

"Feeth," the driver said through the Plexiglas slot. "Thee Plaza eez on Feeth."

"Thank you, sir," his mother yelled.

Brendan glared at her, hardly able to stand the sight: tan sneakers, stonewashed jeans, a green fleece sweater. Under his rule her entire wardrobe would be drowned in a vat of black dye. But none of these dreadful choices came close to the offense of the item strapped to her waist. His eyes snared on the teal nylon of the fanny pack, and it felt as if all sixteen years of his life he'd worn her naiveté through the streets like a crown of thorns. He'd pleaded with her since yesterday not to carry her valuables in that eyesore. He'd even recited the latest crime statistics; forced her to acknowledge that New York was one of the safest cities in the country, and that more people per capita had been murdered in their own state of Missouri than in the five boroughs last year. But still she wouldn't relent. Having to share his first entrance into a world-class hotel with that placard of ignorance struck him as more than anyone should have to bear.

"Won't you please take it off?" he implored again now, glaring down at her hand, which seemed to have unconsciously migrated to the defense of the wretched bulge.

A year ago she would have looked him in the eye and told him he was on thin ice. Now she just turned her head away and said, "Brendan, you need to calm down."

As if calm were an option! Every waking hour for two months had been burned up in anticipation of this weekend. The day his sad-sack, pale-faced, depresso father had finally moved out of the house and into an apartment closer to his job, his mother had got on the phone to his grandmother, and when she hung up she told Brendan he was getting the present he'd asked for each birthday and Christmas for the past two years: they were going to New York City, and they were staying in a hotel.

That same evening he'd sent an e-mail to Tom, the guy he'd spent so much time imagining since they'd met on the Web a few months before, whose pictures were so gorgeous: curly black hair, green eyes, a chest sculpted and smooth and strong. This wasn't one of those pathetic online nonaffairs his friend Tanya was still having, where you fell in love with some 400-pound food-service worker in Jefferson City, believing he was Brad Pitt's nephew. Brendan had taken a bus to a few of those dates. The only relief they'd given him was the knowledge that some people on this earth were more desperate than himself. Sitting in the back row of Language Arts on the first day of school this year, the pothead despera-does nodding beside him, he'd watched the teacher shift his saucer-sized red-plastic glasses up the bridge of his nose, and it seemed as obvious as the sentence diagrammed on the board that Brendan could become either a lonely, sad-assed middle-aged fag like Mr. Growley, up there in his cardigan, his perm, his yellowed mustache, as anxious and bitter an inmate of that place as the worst of them; or someone who got out, someone who lived in an apartment in a famous city.

Since Tom had replied, saying this weekend would be fine, his greatest fear had been that he would go all the way to New York City and be unable to lose his mother long enough to get down to the East Village on his own. To his surprise, what had seemed the most difficult step turned out to be the easiest. A week after she'd booked their tickets, he asked her if on the Saturday afternoon of their visit he could go to Tanya's nonexistent cousin's house, ten blocks from the hotel. He'd anticipated a grilling, and had a map ready to show her. But rather than asking questions, she'd kept on with the dinner dishes, this resigned look on her face, as if she'd expected him to ask such a thing.

As the cab descended from the bridge and turned on to the avenue, Brendan looked at his watch and realized he had less than twenty hours left to wait.

Life at the Plaza consisted mainly of trying to keep at least ten yards between him and his mother when they were not either in the room with the door closed or forced into proximity by a restaurant table. As soon as they'd pulled up, he'd leaped out of the taxi and ascended the steps past the doorman. As he looked back from the doorway, he could almost believe that the miserably attired woman looking frantically over her shoulder, as if bracing for the onslaught of al-Qaeda, was just some tourist one had to expect at such places. After she registered them and handed him a key, they rode the elevator to their floor and he walked well ahead of her down the plush hallway and into the room. The sound of her knocking after repeated failure to operate the lock properly led him to contemplate what she would do if he simply didn't respond. She would either begin one of her shouting whispers or call a manager, he decided, crossing to the door to let her in.

"Well, I think it'll be very good," she said, when he protested her hotel-dining plans. "I'm sure a place as nice as this is very reliable." For two short days they would reside on an island with perhaps the greatest variety of food in the world. But no. Not for the Blankenburgs. The Blankenburgs would eat chicken Kiev in a foyer.

"You're just afraid you're going to be shot," he said. "You might as well take that fleece off and put on a bulletproof vest. At least it would be the right color."

As it turned out, the Oak Room was pretty fancy, and when he saw the prices of the entrees Brendan became alarmed. He waited for his mother to whisper something about how they might need to find another restaurant, but she said nothing. They weren't poor, but they didn't eat out and they didn't travel, and his mother was always stressed about the bank account, about any purchases more significant than groceries. It wasn't as if his dad could afford to pitch in, and his mother's job at the mall didn't pay much more than Brendan's at OfficeMax.

Ever since a year ago, when his father lost his sales job and started sleeping half the day, she'd gone sort of quiet, not even getting after Brendan to do his schoolwork the way she used to. She'd started going to church three or four days a week, and praying more at home. On the kitchen table he'd see the literature she brought back, encouraging people to support the marriage amendment because homosexuals were trying to undermine Missouri families. He couldn't remember her ever voting before, but she'd gone down to his old elementary school on primary day, back in August, and when she came home she sat at the kitchen table and cried. Brendan had paid for the pizza that night and rented her favorite movie, this old black-and-white thing she loved called *The Philadelphia Story*.

Their entrees arrived, and they ate together in silence in the windowless, paneled room, glancing around at the other diners. She shook her head no when the waiter asked if she'd like dessert, but said Brendan should go ahead if he wanted to. As he sometimes did when she became silent, he felt his chest go tight, a kind of caged feeling. He hadn't meant to yell at her so much today; it was just that he'd been so nervous.

"Thanks for the trip," he said. His twelve-dollar brownie sundae was placed before him in a white bowl set on a gold-rimmed plate.

She nodded, looking over his shoulder, sipping her Diet Coke.

After dinner they took a brief walk along Fifty-ninth Street, and he managed to drag her six yards into the bottom entrance to Central Park before she mentioned some woman who'd been raped while jogging at night and said, "You know, we really shouldn't." The fanny pack had been left in the room's safe, replaced by a hooded Windbreaker tied around her waist in case of bad weather. Looking back at her in the lamplight as she peered into the trees, her head covered with a rain hat, Brendan felt the anger flaring again, that leading edge of the bitter promise to himself never to become her, never to stay in the middle of nowhere as she had, never to live like this family, with money so tight. His grandfather watched C-SPAN in a nursing home in St. Louis, damning the spineless Democrats, telling Brendan whenever they visited that in the fifties the union knew how to get things done—crack a few heads when the time came, none of this liberal crap, solid people on a pay scale they were willing to stand up and defend. And when the set-piece tirade was over, he'd stare bewildered at his semiemployed, divorcing daughter as though she were some strange inhabitant of the ruined future. Hurrying back down those corridors of airless linoleum cells, Brendan felt like Sigourney Weaver in *Alien*, fleeing the menaced ship, life clarifying itself into the pure struggle for survival, only to get into the escape car with his mother and realize that the beast of anonymity and defeat remained nestled right there beside him.

He kept three steps ahead all the way back to the hotel.

At one o'clock the next day he carried all his outfit choices into the bathroom, locked the door, took a long, soapy shower, and then tried to decide. For the past week he'd been set on the plan of dark jeans, a gray sweatshirt, and a no-logo baseball cap. But now he saw that the sweatshirt came down too far past his waist, and tucked in it looked totally retarded. The blue button-down was cute in a way, preppy, which given that Tom was a law student, seemed okay. But everything he'd read about the East Village made him think you should look as much like Lou Reed as possible, at least clothingwise. He decided on a long-sleeved dark-blue T-shirt and his black waist-length zip-up jacket. He put some gel in his hair, but other than some moisturizer to keep his skin from flaking he couldn't do much about his face. At least the clothing covered his spindly body for now.

He grabbed his wallet from the bedside table and stuffed it deep in his pocket. Across the room his mother sat in one of the overstuffed chairs, facing out the window that overlooked the park.

"It's your grandmother you have to thank for all this, you know," she said. "She wanted to give us—you and me—she wanted to give us a treat after your father left. You're going to write her a thank-you note."

"Sure," he said, wishing she'd look at him when she spoke. "I'll be back later, okay?"

The white-brick building at 228 East Thirteenth Street stood five stories high, across from an empty lot. Steps led up to a silver panel of buzzers. Tom Fairly's name didn't appear on the list. Brendan had been told to expect this. A sublet, Tom had said. He just had to ring buzzer no. 12 and he'd be let in. He sat on a stoop a few doors down, not wanting Tom to see him out the window and think him a nerd for arriving early. Checking to make sure no one suspicious was looking on, he took out his wallet and counted the money again. Tom charged $200 for a date, but he'd brought the extra hundred just in case he wanted more, given Brendan's looks. The money helped pay for law school and Tom's debt from college.

Sounds like you just need to get your confidence going. I can be gentle like that. Don't worry. His breath went shallow at the memory of the words in the e-mail. He'd jacked off so many times to the idea of being kissed by Tom that he didn't know what he'd do when he got in there. The last minutes remaining between him and their meeting felt as if they would never pass. Then suddenly they had, and he was standing in the entryway holding his finger to the buzzer.

"Who is it?" a man's low, garbled voice asked through the speaker grate.

"Brendan. Brendan Blankenburg."

"All right. Come on up. Fourth floor."

He pushed the door open and walked down the black-and-white-tiled hall.

Every night for months he'd visited the Web site, read Tom's journals, looked at pictures of Tom in his baseball cap and Columbia sweatshirt, or in the shower, water running down his smooth, rippling back. He'd met lots of guys in chat rooms who advertised with home pages like Tom's, but most of them were older, and all they had were pictures and a cell-phone number, maybe some lame paragraph about how hot they were. Tom was the only one he'd found who had a story: Growing up in a banker's family in Ohio. His father discovering him with another boy senior year in high school, cutting him off from the money. Coming to New York, finding a job working for a film director, putting himself through college and now law school. Some of the journal entries were dated a while ago, but they talked about how hard it had been at first, not knowing how the city worked, the parties and the clothes, how everyone seemed to know everything already and be bored with it. Brendan knew from the site that Tom dated other guys in a normal, romantic way; that he never mixed that up with dates like Brendan. He kept reminding himself of this. A jolting, shaking motion rattled in his chest as he climbed the stairs.

The door of 4F stood slightly ajar. As he knocked, it swung farther open.

"Come on in," Tom said, stepping into the kitchen from the next room. He reached out his hand and they shook, Brendan managing through an extreme force of will to keep his arm steady. Tom wore a pair of shiny red track pants with a white stripe running down the leg, and a white T-shirt that hugged the muscles of his chest and arms. He seemed a little older than in the pictures—maybe twenty-six or twenty-seven, Brendan guessed—but just as beautiful, his hair moist and curly, his eyes greener than on the Web, the lightly tanned skin of his face perfectly smooth. No one in Moberly, Missouri, looked anything like this. Like they could be in a magazine.

"Thanks for having me over."

"No problem," he said, reaching behind Brendan to close the door. "Want something to drink?"

Brendan looked quickly around the room for a cue about what to request at three in the afternoon in the East Village. Finding none, he said in a voice as casual as he could muster, "I'll have a Seven-and-Seven." Tom smiled. "Let's see. I don't think I have any Seagram's. How about a Tanqueray and tonic?"

"That's cool."

His host turned to the refrigerator, giving Brendan a chance to take in the apartment. The kitchen they stood in was tiny but immaculate, the counters nearly bare, the cabinets polished steel. Through the doorway Tom had emerged from Brendan could see into a small living room with a wood floor and a bright-red sofa, a modern-looking, colorful abstract painting on the wall above it. Beyond that, through another open door, was a large bed made up like the ones in the hotel—a beige comforter, lots of pillows arranged upright against the headboard. The place looked like a miniature version of something you'd see in a decorating magazine. He'd imagined Tom's apartment as a college dorm room: sports stuff lying around, sweatshirts and sneakers, law books, posters of his favorite bands on the wall. This seemed like an older person's home.

"This your first time in the city?" Tom asked, handing Brendan a glass.

"No, I came once with my dad when I was nine. We live in Missouri." Jesus! he thought. Could he say anything dorkier?

"Yeah, you mentioned that in your e-mail," Tom said. "Here, let's go in the other room." He led Brendan through and took a seat on the red couch. An armchair was on the other side of the coffee table. Brendan froze, not knowing where to go. Tom looked up at him and patted the couch with his hand. "Come over here." Feeling the shaking again, he perched on the opposite end of the sofa.

Since steeling his courage that evening two months ago to send Tom an e-mail asking for a date, he'd wondered again and again if his horny loneliness had driven him temporarily insane. Going to New York City and paying a guy to have sex? What the fuck was he doing? I think it's gutsy, Tanya had said in the cafeteria the day he told her. You're a freak, of course, but it's gutsy. The subway map and condoms she'd bought him as a going-away gift were tucked in the inside pocket of his jacket. Just don't let him murder you, okay?

Okay.

He took another swallow of his drink.

"So . . . have you ever been with a guy?" Tom asked.

He'd rehearsed an answer for this and, not looking up, managed to get it out without his voice breaking. "A couple times," he lied. "No serious boyfriend right now."

"It's cool either way. I've had guys come for their first time. I think it's hot."

He slid closer to Brendan and put an arm over his shoulders. "Come here," he said. "Give me a hug." Brendan put down his drink and leaned into him, his head over Tom's shoulder, Tom's arms coming around his back.

He'd never in his life been held like this before.

The sensation made him suddenly woozy. He thought he was going to pass out, but then the months of waiting burst inside and he had to scrunch his eyes closed and clench the muscles deep in his groin to prevent himself from coming in his jeans.

"This is, like, your exam period, right?" he whispered.

"How do you mean?" Tom asked softly in his ear.

They sat back from their hug, close together still, facing each other.

"On the Columbia Web site. It said you guys had your exams next week."

Tom put a hand on Brendan's bouncing knee. "You're cute," he said.

"Really?"

Tom nodded. Brendan could feel his cheeks burning, and he bowed his head. "It must be really hard to remember all the laws. My friend Tanya's stepdad's a lawyer, and he says they change all the time." Tom's hand touched the back of Brendan's neck, fingers brushing through his hair, pressing gently on his scalp.

"Is it all right," Brendan whispered even more quietly now, "is it all right if we don't go all the way?"

"Of course. Only what you want. Go ahead and finish up your drink."

Brendan drained the rest of his glass and looked back into Tom's face, which seemed more serious now, his lips closed in a flat line. "You go in there," he said, nodding toward the bedroom. "Take off your jacket and shoes. I'll be in in a minute."

Brendan walked into the bedroom and, doing as he was told, removed his jacket and laid it down on a chair in the corner. It would be all right, he told himself, looking at the tidy surface of the dresser: a bowl of change, keys, a tray of cufflinks, a bottle of what looked like some kind of fancy aftershave. Next to these lay a small, neat stack of envelopes. Glancing down, he saw the name Greg DeMarino printed above the address of the apartment. A boyfriend, probably? Someone who'd lived here once? Together there on the dark wood surface, the objects appeared so masculine somehow. It was nothing like his father's dresser, with its crumpled receipts and dog-eared copies of the catalogues he used to sell to his customers from. His mind leaped to the forbidden idea that Tom might be more of a man than his father: stronger, more powerful, richer. At that moment, more than wanting to be touched by Tom, Brendan wanted to *be* him, to live inside the sculpture of his body, inside the life he'd made here, surrounded by these clean things. When the older kids had pushed him against the lockers last year and started kicking, they kept saying *she*. "She's a pussy." "She's a fag." "Look at her." He couldn't forget that word: *she*. It wasn't true.

He took off his shoes and sat on the edge of the bed. From there he could see through into the kitchen, into the mirror on the back of the bathroom door, and in the mirror Tom standing at the sink, lighting a small pipe close to his mouth, tilting his head back and releasing a stream of white smoke. Brendan looked away, out the window, across an airshaft to a brick wall and a strip of sky above. He was probably just smoking pot, which Brendan wouldn't have minded doing himself right now, but asking would be too awkward. When he looked back a minute later, Tom was standing in the doorway. He'd taken his T-shirt off and stood with his arms hanging at his sides, a little trail of dark hair leading down from his belly button into the waist of his track pants.

A lot of the pictures of sex that Brendan had seen on the Web left him scared or grossed out, especially the close-ups; they looked more like photographs out of some veterinary textbook than something two people would want to do together. The ones he liked were of two cute boys, their faces visible, some of their clothing still on—a T-shirt, or maybe their jeans, pulled down—kissing or about to kiss. On countless nights when he had nothing to do he'd spend hours searching for the right image, clicking again and again, waiting for the stupid dial-up connection so that he could download one gallery after another, scanning the faces and bodies, his brain twitching forward like some small caged animal trapped on an endlessly turning wheel, his saliva stale with impatience. And when he was done, he'd feel nothing but dull-headed and alone. He thought of all the men in the chat rooms, the ones who, excited by how young he was, wanted to meet up, and who wrote line after dirty line about all the things they wanted to do to him. Disgusting things, sometimes. Things he wished he didn't know lived in other people's hearts.

"You should take off your shirt," Tom said, coming to stand at the edge of the bed, between Brendan's legs. He could smell the musky, slightly perfumed warmth of Tom's bare stomach and chest. It was *stupid*, so *stupid*, but all he could think now was that if he took his shirt off, Tom would see his skinny body and never fall in love with him, never want Brendan to come back and help him study, or help him as he started out as a lawyer or tried one day to reconcile with his father, traveling back to the family in Ohio to let them know who he was and that he had a boyfriend now.

When Brendan made no move to lift his shirt off, Tom rested his hands on his shoulders.

"It's your first time, isn't it?"

Brendan nodded, looking down at the floor. "I guess it was different for you, being with that guy from high school. More natural, I guess."

For a moment Tom didn't say anything, and Brendan wondered if he had hurt him by reminding him of something painful.

"You're talking about the journals?"

He nodded again, looking up for the first time into Tom's eyes, which he noticed were now bloodshot.

"Brendan. Listen. A lot of guys who visit me, guys older than you, they like to pretend stuff, pretend they're different than they are. Or they like me to act a certain way. That home page—it's one of the ones I keep up because some guys like that student thing. It turns them on. I'm not in law school or anything, but I've got all the sweatshirts—the undergrad ones, too. It's weird—some guys actually want to sleep with someone from a particular school. All I'm saying is, we don't need to do any of that. You seem like a sweet kid. You just need to know you look okay, and maybe you can learn how to suck a guy's cock so that when you get with some-one, you won't be as nervous. Does that sound okay?"

Brendan fixed his eyes on the dresser: the polished cherry wood, the opaque glass of the aftershave bottle, the dark leather box that might once have contained cigars like the ones his grandfather wasn't allowed to smoke anymore. As Tom's words filtered into his mind, he felt as if a heavy serum that must have long been pooled beneath the crown of his head was beginning to soak down now into his brain, filling in around the backs of his eyes, pressing against his skull—some primitive inoculant against sud-den loss.

He made no reply. Tom took Brendan's hand and pressed it against the bulge in his track pants.

"How does that feel?" he said in a low voice.

Frightening, actually, Brendan wanted to say, but didn't. The scent of Tom he'd noticed before was gone. Now it was as if he were watching the image before him on a monitor: a pretty man with a bare chest, a hand coming up from the bottom of the frame—an image he'd like if he found it late enough in his hunt and was tired of searching for the perfect kiss. No one in his life, except maybe Tanya, would recognize him now, sitting on this stranger's bed, about to have sex with a man. He didn't have to do it. He could get up and leave. But as soon as this thought occurred, he saw Mr. Growley, his teacher, in a room a thousand miles away, sitting in front of his own computer, pictures of naked men flashing on the surface of his giant lenses. Brendan wished he could reach into his mind and stab the image dead, but it persisted as he kept going, letting his other hand touch Tom's stomach.

"And what if I want to pretend?" he said.

Tom looked down at him with a curious tilt of the head. His expression had gone bleary, his pupils dilated.

The words Brendan had just uttered felt like the most adult he'd ever spoken, coldly thrilling, lonely in a new, more masculine way. He was hard now, very hard.

"We could do that, I guess," Tom said. "It's your hour."

"Kiss me, then," Brendan said. "Kiss me."

And then, with some of their clothes still on, the light from the window slanting across Tom's smooth muscled arm, the picture just about right, Brendan closed his eyes and waited.

Along Third Avenue twilight had fallen; people were speeding past him, carting grocery bags, or knapsacks slung over their shoulders. Some wore headsets; others talked into phones; two balding men in brown suits jabbered in some clipped foreign tongue, hands poking the cold air. The only people standing still were some Latino grocery boys smoking cigarettes by a stack of milk crates and, next to them, an old black man with a whitened beard mumbling at the pavement.

Brendan crossed Fourteenth Street with the light and stood under the bus shelter. Beside him was an ancient woman who came barely above his waist, her head covered with a polka-dotted scarf; under her arm she held a perforated box with a whining cat inside. The bus arrived soon enough and carried them slowly up the avenue, block after block of restaurants, pet stores, pharmacies, as anonymous, it struck him, as the strip malls out on the highway near his school. Taller buildings began filling the view as they entered midtown, the sidewalks emptier here late on a Saturday afternoon. Through plate-glass windows he could see into darkened hair salons and sandwich shops, stools turned upside down on the counters. Every few blocks men in red-and-white vests were moving slowly past the storefronts, sweeping litter into little boxes dangling from the ends of poles. The old woman had fallen asleep in one of the handicapped seats at the front. Brendan moved by her as he stepped off the bus, and turned past Bloomingdale's toward the hotel.

He was halfway through the lobby when he realized he'd forgotten to notice what it felt like coming up the steps, past the doorman, through the revolving door on his own, a guest like any other. Recessed bulbs lit the plush hall; his footsteps were silent on the carpet. He inserted the key into its slot, opened the door to their room, and paused on the threshold.

If his mother had moved, she showed no sign of it. She was sitting in the same chair, facing the window, looking out at the expanse of bare trees in the park and the low, dimming sky. She hadn't turned at the sound of his entrance.

Back in the spring the vice principal had called her the day Brendan was caught fighting with the kids who'd kicked him up against the lockers. Though he had no way of knowing what the man had reported to her, he sensed it was enough to blow whatever cover he'd managed until then. Her only child. But she'd never said anything, never demanded to know, never told him he had to go to church when he didn't want to. The men in the congregation were almost all married, and sometimes, when Brendan got tired of dogging in his own mind the awful suits his mother wore on Sunday mornings, he'd think it must sort of suck for her, too, how the others might look at her and feel pity.

"How was your visit?" she asked, still without turning to see him.

Could she ever know him now? After what he'd done? How could the raw facts of the past few hours of his life exist in the same world as her?

"Fine," he said. "It was fine."

"You know I'll always love you," she said.

To prevent himself from crying, he took a step backward into the hallway and closed the door.

Opposite the elevators two chairs stood on either side of a table decked with flowers. He unzipped his jacket and sat, his legs stretched out in front of him, his head resting against the cushioned upholstery. At the apartment he'd left his $200 on the kitchen counter while the guy, whose name turned out to be Greg, was still in the shower, and then he'd shut the front door behind himself as he left. In the moments before he came, he'd experienced giddiness and this awful fear, a disbelief that someone so handsome would touch him along with the sensation that he was departing forever a world he understood. Lying on his back afterward, listening to the stranger wash his hands in the bathroom, a rectangle of the fading sky visible above the parapet, he'd thought of how invincible the glittering towers looked when they came over the bridge, how total seemed their promise of fame.

The elevator doors slid open before him and a couple in their thirties, dressed in elegant coats and scarves, emerged with bright cheeks and shopping bags. The man smiled and offered a nod as they passed by, and the thought occurred to Brendan that it probably gave this guy some small, barely recognized satisfaction to make such a gesture, to meet another person in this world of the hotel, to give and briefly gain the sense that yes, here is where we all belong.

Christine Schutt

The Duchess of Albany

"THE GARDEN dies with the gardener" was what Owen had said, but when, years later, he died, she faced the garden with a will to keep it alive—as who would not? But the twins urged her to sell. They thought it would be wise to move out of the house (for too long too large) and into Wax Hill with its assisted-care conveniences and attached hospital: Wax Hill, that short line to the furnace and the thoroughfare.

She had carried Owen's chalky bones in a bag. She had tossed him into every part of the garden. How could she sell the house when from every window in the house—and there were lots of windows—she could see some part of him, Owen, her well-named spirit with meaty gardener's hands and other contradictions. He liked the slow and melancholy; he listened to the St. Matthew Passion long after Easter. But God? He didn't believe. Young once, he saw himself alone when he was old with just a daughter. He left behind two, not of his own making but full of reverence for him, nonetheless.

He was a schoolteacher, and the luggage-colored oak leaves signaled his season, but it had come around so fast. He had had nuns for cousins— nuns! Sisters of Charity, how queer they seemed now; their menace, vanished. Mustachioed Agnes Gertrude and arthritic Mary Agnes, they had taught at the Mount for forty-odd years, wimpled and sudden, full of authority.

She said, "I haven't seen a nun in such a long, long time."

The twins, on conference call, were hard to tell apart except when they laughed.

She didn't have a lot to say and lapsed into what the weather was doing. Today snow, the second snowstorm of the new year—and Owen once in it. She could see him, lopsided, clowny, a scarf around his head. Blizzardy weather was wonderful to walk in.

"Oh, Mother," from the twins when she cried. Overly dramatic, yes, she knew she was being, but she missed him. The wide road he had offered her each morning, saying, "What's on your agenda?" Now the wide road had all the charm of a freeway.

"But take a walk," the twins said, "if it's snowing."

Inward would be a nice word for what she was, *self-absorbed* would be more accurate.

"I know the country is at war," she said; nevertheless, she missed him. "Besides, when I look at the larger world, I cry almost as much."

But there was Owen, his voice, the sound of him in another room, off-key hummer, cracking nuts over the paper, singing or whistling a patter song. A Gilbert and Sullivan tune twiddled for days: "The lady novelist . . . I'm sure she'd not be missed." Whatever he thought to play or heard was his favorite. "I've got a little list . . . I'm sure she'd not be missed."

Some nights now she plunged into working, but vodka some mornings was preferred. She had to admit it—to herself but not to the twins.

She told them, "I have started a sestina." She said she was inspired by Elizabeth Bishop's "Sestina," and she was using two of the same words. "The line '*Time to plant tears*' was what moved me."

"Sestinas are difficult," the twins said. Her educated daughters, they knew, they had tried. "In high school, Mother. Remember Miss Byrd?"

"Oh, Miss Byrd!" And they had a rare good laugh, the three of them, she and the twins, remembering the ethereal Miss Byrd, giddy and over-worked and walking into walls. The twins laughed about Miss Byrd getting lost in the mall on the Boston trip. The twins were laughing, and she was laughing a little, too, when the sight of the old dog asleep alarmed her. And on a sudden, in the whiplash moodiness of youth, she was mad at Owen. Damn him. "There's no pleasure to be had in discipline and restraint," she said to the twins. "That's what a fucking sestina is all about," and so the pleasure of laughing was over.

"Why, Mother?" One voice.

The other said, "You've been drinking."

She said, "I don't have to defend myself." Besides, she explained, the drinking was only a problem if she drove, "and I don't." She stayed at the table or slept in the big chair and no one need worry. She might die there—no mess.

"Mother!"

"All I am saying is you can't have much of an accident if you sit somewhere with a drink."

"You have to get up for the bottle." Only Clarissa would say that. Here was the difference between her girls: one was meaner than the other.

"I bring the bottle to the table."

"Great, Mother. That's just great. Now do you see why we don't want to call?"

"Then don't. Leave me alone." And she hung up the phone and almost kicked at the dog, but she refrained. The dog was her friend. Pink. "Poor, old Pink," she said, "you scared the shit out of me," and she leaned out to pat a shapeless pile of fuzz and spoke nonsense to it, Owen's dog, Pink, adopted, a miniature mix of something abandoned and abused. Pink was hairless at the start. "Look at you now, you little dust cloth, baby Pink, old sweetie. I wouldn't hurt you. You're my pal.

"I'm on the move today," she said to Pink, but the dog lay unperturbed, sure she would come back.

A snowstorm, a thaw, a brilliant sun, snow, freezing temperatures, snow, then better, warmer, promising weather arrived, and she looked back at Pink and then to the rake and the garden, where the wet, mahogany islands of leaves, submerged for months in snow, now floated. All the snow pelted away by a rain the night before and only a mist this morning, something more than fog. She liked to work in it. She thought of Owen's hair—water-beaded and in the sun brightly netted. She raked and thought if the twins could see. If they could live with the garden the way she did. Covered or uncovered, leafed or bare, the garden was restorative in any season. The persistent mist was turning into rain. March, late March. Somebody's birthday—whose?

She abandoned Pink to the mud. She raked the beds; she swept the pavers. "Dirty girl!" she said when the dog wobbled toward her. Why had she even taken the poor mutt out? The dog trembled and squeaked.

The six words in her sestina are *garden, widow, husband, dog, almanac, tears*. "The envoy is an oncoming train." She said, "Restrain the wild element of mourning and what you get is sentimentality."

The twins, she should listen to them, sell, move, secure what there was to secure for them. Poor girls, in the disarray of single life, the yap, yap, yap of the dryer at the Laundromat beating up their tired clothes. Few single men where they lived, and the best of them gay.

The rain was cold, but she let herself get wet the way Owen did until she was soaked.

In the kitchen again she lit up the stove and watched the rain wash the garden into its outline. Green spikes stippled the beds she had raked, and the cropped crowns of established plants, the wheat-colored stalks of hydrangea, poked out polished in a design of circles mostly.

If her daughters could only see.

How is it possible that in caring for the garden she could miss summer? How is it possible, but she did.

Up at four and again at five, and at five-thirty up for good. Pink was awake; she heard him tick against the bare floor, circling the bed; she heard him yawn. "Good morning," she said, and she went on talking to Pink as she carried the dog down the stairs and to the paper. "Because it's too cold outside, isn't it, Pinkie? I'm not going to do what I did yesterday. Too cold and wet this morning." She saw forty-five on the thermometer. The radio said it was colder. Too cold. She got water, aspirin, more water. She put on deodorant, then went back to bed. For how long? Who cared? She was up again besides. She washed her hair and dried it in the heat of the open oven.

Once she had thought it would be hard to let go of life, but it will not be so hard.

She read; she wrote; she must have had lunch but she could not remember. The scenes that blew past came out in bands of color. The wispy complication of bare branches was added magic; the shadows were dark and sure. She put Owen in her poem, Owen or the shape of him, on the deck in his coat and pom-pommed hat, a passenger on a steamer, a blanket over his legs, heavy sweater, scarf—the pom-pommed hat. The garden beyond him she turned into straw.

Why did she lie to the twins? Why, when they called, did she say, "I am not drinking. I am working." Why didn't she tell them, "I'm doing both"?

The brief hello of summer and its long, long good-bye. Great piles of death she hauled to the woods to the dead pile. Farewell to the flowers of summer, to plume poppy and *Vernonia*. Turk's-cap lilies, delicate as paper lanterns at the height of their glowing, good-bye.

"Anytime you care to look," Owen said whenever he caught her watching his quick strip at the back door. She liked to look at his secreted machinery from behind when he bent over or stood one-legged getting out of his shorts. There it was, the long, dark purse of him asway. The head of his cock was the color of putty. Its expression was aloof most of the time, a self-satisfied indifference. When he was seated in some other ablution, the head of his cock was rosy and large and also arousing.

All she ever had to do was ask when what she liked to do most was look. Look!

"It's yours," he said, and with a flourish held out the bouquet of himself, "be my guest."

Overnight, age seemed to happen to him, then a few years of *ifs*, poorer health, and medication.

"Don't talk of moving just yet, please," she told the twins. "Not tonight."

Why, except for loneliness, did she answer the phone? (Owen at the long table, saying to the ringing phone, "Go away, people. Leave us alone," and people pretty much did.) To get off the phone she used the excuse of Pink somewhere sick. The odd thing was when she did hang up, she found Pink in the closet, sick.

"Poor baby," she said.

"Old age," said the vet.

He gave Pink pills that worked to ward off motion sickness, which sometimes happened to old pets, despite their stationary lives. "He will sleep a little bit more."

"A good night's sleep," she said. "Wouldn't that be nice?"

They talked a little, she and the old vet, for he, too, was old. They talked about Owen, or she did, and he asked, "Have you looked for any groups?" On the swizzling drive home in the rain, she cried, and she couldn't see to drive and had to pull over. "Fucking old vet!" She put her face in her hands and cried. She petted Pink and cooed at him a little, saying, "We won't go back there again, will we, Pinkie. No, no. But you feel better already, don't you." The little dog was a dust ball; just petting him made her feel awful. "Do I have to outlive everybody?"

"Yes, yes, yes, no," she said. "The lily of the valley is up." She said, "Yes, it was two years ago today."

"We wanted you to know, we're thinking about you," the twins said, and the girls called again later just to see how she was. "How are you, Mommy?" they asked in maternal voices.

"The lily of the valley is up," she said.

May was his birthday month and hers, when she and Owen quietly celebrated with nothing more than mild surprise. He was given to saying, "I think I'm going to see another spring." And he did—just.

Heart.

Of course, his heart, what else?

Now the oppressive immovable quality of objects wore her out.

"Mother!"

Whatever was not in front of her she meant to remember. His shapely head, his small red ear, his hair.

"You've been drinking. We can tell."

"We knew you would."

"So why act so surprised?" She hung up the phone and saw the fucking dog peeing on the floor in front of her. Little fucker!

They had not had enough time, she and Owen.

"I'm no such thing," she said to the twins.

Another night, "I'm tired."

Another, "I'm old is what it is."

. . .

Owen had said that in the garden she would rediscover childhood, but those childhood experiences she remembered were mostly dreadful. She took her nose out of the flower, and her cousin, seeing her, laughed. "Your nose!" The red was hard to get off, as were grass stains on her knees and elbows. Childhood in the garden. The garden was not genteel. The garden was full of thugs, and Owen had shown her some. The "Duchess of Albany" was not a thug, but a racer on a brittle stem, a *Clematis* with deep pink upside-down bells, deceptively frail and well bred, small, timorous bells. The Duchess of Albany was a favorite of hers: how could she sell the house to someone who might kill the Duchess in the earth-moving business of house improvement?

"The men came, yes," she said to her daughters. "But they have such big feet!" she said. "They can't help it, I know."

"Mommy!" the twins said. "We're only trying to help."

So was she. Hadn't she consented to the ugly tub? That ugly tub with the gruff bottom and the grips.

Her children have not visited in years.

"Oh, Mother," they say, "what are you talking about?"

She took her own safety precautions and moved her bedroom, such as it was, downstairs to the sun porch. On the sun porch on the sofa she was not afraid to fall asleep.

What made Pink nest in corners? "What do you think is the matter?" she asked.

"Pink's old, Mommy."

"The dog's ancient. Take him to the vet's."

"Oh, god," she said. Going to the old vet's frightened her as much as it did the dog. "Oh, god," she said. She felt so bogged down and muddled.

"You're drunk is what you are": from the meaner?

"Oh, god," she said. "I don't want to find a stiff dog under the desk. I don't, I don't, I don't." She cried and the twins consoled her.

"Mommy, why don't you crawl into your cream puff and go to sleep for a while?"

"You and the dog have a snooze."

She said, "I think I will." She said, "Pink doesn't realize I have mixed feelings about him."

She had found him in an odd posture tipped against the shed. The hose was squiggled over half the garden, and elsewhere were two full buckets, a shovel, a rake. How she had wished, for his sake, Owen had put away the tools and coiled the hose and achieved a perfect death, although the twins yelled at her for saying such a thing.

But the morning after he died, the terrible morning after, repeats so many times a day: she woke up, dressed, walked downstairs, made her gritty breakfast drink, and took her tea outside. Then she saw it, the grain bin, where he kept his garden clothes, and she fell to her knees and cried. Up to that moment, she had sipped at her tea and believed he was alive and already in the garden and muddy.

The permanence of his absence is a noise she hears when she listens to how quiet it is. How he did and he did and he did for her.

"Can I be of any help?" Always he asked this, "Do you want anything? Can I get you anything?"

She thought it was summer still if not spring, but the day's evidence said it was fall. Again!

"When was the last time you were outside, Mommy?"

"I'm taking care of the garden." She told them her nose was in it, brushing against the staining anthers, freakishly marked, a bald animal, she, a stiff, kinked dog, not unlike the dog she owned. Pink. Pink, what was the matter with that dog? After she got off the phone, she caught him in the act and pulled him away, made him stop, put him out of doors— like that—then wiped up after him. She brought Pink inside and carried Pink to his bed in the kitchen and talked to him. But even as she apologized for the choke hold, a part of her wished him dead and another part feared his dying, and she took Pink upstairs and bathed him in the new tub. His pink skin was so pink he looked scalded. He was thin; he shivered, though she was gentle and the water was warm. She dried him with her own soft towel and when he was dried and happy and at ease, she swaddled and rocked him. He was so pitifully thin. She put him in his cream puff and said, "I'm getting into mine."

Andrew Foster Altschul

A New Kind of Gravity

AROUND ONE in the morning I go out to the alley with Horace to bum a cigarette and trade the evening's tragedies. I'll pick him up at his cage in the basement, rap on the reinforced glass, point to the clock over his head. We check the monitors to make sure all's clear, no belligerent drunks or clever husbands waiting in ambush. Mattie would fire us both in about a minute and a half if she knew we did this. If she looked back at the night's security tapes, saw the steel door propped open with a brick, the two of us leaning against the outside wall like we were on school recess—she'd have no choice, everyone knows that.

"Play with your own life if you want to," she said when she hired me. She looked me in the eye, shook my hand, but didn't raise her voice. "Don't fuck with someone else's. That's our rule here." Mattie always says things that way—real plain, like she's just talking. But Mattie's never just talking.

I tried to laugh about it with Horace once, my first week on the job, trying to get chummy with the other guard. I did a pretty good impression of Mattie's monotone, her cold half-smile, the way she presses her palms together when she's lecturing you. Horace didn't think it was so funny. He unbuttoned his uniform and showed me the thick, brown scar where a husband had knifed him on the sidewalk at eight in the morning and taken his keys. Mattie shot the guy in the vestibule, then gave them both first aid until the ambulance came.

It's not that we can't smoke in the building—nicotine practically holds this place together. There are meeting rooms on the second and fourth floors with big, industrial ash cans that are always overflowing. There's the dingy third-floor kitchen, and there's the roof. But to get there you have to walk down those sad hallways, posters of Paris and the Grand Canyon, "One day at a time" in flowing letters across a sunrise. You can hear the women in their rooms, praying or sobbing or talking in their sleep, yelling at their children or reading bedtime stories. Some of the rooms are dead silent. The meeting room walls are cluttered with photocollages and news clippings and needlepoint, third-grade spelling tests and divorce papers and Spanish prayers. Me and Horace like it better out in the alley, where it's just the Dumpsters and the weather, a few minutes of bare freedom.

The women don't come out here. They don't stand on the roof or stroll in the city park or take their kids to Little League practice. Some of them can't even hold jobs anymore, haven't left the building in two, three, ten weeks. When they do leave, we usually don't see them again for a while, until they come back with their noses broken or their elbows dislocated or worse.

"Look at them," Horace says out in the alley. He doesn't have to look up to know they're there—sleepless faces in the windows above, staring out at the shabby buildings, jealously watching us smoke outside. "Pathetic," he says. "Pathetic specimens."

Horace is on a roll. Sometimes you'd think he hated the women, the way he talks. But he's been here six years. I've helped him and Mattie wrestle a bodybuilder into a four-point restraint, the guy so amped you could smell the crystal. I saw Horace's face while we held the husband down, howling into the concrete. I don't have to ask whose side he's on.

Tonight he's worked up because he saw on the log that Lucille Johnson checked back in. "You explain it to me, Charlie," he says, blowing out the smoke like it insulted him. "You tell me why a woman like that ought to be coming and going from here, wasting her life in this place. Don't she have brothers? Don't she have a father? And nobody doing shit."

Horace gets especially enraged by black women at Skyer House. He says it's a private thing, the community ought to take care of it. "Woman in my neighborhood gets beat up like that she's not gonna need no safe-house. She's not gonna need no restraining order," he says. He flicks his cigarette across the alley, where it bursts into a small orange shower against the Dumpster. "That kinda shit only gonna happen once. You know why?"

I've heard this speech a hundred times. "Because black men know how to treat their women?" I say.

Horace gives a sour laugh. "Black men know how to treat animals," he says. He crosses his arms and nods. I grind out my cigarette with the toe of my shoe.

"Get back?" I suggest, checking my watch. There's a 1:30 A.M. rerun of *The Honeymooners* that I don't want to miss.

"Talk about humane," he's growling as we head for the door. "I'll show you some fucking humanity."

I kick the doorstop away and try not to look up—even though I know I will, even though I know who I'll see when I do: a seven-year-old girl in Wonder Woman pajamas, waving at me from the fourth-floor window. I wave back, point to my watch and pantomime sleep, but Camila only stares from behind the bulletproof glass. It's the same every night: I trudge upstairs to my cage in the lobby, and in the monitors I can still see her standing there, a tiny figure looking at the place I've left, while I triple-check the doors and clean my gun and wonder if the day will come when I'll have to kill her father to keep her safe.

The doorbell chimes at seven in the morning and I don't even need to check the monitors to know what's out there: a husband on the front stoop, fidgeting with his clothes, trying not to eyeball the camera. He'll be freshly shaved, maybe wearing a tie. He'll definitely have flowers, red roses from the Korean shop on the corner—they do a hell of a business. Some of these husbands are big, real big; some of them aren't. Some of them look like the bottom of the barrel, some look like accountants. But when they walk past you, you get the same feeling, like a smell they give off, like something hot and rotten has been packed inside them, crammed down into a space too small to hold it in.

Soon there are footsteps clicking down the stairs and April Pittelli floats past the cage in her best dress and an hour's worth of makeup. She's wearing a big smile, despite her swollen jaw, glowing like a teenager getting picked up for the prom—she's leaving, she says, we can give her bed to someone who really needs it. It's what she always says. She stops to give me a hug before I buzz her out. In the monitors, I watch them embrace, her husband crying, smothering her in kisses. They hold hands as they walk away.

The first time I had to let one of the women go, I started arguing with her, incredulous. Mattie shook her head at me from across the lobby. "It's not your decision," she said later. "No one can take care of them but themselves."

It's true. You can't stop them. Even the fourth or fifth time—when they've come back to lay low awhile, let their bones heal, their hair grow back—when that door chimes they practically fly down the stairs. The caseworkers talk about how scared the women are, how they go back because they don't know what else to do, or they can't support themselves, or for the kids. But it's the smile that gets me, the way they throw open that door and fall into their husbands' arms. You'd think they really believed this time would be different. You might as well tear up the restraining orders in their file, shower them like ticker tape out the second-story window, make a big celebration out of it.

But then you'd just have to call the courthouse for new copies in a week or ten days, when she comes back in a squad car with cigarette burns on her arms or a high wheeze from broken ribs or, worse, injuries you can't see, whatever spirit she'd had left replaced by shaking hands and a self-loathing so deep she won't find the bottom for months.

When Mariana came back the first time, wearing a neck brace and gripping Camila's hand so tight the little girl was trying to pry it off, I opened the door and put an arm around her to bring her inside. She closed her eyes for a second, and I thought she might cry on my shoulder, but then she pulled away and yanked her daughter up the stairs and disappeared. Mattie called me into her office a minute later and gave me another warning. There's no such thing as positive male attention here, she said, slicing the air with clasped hands. You open the door, you close the door. You see a raised hand, you grab it. You see a knife, you shoot it. These women are not your friends, she said. They're not your girlfriends. They're sick. And let me tell you, you don't want to catch what they've got.

For a while it seemed every woman I dated had an ex who hit. For some it was unpredictable, a kind of reflex—the hard shove in the middle of a fight, the drink thrown against the wall; for others it would be premeditated, methodical. It started with Teresa, my old fiancée. Soon after she moved in with me, she told me about her ex, how he used to cry while he wrapped a towel around his fist so he wouldn't bruise her. She sat on the edge of the bed, her back to me, and I held a pillow over my face while she told me how sorry he'd feel afterward, how she believed it was a different person, like something taking over his body.

He put her in the emergency room once, she said, and when she came home the next morning she found him in the bathtub—he had shaved his head and was trying to slash his wrists. When I asked why she didn't let him do it, she closed her eyes and twisted her mouth into a smile, as if there were some things about love I just couldn't understand.

I heard so many of these stories they stopped surprising me. I didn't know what it was about me that attracted women who'd been with such people. I'd have dreams about running into the guy on the street, smashing his face into the pavement. This was when I still worked at the mall, I'd find myself taking it out on some stupid shoplifter, pinning him to the wall by his neck.

What got me was that they all went back. Maybe they'd go into counseling or quit drinking together, but it didn't make a difference, after the first hit it wouldn't stop. None of these assholes went to jail. No one pressed charges. Teresa's ex was the only one who even got arrested, and that was because he pulled the phone out of the wall when she tried to call 911. Apparently pulling the phone out of the wall is a federal offense.

The last thing Horace and I do each morning is put the kids on the bus. The counselors bring them down the back stairs and they file past Horace's cage with their book bags and lunch boxes, when we see the bus pull up in the monitors we stand outside the steel doors and the kids pass between us. It's almost like any other bus stop, just a bunch of kids going to school—except that these kids barely make a sound, they don't tease each other or complain, and they need two men with guns to make sure they get on the bus all right.

Sometimes a father will be out in the alley, but usually he'll just call to his kid and wave. "Tell your mother I love her" is what they usually say. We have lines painted on the pavement at 100 feet and 200 feet, so they can see exactly where they'll be violating their order. Sometimes, watching a father out of the corner of my eye, I catch myself hoping he'll cross the line, give me a reason.

Horace says he's never seen a problem at the bus. The fathers know there's not much to gain here, what with the mother locked inside and armed guards and all. He says they just come to feel like fathers for a few minutes. Maybe they hope their kid will wave. Maybe they think their kid will run over to them, crying, "Daddy, Daddy!" We have to stop them if they do.

I've worked out a deal with Camila's caseworker where I'm allowed to pat her on the head before she gets on the bus. She used to run over to me and hug my legs—her caseworker watching, alarmed, I stood there and tried to gently pry her away. Now I'm allowed to say, "Have a good day at school," and she's allowed to blow me a kiss.

Last week her father showed up in the alley. I knew he was there because Camila walked out the door and froze and immediately started to cry. "Camila," he shouted. *"Te quiero, Camilita. Tu mamá, dile que le amo."* The caseworker had to carry her onto the bus. I turned to see a middle-aged guy in cords and a fisherman's sweater. I figured I'd get some kind of dirty look or Spanish curses, but he wasn't even looking at me. He just stared at the bus pulling away and gnawed miserably at his thumbnail.

In the evenings things are more informal. From eight o'clock, when I come on, until ten, all the women are in meetings. The night counselors are supposed to plan activities for the kids, but mostly they have them do their homework or watch TV. I sit in my cage with the day's logs and drink coffee, read up on any new residents or watch *Wheel of Fortune* on the little black-and-white. Eventually, out of the corner of my eye, I'll see half of a face and a few strands of hair peek around the corner of the stairwell. I'll pretend not to notice, looking over the notes on the console, and she'll sneak down the last stairs to spring up at the door of the cage.

"Boo!" she yells, and I pretend to fall out of my chair.

"You shouldn't sneak up on a man with a gun," I said to her once, thinking that was kind of funny, but I could see from her face that it wasn't. Another time I put my hands in the air and said, "Please, don't hurt me!" like it was a stickup. That wasn't funny either. You really have to watch yourself.

Camila brings her homework downstairs and I let her sit in my chair and swivel around and I help her with math. She has her times tables down cold, but she's completely blocked on long division. Last night I had to tell her again that it doesn't always come out even, that sometimes there's a remainder.

"This is stupid," she said, shoving the book onto the floor. She started pressing buttons on my console and I could hear the electric lock on the front door clicking in and out. I quickly checked the monitors, which thankfully were clear, but I still didn't want her fooling with the doors. I picked up the book and the pencil and put them back in front of her, but she didn't stop.

"Camila, you can't touch those," I said, and when she kept doing it I reached out and put my hands over hers—so gently I didn't even breathe—and moved her arms away. "We have to keep the doors locked," I said, rolling the chair back.

"Why?" she said.

"That's the rule. That way everyone's safe."

"But what if someone wants to come in?" she said.

I pointed to the monitors and said anyone who wants to come in can talk to me through the intercom. She knows all this. We've been through it before. She said she wanted to go outside and use the intercom. She wanted me to buzz her inside. When I said no, she said I should go outside and she would buzz me in. She wanted to make sure it wasn't broken.

"I'm not allowed to go outside," I told her.

"You'd get in trouble?"

"I'd get in trouble."

"You'd get a *castigo*?" she asked. I didn't know what that meant, so I just nodded.

We finished the last problem and I told Camila it was time to brush her teeth. The groups were letting out upstairs, the women spilling out of the meeting rooms, zooming on caffeine and affirmations.

"My daddy wants to visit me," she said, erasing and carefully rewriting her name in the exercise book, brushing eraser shavings all over my console. "He said he wants to take us home."

"You saw your father today?" I asked, trying to sound casual.

"He said he wants to see my room."

I took a deep breath. I'd have to tell her caseworker. Her father's order says he can't come to her school, but they just don't have the staff to keep a lid on these things. Last month one of our first-graders was taken right out of PE. He was missing for almost a week until they found him, in a motel with his father, two towns away. They were just watching TV and ordering pizzas, like they couldn't think of what else to do.

"He says you won't let him visit me," Camila said.

I pictured her father behind me in the alley while Camila got on the bus. I wondered how many mornings he'd been out there, watching, what it would feel like to see your daughter grab a stranger's leg when you called her. I made myself stop thinking about it—Mattie says the worst thing you can do is let yourself identify with these people.

"I can only let in the people they tell me to," I said, taking back my chair. I tried to say it the way Mattie says it, slow and reassuring. "It's so everyone can be safe."

She crossed her arms in the door and glared. "My daddy loves me."

I pretended to straighten some papers, checked the monitors again. I could see the women in the upstairs hallways, leaning against the walls, on line at the pay phones—waiting to call their husbands, to cup the receiver for their allotted fifteen minutes, whisper how much they miss them.

"I know," I said.

"He does."

I saw Mariana in the third-floor stairwell, on her way down. She couldn't have been more than twenty-five, but she looked much older. Her hair was pulled back tightly and she walked with a stoop, her head tilted to one side like she was listening for something. She never talks to any of the other women. Camila stood in the door of the cage and scowled.

"You're stupid," she finally said.

"You need to be careful with Camila Lopez," Mattie said over the phone. She usually checks in around eleven. Now that I'm on nights, I only see her at our monthly supervisions, or when something is really wrong. "Young girls like her behave in very sexualized ways around men. It's how they get attention."

"Sexualized?" I said, too loud. I tried to laugh. "I'm helping her with long division, for Christ's sake."

"Don't be defensive. I'm not accusing you of anything. You're not trained to see these things. You don't know the things I know."

I knew where she was headed. Horace and I are allowed to see the court orders, so we know who can do what—but only caseworkers can read the files. We hear a lot of stuff, but there's always more. I stared at the monitors, at the washed-out olive world surrounding Skyer House, while Mattie talked about positive reinforcement, appropriate buffer zones, and nonverbal cues. I could feel that tightness creeping back, that heat on the back of my neck. At my first weekly supervision, almost a year ago, I told Mattie how angry it made me to think of what these women had been through, what the kids had been through. I twisted a paper clip until it left dark indentations in my fingertips and said if a husband tried anything while I was around he'd end up in worse shape than his wife. Mattie put down my folder and told me to take the next week off to decide whether this was the right job for me. There was nothing angry or disappointed in the way she said it, but nothing encouraging either.

"It's better if you don't care so much," she said. "We don't need another Rambo. That's why most of them are here in the first place."

Out in the alley, I asked Horace if he thought there was anything weird about how Camila hugs me or asks me to pick her up. He propped a foot against the wall and blew smoke up toward the windows.

"Someone gotta treat these kids like kids," he said. "Else they grow up thinking everyone's just as fucked up as their mother and father. Thinking one minute you hug someone, next minute they punch you in the gut."

"Kids are naturally affectionate. You don't want to discourage that," I said, but it came out sounding a lot like a question.

A light drizzle pattered against the Dumpsters and our breath came out in orange clouds. The alley smelled of burned rubber, like someone had just peeled out around the corner. "You ask me, they should lock both of them up, the mother and the father," Horace said. "You let your kid see that kind of shit, see you putting up with it, now what kind of damn message is that?

"It's weakness," he said on the way inside, gearing up for another one of his rants. "Nothing makes someone want to victimize you more than you being a victim already. They can smell it. Like a shark smells blood a mile away. There's no blood, you can swim right next to a shark and he just leave you alone. But show him you weak . . . ," he said and shut the door to his cage. I watched him sit on his chair and cross his arms, his mouth still moving, the raspy, hollow sound of his voice through the two-way speaker.

Upstairs, I checked all the doors and windows and put on *The Honeymooners*—Ralph steamed again, Alice shaking her fist in his face. I watched Camila in the monitor, her back to the camera as she stared out the meeting room window. Some nights she stands there for hours, wrapped in her Wonder Woman cape. Maybe she's worried that her father will come to get her. Or maybe she's hoping he will. In the months before Teresa moved out I used to stand at our kitchen window, watching the street. Sometimes I'd see her ex, driving slowly past the building, squinting up at the windows; by the time I got down there he was always gone. Other times, waiting for her to come home, I'd sit with the light off and pray for her car to appear.

After the kids got on the bus I went home and pulled down the shade and slept through the morning. I had the dream again, the one I've been having for months: I'm up on the fourth floor and I've found a room I've never been in. The windows are open, long curtains fluttering, and I don't know if someone's gotten in or gotten out. I rush downstairs but can't make it fast enough, moving in that excruciating slow motion. That's when I usually wake up, but this time there was more. This time it was Mariana's father down on the street, and then Mattie was shouting at me from the bottom of the stairs and I couldn't find my gun. "It's the end of the week!" she kept yelling, as though this kind of thing shouldn't be happening, and I fumbled at my holster, trying to make it to the bottom but there were so many stairs, my feet so heavy I knew I'd never make a difference.

Mariana's been talking to her husband again, hanging off the fourth-floor pay phone every night this week. Her caseworker got it from the night counselor, though Mariana still denies it in their sessions.

"It's the old pattern," says the caseworker, shrugging as the school bus pulls away. "She doesn't really have anyone else, no skills, no experience being on her own. It's either go back to her husband or go back to El Salvador." She looks up at the brick wall and bulletproof windows, the crumpled gray sky. "Or stay here."

He's coming to Camila's school every morning, says the caseworker, giving her notes to bring to her mother. This is how it happened last time, she says. She's called the school, the police; no one acts very concerned.

"There's gotta be something you can do," I say. She looks at me like I have three heads. "She can't just go back. I mean, there's a little girl involved."

"I'm aware of that, Charlie," she says.

"Maybe I should ride the bus with them," I say. "Make sure they get in the school all right."

She looks at her hands. "The school has security guards."

"Hell of a job they're doing."

"I'm just saying."

She leans against the wall, looks at me over her glasses. She's my age, or maybe a little younger, with a face that would be pretty if she let it, if she didn't pull her hair back so tight, if she smiled once in a while. Her nose looks like it was broken once. When she talks, her eyes don't blink.

"There must be something we can do," I say.

"We're doing it," she sighs, and goes right into the spiel. "We're giving her choices. We're giving her a place she can be safe, for as long as she needs it."

"What about Camila's choices?" I say, as quietly as I can manage.

The caseworker doesn't answer. It's not really a fair question. She pats me on the arm and walks inside. I can tell by the set of her shoulders how tired she is. I try to imagine her outside of Skyer House—walking in the park or driving, or maybe out on a date, sipping a drink, hair down around her shoulders. But all I can see is that exhausted expression, the lines at the corners of her eyes deepening each day. I picture my own face, shaving in the bathroom mirror. Behind me, my silent apartment, the empty refrigerator and broken stereo, one side of the closet bare where Teresa used to hang her clothes.

I got my job at the shelter when Mattie fired the previous guard, a kid named Trevor. She never told me what he actually did to get fired, but she said she'd always known he wouldn't last. In supervision he'd snicker and talk about irony. It was ironic that so many of the women hung crucifixes in their rooms, he told Mattie. It was ironic that their husbands were out there, living normal lives, while these women were locked up like criminals. It wasn't that he didn't have sympathy for them, she said. Just that he saw them as unwitting, the helpless butts of a cruel joke.

But cheap ironies abound at Skyer House and Mattie won't permit you to underestimate the women. "It's mutually assured destruction—just like the bombs," she once told me. We'd just watched an ambulance pull away; one of the women had swallowed a bottle of pills and collapsed at meeting. You can't stop people from fucking up their own lives, Mattie said. You can't even really stop them from fucking up someone else's, if that's what they want to do. All you can do is give them choices, offer them some scaled-down version of freedom, then stand back and cover your ears when they still decide to push the button.

"Now I'm going to stand there and wave and then you press this button to let me back in," I tell her. I make her point to the button three times, until I'm convinced she knows the right one. "No playing around," I say. "I wave, you push."

But Camila wants me to talk to her on the intercom. She says I have to ask permission.

"No. You just press the button. That's it."

She crosses her arms and spins around and around in the chair. "But you have to pretend I don't know you. You have to ask if you can come in," she says. She stops spinning and puts her arms around my waist. "Please?"

I glance up at the monitors. The meeting room doors are still closed, the sidewalks and the alley all empty. Horace is in the third-floor kitchen, taking his first break. "You can't ever tell anyone," I say, showing her how to key the intercom. "I'll get in big trouble."

"Okay."

"Promise?" She nods solemnly.

As I'm opening the front door, I turn back to look at her—sitting in my chair, staring at the console, her lips pursed in concentration. Outside on the stoop, I wait for a few seconds and wave to the camera, press the doorbell, grasp the handle. After a moment, the speaker crackles, but there's no voice. It crackles again, just the tail end of whatever Camila tried to say.

"It's Charlie," I tell the speaker, smiling for the camera. That's when I realize I left my keys in the cage. "Can I come in please?"

There's another crackle of the speaker, a quick clicking in and out of the lock, too fast for me to pull it open. I look up into the camera and wait, and she does it again—in and out—not holding the button long enough to open the door.

"Camila, no messing around," I whisper into the speaker. "Open the door now." But when it crackles again I can hear her laughing, saying my name. The lock keeps clicking, too fast, she's playing with that button like a damned video game, like this whole thing is just a game. Then it stops clicking altogether.

For a moment it's quiet outside Skyer House. The front of the building is patterned with lit windows—if someone looks out and sees me standing here, if they tell Mattie about it tomorrow, I can kiss my job good-bye. "Camila, open this door," I say, trying to keep my voice down, yanking on the reinforced steel. "Open the damn door, or you'll get a *castigo*." I'm starting to sweat. There's still no response, another minute I'm standing out there like a fool, then the lock buzzes steadily and I'm back inside.

"Camila," I'm saying, throwing open the vestibule door, ready to pick her up out of my chair and send her upstairs. But Mariana is standing in front of my cage, holding her daughter tightly by the arm. Camila is bawling, hiding her face against her mother's hip, holding the hem of Mariana's sweatshirt in one hand and hitting her other fist against her mother's leg. She turns to look at me, her face red and miserable, and cries harder.

"She just wanted to see how the door worked," I say, a little out of breath, feeling like I should apologize for something. Mariana looks at the floor, still gripping Camila's shoulder. Her sweatshirt hangs nearly to her knees, over old jeans. She looks so young—she could be anyone, a college girl in a dorm, or someone's little sister. Above her head, the monitors are gray and empty.

"She is a very bad girl," Mariana says quietly. Camila hiccups and sniffles. "She doesn't listen to me, she doesn't listen to her father."

"It was my fault," I say, scanning the console, the inside of the cage. "I shouldn't have let her do it."

"Disculpe," Mariana says. "I keep her in the room. She will not bother you."

"It's okay," I say. "It's no big deal." I reach out to put my hand on Camila's head, but she hides behind her mother. Mariana raises her eyes, and for just a second I can imagine her as a young girl, back in El Salvador, before all this. Then I imagine her upstairs on the fourth floor, in the small room she shares with her daughter, staring out at the alley and wondering what the hell happened.

"She's a good girl," I tell Mariana, who blinks at me from the door of my cage. "She's very nice. Just like her mother."

For a second she looks like she's going to smile. But then, just as quickly, she lowers her eyes and slides past me. She mutters another apology and guides Camila to the stairs; I sit back in my chair, watch them move through the monitors, climbing back up to the fourth floor, where they'll be safe for the rest of the night.

The next night the front-door chime sounds as Horace and I are heading out for our smoke. I freeze up for a second, sure that it's Camila's father. I have to grind my teeth and tell my feet to follow Horace back to his cage. I have to remind myself that I'm a professional, I'm not paid to understand.

But the guy outside is white, in his thirties, jeans and a dress shirt. He stands there with his hands in his pockets, whistling at the sky. Through the monitors he seems almost friendly, like an insurance agent; if you saw this guy in the supermarket you wouldn't think twice. He's no one we've seen before, probably the husband of a new client, just testing the waters, seeing how much we'll let him get away with.

Horace keys the intercom. "Sorry, we didn't order no pizza," he says.

"I want to see my wife," the guy says. He looks right into the camera, leans forward so his face grows large in the monitor, breaks up into green pixels. His pupils are shrunken to pinheads.

"Visiting hours are over," Horace tells him. "You got two minutes to find somewhere else to be." He keeps his voice even but firm, exactly the way we were taught. He's really good at it—I've seen him put a guy in an armlock while the wife clawed at Horace's face, drawing blood, all without raising his voice. I don't know how you do that, how you lock those feelings away. I wonder if it comes out when he gets home, if the walls of his house have big divots in the plaster where he punches them, like mine do.

"You've got two minutes to go fuck yourself," the guy snarls into the camera. "She's my fucking wife, you piece of shit."

The clock on Horace's console reads 1:08 A.M. and I take out the incident log to start a report. Horace leans back and crosses his arms, trying to wait him out. You never want to get into it with a husband—especially when he's flying on something, like this guy. You keep it friendly as long as you can, let him know the limits, and hope he'll show some good sense and let it go. That almost never happens.

The husband hits the chime again, mashing the button and shouting into the intercom. Any minute now, the women will start coming out of their rooms. We'll see them in the monitors—nightgowned ghosts drifting through the hallways. The chime only sounds in our cages, but somehow they just know. It's like a sixth sense.

"Don't make me call the police," Horace says, rolling his eyes. "Make a better decision than that."

"I'm gonna decide to bust down this door and kick your ass," says the husband. He starts pounding against the door, slamming into it with his shoulder. "You hear me, fuckhead?" he screams, pointing his finger into the camera. "When I get in there I'm gonna rip off your head and shit down your neck. I want to see my fucking wife!"

"Two points for the shit-down-the-neck comment," I say. "This one's creative."

"Yeah, he a real poet," Horace says, reaching for the phone. There are women in the halls now, whispering among themselves, shooing their children back into the rooms. This will be over in five minutes when the police arrive. The only thing to worry about is whether the husband will catch a glimpse of his wife or not. If his wife goes to the window, and her husband looks up and sees her, all bets are off. I've seen a 140-pound husband throw off three cops after seeing his wife in the window. I've seen a guy make it halfway up to the third floor by scaling the front of the building—his wife beating against the glass, trying to put her arms around him. I couldn't stop thinking it wasn't human, that normal people don't behave like this. I watched him in the monitors, clinging to the bricks until the fire department came, his wife being restrained by the counselors—they weren't human, they were more like moths hurling themselves against a lightbulb, some frantic, uncontrollable instinct driving them.

This is what Teresa wouldn't say to me, why she couldn't stop going back to her ex, time after time. It's not something that can be explained. It's a force of nature. We were together for two years, and she said she loved me, but I never felt it. They were just words when she said them to me. They had no force.

The cops finally pull up, and after the obligatory struggle—the husband spits in one of their faces, they slam him onto the hood of the cruiser, his legs wild and rubbery as they cuff him—things are under control. Horace and I flip a coin to see who'll go calm the women. I lose, and climb the stairs to the second floor, where they're still whispering in the hall and peering out the windows. Lucille Johnson is on the phone already, slapping her hand against the wall, her face smeared with cold cream. I tell them everything's all right, to go back to bed. I keep my hands open at my sides, like Mattie showed me. I maintain acceptable distance. These women know me, know I'd never hurt them, but it's not a question of what they know. I speak quietly, and do my best not to look at the open bathrobes, the thin nightgowns and worn sweatpants, the shy smile of a woman who leans against the wall and tries to hide the cast on her wrist.

"Who was it, Charlie?" they ask, their eyes nervous, excited. They grab my arms and ask, "Is he going to come back? Where's Mattie?" I don't know whose husband it was, but it seems like she might have slept through it. If not, if she saw her husband downstairs, it could be an even longer night than it's already been.

When I've finally gotten everyone out of the hallways I remember the cigarette in my shirt pocket. Mattie will review tonight's security tapes, so I open the door to the fourth-floor meeting room, look for a pack of matches. As soon as I walk in I can feel the cold breeze—someone left a window open again—and I'm halfway across the room before I notice Mariana standing in the dark, her nightgown camouflaging her against the curtains. She's standing in the same spot Camila always stands in, holding her arms around herself, her cheek damp and reddish-silver from the streetlights.

"Are you okay?" I ask quietly. I start to reach out to touch her shoulder but think better of it. Mariana just nods. "It's over," I tell her. "There's nothing to be scared of."

I shut the window and look for a blanket or a robe to put around her, but there's nothing. There's the faintest of reflections in the glass, doubling her face, and the large darkness looming behind her is just me.

"Do you need anything?" I ask. "Is there any way I can help?" As I'm saying it I can hear Mattie's voice in my head, but I just don't believe what she says. I don't believe you can help another human being by not helping them. It makes no goddamn sense.

"You are very nice," Mariana says, her voice barely audible. Her eyes are swollen from crying, the light on her face makes her look girlish and innocent. "Camila, she likes you. She says you are very intelligent."

"She's the smart one," I tell her. "She really is a bright little girl."

Mariana still won't look at me. "It is from her father. He is very intelligent."

I know I shouldn't say anything but I can't help it. "I don't think he's very smart," I tell her.

She starts to say something but stops, and that's when I see that she's holding something, a picture frame that she's pressing to her belly, the fabric of her nightgown taut against her body. I don't have to look to know what that photo is. There's no sound in the room, only the rise and fall of her chest, a siren somewhere in the city, as she holds it out to me.

"I was only seventeen years old," she says, handing me her wedding photo. Her eyes are dark and liquid, her hair tucked behind one small, ringless ear. And as we stare at each other I realize that she hadn't been scared by the commotion outside. She wasn't frightened—she was crying because it wasn't her husband, because he wasn't the one who tried to force his way inside and take her home. She pushes the frame to me, her gaze finally meeting mine, and her need for me to look at that photo, to see in it what she sees, is a tangible force between us, a new kind of gravity, bodies that somehow repel and attract each other at the same time. I look at the security camera in the corner, the little red light blinking slowly, I take her wrists and gently push them away, her skin warm on my hands, my knuckles brushing the fabric of her nightgown.

I open my mouth and all that comes out, whispered, is "Camila." We're standing much closer than we should be, something pushing us even closer, I should take my hands away but I don't. We both take a breath, and I don't know whether in the next instant I'm going to lean down and press my lips to hers or take her small, pale neck between my hands. I don't know what comes over me, but the image is so clear, so imminent, that I snatch my hands away and take a step back, the frame falls at Mariana's feet and shatters.

"Don't move," I tell her, awake now, bending to grab the frame, collecting the shards in the palm of my hand. "Stay here. I can't see it all, dammit," I tell Mariana, whose bare toes are inches from my fingers. "Just hang on, I'll carry you out or something."

There are already faces in the doorway, drawn to the sound of violence. I'm on my hands and knees, running my fingertips over the carpet, invisible splinters burrowing into my skin. Mariana snatches the frame out of my hand and then, despite my warnings, walks right past me in her bare feet. I want to reach up and grab her arm, pull her back, ask why she would do such a thing. But I keep my eyes on the carpet, scrounging around stupidly, all I see is a flutter of cotton, the flash of her calves as she pulls the door shut behind her.

A few days later, Camila doesn't come down to the school bus with the others. Horace and I stand in the sunshine, a fragile, early-spring morning, and I watch the kids' faces file past. When the bus door closes, I raise an eyebrow to the caseworker, who shrugs and turns away, heads upstairs before I can catch her.

"Smoke?" Horace says, reaching into his pocket. He casually moves between me and the door. The bus turns out of the alley, sunlight warbling off the back windows.

"I think I'll go see what's wrong with Camila," I tell him, but he grabs my elbow as I try to move past.

"Have a cigarette first," he says. "You go in a few minutes." His hand on my arm is friendly but firm, his expression studiously neutral. I know that expression, have seen it on my own face, practiced it in mirrors.

"What's going on?" I say.

Horace looks past me. "What do you mean?"

By the time I'm halfway up the stairs I can hear Mattie's voice in the front hallway and I know something terrible has happened. I take the stairs two at a time, hands clenched, wondering how I could have missed it. At the top of the stairs I nearly barrel into the four people standing outside my cage.

"Good morning, Charlie," says Mattie, taking a half-step forward to look me in the eyes. "Can you wait in my office a moment, please?"

Before I can say anything, Camila runs to me and wraps her arms around my leg, pressing her face into my thigh. Her mother calls to her, but she holds on to me, sniffling into my leg. Her father says nothing, frowning and watching her over his mustache, holding Mariana's hand. Mariana says something in Spanish and he nods. He's shorter than his wife, wearing freshly ironed black pants and a collared shirt. Mariana clutches the roses to her chest. Her suitcase sits by the door, Camila's small backpack slumped on top of it.

"Camila, *ven*," says Mariana, her voice steadier than I've heard it.

Mattie says my name again, but I don't look at her. My hand rests on Camila's head, stroking her hair.

"*Hija, ven,*" says the husband. Camila looks up at me, wanting me to tell her what to do, but I won't take my eyes off her father. Finally, she lets go and straggles back to her parents. Her father crouches to whisper in her ear. She shakes her head, but he turns her around, urges her back to me.

"He said thank you for being my friend," she translates. Mattie has her hands on her hips, watching me intently, but no one can control what's about to happen, least of all me.

"Tell him I'm not his friend," I say.

Camila starts to giggle. "No, stupid," she says. "*My* friend. Me."

Mariana starts to say something, but I've already taken a step forward, drawn myself up—it's like I can see it happening, like I'm watching the whole thing, that fucking animal shrinking away from me, trying to get his arms up, but not in time, and the sting of his face against my open hand sends a shiver through me, the sharp smack ringing in the air as he half-twirls, slides against the wall, stumbles over his wife's suitcase and sprawls to the floor. Then I'm standing over him, just waiting for him to get up, just waiting, Camila is crying, everyone shouting, but it all seems to come from somewhere else. For that instant it's just me and him, staring at each other, one of us stronger than the other, locked in a moment of perfect communication.

"Now you done it," says a voice behind me, there are arms wrapping me into a bear hug, Horace nearly lifts me off the ground, pushes me against the far wall. He stands inches from me, containing me without anger, Mattie shaking her head and Mariana sheltering her sobbing daughter, the roses strewn across the floor.

"Stand right there," Horace says quietly, barring an arm against my chest. "Don't you move." He reaches around and undoes my belt, removes the holster, faces peering from the top of the stairs, tense voices whispering. I stand with my palms flat against the wall, my throat so tight I can't swallow, while Camila's father picks himself up and smooths out his clothes, reaches for his wife's arm. It's hard to tell who's leaning on whom.

Mattie opens the door and the lobby floods with sunshine. Mariana picks up her howling daughter, her husband's arm around both of them as they walk out of Skyer House. Over her mother's shoulder, Camila looks at me one last time, her face smeared with tears, her eyes wide open and afraid.

The door swings shut and Horace backs off, still wary, ready to tackle me if I try to go after them. "Shit, Charlie, what in hell are you thinking," he says, trying to make eye contact. His voice sounds like it's coming through a tunnel. "You know that motherfucker just gonna take it out on her."

There's noise in the stairwell, women applauding, hooting and calling down congratulations. "You're my hero, Charlie!" comes Lucille Johnson's voice. I walk back to my cage—slowly, hands in the air so Horace will know I'm not a danger anymore. I sit at the console and find them in the monitors, watch them move from camera to camera, Camila's face buried in her mother's shoulder, her father's arm across Mariana's back. The image skips from one monitor to the next, the angle changing as a new camera picks them up, so for a second it almost looks like they're coming back.

Soon they've passed beyond the cameras. I can see Mattie on the stoop, catching her breath, waiting to come inside and fire me. I can hear her doing it, that businesslike voice telling me it's for the good of the shelter. I can't blame her. I've given her no choice.

She'll say it's for my own good, too. She'll smile weakly and suggest I think about getting counseling. She'll say it's up to me to decide what to do now. Then she'll ask for my keys and tell me never to come back.

But first she'll bring me into her office and close the door, and from a desk drawer she'll take out the tape from the other night. She'll ask me if I know what's on that tape and I'll nod, unable to speak. She'll put the tape in the player and let herself out, leaving me alone in her tidy, windowless office. And while she's upstairs, setting everything back to normal, I'll watch that tape again and again, sit right up close to the monitor and stare at the grainy image of a man—standing outside the shelter, coming in the door. I'll keep hitting the rewind button, watching him forward and backward, and wonder if that's what I really look like in the flat gray world outside the door.

Ariel Dorfman

Gringos

As THEY passed the man, Orlando gave him a good long stare. Even
though Karina kept telling him not to do that—I don't care,
she had said just a few minutes ago, if people here in Spain or in Latin
America do it all the time, it's rude, Orlando, it's *really* rude, my God, try
to make believe you're back in the States and *behave*—even though Karina
herself, true to her own recent advice, had hurried by the man standing at
the entrance to the old apartment building, resolutely avoiding the temp-
tation of a glance, not even a sneaking sideways dart of the eyes, nothing.

Orlando couldn't help himself. He was always peering at people, sizing
them up, he said, fascinated by what might be hidden and revealed behind
their features, even if he knew he'd never be able to decipher the secrets
inside another human being the way Karina could, not even if instead of
three ephemeral seconds he had had three hours or three eternities to
examine the face, sadly aware as he passed and quickly turned his head in
the man's direction that he would forget each singular detail of this experience almost as soon as it was over, aware that an hour from now, in fact a
few minutes from now, not even the faintest trace of a memory would be
left.

In this case, he was drawn to the man because the man was so out of
place on that lonely Barcelona street, so different from anyone else
Orlando had seen anywhere in this city or anywhere else in Catalonia,

a stocky, almost chubby man, with a moon of a face, almost perfectly round, with a hint of Filipino looks, or Malay maybe, crossed with—what else? Perhaps a vestige of something Negroid way back and, seeping out, a dash of South American Indian, a mix hopelessly impossible to identify, orientally expressionless but somehow gentle, possibly because of the wire glasses on the pudgy nose or the plaintive childlike voice the man was using to call someone named Francisca through the building's rusty inter-com, as if the man knew—or was Orlando projecting again, again allow-ing his imagination to run amok?—that there wasn't a chance in hell that this Francisca would buzz open the door, almost as if the woman called Francisca up there didn't exist and was merely an entity the man had con-jured up in order to make believe he had someone, anyone, to give his body refuge on this cloudy autumn afternoon.

And then, of course, Orlando and Karina had already passed and were on their way, looking for the shortest route to La Boqueria, Barcelona's bustling central market, and the temptations of the Rambla Catalunya beyond it. But not before the man, at the last instant, caught Orlando's eye. Not before the man understood that Orlando had tried to devour him with his eyes, stuffing the man into some attic of experience from whence he would probably never be taken out, dusted off, and put on display. The man must have guessed at a certain pity that crept into Orlando's eyes as they averted his and he continued on with this resplendent hip-shaking woman; as if, in Orlando's view, the poor guy belonged nowhere on this earth and even less in Barcelona, and certainly not in front of that apart-ment building where neither the invisible Francisca of the upper domains nor anybody else was to offer him consolation, only the flash of Orlando's fleeting eyes to keep him company.

And yet, it was not Orlando who realized, a few steps farther on, that the man was calling to them, to Karina in particular, it turned out to be Karina who had heard the innocent flute of that voice at her back, perhaps because she had not been mindful of whom the voice's owner might be, had not noticed him nor openly gawked in his direction. Later on Orlando was to wonder how come he had not been attentive to that call, how bizarre and yet typical that he should have blotted that man out of his memory so immediately after those few pressing seconds of street com-munion, Orlando rushing on to the next experience, the next intense gaze and instantaneous reconstruction and hasty oblivion of some stranger's life. Or maybe the explanation was simpler: Karina had turned when the man had called because she was the object of his interest, it was to her that the words were directed, he had said something like, *"Madama, Madama,"* repeating the words with such quiet urgency that she could not possibly ignore the note of warning. She had turned around and seen the man, still hovering there near the threshold, but now suddenly advancing towards them like a big naïve bear, pointing a finger at her, mumbling something inchoate in a language that might have been Spanish (or maybe Catalan? or Italian?) and gesticulating at the sweater that Karina had draped around her neck. *Tiene algo ahí.* You've got something there, went the automatic translator in Orlando's head. And Karina had reacted with horror, sensing some insect—a spider, *una araña*—she'd cried out and unwound the black velvet sweater from her body with a dexterity born of fear, and her trembling hand had pushed it in the direction of Orlando who, in turn, had held it out at arm's length to the man—he had reached them by now and was explaining *No, no, una araña no, no es eso.* It wasn't that, not a spider, and he pointed to a streak of orange-brown goo clinging to the fabric.

Orlando nevertheless kept the sweater at a safe distance, even while he conjured up the slight faraway smell of shit, a bird must have blessed Karina's sweater from one of the trees of the Montjuic park they had just visited, an extraordinary accident because he and Karina had been admiring merely a half hour before the assortment of mischievous and imaginary birds in the canvasses of the Miró Museum and the flare of faint color on the black velvet of the sweater was not that different from the palette of contours and lines they had so recently enjoyed in the paintings. But this was not the time—Orlando almost scolded himself—for this sort of association. There was the more crucial matter of the shit itself and Karina's ongoing hysterical reaction, which had so disarmed and perplexed the man that he was now pointing a surprisingly slender finger at a building across the street, telling Orlando that there was water there, *allá hay agua*, articulating each word slowly and deliberately as if speaking to children or people foreign to the tongue, *agua*, he said again, and then indicated with another gesture that the bird had not only soiled the sweater but Orlando's shirt as well and his blue jeans, though by the immature way the man spoke, Orlando thought that it was the man who had to be something of a simpleton, certainly an innocent, radiating a childish need to be of service, which was in and of itself a welcome relief in this city where people were aloof and indifferent and extremely ill-mannered to anyone who was not a native, as if they hated the very idea of having to address them and even more so, it seemed, when the Catalans realized that Orlando and Karina were South Americans and therefore spoke the hated Spanish imperial tongue, *We should talk in English and pretend we have nothing to do with Spanish*, Karina had laughingly suggested, *you look like a gringo anyway*, but Orlando had not expected such a reaction in a city where everybody spoke Spanish, he was disturbed by such a degree of hostility. Not the case with this man, at any rate, who was almost pleading to help them, as if he were blaming himself for the accident, even though it was clear from the neutral tone and blurred accent of his words—as if his skin and rotund Asian face had not already revealed the fact—that he was not originally from Barcelona. *Ahí se pueden limpiar*, he said, they could clean off their clothes over there, in that building over there.

What may have decided Orlando and perhaps also Karina to accept the invitation was a quite normal desire to avoid offending the man, but the immediate impulse came from a joke the man had made, a weak one, to be sure, but nevertheless a further attempt to assure the couple of his innocuousness and vulnerability, answering Orlando's comment *It must have been a big bird* with *More like an elephant*, the sort of give and take that is almost intimate and definitely congenial, so that by the time they found themselves being steered to the open threshold across the narrow street and introduced into a darkened *zaguán* filled with detritus and dis-carded construction materials, neither Orlando nor Karina could object. Anything, Orlando thought, to calm Karina down. And if the gloomy and dank atmosphere might, in other circumstances, have sparked their suspi-cions, the man's awkward actions dispelled their doubts before they even had time to formulate them. Displaying the same gentleness and almost idiotic transparency, he had picked up some pieces of newspaper lying on the ground and, apparently forgetting his offer of water or maybe embar-rassed at the fact that there was, inexplicably, not a hint of a faucet or any-thing of the sort anywhere in the penumbra of that building's entrance hall, proceeded to use the paper to wipe their clothes, here and here and here, he said, trying not to be intrusive, careful not to touch the skin or press the flesh, a model of consideration. *Gracias, gracias*, Orlando kept murmuring, embarrassed himself at such kindness, unable to believe that anybody in this day and age would taint his own fingers with bird crap in order to relieve a stranger, but the man was not exactly on the bright side, one could almost venture that he was slightly dim.

Karina, efficient as ever, rummaged in her handbag and came out with some tissues. The man took a few and passed one to Orlando, ordering him in a still-infantile way to clean his wife, while he kept some for himself in order to work assiduously on Orlando's shirt and blue jeans.

Once Karina felt sufficiently cleansed, she examined Orlando, noticed a few smaller stains, but left them alone. There were no tissues left. Suppressing a shudder—*It's like an insect*, she thought, *crawling under my fingernails*—she threw the used tissues in a corner of the building's dusky hallway, leaving them there among a pile of bricks and unidentifiable junk and, yes, even an old tattered mattress.

"We have to get washed," Karina said to Orlando in English, but her husband, instead of answering, had turned to the man and, speaking Spanish, asked him his name. The man was startled, seemed almost taken aback that anyone should be interested in anything as insignificant as his name, but got over his discomfiture and announced, smiling shyly for the first time, "Juan." Orlando said his own name and then introduced Karina, *Esta es mi esposa*, this is my wife, and then shook the hand of the man who had called himself Juan, and all three of them stood there for a while in the murky swirl of the building's hallway, as if they didn't know what to do next, now that the hullabaloo of wild activity that had consumed them for the last frantic minutes had subsided.

"*Somos de Chile originalmente,*" Orlando added—but Juan didn't react to the information that this couple he had befriended was originally from Chile, or rather, Karina thought, he seemed not to believe them, continued to consider them, or at least Orlando, with his blond hair and tall body, a quintessential gringo, what with the Levis and the Nike shoes. Or maybe Juan was so empty-headed—I mean, after all, spending his time giving succor to perfect strangers who had been sullied by Barcelona birds?—that he had no idea where Chile was, did not even know that it was a country in Latin America thousands of miles to the south and in another hemisphere.

"Maybe you'd like to have a drink with us," Orlando said, to Karina's dismay; she could tell that Juan did not want to be thanked so effusively, as usual Orlando was overdoing it, believing that every favor had to be paid back on the spot, or perhaps it was Orlando's usual gambit of trying to delve into the alien lives he kept coming across, add them to his collection, his eternal struggle against forgetfulness. There was, at any rate, nothing Karina could do at that point but cooperate and insist that Juan, there was no arguing, simply had to join them, he'd been *so* courteous and nice, in spite of the alarm that flooded Juan's eyes behind his spectacles and just as soon drained out. But their new friend answered, Yes, of course, an honor, and added, We all need to get cleaned up.

They walked down to the corner in silence and there was a little tavern there, in which some ancient Catalans were playing cards. Karina chose a table near the entrance and watched Orlando and Juan go to the bathroom and when they returned, she herself went to the ladies' room and scrubbed herself over and over, disgusted by the idea that the bird diarrhea might have leaked through the tissues onto her fingers. The streaks were still on her sweater and blouse, hardened and drying, Karina not wanting to bring any of this, fingers or sweater or whatever, to her nose, desperate to scrub it out of her world, away from her skin, away from her memories. Oh God—she thought this as she tried to erase the blotches and poured on more water—now she had to return to entertain this strange man and be reminded, by his presence, of how deeply contaminated she felt. She had a sudden urge to piss but eyed the toilet with distaste and decided not to risk it. The smell of the disinfectant in the bathroom, just to imagine it mingling with the legacy the birds had dropped on her, it was just too much, she managed to stop from gagging, smiled at her perfect teeth in the mirror, and breathed deep, very deep.

Out at the table, her husband and Juan were warily sipping *café con leche*, while a steaming cup of black coffee awaited her. Orlando always knew what to order for her and at what time of day, after so many years together, so many mugs and taverns and dinners and breakfasts since they'd left Chile, so many tables.

Orlando began filling the silence, as he always did, hating the long drawn-out moments when nobody was talking. He was telling Juan about his first visit to Barcelona, when he had been nine. Orlando and his family had gone up the Montjuic, just like today—but no bird shit, he added, no shit at all—and what he remembered most was a fun fair and a labyrinth shaped out of shrubbery, and how he had managed to get to the center of the maze and ring a bell, done it before his elder brother had found the way. Orlando reminisced fondly about how he had returned to his parents' congratulations.

Juan said, "You were always a smart kid, huh?" but he said it vacuously, almost vacantly, as if to snake in some comment, as if he had not really been listening to the story. As if he really wanted to be somewhere else—Karina could see it, but of course Orlando was totally blind to anything but his own enjoyment. Maybe bored, Juan was. Or maybe, not being too intelligent himself, Juan did not particularly like stories about how brilliant others might be. Or maybe he was kicking himself mentally for helping these strangers who now had made him miss an appointment, some important meeting, maybe with the woman of his dreams who was finally going to open herself to his embrace that very afternoon. Whatever the reasons, Juan was obviously nervous, he couldn't wait to get the hell out of there.

"Is that labyrinth still up there, do you think?" Orlando asked now, and Karina interrupted him. "We really should be on our way," she said, wondering yet one more time why her husband was unable to understand what Juan, or anybody else, for that matter, was feeling.

"Right." Orlando, bless him, picked up her cue, put his hand in his pocket, pursed his lips and then suddenly, almost as an afterthought, asked, "How about you paying for this, *mi amor*? It was your sweater, after all."

She was surprised but did not protest. It wasn't at all like Orlando, who loved to pay for things, especially food and especially when another man was present. Perhaps he didn't want Juan to feel under any obligation, thought Juan would not offer to pay himself if the offer came from a woman, particularly one as determined as Karina, so evidently used to getting her way. So while Juan watched her, she took out some bills and left a tip and then, as soon as she had risen, he stood up himself, excused himself, muttering that he also needed to be going.

"Maybe we can meet again," Karina said, because Orlando was not speaking at all, not a word, merely searching Juan's face with that frank and almost flagrant curiosity which had got Orlando into so much trouble so many times before.

"Maybe," Juan said. "But next time, I'll pay. My turn."

It was a strange good-bye, a strange ending to a strange encounter, and neither of them said a word about it as they headed to their hotel, not a word until, ten minutes later, in their room, Orlando said, in English, as soon as he locked the door behind him, "I need your calling card, quick."

She looked at him in bewilderment.

"We've got to call American Express and the banks for the Visa and MasterCard." And as she still said nothing, he added, "The cards. He stole them. Juan or whatever the fuck his name was. He stole them out of my pocket when he was cleaning me up."

She waited. She sat down on the edge of the bed.

"When did you realize it?"

"Right away. As soon as it happened."

"In that building?"

"Of course. As soon as it happened."

"How much money was there?"

"Not much. Just the cards, my driver's license, my social security card. But we're wasting time, Karina."

"And the bird shit?"

"It's paint. He must have smeared us, or maybe he has a buddy who did it in the park. Here. Smell it."

She did not accept the black sweater Orlando was holding out to her.

"And you invited him for a drink?"

Orlando let the sweater fall to the carpet and sat down next to her. He took her hand. Orlando's hand was warm, gentle, excited.

"I didn't want him to know I'd realized he was a pickpocket. He could have done anything to us, to you, in that place. I played the innocent. He also played the innocent. The one role that we would fall for. As if he could read us through and through. You've got to hand it to him. He was superb."

"It can't have been him. You must have lost the cards at the museum, when you paid for the . . . You're always—"

"It was him, all right. A real master. I hate to say it, but he almost deserves my cards."

She knew Orlando was lying. She knew he hadn't known it then, in the ugly womb of that abandoned hallway, she knew that he hadn't done it to protect her, that he had concocted this story to keep some semblance of control over an episode in which he had been duped all the way, up until the moment in the bar when he had put his hand in his pocket to pay the bill and had understood that the wallet was in Juan's pocket, next to a knife or something worse, and that Juan would not hesitate to use whatever it was in a flash, a cut across her face, a razor in her throat or his throat while the old men played cards. Then, only then, had Orlando realized what had happened.

She said, she couldn't stop herself from saying, "And you told him that story about how intelligent you were as a boy? You were playing with him . . ."

"I wanted him to know it was a matter of age," Orlando said. "I wouldn't have fallen for that sort of thing when I was younger. I mean, we've survived—what? Twenty years, twenty-five of exile?—and nothing like this has ever happened to us."

"All those countries," she said, but she was thinking of the infinite phone calls and the things Juan was charging to their account at this very moment and the forms they would have to fill in and the replacement cards and the credit checks and the endless explanations and the ruined vacations and their son and daughter and son-in-law in the States shaking their heads in wonderment and the friends in New York enjoying the story over dinner and commiserating and the visit tomorrow to American Express to get cash and the new driving license once they got back home and the new social security number and—she cut the stream of thoughts off. "A couple of Chileans being conned in Barcelona."

"I'd read about that con in the *Time Out* guide," Orlando said, standing up, going to his drawer, sifting through his address book for phone numbers. "A few weeks ago, when I was preparing our itinerary."

"You read about it?"

"They said to be wary of the bird-shit trick."

"So?"

"I forgot about it. We speak Spanish. We're survivors. It wasn't meant for us, you know, that sort of warning."

Karina smiled, but it was a weary smile. "Yes. It's supposed to happen to *gringos*."

"Maybe we're turning into *gringos*."

She too stood up. So suddenly that she surprised even herself, she said, "What am I going to do with you?"

"With me? You're the one who panicked. If you hadn't gone crazy because you thought you had a spider—"

"We're wasting time. You should be calling. Who knows what that bastard's buying right now."

"I need your calling card."

"My calling card."

"Your MCI Card. You know that I—"

"Right," she said. "One thing that poor stupid Juan didn't get. That somebody else must be using right now, trying out PIN numbers on his computer." She opened her handbag, fished inside it, took out the card, tossed it to him. It lay on the bed between them, black and shiny on the sheets. "Lately you've been forgetting everything, you know," she said.

"I know," he said.

"Just on this trip. First your medicine on the plane, then your jacket with the calling card at that restaurant in London, then your George Eliot novel on the train in Lyons. You've lost everything on this trip."

She knew what he would say next.

"Except you," he said. "Not you."

"Right," she said, picking up the card and putting it into his hand, closing his fingers over it one by one. "I'm the only thing you haven't lost."

"We're growing old," Orlando said.

He began to dial. She listened to the click of the buttons for a while before she answered him.

"Yes," she said. "We're growing old."

But she knew it wasn't true. She knew it had always been like this.

Susan Straight

El Ojo de Agua

IT WASN'T dreaming, because he wasn't in his bed and he wasn't asleep. He was in his chair, before the fire in winter, or before the screen door in summer, and it was always near midnight.

He was sleeping on the levee, during the flood of 1927, the way they had all curled in on themselves to keep warm there on the mud—even the grown men and women, if they were small and flexible. The big woman called Net couldn't sleep like that. She lay on her back, her stomach to the moon and three children tethered to her by strong fingers in their hair or an arm over their bodies. Gustave watched them in the moonlight, like animal babies angling for food.

But there was no food, after three days. They had been working in the cane when the water came like a carpet unrolling before them. They carried only their hoes and lunch buckets.

His mother had been stung by something in the field the day before. A spider? Her ankle was huge and swollen. She stayed in their room to sleep. The water erased all ten houses near Bayou Becasse, farthest from the fields.

They waited for a boat. The water stopped rising about ten feet from the top of the levee. In the daytime, all they could see was the yellow-brown water, dirty and surging up near the people. The water slapped itself in wavelets and sucked on itself in circles. An entire world was under the water.

Far away, near the edge of sight, he saw two roof spires. The church and the school. The rest of the scattered houses of Sarrat and Bayou Becasse were gone. Oak and pecan trees showed only their crowns, branches laid like veins atop the water. Snakes waited in the branches, measuring the distance to the levee.

Gustave heard the voices: "I ain't eat no snake, me. Ain't no Indian. I want some meat but not no snake." It was not a dream, yet he was not awake. He slept in his chair, upright, before the open screen door.

On the levee, he had curled himself so hard against the cold he felt his backbone bend like wet willow. Dogs and cats covered their faces with their tails, but he had nothing. Just a shirt and pants dirty from cane. No lunch. He'd been hoping to share with someone. Two men sat on boxes, keeping watch. He didn't know them. They were from another place.

They were watching for a boat, for soldiers, for someone.

Sometimes a dead pig or cow floated past. The ears so small. The hooves like gray plates.

The phone was a black cricket in the kitchen, but by the time he realized it was not a cricket, and he'd gotten up from his chair and made his way to the back, the noise stopped. Gustave watched the phone's circular dial. His daughter, Glorette, always made fun of the phone, when she was young and had gone to the houses of school friends in Rio Seco, away from where they lived in Sarrat, the place he and Enrique had made here in California. Princess phones were pink and gold, she said. Wall phones were like house slippers.

Gustave leaned on the counter near the phone, in case it rang again. It would not be Glorette. His daughter had never called him, not in the five years since her mother died. He couldn't give her anything but money, and she only wanted money to buy drugs. But her son, Victor, may have called. In the moving every three months from apartment to apartment, just ahead of eviction, and in the way Glorette lived with thieves and fools, now and then Victor was hungry and desperate. Gustave had bought him a cell phone for emergencies.

He opened the lid on the pot of beans he'd made earlier. The beans breathed when he blew on them to see if they were soft. The hard seeds of beans and rice turned into food. The corn ground into flour for bread. He thought of his mother, standing over the embers of the cook-fire, making corn bread.

His grandson used to stay for a week or so with Gustave and his wife back when he was six or seven, when things got bad. Gustave could still drive, and he'd stop by the rented house and find the boy sitting in the kitchen with his schoolbooks and paper and a mask like Mardi Gras on his face, but not a smiling mask. Only his eyes moved. His mother had been gone all night. He'd eaten Corn Pops dry in a bowl, the yellow dust clinging to his lips.

Anjolie made corn bread every night. Cush-cush in the morning, the corn mush laced with molasses. And on Saturday, beans and rice. Meat attached to a bone. Rib meat. Chicken backs. Neck bones floating like a puzzle on top of the water. His grandson would put the neck bones into his mouth and frown until Gustave said, "Fish them out with your finger, oui, they just the taste now. The meat cook down."

Victor had called three months before. He had the flu, and his mother hadn't been home in three days. He had tests in school. Gustave found the apartment called Las Palmas, and brought money and medicine. Theraflu and Advil. That was what his grandson asked for. In the cupboards, there were packets of noodles that looked like clumsy lace, and in the refrigerator there was soda. Gustave said, "Come and stay with me. Eat some meat and oranges. We get you a ride to that school, there."

His grandson lay on a mattress and said, "I'ma graduate in June. I can walk now. I'm cool, Grandpère. Thanks."

Gustave heard voices now through the open kitchen window, someone talking up the road near Enrique's house. The window was open to catch the cool night air. All the houses except Enrique's were three rooms, shotgun style, like Louisiana even though this was California. The scent of orange blossoms was stronger back here, closer to the trees. When Enrique had brought him here, in the winter of 1957, there were flowers and fruit on the trees at the same time. January. They picked the oranges the next morning and the flowers fell like white stars. Enrique said, "You can have that house, for when you bring Anjolie from Louisiana. When you marry her."

Gustave had eaten a plate of food on the porch that night, the way his own mother had at the end of a hot day when she couldn't stand being inside the two small rooms, one taken up with a stove that radiated heat, one taken up by their beds.

They used to eat their lunch in the cane field, because it was too far to walk home. They had bologna sandwiches on white bread, and his mother put seven drops of Louisiana Gold onto the pink moons of meat between the bread soggy from the heat. She put the tiny bottle back in the pocket of her work dress.

Gustave heated up a tortilla over the burner. Blue crown of flame in the dark. Black spots in a circle on the tortilla.

There were miles of groves—navel and Valencia oranges, lemons and grapefruit—around the city of Rio Seco when Enrique brought him here. The Mexicans had shown him the tortillas. When he first worked the groves, the Mexicans gave him burritos rolled tight like white pipes, hot from having lain on the truck dashboard all morning, baked by the windshield.

He ate the dry soft tortilla, tasting the burned marks. The old gas stove smelled like iron. His mother had sat beside him in the cane the day before she was stung, giving him part of her corn bread softened with cane syrup. His wife cried the first time she saw the blue flames and knew she didn't have to gauge firewood for cooking.

Gustave took a sip of rum from the tiny glass on the counter. Then he carried a handful of pistachios and stood by the screen, cracking the nuts, holding the shells in his palm. Enrique's boys were talking with some others, up at Enrique's wide porch.

The pistachios were green and pink and salty. Nothing else tasted like that. Gustave had refused to eat them the first time someone gave him a bag. A man grew them over in the next town.

When Victor came to stay with him for a few days last year, when Glorette was in the hospital with pneumonia, he would poke at the foods on the counter and say, "How you gon live on tortillas and nuts and coffee and beans?"

Gustave would say, "I made eighty, oui? I eat what I want. When you eighty, eat what you want. Cush-cush in the pot for your breakfast."

His grandson would pour sugar and milk on the hot mush and eat silently, his headphones buzzing as if insects were trapped inside his ears. When he was finished, he would say, "I ain't drinkin no coffee."

Gustave would say, "Oranges on the table. Eat one call it juice. Then I take you to that school, there."

He threw the pistachio shells into a bowl. He had never seen the boy's father. No one had.

Until he was five Gustave had known his own father, who was already dead by the time of the 1927 flood, shot in a bar fight in New Iberia. The men said his father had put his hand on a woman's rump and another man shot him.

He tried to imagine what had bitten his mother to make her ankle so swollen and red she couldn't leave her bed that morning, of the water. Bee or wasp—snakebite would have left marks. Spider? All the things in the cane field, hiding in the forest of cane stalks.

His own mother's ankle. The pigs' feet. Ham hocks. One ham hock could flavor a huge pot of beans, she said. Salted and dried and shriveled, and then floating swollen and revived on the surface of the simmering water. She'd extract every bit of flesh from the cartilage and skin and gristle.

He tried to imagine the buttocks of the woman in the bar. His father's hand on the meat. The bullet in his father's chest. His father had been twenty miles from the bayou, and no one had even known who he was. The body was kept in a morgue. A meat freezer. A man had told his mother two weeks later, but by then he'd been buried. So Gustave had to picture his father's face, frozen in a smile or shout or frown, and his hand, frozen in the shape of rounded meat, and his chest, with a small hole or large.

His own toes and tendons, when he took off the army-issued boots and lay in the field with the others. His daughter's legs, when they grew long and thin. Her dolls. The hair ornaments and beads and makeup and lotions and nail polish like spilled jewels on the dresser.

The voices floated down the dirt road toward his door. Two of Enrique's boys stood on his wooden steps. "Unc Gustave," one said, the two words flowing into one, the name they had always called him though their father was not his blood brother.

Pig blood on Enrique's hands.

"She's here," the son said. Lafayette, the older one, his forearms marked with white dried plaster. Gustave went out onto the steps.

"Glorette?" he said. There was no one else.

Lafayette lifted his chin. "Glorette. We brought her. She—"

Gustave knew. He breathed the sharp dust raised by their feet. Dry and June. No rain. The dust went inside him.

"Someone found her. Over there by the Launderland."

He closed the old screen door behind him, the hiss of the little pump latch, and they let him go first to see her body.

She lay on the couch in Enrique's big front room. Enrique's wife, Marie-Therese, was waiting for him. She was smoothing the small hairs like lace plastered down on Glorette's forehead.

His daughter was on her back. Her mouth was open. Her eyes were closed. Her hair was a tangle like black moss on the couch cushion. Her stomach showed ribs, under the bra she wore. Her skin was pale as raw pecans. She'd slept in the day and gone out in the night. She smoked the small rocks he'd seen. Like grit taken from a chicken's throat.

No blood, no marks, no cuts or bruises. Except three small black half-moons at her collarbone. Like she had scratched herself.

Gustave touched her collarbone. The knob of bone where it had healed, after she'd broken it falling from an orange tree. He couldn't touch her hair. When she was fourteen, the flesh of her body had rearranged itself, and her eyes had grown watchful under the fur of eyebrows and eyelashes. Her hair had come out of the braids and plaits his wife made every morning, and she had coated her eyelashes with crankcase oil and painted her lips, and disappeared into her room. The fear of her beauty wound its way through his entrails. That was where he'd felt it. Inside the tubes that took food through his body.

The collarbone somehow announced her beauty, and the hollow at the base of her throat.

"Some man come up to her at the store ax again do she want to model," his wife would say. "Say she kind of small, but can he take her picture." She would catch her lip between her teeth and hold it until it looked like a staple mark left there. His own wife, with skin like corn tortilla, with hair braided high on her head in a crown, with a French grandfather from Bayou Becasse. She had been hidden in her own mother's house before, when men in cars, their fingers practicing how to pull and hold, came looking for her.

He had asked his wife if she was afraid of Glorette's beauty, and she nodded. He had asked her where she felt the fear, and she said inside the bones of her hips, where Glorette had rested so long.

When Glorette left, with the man who fathered Victor and then disappeared, Gustave had gone inside her bedroom, the first one back from the front. Her Barbies sat on the windowsill, their legs dangling into the air. His wife had bought the dolls for years, saying, "All the girls have them doll. Barbie and all them clothes. Got her own closet. Got bitty hangers inside, oui."

He picked up his daughter's hand and knelt beside the couch. The skin was not soft. It was not hard. It felt smudged. She had broken her wrist, too, and he felt the bones there. He had brought home from Kmart a long piece of plastic and attached a hose so that water ran in a stream. All these children—all these grown men standing on the porch waiting for him— threw themselves down the blue furrow and screamed. The bones were so small. "Calcium collects at the site of a break," the doctor had said, his eyes avoiding Gustave's blackened hands, thick with citrus oil and dirt and rind from the navels he'd crated all day.

Marie-Therese said, "I know you, Gustave. I won't say it."

He nodded. She had been his wife's best friend. Her cousin. She wouldn't say, It's a blessing that Anjolie isn't here to see this.

But it wasn't true. Anjolie had known, the whole time, ever since Glorette had not wanted to go to school or walk to Rio Seco with the others. She was too beautiful, and no one would leave her alone.

That was how these women of Sarrat, Louisiana, had come to be here, on this land Enrique had bought in California. After the flood, when the cane was planted again and the houses had been cleaned of water trash and dead animals, and the people had come back to work, they'd had daughters. Mr. McQuine, who owned Bayou Becasse and Sarrat lands, had stalked them in the fields and dirt roads and woods. He was like a dog who'd tasted chicken blood, Enrique said.

Enrique Antoine had killed him, and Gustave had known, because Gustave had taught him everything. Ever since he fed him meat still smoking and half raw on the levee, in the dark, Gustave had taken care of Enrique. Then, Enrique had taken care of Gustave.

Now Enrique said, "Let Marie-Therese sit with her," and he took Gustave's arm as if they were married and led him toward the barn.

Enrique's sons, Lafayette and Reynaldo, had parked their truck under the big sycamore tree near the barn. Enrique and Gustave sat at the wooden table where they worked on engine parts. Gustave picked up a new air filter from the bench. Glorette had put one around her throat when she was small and said it looked like a queen collar she had seen in history class.

"How you bring her?" he asked now.

Lafayette was thirty-seven, two years older than Glorette. He said, "The truck."

"How you find her?"

Lafayette nodded to the third man, the one Gustave didn't recognize. He wasn't from Sarrat.

"I found her in the alley behind a taqueria, Mr. Picard," the man said. "I'm Sidney Chabert. My papa used to work on your refrigerators and washers."

Gustave looked at the man's dark bare chest, his ribs, a name tattooed over his heart. "Who that?"

"My daughter."

He said, "Who kill Glorette?"

Sidney squatted before him, forearms on his knees, and said quietly, "Mr. Picard. I knew Glorette way back in school. I saw her around the alley before. You know. I'm sorry." He paused for balance, and said, "I work at the video store, and I was walking home, and she was in the alley. First she was—she was waiting for some dude, looked like, near a shopping cart. Then her friend came by."

"Tall one?" Gustave said. His daughter had always run with a tall, dark, scar-faced woman, always friends with that one and never the other girls from Sarrat.

"Yeah," Sidney said. "They were talking in the alley. I mean, that woman was talking, and Glorette didn't say nothing. So maybe she was already—you know. When I went back out to the alley, no one was around, and Glorette was in the shopping cart."

"Who put her there?"

Sidney shook his head. "But I know who didn't do it. Them drug dealers didn't do it—cause they woulda just shot her, from a distance. That's how they do. They don't get up close and touch nobody. And I don't think some—customer—did it, cause he woulda left a mark. Maybe Sisia. Her friend. Maybe they had a fight. But the way Glorette looked—I think she smoked too much rock and had a heart attack."

Gustave watched Sidney rise and bend over as if he couldn't breathe himself. "Chabert. From New Orleans?"

Sidney sighed. "You know what? My papa was from New Orleans. But I'm from here. Rio Seco. We're all from here."

Gustave stared at him. Not a boy. A man. It was hard to see that sometimes. "Why you didn't call the police?"

Sidney threw back his head like he was studying the stars. But these young men didn't know the stars. Then he said, "I didn't want them to disrespect her. The way they would talk about her, poke around. They wouldn't care who killed her. So I took her to Lafayette and Reynaldo. They could take her home." He folded his arms and his daughter's name was gone. "But we could all get arrested. Me for sure. Moving a body. Suspicious. I need to get my ass home now. And I don't even know what you think."

"You touch her? Earlier?"

"Mr. Picard," Sidney said. "I always looked at Glorette. I ain't gon lie. Every brotha in Rio Seco looked at her. But I never touched her. I ain't had nothin she wanted."

Then he walked from the barnyard and headed out the narrow dirt road through the groves toward the canal, where Enrique had put a gate all those years ago. The canal bridge was the only way in or out of Sarrat, and the gate was locked. Only people who lived in Sarrat had a key.

"He gon climb out and walk back to Rio Seco," Lafayette said. "Man, that brotha was sprung on Glorette all his life, and he ain't talked to her but twice, he told me."

"Sprung?" Gustave said, watching the small figure enter the tunnel of orange trees.

"Serious love," Reynaldo finally spoke. "Like a disease."

Gustave drank some of the coffee from Enrique's old silver thermos. Sprung. That's what they called his daughter. Sprung for something that looked as inconsequential as oyster shell and entered her throat and lungs and brain to make the world look like—like what? What had that smoke done, all those years? He tasted the coffee. Dark, roasted black every morning when Marie-Therese moved the pan over the flames. The same way his wife Anjolie had done, even the week before she died. He had smelled these beans all his life. His first memory: his mother roasting the beans and putting one in her mouth, and Gustave tasting one and nearly choking at the burnt bitterness.

Enrique poured himself a cup and they waited. Gustave could hear Enrique's throat work.

Coffee beans and rice and sugar cane. What they had lived on in Louisiana.

Pig. Pig meat.

Gustave put his head down on his arms like a child, on the smooth, oily table. The smell of wood.

The woman named Net. Her body floating down the water with trees and snakes and cows and foam.

Enrique drank the last of the coffee and set his cup down so gently that Gustave heard the tap like a child's finger on the wood. The men waited. Gustave lifted his head and said, "I come right back. I try to call her boy."

He walked unsteadily to his house. He could feel himself leaning to the left. He needed a Swisher Sweet. Then the smoke would gather tears onto his face and hold them until they dried like spiderwebs on his cheeks.

The small cigar made the sounds of tiny coals glistening. Fire. The coyotes in the river bottom laughed their eerie song, so different from the night sounds of Louisiana.

The Barbie dolls sat on the windowsill with their tiny shoes, heels pointing down like needles. He hadn't wanted to live with anyone, to marry anyone, because then there would be a body someday. Enrique had known that. Gustave was near forty when Enrique told him about Anjolie, and he went to Louisiana to see her.

Now Glorette's body lay inside the house. The coyotes laughed again, maybe ten or twelve of them. What did they smell?

Night was when he'd killed the pig. He could smell the blood. The people left on the levee were starving. Meat had floated past for days, but nobody would touch it. The big woman named Net watched the babies cry and cry until the sound was like a saw rasping in the wood she cut up for a fire, and then the cries faded while their eyes grew bigger and sunk into holes in their skulls.

Skulls didn't surface until months after the water had gone down. The memory was eighty years old, and yet at night he could smell the water, and the sickly sweetness of unwashed bodies and death, and the blood in the smoke near him and Enrique. Enrique's eyes wide and flat and dull.

The soldiers had come. They pointed their rifles at the men and herded them into their boats, told them they were headed to weak points in the levee overlooking Mr. McQuine's plantation fields. They would fill sandbags all day and into the night, and then they could come back for Red Cross beans boiled with some oil and salt. That was what they left for the Negroes. That was marked on the boxes. Everyone knew what the *N* really meant.

The soldiers stood up in the boats like tall herons, one pointing his gun at Gustave's head. "That one ten or so. Worked in the field. He can work now."

The woman named Net pulled Gustave to her, next to her son Enrique. "Seven," she said. "Only seven."

The one man left behind was old, his legs thin and shiny, the skin stretched too tight over his ankle bones. He slept without moving.

The women broke up their chairs and lit the legs under the one huge pot. They waited for the men, who never came back.

The two soldiers who had stayed sat on the far end of the levee, smoking, talking to each other, their guns held loose and slanted. They'd told the women and old man not to touch the pigs, or any of the animals in the water.

Those cows and pigs and horses—Gustave knew whose they were, and so did everyone else. The men had known, before the soldiers took them away. He'd heard them talking up on the levee, with chairs and blankets and children piled around them, waiting for a barge to move them to dry ground because someone had gone past in a small pirogue and said the steamboats took only white people. The men couldn't pull out a cow still alive and bawling; they couldn't shoot a pig from the small bunch that had gathered at the far end of the levee, couldn't do the boucherie right there and feed all the people because that was stealing from Mr. McQuine or Msieu Armand, and the police would arrest them even if the animals had swum right out of their fences and would end up in the Gulf or die on the levee because no grass was left.

But the men were gone, and then the beans had been eaten and the people were hungry again. The two soldiers looked bored and afraid, but they ate something from their bags. Then they slept, sitting up, their white chins like stone in the hard moonlight off the water.

Gustave pulled the smoke deep into his lungs. The soft, soft lungs that filled with smoke, or water, or air, or nothing. The old man had died that night. When they rolled his body into a blanket and left it there near the boxes, Gustave found a hammer. He lay with it under his arm, and the next night he crept down the levee to the place where the pigs had gathered, and with the hammer he hit the small mud-covered skull of the one close to him. The pig was young, the size of a sack of rice, and it jerked and snuffled and squealed and then looked into his eyes. Black seeds. He hit and hit until the skull melted into the mud and the snuffling stopped and the other pigs screamed; he dragged the small pig behind him into the shelter of the weeds. He ran back to the levee camp and shook the huge shoulder of Antoinette.

The others just called her Net. Her apron had once been white and was now gray and brown and even red with blood, where one of her babies had a nosebleed from crying for too long. She was not soft. Her shoulder was hard like the pig's ham, the top of the leg.

Gustave said, "I seen your knife. I got a pig."

Crouched in the weeds beside him, she slit the pig's belly, and the entrails steamed until she threw them into the swaying water. Oil slicks washed past like islands of rainbow. Branches and roof shingles and sometimes a body, floating facedown, brought to the surface by the air trapped under the shirt, like pillows sewn under the cloth. Only the back and shoulders and thighs showed. Dress or coat stretched tight.

Gustave watched the ribs. Net wrenched the knife into the side meat. "Them soldiers come back, they smell smoke. Hurry."

She chopped at the soft flesh and he held up the hams that were not ham yet. Ham was pink and feathery and salty. This meat was slippery, and somehow he could see through the thin parts to the bone.

Net cradled more bloody meat in her apron and headed up the levee to the embers she had never let die since the boat had dropped them there, on the narrow rise of land that looked like a long road. Gustave had tried to walk it once when the soldiers first left, but when he looked back and couldn't see anything of the people—Net's tignon like a puff of smoke rising from her head, the old man's white handkerchief laid on his forehead—he stopped. Ahead was nothing, only the levee thin and green, drowned trees on one side and brown water sliding past near his feet.

He washed his face now, in his kitchen, and leaned over the sink. Then he got out the piece of paper from the top drawer. The ten numbers. He dialed carefully, his finger barely fitting inside the circle, the metal pinching his skin. The cricket trill of ringing. Then a voice. "Hey."

Gustave said, "Hello. Victor. This your grandpère."

Then the voice said, "Gotcha. If you getting this message, you ain't getting me. Leave me the digits and I'll get with you when I can."

He walked back toward Enrique's house. The men were still at the table, waiting for him, their own cigarettes only red embers in the dark.

Was his grandson sleeping? Hungry? Where was he? In a car? Wearing his headphones? If he woke up and his mother wasn't there, it wouldn't be the first time.

Inside the house, Marie-Therese hadn't moved. Glorette's mouth and eyes were closed. "No purse? Nothing?" he asked, and Marie-Therese shook her head.

Gustave didn't even know where she lived. No address, no license on his daughter. He looked at her bare toes, her cracked heels. She'd walked enough miles, as if she lived in another time. The men had gathered around Lafayette's truck now. If they didn't go get Victor, and no one called the police, how would he learn about his mother?

Sidney Chabert might know.

They saw him walking along the road that led back into Rio Seco, and Gustave said, "Where his shirt, now?"

Reynaldo said, "In the back. He wrapped her up in it, when he was carrying her."

As Lafayette's truck came upon Sidney, he stopped and stared straight ahead, as if at a rabbit. He was afraid they didn't believe his story. He was afraid they would kill him. Rio Seco people knew Sarrat was another world. Some of them knew how Enrique and Gustave had gotten here, about the man they'd killed in Louisiana, from the stories Sarrat daughters had told to Rio Seco fools who thought the girls were country and pretty and light skinned and dim witted.

Gustave was sitting in the truck bed, on a crate, his back to the cab. "Where she live now?" he called hoarsely to Sidney.

"Jacaranda Gardens," Sidney said. "That's what somebody told me."

"Show me where," Gustave said. "I want my grandson."

Sidney climbed into the truck bed, and Gustave threw him his shirt.

They were silent while the truck moved along the asphalt road toward the city. Only two miles. All the Sarrat children walked to school in Rio Seco along this road, and walked home, for years. Lafayette and Reynaldo had married Sarrat girls, but they lived in the city now. Only a few people were left in the ten bungalows along Gustave's street.

"You ever touch a dead body?" Sidney asked.

Gustave listened to the tires popping over fallen palm fronds. "Oui," he said. "Only one time. I was seven, and Enrique was three. Flood of 1927 come and kill everyone. Take my maman body and our house, and I never see her again. Some of us stay on the levee. High ground. About a hundred people, wait for days for a boat. Then soldiers come and take the men, say they have to work the crevasse. Where the water run into the farms. They point the gun for the men get in the boat, say, Time to work, nigger."

Sidney was silent.

"Then we have no food. We wait for the food, or the boat. One baby die, and then an old man. I touch him. We wrap him in blankets, and the baby, and we can't bury."

Enrique's head leaned against the glass of the cab window. His hair was flattened and gray. His son turned the wheel and the truck moved onto Palm Avenue, the main street, past the packinghouse where they delivered the citrus, and then into the business district, where markets and dry cleaners and taco places had darkened windows.

Gustave wanted to see the alley. Allée. A lane of trees that led to Mr. McQuine's and Msieu Armand's homes, the white homes with black shutters, behind the long allée of oaks.

"Tell Lafayette where you find her," he said, and Sidney said Spanish words to Lafayette through the cab window.

"El Ojo de Agua."

"What that say?" Gustave asked.

"The Eye of Water," Sidney said. "I don't know what it means. What they named the taqueria. Must be something from Mexico."

No shopping cart in the alley behind the taco place. The truck idled at the mouth of the dirt lane, the chain-link fence, the closed doors of buildings, the trash bin. Sidney said, "I took the cart to Sundown Liquor because I knew I'd see Lafayette and Reynaldo there."

His daughter's body floating in the cart, like a metal pirogue, down the dusty alley. His mother's body, floated from her bed to the Gulf. His father's body, buried before anyone knew who he was. His daughter, lying on the couch with Marie-Therese humming beside her, as if she were only napping. His wife, Anjolie, dead of a diabetic coma, lying in the cemetery at the edge of this Sarrat, inside the groves.

Sidney had done the right thing. The empty alley—no police would care, and the men who drive cars around the alleys to look for women like Glorette would find other women, her friend maybe, and only Victor would know.

Enrique said, "No place to die." His eyes were red and muddy when he looked at Gustave. Enrique said to Sidney, "You find her here? You ain't play with us? You ain't touch her?"

Sidney said, "I ain't lying. I found her right there." He pointed to a spot near some weeds, at the fence. "Her son came into the video store last month. Said they didn't even have a TV at his place, but he had to watch some history movie at his friend's house. I asked if he was okay, and he said you gave him a cell in case of emergency."

"I call. Nobody there."

Gustave looked up at the palms, electric in the moonlight. Sidney stared up too. He said, "You know why I took her? Cause I saw rats running across the phone wires, and I couldn't hang. No. I just took her."

Gustave said, "You did right. You take me to where she live. I tell her boy she called me, and I came and got her, and she died at home. On the couch. She just give out."

Enrique nodded. "Her heart just stop on her." He threw his cigarette butt into the dirt.

Gustave and Enrique and the others would build a coffin for Glorette, and they would dig the hole in the old cemetery where no one but Sarrat people came. Victor would say good-bye to her. The only church would be their words, the way it had been on the levee. Then Victor would sleep in her room.

Sidney took them to the Jacaranda Gardens apartment building, a few blocks away. The stucco walls were gray. The wrought iron railings were black. The windows were shuttered with old sheets and broken shades. The word PICARD was written in pen on the mail slot for number sixteen.

Gustave climbed the pebbled stairs slowly. The railing felt rough and pitted, as if someone had cooked on the iron. But he smelled no food here.

The door was flimsy when he knocked. He called softly, "Victor. Victor." But no one answered.

He pushed, and the catch on the door gave way. The lock had been broken many times. In the living room a futon lay in the corner near the heating vent. A glass-topped table and two chairs sat near the window. The Formica counter held nothing but Shasta cola and a plain paper bag. Inside were empty corn husks streaked with orange grease—tamales.

The bedroom door was closed. He went inside quietly, wondering, *What if Victor has a gun?*

But his grandson was asleep. His ears were covered with headphones, and his arms were tightly gripping something to his chest, under the blanket. Sharp corners. Maybe CD cases. A pile of books lay close to his head. The cell phone must be under his pillow, or his back, Gustave thought, and he sat down on the carpet.

A bowl beside him on the floor, a lone dried noodle like a worm trying to crawl up the side. Carpet with strands tangled and dirty like more worms. He would take Victor to his house, and Victor would hate it, and hate the oranges, and the beans. He would want hamburgers, and Gustave would buy them. He wouldn't say what he said last time. "I make my meat in fall, when Lanier bring me some pig for Marie-Therese freezer. We buy a whole pig. Not no piece of pink sponge in some plastic. Enrique and me have to have some good meat."

Net had carried the meat to her fire, laid it on a pan there, and when her baby woke she'd tied the baby to her breast, inside her shirt, to keep him quiet. But the soldiers smelled the smoke. The fat rising in the black. They came with their guns and said, "Where you get that meat? That a knife?" Net went toward them with the knife and they shot her. She fell into the water and went under, and only her broad back showed when she surfaced and floated away from the levee.

The other women screamed and screamed and the soldiers pushed at the people surging toward them. They didn't shoot again. Gustave pulled the half-burned meat from the fire and squatted near Enrique. He tore pieces from the ham and pushed them into Enrique's mouth, shielding him from the people. Enrique pulled at Gustave's hands, and he saw the blood glistening on his knuckles.

Victor's shoes, under the covers, made lumps like bread loaves. Gustave cupped his palms over his eyebrows, moving the loose skin there back and forth, like he always had when he waited, on the levee, in the barracks, in the cane fields.

His grandson slept like the dead.

Seventeen. Never had a job. Half grown. That was what the soldiers called the boys on the levee. "Take the grown ones. They don't want to come, get them half-grown niggers. They got small hands but they got two. Shovel take two hands."

He didn't want to frighten the boy. Something like seashells lay on the floor near the mattress. Gustave leaned down to touch them. When had he gone to the ocean? No—these were pistachio shells. A small bag, like you'd get at the liquor store. He held the shells in his palm. He could hear the engine of Lafayette's truck outside. He could see the palm fronds up close from this second-floor window. Dates like small gold worlds, way too high for anyone to pick.

Alice Munro

The View from Castle Rock

O N A visit to Edinburgh with his father when he is nine or ten years old, Andrew finds himself climbing the damp, uneven stone steps of the Castle. His father is in front of him, some other men behind—it's a wonder how many friends his father has found, standing in cubbyholes where there are bottles set on planks, in the High Street—until at last they crawl out on a shelf of rock, from which the land falls steeply away. It has just stopped raining, the sun is shining on a silvery stretch of water far ahead of them, and beyond that is a pale green and grayish-blue land, a land as light as mist, sucked into the sky.

"America," his father tells them, and one of the men says that you would never have known it was so near.

"It is the effect of the height we are on," another says.

"There is where every man is sitting in the midst of his own properties and even the beggars is riding around in carriages," Andrew's father says, paying no attention to them. "So there you are, my lad"—he turns to Andrew—"and God grant that one day you will see it closer, and I will myself, if I live."

Andrew has an idea that there is something wrong with what his father is saying, but he is not well enough acquainted with geography to know that they are looking at Fife. He does not know if the men are mocking his father or if his father is playing a trick on them. Or if it is a trick at all.

. . .

Some years later, in the harbor of Leith, on the fourth of June, 1818, Andrew and his father—whom I must call Old James, because there is a James in every generation—and Andrew's pregnant wife, Agnes, his brother Walter, his sister Mary, and also his son James, who is not yet two years old, set foot on board a ship for the first time in their lives.

Old James makes this fact known to the ship's officer who is checking off the names.

"The first time, serra, in all my long life. We are men of the Ettrick. It is a landlocked part of the world."

The officer says a word which is unintelligible to them but plain in meaning. *Move along*. He has run a line through their names. They move along or are pushed along, Young James riding on Mary's hip.

"What is this?" Old James says, regarding the crowd of people on deck. "Where are we to sleep? Where have all these rabble come from? Look at the faces on them—are they the blackamoors?"

"Black Highlanders, more like," Walter says. This is a joke, muttered so that his father cannot hear, Highlanders being one of the sorts the old man despises.

"There are too many people," his father continues. "The ship will sink."

"No," Walter says, speaking up now. "Ships do not often sink because of too many people. That's what the fellow was there for, to count the people."

Barely on board the vessel and this seventeen-year-old whelp has taken on knowing airs; he has taken to contradicting his father. Fatigue, astonishment, and the weight of the greatcoat he is wearing prevent Old James from cuffing him.

The business of life aboard ship has already been explained to the family. In fact, it has been explained by the old man himself. He was the one who knew all about provisions, accommodations, and the kinds of people you would find on board. All Scotsmen and all decent folk. No Highlanders, no Irish.

But now he cries out that it is like the swarm of bees in the carcass of the lion.

"An evil lot, an evil lot. Oh, that ever we left our native land."

"We have not left yet," Andrew says. "We are still looking at Leith. We would do best to go below and find ourselves a place."

More lamentation. The bunks are narrow planks with horsehair pallets that are both hard and prickly.

"Better than nothing," Andrew says.

"Oh, that ever I was enticed to bring us here, onto this floating sepulchre."

Will nobody shut him up? Agnes thinks. This is the way he will go on and on, like a preacher or a lunatic, when the fit takes him. She cannot abide it. She is in more agony herself than he is ever likely to know.

"Well, are we going to settle here or are we not?" she says.

Some people have hung up their plaids or shawls to make a half-private space for their families. She goes ahead and takes off her outer wrappings to do the same.

The child is turning somersaults in her belly. Her face is hot as a coal, her legs throb, and the swollen flesh in between them—the lips the child must soon part to get out—is a scalding sack of pain.

Her mother would have known what to do about that. She would have known which leaves to mash to make a soothing poultice. At the thought of her mother such misery overcomes her that she wants to kick somebody.

Why does Andrew not speak plainly to his father, reminding him of whose idea it was, who harangued and borrowed and begged to get them just where they are now? Andrew will not do it, Walter will only joke, and as for Mary, she can hardly get her voice out of her throat in her father's presence.

Agnes comes from a large Hawick family of weavers, who work in the mills now but worked for generations at home. Working there they learned the art of cutting one another down to size, of squabbling and surviving in close quarters. She is still surprised by the rigid manners, the deference and silences in her husband's family. She thought from the beginning that they were a queer sort and she thinks so still. They are as poor as her own folk but they have such a great notion of themselves. And what have they got to back it up?

Mary has taken Young James back up to the deck. She could tell that he was frightened down there in the half-dark. He does not have to whimper or complain—she knows his feelings by the way he digs his little knees into her.

The sails are furled tight. "Look up there, look up there," Mary says, and points to a sailor who is busy high up in the rigging. The boy on her hip makes his sound for bird—"peep." "Sailor-peep, sailor-peep," she says. She and he communicate in a half-and-half language—half her teaching and half his invention. She believes that he is one of the cleverest children ever born into the world. Being the eldest of her family, and the only girl, she has tended to all her brothers, and been proud of them all at one time, but she has never known a child like this. Nobody else has any idea how original and independent he is. Men have no interest in children so young, and Agnes, his mother, has no patience with him.

"Talk like folk," Agnes tells him, and if he doesn't she gives him a clout. "What are you?" she says. "Are you a folk or an elfit?"

Mary fears Agnes's temper, but in a way she doesn't blame her. She thinks that women like Agnes—men's women, mother women—lead an appalling life. First with what the men do to them—even as good a man as Andrew—and then with what the children do, coming out. She will never forget the way her own mother lay in bed, out of her mind with a fever, not knowing anyone, till she died, three days after Walter was born. She screamed at the black pot hanging over the fire, thinking it was full of devils.

Mary—her brothers call her "poor Mary"—is under five feet tall and has a tight little face with a lump of protruding chin, and skin that is subject to fiery eruptions that take a long time to fade. When she is spoken to, her mouth twitches as if the words were all mixed up with her spittle and her crooked teeth, and the response she manages is a dribble of speech so faint and scrambled that it is hard for people not to think her dim witted. She has great difficulty looking anybody in the eyes—even the members of her own family. It is only when she gets the boy hitched onto the narrow shelf of her hip that she is capable of some coherent and decisive speech—and then it is mostly to him.

She hears the cow bawling before she can see it. Then she looks up and sees the brown beast dangling in the air, all caged in ropes and kicking and roaring frantically. It is held by a hook on a crane, which now hauls it out of sight. People around her are hooting and clapping their hands. A child cries out, wanting to know if the cow will be dropped into the sea. A man tells him no—she will go along with them on the ship.

"Will they milk her, then?"

"Aye. Keep still. They'll milk her," the man says reprovingly. And another man's voice climbs boisterously over his.

"They'll milk her till they take the hammer to her, and then ye'll have the blood pudding for yer dinner."

Now follow the hens, swung through the air in crates, all squawking and fluttering in their confinement and pecking one another when they can, so that some feathers escape and float down through the air. And after them a pig trussed up like the cow, squealing with a human note in its distress and shifting wildly in midair, so that howls of both delight and outrage rise below, depending on whether they come from those who are hit or those who see others hit.

James is laughing, too. He recognizes shite, and cries out his own word for it, which is "gruggin."

Someday he may remember this, Mary thinks. *I saw a cow and a pig fly through the air.* Then he may wonder if it was a dream. And nobody will be there—she certainly won't—to tell him that it was not, that it happened on this ship. It's possible that he will never see a ship like this again in all his waking life. She has no idea where they will go when they reach the other shore, but she imagines that it will be someplace inland, among the hills, someplace like the Ettrick.

She does not think that she will live long, wherever they go. She coughs in the summer as well as the winter, and when she coughs her chest aches. She suffers from sties, and cramps in the stomach, and her bleeding comes rarely but may last a month when it does. She hopes, though, that she will not die while James is still in need of her, which he will be for a while yet. She knows that the time will come when he will turn away, as her brothers did, when he will become ashamed of the connection with her. At least, that is what she tells herself will happen, but like anybody in love she cannot believe it.

On a trip to Peebles, Walter bought himself a notebook to write in, but for several days he has found too much to pay attention to and too little space or quiet on the deck even to open it. Finally, after some investigating, he has discovered a favorable spot, near the cabins on the upper deck.

We came on board on the 4th day of June and lay the 5th, 6th, 7th, and 8th in the Leith roads getting the ship to a place where we could set sail, which was on the 9th. We passed the corner of Fifeshire all well nothing occurring worth mentioning till this day the 13th in the morning when we were awakened by a cry, John o'Groat's House. We could see it plain and had a fine sail across the Pentland Firth having both wind and tide in our favour and it was in no way dangerous as we had heard tell. There was a child had died, the name of Ormiston and its body was thrown overboard sewed up in a piece of canvas with a large lump of coal at its feet.

He pauses in his writing to think of the weighted sack falling down through the water. Would the piece of coal do its job, would the sack fall straight down to the very bottom of the sea? Or would the current of the sea be strong enough to keep lifting it up and letting it fall, pushing it sideways, taking it as far as Greenland or south to the tropical waters full of rank weeds, the Sargasso Sea? Or might some ferocious fish come along and rip the sack and make a meal of the body before it had even left the upper waters and the region of light?

He pictures it now—the child being eaten. Not swallowed whole as in the case of Jonah but chewed into bits as he himself would chew a tasty chunk from a boiled sheep. But there is the matter of a soul. The soul leaves the body at the moment of death. But from which part of the body does it leave? The best guess seems to be that it emerges with the last breath, having been hidden somewhere in the chest, around the place of the heart and the lungs. Though Walter has heard a joke they used to tell about an old fellow in the Ettrick, to the effect that he was so dirty that when he died his soul came out his arsehole, and was heard to do so with a mighty explosion.

This is the sort of information that preachers might be expected to give you—not mentioning anything like an arsehole, of course, but explaining something of the proper location and exit. Yet they shy away from it. Also they cannot explain—at least, he has never heard one explain—how the souls maintain themselves outside of bodies until the Day of Judgment and how on that day each one finds and recognizes the body that is its own and reunites with it, though it be not so much as a skeleton at that time. *Though it be dust.* There must be some who have studied enough to know how all this is accomplished. But there are also some—he has learned this recently—who have studied and read and thought till they have come to the conclusion that there are no souls at all. No one cares to speak about these people, either, and indeed the thought of them is terrible. How can they live with the fear—indeed, the certainty—of Hell before them?

On the third day aboard ship Old James gets up and starts to walk around. After that, he stops and speaks to anybody who seems ready to listen. He tells his name, and says that he comes from Ettrick, from the Valley and Forest of Ettrick, where the old kings of Scotland used to hunt.

"And on the field at Flodden," he says, "after the battle of Flodden, they said you could walk up and down among the corpses and pick out the men from the Ettrick, because they were the tallest and the strongest and the finest-looking men on the ground. I have five sons and they are all good strong lads, but only two of them are with me. One of my sons is in Nova Scotia. The last I heard of him he was in a place called Economy, but we have not had any word of him since and I do not know whether he is alive or dead. My eldest son went off to work in the Highlands, and the son that is next to the youngest took it into his head to go off there, too, and I will never see either of them again. Five sons and, by the mercy of God, all grew to be men, but it was not the Lord's will that I should keep them with me. A man's life is full of sorrow. I have a daughter as well, the oldest of them all, but she is nearly a dwarf. Her mother was chased by a ram when she was carrying her."

On the afternoon of the 14th a wind from the North and the ship began to shake as if every board that was in it would fly loose from every other. The buckets overflowed from the people that were sick and vomiting and there was the contents of them slipping all over the deck. All people were ordered below but many of them crumpled up against the rail and did not care if they were washed over. None of our family was sick however and now the wind has dropped and the sun has come out and those who did not care if they died in the filth a little while ago have got up and dragged themselves to be washed where the sailors are splashing buckets of water over the decks. The women are busy too washing and rinsing and wringing out all the foul clothing. It is the worst misery and the suddenest recovery I have seen ever in my life.

A young girl ten or twelve years old stands watching Walter write. She is wearing a fancy dress and bonnet and has light-brown curly hair. Not so much a pretty face as a pert one.

"Are you from one of the cabins?" she says.

Walter says, "No. I am not."

"I knew you were not. There are only four of them, and one is for my father and me and one is for the captain and one is for his mother, and she never comes out, and one is for the two ladies. You are not supposed to be on this part of the deck unless you are from one of the cabins."

"Well, I did not know that," Walter says, but does not bestir himself to move away.

"I have seen you before writing in your book."

"I haven't seen you."

"No. You were writing so you didn't notice. I haven't told anybody about you," she adds carelessly, as if that were a matter of choice and she might well change her mind.

When she leaves, Walter adds a sentence.

And this night in the year 1818 we lost sight of Scotland.

The words seem majestic to him. He is filled with a sense of grandeur, solemnity, and personal importance.

16th was a very windy day with the wind coming out of the SW the sea was running very high and the ship got her gib-boom broken on account of the violence of the wind. And our sister Agnes was taken into the cabin.

"Sister," he has written, as if she were all the same to him as poor Mary, but that is not the case. Agnes is a tall well-built girl with thick dark hair and dark eyes. The flush on one of her cheeks slides into a splotch of pale brown as big as a handprint. It is a birthmark, which people say is a pity, because without it she would be handsome. Walter can hardly bear looking at it, but this is not because it is ugly. It is because he longs to touch it, to stroke it with the tips of his fingers. It looks not like ordinary skin but like the velvet on a deer. His feelings about her are so troubling that he can speak to her only unpleasantly, if he speaks at all. And she pays him back with a good seasoning of contempt.

Agnes thinks that she is in the water and the waves are heaving her up and slamming her down. Every time they slap her down it is worse than the time before, and she sinks farther and deeper, the moment of relief passing before she can grab it, for the next wave is already gathering its power to hit her.

Then sometimes she knows that she is in a bed, a strange bed and strangely soft, but it is all the worse for that because when she sinks down there is no resistance, no hard place where the pain has to stop. People keep rushing back and forth in front of her. They are all seen sideways and all transparent, talking very fast so she can't make them out, and maliciously taking no heed of her. She sees Andrew in the midst of them, and two or three of his brothers. Some of the girls she knows are there, too— the friends she used to lark around with in Hawick. And they do not give a poor penny for the plight she is in now.

She never knew before that she had so many enemies. They are grinding her down and pretending they don't even know it. Their movement is grinding her to death.

Her mother bends over her and says in a drawling, cold, lackadaisical voice, "You are not trying, my girl. You must try harder." Her mother is all dressed up and talking fine, like some Edinburgh lady.

Evil stuff is poured into her mouth. She tries to spit it out, knowing it is poison.

I will just get up and get out of this, she thinks. She starts trying to pull herself loose from her body, as if it were a heap of rags on fire.

She hears a man's voice, giving some order. "Hold her," he says, and she is split and stretched wide open to the world and the fire.

"Ah—ah—anh," the man says, panting as if he had been running in a race.

Then a cow that is so heavy, bawling heavy with milk, rears up and sits down on Agnes's stomach.

"Now. Now," the man says, and he groans at the end of his strength as he tries to heave it off.

The fools. The fools, ever to have let it in.

> She was not better till the 18th when she was delivered of a daughter. We having a surgeon on board nothing happened. Nothing occurred till the 22nd this was the roughest day we had till then experienced. Agnes was mending in an ordinary way till the 29th we saw a great shoal of porpoises and the 30th (yesterday) was a very rough sea with the wind blowing from the west we went rather backwards than forwards.

"In the Ettrick there is what they call the highest house in Scotland," Old James says, "and the house that my grandfather lived in was a higher one than that. The name of the place is Phauhope—they call it Phaup. My grandfather was Will O'Phaup, and fifty years ago you would have heard of him if you came from any place south of the Forth and north of the Debatable Lands."

There are people who curse to see him coming, but others who are glad of any distraction. His sons hear his voice from far away, amid all the other commotion on the deck, and make tracks in the opposite direction.

For the first two or three days, Young James refused to be unfastened from Mary's hip. He was bold enough, but only if he could stay there. At night he slept in her cloak, curled up beside her, and she wakened aching along her left side, because she had lain stiffly all night so as not to disturb him. Then in the space of one morning he was down and running about and kicking at her if she tried to hoist him up.

Everything on the ship calls out for his attention. Even at night he tries to climb over her and run away in the dark. So she gets up aching not only from her position but from lack of sleep altogether. One night she drops off and the child gets loose, but most fortunately stumbles against his father's body in his bid for escape. Henceforth, Andrew insists that he be tied down every night. He howls, of course, and Andrew shakes him and cuffs him and then he sobs himself to sleep. Mary lies by him softly explaining that this is necessary so that he cannot fall off the ship into the ocean, but he regards her at these times as his enemy, and if she puts out a hand to stroke his face he tries to bite it with his baby teeth. Every night he goes to sleep in a rage, but in the morning when she unties him, still half asleep and full of his infant sweetness, he clings to her drowsily and she is suffused with love.

Then one day he is gone. She is in the line for wash water and she turns around and he is not beside her. She was just speaking a few words to the woman ahead of her, answering a question about Agnes and the infant, she had just told the woman its name—Isabel—and in that moment he got away.

Everything in an instant is overturned. The nature of the world is altered. She runs back and forth, crying out James's name. She runs up to strangers, to sailors who laugh at her as she begs them, "Have you seen a little boy? Have you seen a little boy this high, he has blue eyes?"

"I seen fifty or sixty of them like that in the last five minutes," a man says to her. A woman trying to be kind says that he will turn up, Mary should not worry herself, he will be playing with some of the other children. Some women even look about, as if they would help her search, but of course they cannot, they have their own responsibilities.

This is what Mary sees plainly in those moments of anguish: that the world which has turned into a horror for her is still the same ordinary world for all these other people and will remain so even if James has truly vanished, even if he has crawled through the ship's railings—she has noticed everywhere the places where this would be possible—and been swallowed by the ocean.

The most brutal and unthinkable of all events, to her, would seem to most others like a sad but not extraordinary misadventure. It would not be unthinkable to them.

Or to God. For in fact when God makes some rare and remarkable, beautiful human child is He not particularly tempted to take His creature back, as if the world did not deserve it?

Still, she is praying to Him all the time. At first she only called on the Lord's name. But as her search grows more specific and in some ways more bizarre—she is ducking under clotheslines that people have contrived for privacy, she thinks nothing of interrupting folk at any business, she flings up the lids of their boxes and roots in their bedclothes, not even hearing them when they curse her—her prayers also become more complicated and audacious. She tries to think of something to offer, something that could equal the value of James's being restored to her. But what does she have? Nothing of her own—not health or prospects or anybody's regard. There is no piece of luck or even a hope that she can offer to give up. What she has is James.

And how can she offer James for James?

This is what is knocking around in her head.

But what about her love of James? Her extreme and perhaps idolatrous, perhaps wicked love of another creature. She will give up that, she will give it up gladly, if only he isn't gone.

If only he can be found. If only he isn't dead.

She recalls all this an hour or two after somebody has noticed the boy peeping out from under a large empty bucket, listening to the hubbub. And she retracts her vow at once. Her understanding of God is shallow and unstable, and the truth is that, except in a time of terror such as she has just experienced, she does not really care. She has always felt that God or even the idea of Him was more distant from her than from other people. There is a stubborn indifference in her that nobody knows about. In fact, everybody may imagine that she clings secretly to religion because there is so little else available to her. They are quite wrong, and now that she has James back she gives no thanks but thinks what a fool she was and how she could not give up her love of him any more than stop her heart beating.

After that, Andrew insists that James be tied down not only by night but also by day, to the post of the bunk or to their clothesline on the deck. Andrew has trounced his son for the trick he played, but the look in James's eyes says that his tricks are not finished.

Agnes keeps asking for salt, till they begin to fear that she will fuss herself into a fever. The two women looking after her are cabin passengers, Edinburgh ladies, who took on the job out of charity.

"You be still now," they tell her. "You have no idea what a fortunate lassie you are that we had Mr. Suter on board."

They tell her that the baby was turned the wrong way inside her, and they were all afraid that Mr. Suter would have to cut her, and that might be the end of her. But he had managed to get it turned so that he could wrestle it out.

"I need salt for my milk," says Agnes, who is not going to let them put her in her place with their reproaches and their Edinburgh speech. They are idiots, anyway. She has to explain to them how you must put a little salt in the baby's first milk, just place a few grains on your finger and squeeze a drop or two of milk onto it and let the child swallow that before you put it to the breast. Without this precaution there is a good chance that it will grow up half-witted.

"Is she even a Christian?" one of them says to the other.

"I am as much as you," Agnes says. But to her own surprise and shame she starts to weep aloud, and the baby howls along with her, out of sympathy or hunger. And still she refuses to feed it.

Mr. Suter comes in to see how she is. He asks what all the grief is about, and they tell him the trouble.

"A newborn baby to get salt in its stomach—where did she get the idea?"

He says, "Give her the salt." And he stays to see her squeeze the milk on her salty finger, lay the finger to the infant's lips, and follow it with her nipple.

He asks her what the reason is and she tells him.

"And does it work every time?"

She tells him—a little surprised that he is as stupid as they are, though gentler—that it works without fail.

"So where you come from they all have their wits about them? And are all the girls strong and good-looking like you?"

She says that she would not know about that.

Sometimes visiting young men, educated men from the town, used to hang around her and her friends, complimenting them and trying to work up a conversation, and she always thought that any girl who allowed it was a fool, even if the man was handsome. Mr. Suter is far from handsome— he is too thin, and his face is badly pocked, so that at first she took him for an old fellow. But he has a kind voice, and if he is teasing her a little there is no harm in it. No man would have the nature left to deal with a woman after looking at her spread wide, her raw parts open to the air.

"Are you sore?" he asks, and she believes there is a shadow on his damaged cheeks, a slight blush rising. She says that she is no worse than she has to be, and he nods, picks up her wrist, and bows over it, strongly pressing her pulse.

"Lively as a racehorse," he says, with his hands still above her, as if he did not know where to put them next. Then he decides to push back her hair and press his fingers to her temples, as well as behind her ears.

She will recall this touch, this curious, gentle, tingling pressure, with an addled mixture of scorn and longing, for many years to come.

"Good," he says. "No sign of a fever."

He watches, for a moment, the child sucking.

"All's well with you now," he says, with a sigh. "You have a fine daughter, and she can say all her life that she was born at sea."

Andrew arrives later and stands at the foot of the bed. He has never looked on her in such a bed as this (a regular bed, even though bolted to the wall). He is red with shame in front of the ladies, who have brought in the basin to wash her.

"That's it, is it?" he says, with a nod—not a glance—at the bundle beside her.

She laughs in a vexed way and asks what did he think it was. That is all it takes to knock him off his unsteady perch, to puncture his pretense of being at ease. Now he stiffens up, even redder, doused with fire. It isn't just what she said. It is the whole scene—the smell of the infant and the milk and the blood, and most of all the basin, the cloths, the women standing by, with their proper looks that might seem to a man both admonishing and full of derision.

He looks as if he can't think of another word to say, so she has to tell him, with rough mercy, to get on his way, there's work to be done here.

Some of the girls used to say that when you finally gave in and lay down with a man—even granting he was not the man of your first choice—it gave you a helpless but calm and even sweet feeling. Agnes does not recall that she felt that with Andrew. All she felt was that he was an honest lad and the right one for her in her circumstances, and that it would never occur to him to run off and leave her.

Walter has continued to go to the same private place to write in his book and nobody has caught him there. Except the girl, of course. One day he arrives at the place and she is there before him, skipping with a red-tasselled rope. When she sees him she stops, out of breath. And no sooner does she catch her breath than she begins to cough, so that it is several minutes before she can speak. She sinks down against the pile of canvas that conceals the spot, flushed, her eyes full of bright tears from the coughing. He simply stands and watches her, alarmed at this fit but not knowing what to do.

"Do you want me to fetch one of the ladies?"

He is on speaking terms with the Edinburgh women now, on account of Agnes. They take a kind interest in the mother and baby and Mary and Young James, and think that the old father is comical. They are also amused by Andrew and Walter, who seem to them so bashful.

The coughing girl is shaking her curly head violently.

"I don't want them," she says, when she can gasp the words out. "I have never told anybody that you come here. So you mustn't tell anybody about me."

"Well, you are here by rights."

She shakes her head again and gestures for him to wait till she can speak more easily.

"I mean that you saw me skipping. My father hid my skipping rope but I found where he hid it."

"It isn't the Sabbath," Walter says reasonably. "So what is wrong with you skipping?"

"How do I know?" she says, regaining her saucy tone. "Perhaps he thinks I am too old for it. Will you swear not to tell anyone?"

What a queer, self-important little thing she is, Walter thinks. She speaks only of her father, so he thinks it likely that she has no brothers or sisters and—like himself—no mother. That condition has probably made her both spoiled and lonely.

The girl—her name is Nettie—becomes a frequent visitor when Walter tries to write in his book. She always says that she does not want to disturb him, but after keeping ostentatiously quiet for about five minutes she interrupts him with some question about his life or a bit of information about hers. It is true that she is motherless and an only child. She has never even been to school. She talks most about her pets—those dead and those living at her house in Edinburgh—and a woman named Miss Anderson, who used to travel with her and teach her. It seems that she was glad to see the back of this woman, and surely Miss Anderson, too, was glad to depart, after all the tricks that were played on her—the live frog in her boot and the woollen but lifelike mouse in her bed.

Nettie has been back and forth to America three times. Her father is a wine merchant whose business takes him to Montreal.

She wants to know all about how Walter and his people live. Her questions are, by country standards, quite impertinent. But Walter does not really mind. In his own family he has never been in a position that allowed him to instruct or teach or tease anybody younger than himself, and it gives him pleasure.

What does Walter's family have for supper when they are at home? How do they sleep? Are animals kept in the house? Do the sheep have names, and what are the sheepdogs' names, and can you make pets of them? What is the arrangement of the scholars in the schoolroom? Are the teachers cruel? What do some of his words mean that she does not understand, and do all the people where he is from talk like him?

"Oh, aye," Walter says. "Even His Majesty the duke does. The Duke of Buccleuch."

She laughs and freely pounds her little fist on his shoulder.

"Now you are teasing me. I know it. I know that dukes are not called Your Majesty. They are not."

One day she arrives with paper and drawing pencils. She says that she has brought them to keep herself busy, so she will not be a nuisance to him. She offers to teach him to draw, if he wants to learn. But his attempts make her laugh, and he deliberately does worse and worse, till she laughs so hard she has one of her coughing fits. Then she says that she will do some drawings in the back of his notebook, so that he will have them to remember the voyage by. She draws the sails up above and a hen that has somehow escaped its cage and is trying to travel like a seabird over the water. She sketches from memory her dog that died. And she makes a picture of the icebergs she saw, higher than houses, on one of her past voyages with her father. The setting sun shone through these icebergs and made them look—she says—like castles of gold. Rose-colored and gold.

Everything that she has drawn, including the icebergs, has a look that is both guileless and mocking, peculiarly expressive of herself.

"The other day I was telling you about that Will O'Phaup that was my grandfather, but there was more to him than I told you. I did not tell you that he was the last man in Scotland to speak to the fairies. It is certain that I have never heard of any other, in his time or later."

Walter is sitting around a corner, near some sailors who are mending the torn sails, but by the sounds that are made throughout the story he can guess that the out-of-sight audience is mostly women.

There is one tall well-dressed man—a cabin passenger, certainly—who has paused to listen within Walter's view. There is a figure close to this man's other side, and at one moment in the tale this figure peeps around to look at Walter and he sees that it is Nettie. She seems about to laugh, but she puts a finger to her lips as if warning herself—and Walter—to keep silent.

The man must, of course, be her father. The two of them stand there listening quietly till the tale is over. Then the man turns and speaks directly, in a familiar yet courteous way, to Walter. "Are you writing down what you can make of this?" the man asks, nodding at Walter's notebook.

Walter is alarmed, not knowing what to say. But Nettie looks at him with calming reassurance, then drops her eyes and waits beside her father as a demure little miss should.

"I am writing a journal of the voyage," Walter says stiffly.

"Now, that is interesting. That is an interesting fact, because I, too, am keeping a journal of this voyage. I wonder if we find the same things worth writing of."

"I only write what happens," Walter says, wanting to make clear that this is a job for him and not an idle pleasure. Still, he feels that some further justification is called for. "I am writing to keep track of every day so that at the end of the voyage I can send a letter home."

The man's voice is smoother and his manner gentler than any address Walter is used to. He wonders if he is being made sport of in some way. Or if Nettie's father is the sort of person who strikes up an acquaintance in the hope of getting hold of your money for some worthless investment.

Not that Walter's looks or dress would mark him out as a likely prospect.

"So you do not describe what you see? Only what, as you say, is happening?"

Walter is about to say no, and then yes. For he has just thought, if he writes that there is a rough wind, is that not describing? You do not know where you are with this kind of person.

"You are not writing about what we have just heard?"

"No."

"It might be worth it. There are people who go around now prying into every part of Scotland and writing down whatever these old country folk have to say. They think that the old songs and stories are disappearing and that they are worth recording. I don't know about that—it isn't my business. But I would not be surprised if the people who have written it all down will find that it was worth their trouble—I mean to say, there will be money in it."

Nettie speaks up unexpectedly.

"Oh, hush, Father. The old fellow is starting again."

This is not what any daughter would say to her father in Walter's experience, but the man seems ready to laugh, looking down at her fondly.

And indeed Old James's voice has been going this little while, breaking in determinedly and reproachfully on those of his audience who might have thought it was time for their own conversations.

"And still another time, but in the long days in the summer, out on the hills late in the day but before it was well dark . . ."

Walter has heard the stories his father is spouting, and others like them, all his life, but the odd thing is that until they came on board this ship he had never heard them from his father. The father he knew until a short while ago would, he is certain, have had no use for them.

"This is a terrible place we live in," his father used to say. "The people is all full of nonsense and bad habits, and even our sheep's wool is so coarse you cannot sell it. The roads are so bad a horse cannot go more than four miles an hour. And for plowing here they use the spade or the old Scotch plow, though there has been a better plow in other places for fifty years. 'Oh, aye, aye,' they say when you ask them. 'Oh, aye, but it's too steep hereabouts, the land is too heavy.'

"To be born in the Ettrick is to be born in a backward place," he would say, "where the people is all believing in old stories and seeing ghosts, and I tell you it is a curse to be born in the Ettrick."

And very likely that would lead him on to the subject of America, where all the blessings of modern invention were put to eager use and the people could never stop improving the world around them.

But hearken at him now.

"You must come up and talk to us on the deck above," Nettie's father says to Walter when Old James has finished his story. "I have business to think about and I am not much company for my daughter. She is forbidden to run around, because she is not quite recovered from the cold she had in the winter, but she is fond of sitting and talking."

"I don't believe it is the rule for me to go there," Walter says, in some confusion.

"No, no, that is no matter. My girl is lonely. She likes to read and draw, but she likes company, too. She could show you how to draw, if you like. That would add to your journal."

So they sit out in the open and draw and write. Or she reads aloud to him from her favorite book, which is *The Scottish Chiefs*. He already knows the story—who does not know about William Wallace?—but she reads smoothly and at just the proper speed and makes some things solemn and others terrifying and others comical, so that soon he is as much in thrall to the book as she is. Even though, as she says, she has read it twelve times already.

He understands a little better now why she has so many questions to ask him. He and his folk remind her of the people in her book, such people as there were out on the hills and in the valleys in the olden times. What would she think if she knew that the old fellow, the old tale-spinner spouting all over the boat and penning people up to listen as if they were sheep—what would she think if she knew that he was Walter's father?

She would be delighted, probably, more curious about Walter's family than ever. She would not look down on them, except in a way that she could not help or recognize.

> We came on the fishing bank of Newfoundland on the 12th of July and on the 19th we saw land and it was a joyful sight to us. It was a part of Newfoundland. We sailed between Newfoundland and St. Paul's Island and having a fair wind both the 18th and the 19th we found ourselves in the river on the morning of the 20th and within sight of the mainland of North America. We were awakened at about 1 o'clock in the morning and I think every passenger was out of bed at 4 o'clock gazing at the land, it being wholly covered with wood and quite a new sight to us. It was a part of Nova Scotia and a beautiful hilly country.

This is the day of wonders. The land is covered with trees like a head with hair and behind the ship the sun rises, tipping the top trees with light.

The sky is clear and shining as a china plate and the water playfully ruffled with wind. Every wisp of fog has gone and the air is full of the resinous smell of the trees. Seabirds are flashing above the sails all golden like creatures of Heaven, but the sailors fire a few shots to keep them from the rigging.

Mary holds Young James up so that he may always remember this first sight of the continent that will be his home. She tells him the name of this land—Nova Scotia.

"It means New Scotland," she says.

Agnes hears her. "Then why doesn't it say so?"

Mary says, "It's Latin, I think."

Agnes snorts with impatience. The baby was woken early by all the hubbub and celebration, and now she is miserable, wanting to be on the breast all the time, wailing whenever Agnes tries to take her off. Young James, observing all this closely, makes an attempt to get on the other breast, and Agnes bats him off so hard that he staggers.

"Suckie-laddie," Agnes calls him. He yelps a bit, then crawls around behind her and pinches the baby's toes.

Another whack.

"You're a rotten egg, you are," his mother says. "Somebody's been spoiling you till you think you're the Laird's arse."

Agnes's roused voice always makes Mary feel as if she were about to catch a blow herself.

Old James is sitting with them on the deck, but pays no attention to this domestic unrest.

"Will you come and look at the country, Father?" Mary says uncertainly. "You can have a better view from the rail."

"I can see it well enough," Old James says. Nothing in his voice suggests that the revelations around them are pleasing to him.

"Ettrick was covered with trees in the old days," he says. "The monks had it first and after that it was the Royal Forest. It was the king's forest. Beech trees, oak trees, rowan trees."

"As many trees as this?" Mary says, made bolder than usual by the novel splendors of the day.

"Better trees. Older. It was famous all over Scotland. The Royal Forest of Ettrick."

"And Nova Scotia is where our brother James is," Mary continues.

"He may be or he may not. It would be easy to die here and nobody know you were dead. Wild animals could have eaten him."

Mary wonders how her father can talk in this way, about how wild animals could have eaten his own son. Is that how the sorrows of the years take hold of you—turning your heart of flesh to a heart of stone, as it says in the old song? And if it is so, how carelessly and disdainfully might he talk about her, who never meant to him a fraction of what the boys did?

Somebody has brought a fiddle onto the deck and is tuning up to play. The people who have been hanging on to the rail and pointing out to one another what they can all see on their own—likewise repeating the name that by now everyone knows, Nova Scotia—are distracted by these sounds and begin to call for dancing. Dancing, at seven o'clock in the morning.

Andrew comes up from below, bearing their supply of water. He stands and watches for a little, then surprises Mary by asking her to dance.

"Who will look after the boy?" Agnes says immediately. "I am not going to get up and chase him." She is fond of dancing, but is prevented now not only by the nursing baby but by the soreness of the parts of her body that were so battered in the birth.

Mary is already refusing, saying she cannot go, but Andrew says, "We will put him on the tether."

"No. No," Mary says. "I've no need to dance." She believes that Andrew has taken pity on her, remembering how she used to be left on the sidelines in school games and at the dancing, though she can actually run and dance perfectly well. Andrew is the only one of her brothers capable of such consideration, but she would almost rather he behaved like the others and left her ignored as she has always been. Pity galls her.

Young James begins to complain loudly, having recognized the word "tether."

"You be still," his father says. "Be still or I'll clout you."

Then Old James surprises them all by turning his attention to his grandson.

"You. Young lad. You sit by me."

"Oh, he will not sit," Mary says. "He will run off and then you cannot chase him, Father. I will stay."

"He will sit," Old James says.

"Well, settle it," Agnes says to Mary. "Go or stay."

Young James looks from one to the other, cautiously snuffling.

"Does he not know even the simplest word?" his grandfather says. "Sit. Lad. Here."

Young James lowers himself, reluctantly, to the spot indicated.

"Now go," Old James says to Mary. And all in confusion, on the verge of tears, she is led away.

People are dancing not just in the figure of the reel but quite outside of it, all over the deck. They are grabbing anyone at all and twirling around. They are even grabbing some of the sailors, if they can get hold of them. Men dance with women, men dance with men, women dance with women, children dance with one another or all alone and without any idea of the steps, getting in the way—but everybody is in everybody's way already and it is no matter.

Mary has caught hands with Andrew and is swung around by him, then passed on to others, who bend to her and fling her undersized body about. She dances down at the level of the children, though she is less bold and carefree. In the thick of so many bodies she is helpless, she cannot pause—she has to stamp and wheel to the music or be knocked down.

"Now, you listen and I will tell you," Old James says. "This old man, Will O'Phaup, my grandfather—he was my grandfather as I am yours—Will O'Phaup was sitting outside his house in the evening, resting himself. It was mild summer weather. All alone, he was. And there was three little lads hardly bigger than you are yourself, they came around the corner of Will's house. They told him good evening. 'Good evening to you, Will O'Phaup,' they says. 'Well, good evening to you, lads. What can I do for you?' 'Can you give us a bed for the night or a place to lie down?' they says. And 'Aye,' he says. 'Aye, I'm thinking three bits of lads like yourselves should not be so hard to find room for.' And he goes into the house with them following and they says, 'And by the bye, could you give us the key, too, the big silver key that you had of us?' Well, Will looks around, and he looks for the key, till he thinks to himself, What key was that? For he knew he never had such a thing in his life. Big key or silver key, he never had it. 'What key are you talking about?' And turns himself around and they are not there. Goes out of the house, all around the house, looks to the road. No trace of them. Looks to the hills. No trace. Then Will knew it. They was no lads at all. Ah, no. They was no lads at all."

James has not made any sound. At his back is the thick and noisy wall of dancers, to the side his mother, with the small clawing beast that bites into her body. And in front of him is the old man with his rumbling voice, insistent but remote, and his blast of bitter breath.

It is the child's first conscious encounter with someone as perfectly self-centered as he is.

He is barely able to focus his intelligence, to show himself not quite defeated. "Key," he says. "Key?"

Agnes, watching the dancing, catches sight of Andrew, red in the face and heavy on his feet, linked arm to arm with various jovial women. There is not one girl whose looks or dancing gives Agnes any worries. Andrew never gives her any worries, anyway. She sees Mary tossed around, with even a flush of color in her cheeks—though she is too shy, and too short, to look anybody in the face. She sees the nearly toothless witch of a woman who birthed a child a week after her own, dancing with her hollow-cheeked man. No sore parts for her. She must have dropped the child as slick as if it were a rat, then given it to one or the other of her weedy-looking daughters to mind.

She sees Mr. Suter, the surgeon, out of breath, pulling away from a woman who would grab him, ducking through the dance and coming to greet her.

She wishes he would not. Now he will see who her father-in-law is; he may have to listen to the old fool's gabble. He will get a look at their drab, and now not even clean, country clothes. He will see her for what she is.

"So here you are," he says. "Here you are with your treasure."

It is not a word that Agnes has ever heard used to refer to a child. It seems as if he is talking to her in the way he might talk to a person of his own acquaintance, some sort of a lady, not as a doctor talks to a patient. Such behavior embarrasses her and she does not know how to answer.

"Your baby is well?" he says, taking a more down-to-earth tack. He is still catching his breath from the dancing, and his face is covered with a fine sweat.

"Aye."

"And you yourself? You have your strength again?"

She shrugs very slightly, so as not to shake the child off the nipple.

"You have a fine color, anyway. That is a good sign."

He asks then if she will permit him to sit and talk to her for a few moments, and once more she is confused by his formality but tells him that he may do as he likes.

Her father-in-law gives the surgeon—and her as well—a despising glance, but Mr. Suter does not notice it, perhaps does not even realize that the old man and the fair-haired boy who sits straight-backed facing the old man have anything to do with her.

"What will you do in Canada West?" he asks.

It seems to her the silliest question. She shakes her head—what can she say? She will wash and sew and cook and almost certainly suckle more children. Where that will be does not much matter. It will be in a house, and not a fine one.

She knows now that this man likes her, and in what way. She remembers his fingers on her skin. What harm can happen, though, to a woman with a baby at her breast? She feels stirred to show him a bit of friendliness.

"What will you do?" she says.

He smiles and says that he supposes he will go on doing what he has been trained to do, and that the people in America—so he has heard—are in need of doctors and surgeons, just like other people in the world.

"But I do not intend to get walled up in some city. I'd like to get as far as the Mississippi River, at least. Everything beyond the Mississippi used to belong to France, you know, but now it belongs to America and it is wide open—anybody can go there, except that you may run into the Indians. I would not mind that, either. Where there is fighting with the Indians, there'll be all the more need for a surgeon."

She does not know anything about this Mississippi River but she knows that Mr. Suter does not look like a fighting man himself—he does not look as if he could stand up in a quarrel with the brawling lads of Hawick, let alone red Indians.

Two dancers swing so close to them as to put a wind into their faces. It is a young girl, a child, really, whose skirts fly out—and who should she be dancing with but Agnes's brother-in-law Walter. Walter makes some sort of silly bow to Agnes and the surgeon and his father, and the girl pushes him and turns him around and he laughs at her. She is dressed like a young lady, with bows in her hair. Her face is lit up with enjoyment, her cheeks are glowing like lanterns, and she treats Walter with great familiarity, as if she had got hold of a large toy.

"That lad is your friend?" Mr. Suter says.

"No. He is my husband's brother."

The girl is laughing quite helplessly, as she and Walter—through her heedlessness—have almost knocked down another couple in the dance. She is not able to stand up for laughing, and Walter has to support her. Then it appears that she is not laughing but coughing. Walter is holding her against himself, half carrying her to the rail.

"There is one lass that will never have a child to her breast," Mr. Suter says, his eyes flitting to the sucking child before resting again on the girl. "I doubt if she will live long enough to see much of America. Does she not have anyone to look after her? She should not have been allowed to dance."

He stands up so that he can keep the girl in view as Walter holds her by the rail.

"There, she has stopped," he says. "No hemorrhaging. At least not this time."

Agnes can see that he takes a satisfaction in the verdict he has passed on this girl. And it occurs to her that this must be because of some condition of his own—that he must be thinking that he is not so bad off by comparison.

There is a cry at the rail, nothing to do with the girl and Walter. Another cry, and many people break off dancing and rush to look at the water. Mr. Suter rises and goes a few steps in that direction, following the crowd, then turns back.

"A whale," he says. "They are saying there is a whale to be seen off the side."

"You stay here!" Agnes shouts in an angry voice, and he turns to her in surprise. But he sees that her words are meant for Young James, who is on his feet.

"This is your lad, then?" Mr. Suter exclaims, as if he had made a remarkable discovery. "May I carry him over to have a look?"

And that is how Mary—happening to raise her face in the crush of passengers—beholds Young James, much amazed, being carried across the deck in the arms of a hurrying stranger, a pale and determined dark-haired man who is surely a foreigner. A child stealer, or child murderer, heading for the rail.

She gives so wild a shriek that anybody would think she was in the Devil's clutches herself, and people make way for her as they would for a mad dog.

"Stop, thief! Stop, thief!" she is crying. "Take the boy from him. Catch him. James! James! Jump down!"

She flings herself forward and grabs the child's ankles, yanking him so that he howls in fear and outrage. The man bearing him nearly topples over but doesn't give him up. He holds on and pushes at Mary with his foot.

"Take her arms," he shouts to those around them. He is short of breath. "She is in a fit."

Andrew has pushed his way in, through people who are still dancing and people who have stopped to watch the drama. He manages somehow to get hold of Mary and Young James and to make clear that one is his son and the other his sister and that it is not a question of fits.

All is shortly explained with courtesies and apologies from Mr. Suter.

"I had just stopped for a few minutes' talk with your wife, to ask her if she was well," the surgeon says. "I did not take time to bid her good-bye, so you must do it for me."

Mary remains unconvinced by the surgeon's story. Of course he would have to say to Agnes that he was taking the child to look at the whale. But that does not make it the truth. Whenever the picture of that devilish man carrying Young James flashes through her mind, and she feels in her chest the power of her own cry, she is astonished and happy. It is still her belief that she has saved him.

> We were becalmed the 21st and 22nd but we had rather more wind the 23rd but in the afternoon were all alarmed by a squall of wind accompanied by thunder and lightning which was very terrible and we had one of our mainsails that had just been mended torn to rags again with the wind. The squall lasted about 8 or 10 minutes and the 24th we had a fair wind which sent us a good way up the River, where it became more strait so that we saw land on both sides of the River. But we becalmed again till the 31st when we had a breeze only two hours.

Nettie's father's name is Mr. Carbert. Sometimes he sits and listens to Nettie read or talks to Walter. The day after the dancing, when many people are in a bad humor from exhaustion and some from drinking whiskey, and hardly anybody bothers to look at the shore, he seeks Walter out to talk to him.

"Nettie is so taken with you," he says, "that she has got the idea that you must come along with us to Montreal."

He gives an apologetic laugh, and Walter laughs, too.

"Then she must think that Montreal is in Canada West," Walter says.

"No. No. I am not making a joke. I looked out for you on purpose when she was not with me. You are a fine companion for her and it makes her happy to be with you. And I can see that you are an intelligent lad and a prudent one and one who would do well in my office."

"I am with my father and my brother," Walter says, so startled that his voice has a youthful yelp in it. "We are going to get land."

"Well, then. You are not the only son your father has. There may not be enough good land for all of you. And you may not always want to be a farmer."

Walter tells himself that this is true.

"My daughter, now, how old do you think she is?"

Walter cannot think. He shakes his head.

"She is fourteen, nearly fifteen," Nettie's father says. "You would not think so, would you? But it does not matter—that is not what I am talking about. Not about you and Nettie, anything in years to come. You understand that? There is no question of years to come. But I would like for you to come with us and let her be the child that she is and make her happy now with your company. Then I would naturally want to repay you, and there would also be work for you in the office, and if all went well you could count on advancement."

Both of them at this point notice that Nettie is coming toward them. She sticks out her tongue at Walter, so quickly that her father apparently does not notice.

"No more now. Think about it and pick your time to tell me," her father says. "But sooner rather than later would be best."

Walter does not take long to make up his mind. He knows enough to thank Mr. Carbert, but says that he has not thought of working in an office, or at any indoor job. He means to work with his family until they are set up with land to farm and then when they do not need his help so much he thinks of being a trader to the Indians, a sort of explorer. Or a miner for gold.

"As you will," Mr. Carbert says. They walk several steps together, side by side. "I must say I had thought you were rather more serious than that. Fortunately, I said nothing to Nettie."

But Nettie has not been fooled as to the subject of their talks together. She pesters her father until he has to let her know how things have gone and then she seeks out Walter.

"I will not talk to you anymore from now on," she says, in a more grown-up voice than he has ever heard from her. "It is not because I am angry but just because if I go on talking to you I will have to think all the time about how soon I'll be saying good-bye to you. But if I stop now I will have already said good-bye, so it will all be over sooner."

She spends the time that is left walking sedately with her father, in her finest clothes.

Walter feels sorry to see her—in these fine cloaks and bonnets she looks more of a child than ever, and her show of haughtiness is touching—but there is so much for him to pay attention to that he seldom thinks of her when she is out of sight.

Years will pass before she will reappear in his mind. But when she does he will find that she is a source of happiness, available to him till the day he dies. Sometimes he will even entertain himself with thoughts of what might have happened had he taken up the offer. He will imagine a radiant recovery, Nettie's acquiring a tall and maidenly body, their life together. Such foolish thoughts as a man may have in secret.

> Several boats from the land came alongside of us with fish, rum, live sheep, tobacco, etc. which they sold very high to the passengers. The 1st of August we had a slight breeze and on the morning of the 2nd we passed by the Isle of Orleans and about six in the morning we were in sight of Quebec in as good health I think as when we left Scotland. We are to sail for Montreal tomorrow in a steamboat.

> My brother Walter in the former part of this letter has written a large journal which I intend to sum up in a small ledger. We have had a very prosperous voyage being wonderfully preserved in

health. We can say nothing yet about the state of the country. There is a great number of people landing here but wages is good. I can neither advise nor discourage people from coming. The land is very extensive and very thin-peopled. I think we have seen as much land as might serve all the people in Britain uncultivated and covered with wood. We will write you again as soon as settled.

When Andrew has added this paragraph, Old James is persuaded to add his signature to those of his two sons before the letter is sealed and posted to Scotland from Quebec. He will write nothing else, saying, "What does it matter to me? It cannot be my home, it can be nothing to me but the land where I will die."

"It will be that for all of us," Andrew says. "But when the time comes we will think of it more as a home."

"Time will not be given to me to do that."

"Are you not well, Father?"

"I am well and I am not."

Young James is now paying occasional attention to the old man, sometimes stopping in front of him and looking straight into his face, with a sturdy insistence.

"He bothers me," Old James says. "I don't like the boldness of him. He will go on and on and not remember a thing of Scotland, where he was born, or the ship he travelled on. He will get to talking another language the way they do when they go to England, only it will be worse than theirs. He looks at me with the kind of look that says he knows that me and my times is all over with."

"He will remember plenty of things," Mary says. Since the dancing and the incident of Mr. Suter she has grown more forthright within the family. "And he doesn't mean his look to be bold," she says. "It is just that he is interested in everything. He understands what you say, far more than you think. He takes everything in and he thinks about it."

Her eyes fill with tears of enthusiasm, but the others look down at the child with sensible reservations.

Young James stands in the midst of them—bright-eyed, fair, and straight. Slightly preening, somewhat wary, unnaturally solemn, as if he had indeed felt descend upon him the burden of the future.

The adults, too, feel the astonishment of the moment. It is as if they had been borne for these past six weeks not on a ship but on one great wave, which has landed them with a mighty thump on this bewildering shore. Thoughts invade their heads, wheeling in with the gulls' cries, their infidel commotion.

Mary thinks that she could snatch up Young James and run away into some part of the strange city of Quebec and find work as a sewing woman (talk on the boat has made her aware that such work is in demand). Then she could bring him up all by herself, as if she were his mother.

Andrew thinks of what it would be like to be here as a free man, without wife or father or sister or children, without a single burden on his back. What could he do then? He tells himself that it is no harm, surely, it is no harm to think about it.

Agnes has heard women on the boat say that the officers you see in the street here are surely the best-looking men anywhere in the world, and that they are ten or twenty times more numerous than the women. Which must mean that you can get what you want out of them—that is, marriage. Marriage to a man with enough money that you could ride in a carriage and send presents to your mother. If you were not married already and dragged down with two children.

Walter thinks that his brother is strong and Agnes is strong—she can help him on the land while Mary cares for the children. Who ever said that he should be a farmer? When they get to Montreal he will go and attach himself to the Hudson's Bay Company and they will send him to the frontier, where he will find riches as well as adventure.

Old James has sensed defection and begins to lament openly, "How shall we sing the Lord's song in a strange land?"

These travellers lie buried—all but one of them—in the graveyard of Boston Church, in Esquesing, in Halton County, Ontario, almost within sight, and well within sound, of Highway 401, which at that spot, just a few miles from Toronto, may be the busiest road in Canada.

Old James is here. And Andrew and Agnes. Nearby is the grave of Mary, married after all and buried beside Robert Murray, her husband. Women were scarce and so were prized in the new country. She and Robert did not have any children together, but after Mary's early death he married another woman and with her he had four sons who lie here, dead at the ages of two, and three, and four, and thirteen. The second wife is here, too. Her stone says "Mother." Mary's says "Wife."

Agnes is here, having survived the births of many children. In a letter to Scotland, telling of the death of Old James in 1829 (a cancer, not much pain until near the end, though "it eat away a great part of his cheek and jaw"), Andrew mentions that his wife has been feeling poorly for the past three years. This may be a roundabout way of saying that during those years she bore her sixth, seventh, and eighth children. She must have recovered her health, for she lived into her eighties.

Andrew seems to have prospered, though he spread himself less than Walter, who married an American girl from Montgomery County, in New York State. Eighteen when she married him, thirty-three when she died after the birth of her ninth child. Walter did not marry again, but farmed successfully, educated his sons, speculated in land, and wrote letters to the government complaining about his taxes. He was able, before he died, to take a trip back to Scotland, where he had himself photographed wearing a plaid and holding a bouquet of thistles.

On the stone commemorating Andrew and Agnes there appears also the name of their daughter Isabel, who, like her mother, died an old woman.

Born at Sea.

Here, too, is the name of Andrew and Agnes's firstborn child, Isabel's elder brother.

Young James was dead within a month of the family's landing at Quebec. His name is here, but surely he cannot be. They had not yet taken up their land when he died; they had not even seen this place. He may have been buried somewhere along the way from Montreal to York or in that hectic new town itself. Perhaps in a raw temporary burying ground now paved over, perhaps without a stone in a churchyard, where other bodies would someday be laid on top of his. Dead of some mishap in the busy streets, or of a fever, or dysentery, or any of the ailments, the accidents, that were the common destroyers of little children in his time.

Reading *The O. Henry Prize Stories 2007*

The Jurors on Their Favorites

Charles D'Ambrosio on "The Room" by William Trevor

As a reader I rarely feel the need to judge the books and stories I encounter; in fact I can measure my distance from the experience of a work by counting up the opinions I hold about it. And then the writer in me reads almost entirely without opinions, I get so lost in rhythms and colors, the shape and sensation of sentences; it all feels so close to music, loosed from the material, that an opinion would only seem a kind of dross, one of the forms feeling takes as it cools and hardens over. Probably the true encounter for any reader is not through opinion but its opposite: reserving judgment, living with uncertainty, accepting the unknown, and keeping the mystery fully intact until it is absorbed by some means other than your own interfering mind. Very often the best we can do for others, and for stories, too, is to admit that we don't understand them. That's not a failure, I don't think, unless you're in the business of writing reviews or running a blog.

Each story in the collection gave me something generously—the mandarin rolling over the dust in "Djamilla" and the lovely, utterly convincing poetry of that first passage of dialogue, sung like a duet; or in "Summer, with Twins," the wonderful control of the comedy, the tension created by a surface that won't give way to depth, the author's keen accuracy in finding the echo of a cruelty in people that is also in the universe itself; or in the elegantly constructed "El Ojo de Agua," written in half-sentences that evoke the fitful mood and music of a dream and offer in turn a metaphysic for the story as a whole, as Gustave, the elderly main character, never quite manages to complete a life or wake fully to this world, remaining submerged in terror, tragedy. With regret, I can't run through the entire catalog of loves encountered along the way. The story that chose me—for that's the way it feels, as if the narrative had been lying in wait—is "The Room."

The story begins with a bluntly thematic question, the sort of thing that might cause me to hesitate. Why is it so hard to begin a story with dialogue? A weight falls on the words, forcing them into something beyond ordinary speech, and the writer risks perverting the tone in order to carry the added burden of sense—but here it works. So the line is self-consciously thematic, which in turn takes a special bravery—the question can't be resolvable—not in the story, not in the mind of the writer, not in the universe. A similar bravura move comes in the homophonously named husband, Phair. The author uses this personified abstraction, like the allegorical Envy or Despair, in a modern, postsymbolic world that won't support the one-to-one correspondences of an allegory. There's a strange atavism in the name, and I'm still trying to puzzle out how it works. It can't be simple irony, for that would be no better than an innocent, straight usage of Phair/Fair. Something of its literal bluntness weighs against the maddeningly inconclusive nature of the story. It's almost as if the name must retain all its possible suggestiveness—straight and ironic, serious and ridiculous, sly and obvious—and carry each of its canceling contradictions in order to work. Something like that—and I love it, at any rate, particularly the way it challenges the reader, warning us away from settling on a premature and simplistic understanding.

Katherine barely knows the man she's having an affair with, yet she hardly knows her husband either. Lies, and liars, still corrupt, even in this old, already corrupted world. There is a murder but the case is dismissed—the witness summoned for this most unwitnessed life proves unreliable. These are not exotic or intriguing people; their small adventures play out, one imagines, in the streets of their hometown. As familiar as the world is, everyone in this story is anonymous, deeply unknown, existing without the support of facts or validation. Katherine's trysts take place above a betting shop. Chance and circumstance form fate, and, some

God—some adhesive unifying love—is felt as an absence, though this is not an overtly religious story. Late in the story, Katherine finds herself bewildered, wondering "how she knew what she seemed to know," and yet, stripped of certainty, there is a sense in which all of these characters—Katherine and Phair, but others too—pursue deception as a means to enrich their lives. There is excitement in it, there is storytelling, the hint of narrative control. The lies lead them toward romance and yet suspend them above the truth, which makes "The Room" the saddest of love stories—a frank and somewhat brutal collision of bodies. And that's very near the thing that decided me on this story. Every time I read it I'd wait for a simple image near the end, of a barge that struggles upriver, the prow painted with roses; the author notes it twice in a short span. Something about the handling seems particularly deft, the suddenly appearing barge treated as an important symbol that, like the lives of these characters, like our own ordinary lives, can't quite approach significance.

Charles D'Ambrosio is the author of *The Point and Other Stories*, and *The Dead Fish Museum*. His fiction has appeared in *The New Yorker*, *Zoetrope: All-Story*, *The Paris Review*, *A Public Space*, and various anthologies, including *The Pushcart Prize*, *Best American Short Stories*, and *The O. Henry Prize Stories 2005*. *Orphans* is a book of his essays. D'Ambrosio lives in Portland, Oregon.

Ursula K. Le Guin on "Galveston Bay, 1826" by Eddie Chuculate

As I read these stories, I found myself asking each one: are you a literary performance or a story? Of course, I assured them, you can and should be both. But if you're only a fine, artful performance you'll fade out of my mind as I put you down; if you're a story too, I will never entirely forget you.

Many of the pieces in this book met my question bravely. Four answered it to my complete satisfaction. One of the four is about two mad, peaceable engineers dumped into the Vietnam war; another is about an old man in California who has lived his whole life just barely above floodwater; one is about a man who guards women who will not guard themselves from the men who destroy them; and then there's the one about some crazy tourists. I picked this last one to talk about, but I tell you, it was a hard pick.

"Galveston Bay, 1826" won me first, and last, by surprising me: every sentence unexpected, yet infallible. On rereading, both qualities remain.

Where are we, among these coyote mirages, this endless herd of antelope? What is this beautiful place? Is it the land of magical realism? Not exactly. It's a bit north of that. It's nearer home. It's the way things were, and aren't. So, who are these fellows we're riding with, and where are they going? War party, no? No. They're tourists, off to see the Great Lake. Like any tourists, they have to get along with semicomprehending foreigners, and their experience will be a mixture of shock, enjoyment, and endurance—a rattlesnake, a crazy dance, a huge shrimp feast, a prairie on fire. Unlike some sightseers, they accept and admire whatever they see, being perfectly secure in the knowledge of who they are themselves. And so they arrive at the end of the Earth, and have a swim there.

The tone of the narration is serene and buoyant, a rare mood at present and one that might lead a reader, thinking it accidental, to underestimate the weight and strength of the piece. Particularly in the short story, we're so used to expressivist angst that we may mistake the absence of it for triviality. In that case, Mozart might be a useful model to think of; or the quiet, understated way so many American Indians talk.

The calm, beautiful, unexplaining accuracy of description carries us right through the madness of the final adventure: "Three arrows pointing upward floated past Old Bull at eye level, followed by a limp swamp rat and Red Moon's appaloosa, upside down." And so the survivor of journey and cataclysm comes home, alone, to tell his tale—perhaps, as an old hero, to embellish it a little. The ultimate aim of the short story, like the arrow, is to end exactly where it should. In art, the satisfaction of hitting the bull's-eye is not a simple one. It goes deep.

Ursula K. Le Guin was born in 1929 in Berkeley, California. Her novel *The Left Hand of Darkness* (1969) is an American classic, and she has been honored for her fiction by the American Academy of Arts and Letters, shortlisted for the National Book Award, and has won the PEN/Malamud Award for short fiction, as well as the Nebula, Hugo, Gandalf, Pushcart, Newbery Silver Medal, and many other prizes. Her short fiction has appeared in periodicals ranging from *The New Yorker* to *Fantasy and Science Fiction*. Le Guin lives in Portland, Oregon.

Lily Tuck on "The Room" by William Trevor

"'Do you know why you are doing this?' he asked, and Katherine hesitated, then shook her head, although she did know" is how this remarkable story begins, introducing a double deception—the act of adultery and that of deceiving the lover. Or perhaps a triple one—self-deception—since the reader is right away alerted to the fact that Katherine may not really know *yet*.

Ostensibly the story is about a woman who has embarked in a rather calculating manner on a loveless affair with an unnamed man—whose own marriage is failing—in order to know what it is like to deceive. Nine years earlier, her husband, Phair, had been accused of murdering a woman he had been seeing and deceiving his wife with. Thanks in part to his wife's testimony, based on her own lie, Phair was acquitted of the crime. The couple has been living quietly with this "deception" and Katherine, the wife and the protagonist of the story, even makes the claim: "I love him more, now that I feel so sorry for him, too," a sentiment further complicated by the fact that, originally, her husband had felt sorry for her since she could not have children and the marriage would be childless. It is also a story of how Katherine has tried to be a good, loyal, loving wife, about her restraint and discretion; a story about trust, but like all good stories it is not easily reducible.

As one reads further one learns that Katherine's affair may not just be based on wanting to know what it is like to deceive but rather on a multitude of reasons that she may not understand or try to define to herself (and are only suggested to the reader): curiosity, revenge, and also idleness since she has just been fired from her job. Not only is Katherine at loose ends but she seems to be at a turning point in her life as she takes physical stock of herself in the mirror: "Her beauty was ebbing—but slowly, and there was beauty left." She also is passive and passionless; there is nothing heady or exciting about the affair. Before going home to her husband to cook their dinner, she sits in a café and drinks a latte, taking more pleasure in drinking the coffee than in anything else that had occurred that afternoon—in the sex.

The characters in this story seem to have settled into a routine of stoic acceptance and hopelessness; Katherine and her husband no longer seem to have any expectations for happiness—they are merely soldiering on. At the same time their lives, the daily domestic routines—buying and cooking food, ironing a shirt—that shore up the marriage are portrayed without cynicism and with compassion and sensitivity, particularly for Katherine.

The room rented by the nameless man, in which the affair is conducted, is central and symbolic. It is described as squalid, messy, and temporary: "cardboard boxes, suitcases open, not yet unpacked. A word processor had not been plugged in, its cables trailing on the floor . . ." The most unusual item does not belong to the man: "an anatomical study of an elephant decorated one of the walls, with arrows indicating where certain organs were beneath the leathery skin." It is of course the most telling. The room is not so much a place for sex as for emotional release; it is where Katherine suddenly feels compelled to tell her lover about the nine-year-old murder case and where she speaks of it for the first time. It is both cathartic and a test. The room is where Katherine allows herself to think about what happened in the past, about her marriage, and finally it is the place where she stops deceiving herself.

Rain, too, plays a part in the story. Rain as cleansing and as revealing: the woman who identified Phair as the murderer does so because she saw him on the stairs while she went there to shut the window when it began to rain; the rain was the excuse Phair gave the night of the murder for coming home late; likewise a rainstorm that ends the period of excessive heat finds Katherine in the café drinking her latte and lying to her husband about how she spent the afternoon. The affair lasts six months before the nameless man decides to go back to his wife, and during this time, in spite of herself, Katherine thinks back on events—the police questioning her, her husband's part, his denial of the murder and his unquestioning acceptance of her lying about what time he came home on that particular evening—that are fine examples of the author's deft handling of information in both the past and the present.

Also, inevitably during those six months, the truth will out: not necessarily the truth about whether or not Phair killed the woman but the truth about how Katherine feels about not knowing whether or not Phair killed her. The day comes when Katherine and her lover meet for what will be the last time, and after he has gone, she does not want to leave the room; instead she falls asleep for a few minutes, and when she wakes up she does not know where she is. Katherine then goes on a walk that is described as a "wasteland, it seemed like where she walked, made so not by itself but by her mood. She felt an anonymity, a solitude here where she did not belong, and something came with that which she could not identify. Oh, but it's over, she told herself . . ." And here the reader is not certain whether she is referring to the affair or to her marriage. Both probably. The ambiguity is stunning and Katherine's realization too comes with a heavy price that is applicable to both: "The best that love could do was not enough . . ."

In spare and deceptively simple prose and in an uninflected and composed tone, the author is able to evoke the fraught atmosphere of a bad marriage and to dissect unhappiness and establish a mood, a sense of place, an atmosphere of expectations or the lack of them. More impressive still and a testament to his skill, the author is able to both infuse this story with authorial knowledge and disappear as an authorial presence so that his character can achieve a certain freedom based on self-knowledge. Never does the author draw any conclusions from either Katherine's lies or her truths. Her realization occurs as a result of the reality of the story. Where—the reader cannot help but wonder—did the germ for this story come from? And how did such a seamless structure arise out of the incipient idea? How did the author capture the complexity of reality in such artful and unexpected ways and yet have it be so profoundly like life?

Born in Paris, Lily Tuck is the author of four novels: *Interviewing Matisse, or The Woman Who Died Standing Up*, *The Woman Who Walked on Water*, and *Siam, or The Woman Who Shot a Man*, which was nominated for the 2000 PEN/Faulkner Award for Fiction. Her fourth novel, *The News from Paraguay*, won the National Book Award. Her short stories have appeared in *The New Yorker* and are collected in *Limbo, and Other Places I Have Lived*. Her biography of the Italian writer Elsa Morante is forthcoming. Tuck divides her time between Maine and New York City.

Writing *The O. Henry Prize Stories 2007*

The Writers on Their Work

Andrew Foster Altschul, "A New Kind of Gravity"

When I was just out of college, I spent three summers working at a camp for emotionally and behaviorally disordered kids, mainly from New York City's poorest neighborhoods. The counselors heard story after atrocious story of abuse and neglect, saw the physical and emotional violence play itself out in hourly horrors, and then on visitors day we walked in the woods and swam in the lake with the parents, smiling and trying to sound encouraging about their children's progress. Our emotions on that day, as every other day, were grim and confusing; often the counselors would privately break down or drink ourselves to sleep that night. The question we asked ourselves, and that I suppose I've tried to ask here, is: what is the proper response to brutality?

I didn't know I wanted to write a story about it until years later, when I heard Charlie's voice on a morning when I didn't know what I was going to write. Most of the story came fairly quickly, but it was Charlie's inner life that had to be teased out over a few drafts. I still can't read it without feeling sorry for him.

Andrew Foster Altschul is a Jones Lecturer in Creative Writing at Stanford University. His short stories have appeared in *Fence*, *Swink*, *StoryQuarterly*, *One Story*, *Pleiades*, and the anthology *Best New American Voices*

2006. His first novel, *Lady Lazarus*, will be published in 2007. He lives in San Francisco.

Bay Anapol, "A Stone House"

The story began as an ode to a wonderful stone house for sale near Bisbee, Arizona, a house I fell in love with the way I used to fall in love with men—captivated by beauty and a vague feeling of destiny. Now I know enough about real estate to assume that the place probably suffered from a leaky roof or fire-ant infestation, but it remains golden in my memory, and I later uprooted it from the desert to a beach in the south of France. I think the house would have liked that.

My own mother had been dead for at least six years before I wrote this story. She had never left me alone on any beach, nor could we have afforded a Florida vacation, and, happily, I've never had a boyfriend who dated movie stars or ran with bulls. What is true in the story is the odd relief I felt in the first days after my mother's death from cancer. It took a long time before it sank in that she was gone and never coming back, and that grief is a living thing and continues evolving long past the event.

When I begin to write a story I'm never sure exactly where it will go. On the theory that I want my characters to be much more interesting than I am, I rarely write autobiographically. So at first this story was only about a stone house. The family was at war, not the country. As they battled, the house began to recede and the Nazis entered. The character of the young girl visiting the house grew up and became a character much like my real mother, although not exactly. While each of my many revisions embellished the details of her life into fiction, it also made me realize how many of those details concerned what I really wanted to know, and never would.

When I think about it now, I'm sure I wrote "A Stone House" in an effort to bring my mother back to life. I wanted to calm our stormy relationship although it had ended, and to assure her that despite our battles she was both loved and valued. A story does not have this power, but I'd like to believe that she knew everything, and so she surely knows how very much I miss her.

Bay Anapol received her M.F.A. from the University of Arkansas and is the recipient of a Wallace Stegner Fellowship, Rona Jaffe Writer's Award, Pushcart Prize, and a National Endowment for the Arts Creative Writing

Fellowship. Her work has been published in *Story*, *Michigan Quarterly Review*, and *Gulf Coast*. She lives in Santa Fe, New Mexico.

Eddie Chuculate, "Galveston Bay, 1826"

A friend, a Southern Cheyenne, told me the skeleton of this story, how one of her grandfathers and other men in the tribe had made this trip from Oklahoma to the Gulf of Mexico, and how this group had encountered a cannibalistic Indian tribe at the end of their journey. Her story had been handed down orally through generations, and I was honored and fascinated to hear it. I tried to use the material in a novel I began to write years later, but it came off flat on the page—a character simply telling the story to someone else over the course of a few paragraphs. Interesting stuff, but not necessarily riveting. I quit the novel eventually, but that story wouldn't leave me alone. I sat down—again, years later—with a blank slate, and rewrote it, using the painting *Prairie Fire* by Kiowa-Comanche artist Blackbear Bosin as inspiration for the opening. I cut the cannibalistic aspect for fear it would be read as sensationalistic, and it didn't matter to the core of the story anyway. In earlier work I felt bound by chains of autobiography, but in this refreshing departure I just let the characters live, and relied more on imagination.

Eddie Chuculate is a Creek and Cherokee Indian from Muskogee, Oklahoma, raised in the Creek and Chickasaw nations. He has published stories in *Ploughshares*, *The Iowa Review*, *Blue Mesa Review*, *Weber Studies*, and *Many Mountains Moving*. He is a graduate of the Institute of American Indian Arts in Santa Fe, New Mexico, and held a Wallace Stegner Fellowship at Stanford University. Chuculate lives in Denver, Colorado.

Rebecca Curtis, "Summer, with Twins"

I was raised Catholic, and so as a child I was inundated with a lot of Christian myths and allegories. These stories were always interesting, but many of them confused me. For example the one about the three men who are each given, by God or some god-figure (a wealthy-but-really-nice guy?), a bag of money. The first man gets the least money, the second a middle amount, and the third gets the most. They are each told that the money bag is on loan. The nice-but-wealthy guy is taking a little trip, and he wants the three men to take care of his loot while he's gone. The first guy, really wanting to make sure he doesn't lose the money, buries it under a tree. The second guy, really wanting to please the benefactor, invests it conservatively. And the third guy, having the biggest balls or something, invests it in, let's say, futures. The god-figure goes away, returns, and confronts the men. He is like, Well, guys, what have you done with my money? The first one rather timidly says, Here, Sir. I buried it under a tree. The second says, Hey, I doubled it by investing it conservatively. And the third says proudly, I quadrupled it by investing in futures!! The god-figure is furious at the first guy, mildly pleased with the second, and thrilled with the last. Now this is what I never understood: why do the guys get different amounts of money? That's not nice. Also, why is the god so angry at the first man, who did exactly what I would have done, and was only trying to make sure he'd be able to give the money back? Nothing about the story seemed fair to me. I think when I wrote "Summer, with Twins," I was trying to write my own Christian myth.

Rebecca Curtis was born in Tacoma, Washington, and grew up in New Hampshire. Her first collection of stories, *Twenty Grand and Other Tales of Love & Money*, will be published in summer 2007. Her fiction has appeared in *The New Yorker*, *Harper's*, *McSweeney's Quarterly*, and elsewhere, and she has received a Saltonstall Grant and a Rona Jaffe Writer's Award. She teaches in the graduate writing program at Columbia University. Curtis lives in Brooklyn, New York.

Ariel Dorfman, "Gringos"

A decade ago, when I was working on my novel *Konfidenz*, two characters, Karina and Orlando—only tenuously connected to the plot—kept insinuating themselves into my writing. I toyed with the idea of introducing them into a sequence contrapuntal to the plot and even went so far as to develop that man and that woman, young and madly in love, in several episodes. Finally, however, I decided that *Konfidenz* would suffer irreparably from such an addition, and so Karina and Orlando were sent off into the sad inner exile of the mind (and the more concrete back drawers or boxes) where characters emigrate when they have been denied full literary incarnation. But it is also true that fictional folk do not give up that easily. They know (they do?) that if they are passionately invented by a solitary writer and joyfully received by a community of readers, they could well outlive their progenitors. Desperate for some semblance of immortality, they lie in wait for the occasion to resurrect themselves on some page somewhere, and that is, indeed, what happened when my wife and I were involved in an incident in Barcelona many years later that cried out for a devious literary exploration. Karina and Orlando almost immediately reminded me of their existence, and suggested to me that they were the perfect couple to embody the story that was hovering in my thoughts. They insisted that this street in Barcelona was their destiny, was theirs to live abundantly and ambiguously. Are you sure you want this future for yourselves, I asked them, and they said Yes, oh yes, let us loose. I think that I ultimately agreed to Orlando and Karina's lobbying for their right to a further personification because I did not want to be trapped in a realistic rendering of what my wife and I had gone through, preferred to play with that experience as if it had not happened to me.

Readers might be interested in knowing that Orlando and Karina have generously answered, reciprocated perhaps, my faith in them. Since I completed "Gringos," I have written another story in which they appear, leading me to disinter those old manuscripts and contemplate a possible book overflowing with their misadventures and anchored by their blemished and loyal love.

Ariel Dorfman has written short stories (collected in *My House Is On Fire*) as well as novels, poems, plays, screenplays, essays, and journalism. Of Argentine-Chilean origin, he writes in both English and Spanish, and has received numerous awards, including the Lawrence Olivier for best play (*Death and the Maiden*) and two awards from the Kennedy Center. His latest books are *Desert Memories* (winner of the Lowell Thomas Award for travel writing) and *Burning City*, a novel written with his youngest son, Joaquín. He holds the Walter Hines Page Chair of Literature and Latin American Studies at Duke University.

Tony D'Souza, "Djamilla"

I really did live for an extended period in a West African village. But the story is fiction. The African girl I based Djamilla on kicked away the orange I rolled at her. So, alone in my hut, and later in California where I wrote the story, I had plenty of time to wonder, "What if she'd picked it up?"

A reader recently told me that "djamilla" means "beautiful" in Arabic. I didn't know that when I wrote the story.

Tony D'Souza was born in Chicago. His fiction and essays have appeared in *The New Yorker*, *Playboy*, *Tin House*, *Esquire*, *Salon*, *The Literary Review*, *McSweeney's Quarterly*, and elsewhere. His first novel was *Whiteman*. He received a National Endowment for the Arts Creative Writing Fellowship. From 2000 to 2003, he was a rural AIDS educator in West Africa with the Peace Corps. D'Souza lives in Sarasota, Florida.

Justine Dymond, "Cherubs"

I have long wanted to write the story of this French house that was occupied by three different armies in World War II, but it took a while for me to find the right point of view and voice. Then, in March 2003, I was infuriated by the invasion of Iraq and for some reason that anger made it all click and was the impetus for the first-person plural. I sat down and wrote the story in a week, the quickest I've ever written a short story.

Justine Dymond was born in Washington, D.C. She holds an M.F.A. in creative writing and a Ph.D. in English from the University of Massachusetts Amherst. Her fiction and poetry have appeared in *The Massachusetts Review*, *Pleiades*, *Cimarron Review*, and WomenWriters.net, among other places. Her short story "The Emigrant" won the *Briar Cliff Review* fiction prize and forms the basis for her in-progress novel of the same title. She lives in western Massachusetts.

Jan Ellison, "The Company of Men"

"The Company of Men" began with an image, plucked from memory, of a drunk and wordless boy hulking through my doorway in King's Cross with a potted plant in his arms. This scene and others, along with the setting and a number of the story's preoccupations—the blessings of oblivion and of being far from home, the indiscriminate longing to be loved, the past viewed from a distance—all this came fairly readily to the page in the first draft. But it came clumsily, when I was just beginning to write, and for five years the story was dragged through the muck of learning the craft and finding a voice. At first this learning was fixed less on invention than on reduction; it was like chipping away at a dense block of ice until a shape emerged. Along the way the story's narrator became bolder and looser—and perhaps braver—than her real-life counterpart, and the facts began to move aside to give her room.

It was during those same years that, after a decade of traveling, living alone, and pursuing a career, I was learning a new kind of life—as a wife and mother. I wrote and rewrote "The Company of Men" and other stories as I struggled to find for myself a comfortable, even a joyful place in the larger landscape of suburban motherhood. It was a long time before I could feel what that life, and what Catherine and her story, wanted: a private celebration of what is vivid and precious in memory—the people we knew, the people we were—within the borders of a laden but equally brilliant present.

Jan Ellison was raised in Los Angeles. "The Company of Men" is her first published story, and a second story has appeared in *The Hudson Review*. Ellison lives in the Bay Area.

Brian Evenson, "Mudder Tongue"

"Mudder Tongue" is one of a series of stories that I've been writing over the last few years about the relationship of children to parents, about the sorts of revolutions those relationships go through when under pressure or under stress.

After I went through a divorce several years ago, I began increasingly to wonder what my two daughters were experiencing, what sort of effect the experience was having on them, and how it was changing our relationship. This led to several stories about girls in difficult circumstances trying to figure out ways to make sense of what was going on around them. In "Mudder Tongue," the narration stays much closer to the father than to the daughter as he tries to hide his illness from her. I was most interested in the strange mix of motivations that went into his attempt to hide his illness from her and others close to him, the combination of his fear, his selfishness, his love, and his desire not to be a burden that come together in troubling and disturbing ways to lead to the final confrontation. I'd originally written past the current ending, but could never get something I was satisfied with, and felt the story needed to end at a point of tension that was also potentially a turning point, a moment that could either lead to understanding and recognition or that could intensify the terror of the situation itself.

. . .

Brian Evenson was born in Ames, Iowa, and raised in Provo, Utah. His short fiction has appeared in *The Paris Review*, *Conjunctions*, *McSweeney's Quarterly*, and *Prairie Schooner*, and he was the recipient of fellowships from the National Endowment for the Arts, Howard Foundation, and Camargo Foundation. He is the author of four collections of stories, a novella, and two novels, most recently *The Open Curtain*. He teaches creative writing at Brown University. Evenson lives in Providence, Rhode Island.

Adam Haslett, "City Visit"

The writing began, as story writing most often does for me, with a character taking in a view. In this case, a teenage boy in the back of a taxicab seeing the skyline of Manhattan for the first time as he crosses over the East River. During the three months or so that I worked on the story, I edited that first paragraph virtually every day, trying to fine-tune the rhythm of the prose to capture his initial moment of awe. The plot of the story developed as a series of answers to the questions this first image posed. Was anyone with him in the cab? (Yes, his mother.) Why were they coming to New York? (A vacation she had long promised him.) What accounted for the intensity of his desire to be in the city? (A planned assignation about which his mother knew nothing.) Each answer required further writing to develop the story and editing to prepare the ground for what came next. But wherever those developments led, the emotional key to the story remained for me the pent longing in that first look, and what would become of it.

Adam Haslett grew up in Massachusetts. He is the author of the short story collection *You Are Not a Stranger Here*, which was a finalist for the Pulitzer Prize and National Book Award. He has received fellowships from the John Simon Guggenheim Foundation and the Provincetown Fine Arts Work Center, and received the PEN/Malamud Award for short fiction. His work has appeared in *The New Yorker*, *The Atlantic Monthly*, *The Nation*, *Zoetrope: All-Story*, *The Best American Short Stories*, and on *Selected Shorts*. He lives in New York City.

Sana Krasikov, "Companion"

I began to gather the threads of this story while rereading some of my favorite nineteenth-century novels. I was intrigued by how gossip and innuendo could undercut a person's social position. I also wanted to evoke a more modern version of the shabby gentility one finds among tragic heroines—these complicated women who maintain a veneer of beauty in their daily lives, but who are still burdened by minds that prevent them from fully making their bargains. In a larger sense, I wanted Ilona's impulse toward extravagance and charm to be a counterpoint to the echoes of great devastation she's left behind.

Sana Krasikov was born in Rustavi, Georgia, and grew up in New York State. She attended the Iowa Writer's Workshop and is currently a Fulbright Fellow at the National Academy of Sciences in Moscow.

Charles Lambert, "The Scent of Cinnamon"

The story was originally conceived as an entry for the Daphne du Maurier short story competition, which meant that it had to involve a haunting. I was interested in loneliness and the need for companionship, and I started to wonder if a ghost might be enough to satisfy that need. But I also wanted to write a ghost story in which the senses played a strong part and this meant reversing both my own expectations, as a writer, and those of my reader by making ghosts that were capable of sensuality and by making the spirit world a place of heat and light. The most challenging aspect of writing the story was to both set up and conceal the ambiguity of the central event so that whoever finishes the story has to retrace, or at least rethink, what's just been read in the light of it. The strongest visual influence came from the wonderfully odd film *Mississippi Mermaid* by Truffaut.

Charles Lambert was born in England. He was among the winners of the 1997 *Independent on Sunday*/Bloomsbury Short Story Competition. Other stories have been published in various print and online magazines, including *Harrington Gay Men's Literary Quarterly*, *In Posse Review*, and *The Barcelona Review*. His novel *Fern Seed* will be published in the United Kingdom in 2008. He has lived in Italy since 1980.

Richard McCann, "The Diarist"

Most often, I've written each of my stories over a period of at least a few years, working on each obsessively until I am so confounded that I have no choice but to abandon it for later. That is, as a writer, I tend to lurch along, with quite a bit of stumbling. Certainly this was true of "The Diarist," which took me more time to complete than anything else I have ever written. Fifteen years, to be specific.

For a long time, "The Diarist" (as it's now called) consisted only of several long, descriptive recollections of the weeks my family used to spend each August in a shabby cabin in rural Pennsylvania, where my father liked to go fishing. Initially, I wanted to write about my father, who died suddenly when I was eleven, not long after returning from one of our fishing trips. But the writing was sluggish. Nothing happened.

Of course, stories are often born of unforeseen convergences. One winter afternoon, more than a dozen years after starting "The Diarist," I found myself looking again through my failed pages. As it happens, I had been thinking earlier that day about a girl's pink diary that I had seen for sale at the local five-and-dime in the months before my father's death and how I had coveted that diary so badly I couldn't stop thinking about it for weeks. I knew I'd never be able to buy it and bring it home. By that time, my parents had already begun telling me to stop playing so much with the neighbor girls and to stop talking so much with my hands.

But what might I have written in that diary, I started to wonder, if I had somehow managed to possess it? It wasn't long before I began wondering what would happen to the boy in my failed story if he somehow purchased the girl's diary that I had wanted and secretly brought it along on one of the family's fishing trips to Pennsylvania. And what if the mother didn't go with them? And what if that trip proved to be the last one, before his father's death?

What surprised me in the writing of "The Diarist" was that a story about a father and a son eventually became a story about writing itself, about the competing desires for exposure and concealment, for instance, and the ways in which the act of writing necessarily calls into existence even the most hidden and frightened of selves.

Richard McCann grew up in Silver Spring, Maryland, and he's lived in a lot of places over the years, including Germany, Spain, and Sweden. McCann is the author of *Mother of Sorrows*, a collection of linked stories, and *Ghost Letters*, a collection of poems. He is also the editor (with Michael Klein) of *Things Shaped in Passing: More "Poets for Life" Writing from the AIDS Pandemic*. His fiction, nonfiction, and poems have appeared in such magazines as *The Atlantic Monthly*, *Esquire*, *Ms.*, and *Tin House*, and in numerous anthologies, including *The Penguin Book of Gay Short Stories* and *The Best American Essays 2000*. His awards include fellowships from the John Simon Guggenheim Foundation, the National Endowment for the Arts, the Rockefeller and Fulbright foundations, and the Fine Arts Work Center in Provincetown. He is a professor in the graduate creative writing program at American University. McCann lives in Washington, D.C.

Alice Munro, "The View from Castle Rock"

My family came to Canada from Scotland in 1818, on a sailing ship. The journal is the one actually written by Walter Laidlaw and preserved by our family. The names and ages of those in the party have not been changed. The letters of "Old James" were printed in a) *Blackwood Magazine* and b) *the Colonial Advocate*. I have abridged these slightly. Old James's character and self-presentation is very well recorded by his cousin, the Scottish writer, James Hogg. It is Hogg who reports that James (perhaps drunkenly, or perversely) gets America mixed up with Fife.

This is a great deal more "reality" than I usually work with, but once I got them on board the ship, the characters took over in a way that delighted me. I don't know what they would say about my rendition of them (well, I think I have a pretty good idea of what Old James would say), but I felt privileged to know what I did know about people who were obscure and poor and had lived two centuries ago. So I thought that they—maybe even Old James, under his ranting—would forgive my invention.

Alice Munro was born in 1931 in Wingham, Ontario. Her most recent short-story collection is *The View from Castle Rock*. She is a three-time winner of the Governor General's Literary Award, the Lannan Literary Award, the WHSmith Award, and the Rea Award. Her stories have appeared in *The New Yorker*, *The Atlantic Monthly*, *The Paris Review*, and other publications, and her collections have been translated into thirteen languages. In 2006, Munro received the Edward MacDowell Medal. She divides her time between Clinton, Ontario, and Comox, British Columbia.

Yannick Murphy, "In a Bear's Eye"

When a friend of mine died there was a strange twilight period. Because she hadn't been gone for long, I could still think of her as being there. In my mind, I could still talk to her. But how could she be gone if I was still talking to her? It is this twilight period, where in it the person somehow still exists, that I wanted to render on the page.

Yannick Murphy was born in New York City and raised in Armonk, New York. She is the author of *Stories in Another Language*, *The Sea of Trees*, *Here They Come*, and *Signed, Mata Hari*, which will be published in 2007. Her stories have appeared in *McSweeney's Quarterly* and *AGNI* online. She's the author of the children's book *Ahwoooooooo!* Murphy lives in Reading, Vermont.

Christine Schutt, "The Duchess of Albany"
By way of explaining how he could turn his back on the first of two gardens, my husband once said, "The garden dies with the gardener." This was a scary notion to me, the possibility of losing both my own garden and gardener, and so began "The Duchess of Albany." I lived through the dread event with the widow and her daughters.

Christine Schutt is the author of two short story collections and a novel, *Florida*, which was a National Book Award finalist. She lives and teaches in New York City.

Joan Silber, "War Buddies"
For a while I had the vague but persistent idea that I wanted to write about the lure of solitude. I grew up with a very reclusive brother, the model for Ernst in this story, and once I began writing, I wanted to make Toby, his sidekick, a man as conflicted on the subject as I am. Vietnam provided the pressure of fear and emergency to test and mold Toby's own emotional logic. My brother (who died some years ago) spent six months as a civilian in wartime Vietnam, and I've always wanted to think about what he never spoke about.

"War Buddies" became the first part of a composite novel, currently titled "Independence." Other parts are set in Thailand, Mexico, and Sicily, as well as the United States. The experience of a wider world, and the often uncomfortable contact with history, was something I wanted to put my characters through, since the time when local knowledge was enough seems to be over.

Joan Silber is the author of *Ideas of Heaven: A Ring of Stories*, a finalist for the National Book Award and the Story Prize, and four other books of fiction, including *Household Words*, winner of a PEN/Hemingway Award. Her work was chosen for *The O. Henry Prize Stories 2003* and has appeared in *The Pushcart Prize*, *The New Yorker*, *Ploughshares*, and *The Paris Review*. She's received fellowships from the John Simon Guggenheim Foundation, National Endowment for the Arts, and the New York Foundation for the Arts. She teaches at Sarah Lawrence College. Silber lives in New York City.

Susan Straight, "El Ojo de Agua"

For thirty years, the older men of my marriage family and neighborhood have told me stories of survival, most often in Louisiana, Oklahoma, and Florida. Floods, famine, evil, and always animals. Twenty years ago, a young pregnant girl was found dead in a shopping cart on the street where I drive to work every day. Her mother said that no one, including the police, cared enough to find out how it had happened. Four years ago I started working on stories about Glorette, and the small place called Sarrat, to look at beauty and desperation and fierce loyalty. Many of the characters are descendants of the freed slave woman in my novel *A Million Nightingales*.

Susan Straight has published six novels, including *A Million Nightingales* and *Highwire Moon*, a finalist for the National Book Award. Her short fiction has won a Pushcart Prize, been published in *Zoetrope: All-Story*, *Black Clock*, *McSweeney's Quarterly*, *The Cincinnati Review*, *Story*, *Ontario Review*, and *TriQuarterly*, among other periodicals, and has been included in *The Best American Short Stories*. She was born in Riverside, California, and lives there still.

Vu Tran, "The Gift of Years"

During my first trip back to Vietnam in 1996, one of my aunts—whom I hadn't seen in sixteen years—was telling me about her husband, an awkward taciturn man who enjoyed drinking more than taking care of her and my cousins. She spoke of one drunken episode where he slapped her and she promptly slapped him back, much harder, and sent him, stunned, out of the house. At least I knew she could take care of herself. Her moment of power reversal ended up in "The Gift of Years," a story essentially about our ingrained expectations of what a woman should be and what a man should be. The expectations of the father in the story are naturally those of his culture, only his are complicated by a war, a possible murder in the family, and the beloved daughter who simply won't behave the way "normal" girls do. My aunt has none of her violent tendencies, and her marriage has turned out a little better, but the disappointment with which she told me her real-life story very much pervades this fictional one.

Vu Tran was born in Saigon in 1975 and grew up in Tulsa, Oklahoma. He is a graduate of the Iowa Writers' Workshop and was a Glenn Schaeffer Fellow at the University of Nevada, Las Vegas, where he currently teaches. His stories have appeared in *The Southern Review, Glimmer Train, Harvard Review, Michigan Quarterly Review*, and other magazines. Tran lives in Las Vegas, Nevada.

William Trevor, "The Room"
William Trevor was born in 1928 at Mitchelstown, County Cork, and spent his childhood in provincial Ireland. He has written many novels, including *Fools of Fortune, Felicia's Journey*, and most recently *The Story of Lucy Gault*. He is a renowned short story writer and has published thirteen collections, from *The Day We Got Drunk on Cake* to *A Bit on the Side*. Trevor lives in Devon, England.

Recommended Stories

David Bezmozgis, "A New Gravestone for an Old Grave," *Zoetrope: All-Story*
Jenny Burman, "The Catherine School," *Tin House*
Lilian Crutchfield, "The Depth of All Things," *Black Warrior Review*
Gary Fincke, "There's Worse," *Witness*
Joshua Furst, "Close to Home," *Conjunctions*
Joanna Hershon, "Crawl," *Tin House*
Philip Holden, "September Ghosts," *Prism International*
Keith Scribner, "Paradise in a Cup," *TriQuarterly*

Publications Submitted

Because of production deadlines for the 2008 collection, it is essential that stories reach the series editor by May 1, 2007. If a finished magazine is unavailable before the deadline, magazine editors are welcome to submit scheduled stories in proof or in manuscript. Work received after May 1, 2007, will be considered for the 2009 collection. Stories may not be submitted by agents or writers. Please see our Web site http://www. ohenryprizestories.com for more information about submission to *The O. Henry Prize Stories*.

The address for submission is:

Professor Laura Furman
The O. Henry Prize Stories
The University of Texas at Austin
English Department
1 University Station, B5000
Austin, Texas 78712

The information listed below was up-to-date as *The O. Henry Prize Stories 2007* went to press. Inclusion in the listings does not constitute endorsement or recommendation.

580 Split
Erika Staiti, Managing Editor
580 Split
Mills College
P.O. Box 9982
Oakland, CA 94613-0982
editor@580split.com
www.580split.com
Annual

A Public Space
Brigid Hughes, Editor
A Public Space
323 Dean Street
Brooklyn, New York 11217
editors@apublicspace.org
www.apublicspace.org
Quarterly

African American Review
Jocelyn Moody, Editor
African American Review
Saint Louis University
Humanities 317
3800 Lindell Boulevard
St. Louis, MO 63108
keenanam@slu.edu
aar.slu.edu
Quarterly

AGNI Magazine
Sven Birkerts, Editor
AGNI Magazine
Boston University
236 Bay State Road
Boston, MA 02215
agni@bu.edu
www.bu.edu/agni/
Semiannual

Alaska Quarterly Review
Ronald Spatz, Editor
Alaska Quarterly Review
University of Alaska Anchorage
3211 Providence Drive
Anchorage, AK 99508
aqr@uaa.alaska.edu
aqr.uaa.alaska.edu
Semiannual

Alligator Juniper
Editors
Alligator Juniper
Prescott College
220 Grove Avenue
Prescott, AZ 86301
aj@prescott.edu
www.prescott.edu/highlights/
    alligator_juniper/index.html
Annual

**American Letters and
    Commentary**
David Ray Vance and Catherine
    Kasper, Editors
American Letters and Commentary
P.O. Box 830365
San Antonio, TX 78283
AmerLetters@satx.rr.com
www.amletters.org
Annual

American Short Fiction
Stacey Swann
American Short Fiction
P.O. Box 301209
Austin, TX 78703
editors@americanshortfiction.org
americanshortfiction.org
Quarterly

**Antietam Review, A Magazine of
    Literature and Photography**
Philip Bufithis, Editor
*Antietam Review, A Magazine of
    Literature and Photography*
41 South Potomac Street
Hagerstown, MD 21740
info@washingtoncountyarts.com
www.washingtoncountyarts.com/
    antietam_review.htm
Annual

Apalachee Review
Laura Newton, Mary Jane Ryals,
    and Michael Trammel, Editors
Apalachee Review
P.O. Box 10469
Tallahassee, FL 32302
apalacheereview.org
Semiannual

Arkansas Review
Tom Williams, Editor
Arkansas Review
Department of English and
    Philosophy
Box 1890
Arkansas State University
State University, AR 72467
delta@astate.edu
www.clt.astate.edu/arkreview
Triannual

Ascent
W. Scott Olsen, Editor
Ascent
English Department
Concordia College
901 S. 8th Street
Moorhead, MN 56562
ascent@cord.edu
www.cord.edu/dept/english/
    ascent
Triannual

At Length
Jonathan Farmer, Editor
At Length
P.O. Box 594
New York, NY 10185
info@atlengthmag.com
www.atlengthmag.com
Quarterly

Backwards City Review
Editors
Backwards City Review
P.O. Box 41317
Greensboro, North Carolina
    27404-1317
editors@backwardscity.net
www.backwardscity.net
Semiannual

Bat City Review
Editors
Bat City Review
Department of English
The University of Texas at Austin
1 University Station, B5000
Austin, TX 78712
batcity@batcityreview.com
www.batcityreview.com
Annual

Bellevue Literary Review
Ronna Wineberg, J.D., Fiction
    Editor
Bellevue Literary Review
Department of Medicine, Room
    OBV-612
NYU School of Medicine
550 First Avenue
New York, NY 10016
info@BLReview.org
blreview.org
Semiannual

Black Warrior Review
Molly Dowd, Editor
Black Warrior Review
Box 862936
Tuscaloosa, Alabama 35486-0027
bwr@ua.edu
webdelsol.com/bwr
Semiannual

Bloom
Charles Flowers, Editor
Bloom
P.O. Box 1231
Old Chelsea Station
New York, NY 10011
askbloom@earthlink.net
bloommagazine.org
Semiannual

BOMB Magazine
Betsy Sussler, Editor in Chief
BOMB Magazine
80 Hanson Place
Suite 703
Brooklyn, NY 11217
info@bombsite.com
www.bombsite.com
Quarterly

**Boston Review, A Political and
Literary Forum**
Deborah Chasman and Joshua
Cohen, Editors
*Boston Review, A Political and
Literary Forum*
35 Medford Street, Suite 302
Somerville, MA 02143
review@mit.edu
www.bostonreview.net
Published six times per year

Boulevard Magazine
Richard Burgin, Editor
Boulevard Magazine
6614 Clayton Road, Box 325
Richmond Heights, MO 63117
ballymon@hotmail.com
www.richardburgin.net/
   boulevard
Triannual

Briar Cliff Review
Tricia Currans-Sheehen, Editor
Briar Cliff Review
3303 Rebecca Street
P.O. Box 2100
Sioux City, IA 51104-2100
currans@briarcliff.edu
www.briarcliff.edu/bcreview
Annual

Cairn
Lindsay Hess, Editor
Cairn
St. Andrews College
1700 Dogwood Mile
Laurinburg, NC 28352
press@sapc.edu
www.sapc.edu/sapress/index.php
Annual

Callaloo
Charles Henry Rowell, Editor
Callaloo
English Department
Texas A&M University
4227 TAMU
College Station, TX 77843-4227
callaloo@tamu.edu
xroads.virginia.edu/~public/
   callaloo/home/callaloohome.
   htm
Quarterly

**Calyx, A Journal of Art and
    Literature by Women**
Beverly McFarland, Senior Editor
*Calyx, A Journal of Art and
    Literature by Women*
P.O. Box B
Corvallis, OR 97339-0539
calyx@proaxis.com
www.proaxis.com/~calyx/
    journal.html
Semiannual

Chelsea
Alfredo de Palchi, Editor
Chelsea
P.O. Box 773
Cooper Station
New York, NY 10276-0773
www.chelseamag.org
Semiannual

Chicago Review
Joshua Kotin, Editor
Chicago Review
5801 South Kenwood Avenue
Chicago, IL 60637
chicago-review@uchicago.edu
humanities.uchicago.edu/review
Quarterly

Cimarron Review
E. P. Walkiewicz, Editor
Cimarron Review
205 Morrill Hall
English Department
Oklahoma State University
Stillwater, OK 74078
cimarronreview@yahoo.com
cimarronreview.okstate.edu
Quarterly

Colorado Review
Stephanie G'Schwind, Editor
Colorado Review
Colorado State University
Department of English
Fort Collins, CO 80523
creview@colostate.edu
coloradoreview.colostate.edu
Triannual

Confrontation
Confrontation
English Department
C. W. Post Campus of Long
    Island University
720 Northern Boulevard
Brookville, NY 11548-1300
www.liu.edu/confrontation
Semiannual

Conjunctions
Bradford Morrow, Editor
Conjunctions
21 East 10th Street
New York, NY 10003
webmaster@conjunctions.com
www.conjunctions.com
Semiannual

Crab Orchard Review
Allison Joseph, Editor
Crab Orchard Review
Southern Illinois University
   Carbondale
1000 Faner Drive
Faner Hall 2380—Mail Code
   4503
Carbondale, IL 62901
www.siu.edu/~crborchd
Semiannual

Crazyhorse
Editors
Crazyhorse
Department of English
College of Charleston
66 George Street
Charleston, SC 29424
crazyhorse@cofc.edu
crazyhorse.cofc.edu
Semiannual

**Daedalus, Journal of the
   American Academy of Arts &
   Sciences**
James Miller, Editor
*Daedalus, Journal of the American
   Academy of Arts & Sciences*
Norton's Woods
136 Irving Street
Cambridge, MA 02138
daedalus@amacad.org
www.mitpressjournals.org/page/
   editorial/daed
Quarterly

Epoch
Michael Koch, Editor
Epoch
251 Goldwin Smith Hall
Cornell University
Ithaca, NY 14853-3201
www.arts.cornell.edu/english/
   epoch.html
Triannual

Esopus
Tod Lippy, Editor
Esopus
532 Laguardia Place
#486
New York, New York 10012
info@esopusmag.com
www.esopusmag.com
Semiannual

Esquire
David Granger
Esquire
Hearst Corp.
1790 Broadway
New York, NY 10019
esquire@hearst.com
www.esquire.com
Monthly

Event
Billeh Nickerson, Editor
Event
Douglas College
P.O. Box 2503
New Westminster, British
    Columbia V3L 5B2
Canada
event@douglas.bc.ca
event.douglas.bc.ca
Triannual

Faultline
Faultline
Department of English
University of California–Irvine
Irvine, CA 92697-2650
faultline@uci.edu
www.humanities.uci.edu/faultline
Annual

Fence
Lynne Tillman, Fiction Editor
Fence
303 East Eighth Street, #B1
New York, NY 10009
fence@angel.net
www.fencemag.com
Semiannual

Five Points
Editors
Five Points
P.O. Box 3999
Atlanta, GA 30302-3999
info@langate.gsu.edu
webdelsol.com/Five_Points/
Triannual

Folio
Amina Hafiz
Folio
Department of Literature
American University
Washington, DC 20016
folio_editors@yahoo.com
www.foliojournal.org
Semiannual

Fugue
Justin Jainchill and Sara Kaplan,
    Editors
Fugue
University of Idaho
200 Brink Hall
P.O. Box 441102
Moscow, ID 83844-1102
fugue@uidaho.edu
www.uidaho.edu/fugue
Semiannual

Gargoyle
Lucinda Ebersole and Richard
    Peabody, Editors
Gargoyle
3819 North 13th Street
Arlington, VA 22291-4922
gargoyle@gargoylemagazine.com
www.gargoylemagazine.com
Annual

Glimmer Train
Susan Burmeister-Brown and
    Linda B. Swanson-Davies,
    Editors
Glimmer Train
1211 NW Glisan Street
Suite 207
Portland, OR 97209-3054
eds@glimmertrain.org
www.glimmertrain.org
Quarterly

Good Housekeeping
Ellen Levine, Editor in Chief
Good Housekeeping
Hearst Corp.
250 W. 55th St.
New York, NY 10019
www.goodhousekeeping.com
Monthly

Grain Magazine
Kent Bruyneel, Editor
Grain Magazine
P.O. Box 67
Saskatoon, Saskatchewan S7K 3KI
Canada
grainmag@sasktel.net
www.grainmagazine.ca
Quarterly

Granta
Granta
2/3 Hanover Yard
Noel Road
London N1 8BE, UK
editorial@granta.com
www.granta.com
Quarterly

Gulf Coast
Mark Doty, Executive Editor
Gulf Coast
Department of English
University of Houston
Houston, Texas 77204-3013
editors@gulfcoastmag.org
www.gulfcoastmag.org
Semiannual

Hadassah Magazine
Tom Blunt, Editor
Hadassah Magazine
50 West 58th Street
New York, NY 10019
tblunt@hadassah.org
www.hadassah.org
Monthly

Happy
Bayard, Editor
Happy
46 St. Pauls Ave.
Jersey City, NJ 07306-1623
bayardx@gmail.com
Quarterly

Harper's Magazine
Harper's Magazine
666 Broadway, 11th Floor
New York, NY 10012
www.harpers.org
Monthly

Harpur Palate
Catherine Dent, Editor
Harpur Palate
English Department
Binghamton University
P.O. Box 6000
Binghamton, NY 13902-6000
hpalate@binghamton.edu
harpurpalate.binghamton.edu/
    hphome.html
Semiannual

Harvard Review
Christina Thompson, Editor
Harvard Review
Lamont Library
Harvard University
Cambridge, MA 02138
harvard_review@harvard.edu
hcl.harvard.edu/harvardreview
Semiannual

Hayden's Ferry Review
Salima Keegan, Managing Editor
Hayden's Ferry Review
Box 875002
Arizona State University
Tempe, AZ 85287-5002
hfr@asu.edu
haydensferryreview.org
Semiannual

Hemispheres
Randy Johnson, Editor
Hemispheres
Pace Communications
1301 Carolina Street
Greensboro, NC 27401
hemiedit@aol.com
www.hemispheresmagazine.com
Monthly

Hobart
Aaron Burch, Editor
Hobart
P.O. Box 1658
Ann Arbor, MI 48103
submit@hobartpulp.com
www.hobartpulp.com
Semiannual

Hotel Amerika
David Lazar, Editor
Hotel Amerika
Department of English
360 Ellis Hall
Ohio University
Athens, OH 45701
editors@HotelAmerika.net
www.hotelamerika.net
Semiannual

Image, A Journal of the Arts & Religion
Gregory Wolfe, Editor
Image, A Journal of the Arts & Religion
3307 Third Avenue West
Seattle, WA 98119
image@imagejournal.org
www.imagejournal.org
Quarterly

Indiana Review
Tracy Truels, Editor
Indiana Review
Indiana University
Ballantine Hall 465
Bloomington, IN 47405-7103
inreview@indiana.edu
www.indiana.edu/~inreview
Semiannual

Inkwell
Alex Lindquist, Editor
Inkwell
Manhattanville College
2900 Purchase Street
Purchase, NY 10577
inkwell@mville.edu
www.inkwelljournal.org
Annual

Kalliope, A Journal of Women's Literature & Art
Dr. Margaret Clark, Editor in Chief
Kalliope, A Journal of Women's Literature & Art
Florida Community College at Jacksonville
South Campus
11901 Beach Boulevard
Jacksonville, FL 32246
maclark@fccj.edu
opencampus.fccj.org/kalliope/index.html
Semiannual

Karamu
Olga Abella, Editor
Karamu
English Department
Eastern Illinois University
Charleston, IL 61920
www.eiu.edu/~karamu
Annual

Lake Effect
George Looney, Editor in Chief
Lake Effect
Penn State Erie
5091 Station Road
Erie, PA 16563-1501
gol1@psu.edu
www.pserie.psu.edu/academic/
    hss/lakeeffect/index.html
Annual

Lorraine and James
Jasai Madden
Lorraine and James
3227 Magnolia Blvd., Suite 406
Burbank, CA 91505-2818
www.lorraineandjames.com
Triannual

Louisiana Literature
Jack Bedell, Editor
Louisiana Literature
Box 10792
Southeastern Louisiana
    University
Hammond, LA 70402
lalit@selu.edu
www.louisianaliterature.org/
    press
Semiannual

Mānoa
Frank Stewart, Editor
Mānoa
English Department
University of Hawai'i
1733 Donaghho Road
Honolulu, HI 96822
mjournal-l@hawaii.edu
www.hawaii.edu/mjournal
Semiannual

McSweeney's Quarterly
Dave Eggers, Editor
McSweeney's Quarterly
849 Valencia Street
San Francisco, CA 94110
printsubmissions@mcsweeneys.net
www.mcsweeneys.net
Quarterly

Meridian
Fiction Editor
Meridian
University of Virginia
P.O. Box 400145
Charlottesville, VA 22904-4145
meridian@virginia.edu
www.readmeridian.org
Semiannual

Michigan Quarterly Review
Laurence Goldstein, Editor
Michigan Quarterly Review
University of Michigan
3574 Rackham Building
915 East Washington Street
Ann Arbor, MI 48109-1070
MQR@umich.edu
www.umich.edu/~mqr
Quarterly

Mid-American Review
Karen Craigo, Editor
Mid-American Review
Department of English,
   Box W
Bowling Green State University
Bowling Green, OH 43403
karenka@bgnet.bgsu.edu
www.bgsu.edu/studentlife/
   organizations/
   midamericanreview
Semiannual

Ms. Magazine
Michele Kort, Senior Editor
Ms. Magazine
443 South Beverly Drive
Beverly Hills, CA 90212
mkort@msmagazine.com
www.msmagazine.com
Quarterly

**Natural Bridge, A Journal
   of Contemporary
   Literature**
John Dalton, Ruth Ellen Kocher,
   Steven Schriener, Howard
   Schwartz, Nanora Sweet, and
   Mary Troy, Editors
*Natural Bridge, A Journal of
   Contemporary Literature*
Department of English
University of Missouri–St. Louis
One University Boulevard
St. Louis, MO 63121
natural@umsl.edu
www.umsl.edu/~natural
Semiannual

New England Review
Stephen Donadio, Editor
New England Review
Middlebury College
Middlebury, VT 05753
NEReview@middlebury.edu
go.middlebury.edu/nereview
Quarterly

New Letters
Robert Stewart, Editor in Chief
New Letters
University of Missouri–Kansas
   City
5101 Rockhill Road
Kansas City, MO 64110
newletters@umkc.edu
www.newletters.org
Quarterly

New Millennium Writings
Don Williams, Editor
New Millennium Writings
P.O. Box 2463
Room M2
Knoxville, TN 37901
www.newmillenniumwritings
.com/
Annual

New Orleans Review
Christopher Chambers, Editor
New Orleans Review
Box 195
Loyola University
New Orleans, LA 70118
chambers@loyno.edu
www.loyno.edu/~noreview
Semiannual

New York Stories
Daniel Caplice Lynch, Editor in
Chief
New York Stories
English Department, E-103
La Guardia Community
College/CUNY
31-10 Thomson Avenue
Long Island City, NY 11101
nystories@lagcc.cuny.edu
www.newyorkstories.org
Triannual

NFG Magazine
Shar O'Brien, Publisher/Editor in
Chief
NFG Magazine
Sheppard Centre
P.O. Box 43112
Toronto, Ontario M2N 1E1
Canada
nfgmedia@rogers.com,
nfgmag@hotmail.com
www.nfg.ca
Triannual

Night Train Magazine
Rusty Barnes, Editor
Night Train Magazine
212 Bellingham Ave. #2
Revere, MA 02151-4106
rustybarnes@
nighttrainmagazine.com
www.nighttrainmagazine.com
Semiannual

Nimrod
Francine Ringold, Editor in Chief
Nimrod
University of Tulsa
600 South College Avenue
Tulsa, OK 74104-3189
nimrod@utulsa.edu
www.utulsa.edu/nimrod
Semiannual

Ninth Letter
Jodee Stanley, Editor
Ninth Letter
Department of English
University of Illinois, Urbana-
    Champaign
608 South Wright Street
Urbana, IL 61801
ninthletter@uiuc.edu
www.ninthletter.com
Semiannual

Noon
Diane Williams, Editor
Noon
1324 Lexington Avenue
PMB 298
New York, NY 10128
www.noonannual.com/
Annual

**North Carolina Literary
    Review**
Margaret Bauer, Editor
North Carolina Literary Review
Department of English
2201 Bate Building
East Carolina University
Greenville, NC 27858-4353
bauerm@ecu.edu
www.ecu.edu/nclr
Annual

North Dakota Quarterly
Robert W. Lewis, Editor
North Dakota Quarterly
Merrifield Hall, Room 110
276 Centennial Drive, Stop 7209
Grand Forks, ND 58202-7209
ndq@und.nodak.edu
www.und.nodak.edu/org/ndq
Quarterly

Northwest Review
John Witte, Editor
Northwest Review
1286 University of Oregon
Eugene, OR 97403
jwitte@uoregon.edu
darkwing.uoregon.edu/
    ~nwreview/
Triannual

Notre Dame Review
Editors
Notre Dame Review
804 Flanner Hall
Department of English
University of Notre Dame
Notre Dame, IN 46556
english.ndreview.1@nd.edu
www.nd.edu/~ndr/review.htm
Semiannual

One Story
Hannah Tinti, Editor
One Story
P.O. Box 150618
Brooklyn, NY 11215
questions@one-story.com
www.one-story.com
Published about every three weeks

Ontario Review
Raymond J. Smith, Editor
Ontario Review
9 Honey Brook Drive
Princeton, NJ 08540
www.ontarioreviewpress.com
Semiannual

Open City
Thomas Beller and Joanna Yas,
    Editors
Open City
270 Lafayette Street
Suite 1412
New York, NY 10012
editors@opencity.org
www.opencity.org
Triannual

Opium Magazine.print
Todd Zuniga, Founding Editor
Opium Magazine.print
161 W. 15th Street, Suite 6E
New York, NY 10011
todd@opiummagazine.com
www.opiummagazine.com
Semiannual

Orchid
Keith Hood, Editor
Orchid
P.O. Box 131457
Ann Arbor, MI 48113-1457
editors@orchidlit.org
www.orchidlit.org
Semiannual

Oyster Boy Review
Damon Sauve, Publisher
Oyster Boy Review
P.O. Box 299
Pacifica, CA 94044
email@oysterboyreview.com
www.oysterboyreview.com
Quarterly

Paper Street
Dory Adams, Editor
Paper Street
P.O. Box 14786
Pittsburgh, PA 15234-0786
editor@paperstreetpress.org
www.paperstreetpress.org
Semiannual

Parting Gifts
Robert Bixby, Editor
Parting Gifts
3413 Wilshire Drive
Greensboro, NC 27408
rbixby@earthlink.net
www.marchstreetpress.com
Semiannual

Phantasmagoria
Abigail Allen, Editor
Phantasmagoria
English Department
Century Community and
 Technical College
3300 Century Avenue North
White Bear Lake, MN 55110
Semiannual

**Phoebe, A Journal of Literature
 and Art**
Kati Fargo, Editor
*Phoebe, A Journal of Literature and
 Art*
MSN 2D6
George Mason University
4400 University Drive
Fairfax, VA 22030-4444
phoebe@gmu.edu
www.gmu.edu/pubs/phoebe
Semiannual

Pindeldyboz
Whitney Pastorek, Executive
 Editor
Pindeldyboz
23-55 38th Street
Astoria, NY 11105
editor@pindeldyboz.com
www.pindeldyboz.com

**Pleiades, A Journal of New
 Writing**
Kevin Prufer, Editor
Pleiades, A Journal of New Writing
Department of English
Central Missouri State University
Warrensburg, MO 64093
pleiades@cmsu1.cmsu.edu
www.cmsu.edu/englphil/pleiades/
Semiannual

Ploughshares
Don Lee, Editor
Ploughshares
Emerson College
120 Boylston Street
Boston, MA 02116-4624
pshares@emerson.edu
www.pshares.org
Triannual

Post Road
Mary Cotton, Managing Editor
Post Road
P.O. Box 400951
Cambridge, MA 02140
fiction@postroadmag.com
www.postroadmag.com
Semiannual, e-mail submissions
 only

Potomac Review
Julie Wakeman-Linn, Editor
Potomac Review
Montgomery College
51 Mannakee Street
Rockville, MD 20850
potomacrevieweditor@
    montgomerycollege.edu
www.montgomerycollege.edu/
    potomacreview
Annual

Prairie Fire
Andris Taskans, Editor
Prairie Fire
Artspace
423-100 Arthur Street
Winnipeg, Manitoba R3B 1H3
Canada
prfire@mts.net
www.prairiefire.ca
Quarterly

Prairie Schooner
Hilda Raz, Editor in Chief
Prairie Schooner
201 Andrews Hall
University of Nebraska
Lincoln, NE 68588-0334
kgrey2@unlnotes.unl.edu
prairieschooner.unl.edu
Quarterly

Prism International
Ben Hart, Fiction Editor
Prism International
University of British Columbia
Buchanan E-462
1866 Main Mall
Vancouver, BC V6T 1Z1
Canada
prism@interchange.ubc.ca
prism.arts.ubc.ca
Quarterly

Provincetown Arts
Christopher Busa, Editor
Provincetown Arts
P.O. Box 35
650 Commercial Street
Provincetown, MA 02657
cbusa@comcast.net
www.provincetownarts.org
Annual

Rattapallax
Ram Devineni, Editor
Rattapallax
532 LaGuardia Place, Suite 353
New York, NY 10012
info@rattapallax.com
www.rattapallax.com
Semiannual

Red Rock Review
Richard Logsdon, Editor in Chief
Red Rock Review
English Department, J2A
Community College of Southern
    Nevada
3200 East Cheyenne Avenue
North Las Vegas, NV 89030
richard_logsdon@ccsn.nevada
    .edu
www.ccsn.nevada.edu/english/
    redrockreview/index.html
Semiannual

Redivider
Chip Cheek, Editor in Chief
Redivider
Emerson College
120 Boylston Street
Boston, MA 02116
redivider_editor@yahoo.com
pages.emerson.edu/publications/
    redivider/
Semiannual

River Styx
Richard Newman, Editor
River Styx
3547 Olive Street
Suite 107
St. Louis, MO 63103-1014
bigriver@riverstyx.org
www.riverstyx.org
Triannual

Salamander
Jennifer Barber, Editor
Salamander
English Department
Suffolk University
41 Temple Street
Boston, MA 02114
media.cas.suffolk.edu/
    salamander
Semiannual

Salmagundi
Robert Boyers, Editor in Chief
Salmagundi
Skidmore College
815 North Broadway
Saratoga Springs, NY 12866
pboyers@skidmore.edu
www.skidmore.edu/salmagundi
Quarterly

Santa Monica Review
Andrew Tonkovich, Editor
Santa Monica Review
Santa Monica College
1900 Pico Boulevard
Santa Monica, CA 90405
antonkovi@uci.edu
www.smc.edu/sm_review
Semiannual

Shenandoah
R. T. Smith, Editor
Shenandoah
Mattingly House
2 Lee Avenue
Washington and Lee University
Lexington, VA 24450-2116
shenandoah@wlu.edu
shenandoah.wlu.edu
Triannual

Small Spiral Notebook
Felicia C. Sullivan, Editor
Small Spiral Notebook
172 5th Avenue
Suite 104
Brooklyn, NY 11217
editor@smallspiralnotebook.com
www.smallspiralnotebook.com
Semiannual

Sonora Review
Editors
Sonora Review
English Department
University of Arizona
Tucson, AZ 85721
sonora@email.arizona.edu
www.coh.arizona.edu/Sonora
Semiannual

Southern Humanities Review
Editors
Southern Humanities Review
9088 Haley Center
Auburn University
Auburn, AL 36849
shrengl@auburn.edu
www.auburn.edu/english/shr/
home.htm
Quarterly

Southern Indiana Review
Ron Mitchell, Managing Editor
Southern Indiana Review
College of Liberal Arts
University of Southern Indiana
8600 University Boulevard
Evansville, IN 47712
sir@usi.edu
www.southernindianareview.org
Semiannual

Southwest Review
Willard Spiegelman, Editor in
Chief
Southwest Review
Southern Methodist University
P.O. Box 750374
Dallas, Texas 75275-0374
swr@mail.smu.edu
www.southwestreview.org
Quarterly

St. Anthony Messenger
Pat McCloskey, O.F.M., Editor
St. Anthony Messenger
28 West Liberty Street
Cincinnati, OH 45202-6498
samadmin@americancatholic.org
www.americancatholic.org
Monthly

StoryQuarterly
M.M.M. Hayes and Will Hayes,
    Co-editors
StoryQuarterly
431 Sheridan Road
Kenilworth, IL 60043
storyquarterly@yahoo.com
www.storyquarterly.com
Annual, online submissions only

Subtropics
David Leavitt, Editor
Subtropics
P.O. Box 112075
4008 Turlington Hall
University of Florida
Gainesville, FL 32611
www.english.ufl.edu/subtropics
Triannual

Tampa Review
Richard Mathews, Editor
Tampa Review
University of Tampa
401 West Kennedy Boulevard
Tampa, FL 33606-1490
utpress@ut.edu
tampareview.ut.edu
Semiannual

The Antioch Review
Robert S. Fogarty, Editor
The Antioch Review
P.O. Box 148
Yellow Springs, Ohio 45387
review@antioch.edu
www.review.antioch.edu
Quarterly

The Atlantic Monthly
C. Michael Curtis, Senior Fiction
    Editor
The Atlantic Monthly
The Watergate
600 New Hampshire Ave, N.W.
Washington, DC 20037
letters@theatlantic.com
www.theatlantic.com
Annual Fiction Issue

The Baltimore Review
Susan Muaddi Darraj, Managing
    Editor
The Baltimore Review
P.O. Box 36418
Towson, Maryland 21286
www.baltimorereview.org
Semiannual

The Carolina Quarterly
Elena Oxman, Editor
The Carolina Quarterly
Greenlaw Hall CB# 3520
University of North Carolina
Chapel Hill, NC 27599-3520
cquarter@unc.edu
www.unc.edu/depts/cqonline
Triannual

The Chariton Review
Jim Barnes, Editor
The Chariton Review
821 Camino de Jemez
Santa Fe, New Mexico 87501
Semiannual

The Cincinnati Review
Brock Clarke, Editor
The Cincinnati Review
University of Cincinnati
McMicken Hall, Room 369
P.O. Box 210069
Cincinnati, OH 45221-0069
editors@cincinnatireview.com
cincinnatireview.com
Semiannual

The Fiddlehead
Ross Leckie, Editor
The Fiddlehead
University of New Brunswick
P.O. Box 4400
Campus House, 11 Garland
    Court
Fredericton, New Brunswick
    E3B 5A3
Canada
fiddlehd@unb.ca
www.lib.unb.ca/Texts/Fiddlehead
Quarterly

The First Line
David LaBounty and Jeff Adams,
    Editors
The First Line
P.O. Box 250382
Plano, TX 75025-0382
info@thefirstline.com
www.thefirstline.com
Quarterly

The Florida Review
Jeanne M. Leiby, Editor
The Florida Review
Department of English
P.O. Box 161346
University of Central Florida
Orlando, FL 32816
flreview@mail.ucf.edu
www.flreview.com
Semiannual

The Frostproof Review
Kyle Minor, Editor
The Frostproof Review
P.O. Box 21013
Columbus, OH 43221
editor@frostproofreview.com
www.frostproofreview.com
Annual

The Georgia Review
Stephen Corey, Acting Editor
The Georgia Review
University of Georgia
Athens, GA 30606-9009
scorey@uga.edu, garev@uga.edu
www.uga.edu/garev
Quarterly

The Gettysburg Review
Peter Stitt, Editor
The Gettysburg Review
Gettysburg College
Gettysburg, PA 17325
pstitt@gettysburg.edu
www.gettysburg.edu/academics/
    gettysburg_review
Quarterly

The Hudson Review
Paula Deitz, Editor
The Hudson Review
684 Park Avenue
New York, NY 10021
www.hudsonreview.com
Quarterly

The Idaho Review
Mitch Wieland, Editor
    in Chief
The Idaho Review
Boise State University
Department of English
1910 University Drive
Boise, ID 83725
english.boisestate.edu/
    idahoreview/
Annual

The Iowa Review
David Hamilton, Editor
The Iowa Review
308 EPB
University of Iowa
Iowa City, IA 52242-1492
iowareview.org
Triannual

The Journal
Michelle Herman, Fiction
    Editor
The Journal
Department of English
Ohio State University
164 West 17th Avenue
Columbus, OH 43210
thejournal@osu.edu
english.OSU.edu/research/
    journals/thejournal/default
    .cfm
Semiannual

The Kenyon Review
David H. Lynn, Editor
The Kenyon Review
Kenyon College
Walton House
Gambier, OH 43022
kenyonreview@kenyon.edu
www.kenyonreview.org
Quarterly

The Land-Grant College Review
Dave Koch and Josh Melrod,
    Editors
The Land-Grant College Review
P.O. Box 1164
New York, NY 10159
editors@lgcr.org
www.land-grantcollegereview.com/
Semiannual

The Literary Review
René Steinke, Editor in Chief
The Literary Review
285 Madison Avenue
Madison, NJ 07940
tlr@fdu.edu
www.theliteraryreview.org
Quarterly

The Malahat Review
John Barton, Editor
The Malahat Review
University of Victoria
P.O. Box 1700
STN CSC
Victoria, British Columbia
    V8W 2Y2
Canada
malahat@uvic.ca
malahatreview.ca
Quarterly

The Massachusetts Review
David Lenson, Editor
The Massachusetts Review
South College
University of Massachusetts
Amherst, MA 01003-7140
massrev@external.umass.edu
www.massreview.org
Quarterly

The Means
Tanner Higgin, Editor
The Means
Self-Evident Press, LLC
P.O. Box 183246
Shelby Township, MI 48318
tanner@the-means.com
www.the-means.com

The Minnesota Review
Jeffrey J. Williams, Editor
The Minnesota Review
Department of English
Carnegie Mellon University
Pittsburgh, PA 15213
editors@theminnesotareview.org
www.theminnesotareview.org
Semiannual

The Missouri Review
Speer Morgan, Editor
The Missouri Review
357 McReynolds Hall
University of Missouri–
    Columbia
Columbia, MO 65211
tmr@missourireview.com
www.missourireview.com
Quarterly

The New Renaissance
Louise T. Reynolds
The New Renaissance
26 Heath Road
#11
Arlington, MA 02474-3645
tnrlitmag@aol.com
www.tnrlitmag.net
Semiannual

The New Yorker
Deborah Treisman, Fiction Editor
The New Yorker
4 Times Square
New York, NY 10036
fiction@newyorker.com
www.newyorker.com
Weekly

The North American Review
Grant Tracey, Editor
The North American Review
University of Northern Iowa
1222 West 27th Street
Cedar Falls, Iowa 50614-0516
nar@uni.edu
www.webdelsol.com/
   NorthAmReview/NAR/
Published five times per year

The Oxford American
Marc Smirnoff, Editor
The Oxford American
201 Donaghey Avenue
Conway, AR 72035
smirnoff@oxfordamericanmag.com
www.oxfordamericanmag.com/
Quarterly

The Paris Review
Philip Gourevitch, Editor
The Paris Review
62 White Street
New York, NY 10013
queries@theparisreview.com
www.parisreview.com
Quarterly

**The Saint Ann's Review,
   A Journal of Contemporary
   Arts and Letters**
Beth Bosworth, Editor
*The Saint Ann's Review, A Journal
   of Contemporary Arts and
   Letters*
129 Pierrepont Street
Brooklyn, New York 11201
sareview@saintannsny.org
www.saintannsreview.com
Semiannual

The Sewanee Review
George Core, Editor
The Sewanee Review
University of the South
735 University Avenue
Sewanee, TN 37383-1000
www.sewanee.edu/sewanee_review
Quarterly

The Southern Review
Bret Lott, Editor
The Southern Review
Louisiana State University
Old President's House
Baton Rouge, LA 70803-0001
southernreview@lsu.edu
www.lsu.edu/thesouthernreview
Quarterly

The Texas Review
Paul Ruffin, Editor
The Texas Review
English Department
Sam Houston State University
Box 2146
Huntsville, TX 77341
eng_pdr@shsu.edu
www.shsu.edu/~www_trp/
    abouttr2.html
Semiannual

The Threepenny Review
Wendy Lesser, Editor
The Threepenny Review
P.O. Box 9131
Berkeley, CA 94709
wlesser@threepennyreview.com
www.threepennyreview.com
Quarterly

The Virginia Quarterly Review
Ted Genoways, Editor
The Virginia Quarterly Review
1 West Range
Box 400223
Charlottesville, VA 22904-4223
vqreview@virginia.edu
www.vqronline.org
Quarterly

Third Coast
Editors
Third Coast
English Department
Western Michigan University
Kalamazoo, MI 49008-5092
peter.j.geye@wmich.edu
www.wmich.edu/thirdcoast
Semiannual

Timber Creek Review
John M. Freiermuth, Editor
Timber Creek Review
8969 UNCG Station
Greensboro, NC 27413
Quarterly

Tin House
Editors
Tin House
PMB 280
320 Seventh Ave.
Brooklyn, NY 11215
tinhouse.com
Quarterly

Transition Magazine
Editors
Transition Magazine
104 Mt. Auburn St.
3R
Cambridge, MA 02138
transition@fas.harvard.edu
www.transitionmagazine.com
Quarterly

Triquarterly
Susan Firestone Hahn, Editor
Triquarterly
Northwestern University
629 Noyes Street
Evanston, IL 60208
triquarterly@northwestern.edu
www.triquarterly.org/index.cfm
Triannual

Tusculum Review
Mary Boyes, Editor
Tusculum Review
English Department
Tusculum College
Greeneville, TN 37743
mboyes@tusculum.edu
www.tusculum.edu/
    academics/review/
Annual

Washington Square Review
Editors
Washington Square Review
Creative Writing Program
New York University
19 University Place, Room 219
New York, NY 10003-4556
washington.square.journal@nyu
    .edu
cwp.fas.nyu.edu/page/wsr
Semiannual

West Branch
Paula Closson Buck, Editor
West Branch
Bucknell Hall
Bucknell University
Lewisburg, PA 17837
westbranch@bucknell.edu
www.bucknell.edu/westbranch
Semiannual

Whistling Shade
Anthony Telschow, Executive
    Editor
Whistling Shade
P.O. Box 7084
Saint Paul, MN 55107
editor@whistlingshade.com
www.whistlingshade.com
Quarterly

Witness
Peter Stine, Editor
Witness
Oakland Community College
Orchard Ridge Campus
27055 Orchard Lake Road
Farmington Hills, MI 48334
stinepj@umich.edu
www.oaklandcc.edu/witness
Semiannual

Worcester Review
Rodger Martin, Managing Editor
Worcester Review
1 Ekman Street
Worcester, MA 01607
rodgerwriter@tds.net
www.geocities.com/wreview
Annual

Words of Wisdom
J.M. Freiermuth, Editor
Words of Wisdom
8969 UNCG Station
Greensboro, NC 27413
Quarterly

Workers Write!
David LaBounty, Editor
Workers Write!
P.O. Box 250382
Plano, Texas 75025-0382
info@workerswritejournal.com
www.workerswritejournal.com
Annual

Xavier Review
Thomas Bonner, Executive Editor
Xavier Review
110 Xavier University
New Orleans, LA 70125
tbonner@xula.edu
www.xula.edu/review
Semiannual

Zoetrope: All-Story
Michael Ray, Editor
Zoetrope: All-Story
916 Kearny Street
San Francisco, CA 94133
info@all-story.com
www.all-story.com
Quarterly

ZYZZYVA
Howard Junker, Editor
ZYZZYVA
P.O. Box 590069
San Francisco, CA
 94159-0069
editor@zyzzyva.org
www.zyzzyva.org
Triannual

Permissions